Losing What I Never Had

—⚭—

(Uncovering My Authentic Self)

Raphael Heaggans

Please refer all pertinent questions or comments to Raphael Heaggans at: losingwhatIneverhad@gmail.com

ISBN (E-book): 979-8-9901656-0-1
ISBN (Print): 979-8-9901656-2-5

Published by Raphael Heaggans

All scripture quotations are taken from the The Lost Books of the Bible and the Holy Bible, King James Version.

Cover and interior design by Elite Authors

Photo by Daniel McGarrity

Library of Congress Control Number: 2024904511

Endorsements for
Losing What I Never Had

Losing What I Never Had is a poignant exploration of identity, trauma, and struggle for self-acceptance amidst religious intolerance. This novel skillfully navigates the complexities of family dynamics, religious indoctrination, and the quest for authenticity, leaving readers riveted by Bart's courage to confront his past and embrace a new and liberating future.

—Matthew Vialva, Ed.D., LICSW and CEO, Founder, & Therapist of
Multivious Behavioral and Leadership Group

This must-read is a modern day story of one man's emancipation from trauma, suffering, and doubt to reflection, healing, and self-actualization. This text is a blueprint on resiliency and how one can transmute pain, suffering, emotional and psychological duress into purpose.

—Rasheen Powell, MS, LICSW and CEO/Clinical
Director of *New Purpose Counseling, PLLC*

This book should be distributed in communities where individuals may find it a catalyst to improve their own lives. This heartbreaking tale shows how a gentle young man finally escaped the nightmare he was born into. It is a courageous story.

—Deborah DeNicola, MA, award-winning author of *The Future that Brought Her Here* and CEO of *Intuitive Gateways*

This book is a must-read for anyone who is striving to overcome religious indoctrination. This page-turner is descriptive in showing how religion is weaponized to manipulate and shows the reader the best means of escape.

—Charles A. Burt, Ph.D.

Losing What I Never Had speaks to the experiences of many parishioners who fell prey to the rules of overzealous religious leaders. This text exposes the modern day Pharisees and provides spiritual hope for anyone who finds him or herself in a similar situation.

—Dwayne Smith, Founder of *The Gentleman's Network*

Table of Contents

1

The Murder Accusation

The sky cried a monsoon of tears as Montgomery arrived at the parking lot of Fire Baptized Baptist Church. The rain seemed to hover over the church, while the rest of Rhony Street appeared to have sunshine. Montgomery wondered if it was a sign that he should not have attended. "I am so glad that Joe Grabowitz is closing on the mall purchase today. That should net my company over a million dollars after the real-estate commissions and other fees are paid," Montgomery thought as he looked at his watch. "I'll probably have to leave this funeral early to get back in time."

Montgomery entered the church's vestibule, quickly taking off his sunglasses. He casually passed a group of women speaking hushedly about how well Montgomery's designer suit fitted him.

"Please sign the guest book, Sir," welcomed a prepubescent girl ushering in a black-laced dress with white flowers. His coat and gloves were drenched, but Montgomery complied with her wishes, dripping raindrops on the guest book's white pages as he illegibly scribbled his name.

"Are you with the family, sir?" said the thin-faced usher beside the girl. His eyes communicated that Montgomery may remind him of someone he once knew.

"No sir; I am a guest," Montgomery stated apprehensively.

"Right this way, please." Just as the usher escorted him into the entrance of the double-swing doors, Montgomery was shaking the rain off his partially opened umbrella.

"Shhh!" a wide-eyed man about sixtyish groused. "You youngins just dun't half no 'spect for da church."

"Well, I do!" said the young usher as she curtsied to the senior citizen. Montgomery looked at her stone-faced, imagining that he slapped her in her fresh mouth.

"Well may be ya outta teach it to him, makin' all dat noise wit a umbrell-a knowin' the choir is 'bout ta sing. Keep dat noise down and wait here." The other late attendees looked at him for a reaction; Montgomery quietly looked straight ahead through the circular glass panel in the double doors anxiously as the choir sang "What a Fellowship." Brenda Matthews was leading the song.

She was just like Montgomery remembered her: stout, round, and gap-toothed. That woman never needed a choir for backup. Some of the congregants were standing, some rocking, others crying and waving their hands while Brenda growled, "Oh, how bright the path / Grows from day-to-day . . ." Sister Williams, who stood beside her, waving her arms vehemently as if swatting a fly, nearly smacked Brenda across the face. Brenda was a favorite at every church within a 100-mile radius of Catticoro, South Carolina. Her voice combined the emotional charge of Chaka Khan, the belting power of Patti LaBelle, and the melismatic vocals of Jennifer Holliday rolled into one.

Not everyone was moved by her gift. Doris Evans and Mary Howell hated Brenda since they felt their talent was not recognized or utilized. They tried to convince the other twenty choir members to quit the adult choir since they were hardly selected to lead a song. The two times they were each selected, Doris sang like she was gargling gravel while smoking a cigarette, and Mary sang like a cat in pain. Doris would sing louder and faster than the melody from the beginning to the middle of the song. And like clockwork, she would start coughing only later to state, "The devil is trying to attack my voice, and he's a liar." To finish her piece, she would just talk through it, jumping up and down in hopes of a reaction from the churchgoers. The same two people—her elderly mother and aunt—would give her charitable applause while rolling their eyes.

Mary's voice was no better. She started the song twice by saying, "It is such an honor that some people requested that I sing this song. It goes a little something like this . . ." The moment her mousey voice started to make its way into the microphone, congregants knew she would sing the extended version even if she had to repeat a verse twice. They took this time to change their babies, do crossword puzzles, pass notes around, or whisper among themselves. Some closed their eyes, probably praying the song would soon end. On one occasion, Mary gave the organist sheet music for *Wonderful Counselor,* yet Mary sang *Silent Night.* It wasn't even Christmas time. Mary bowed and said, "Hallelujah," as the crowd applauded that the song was over. Mary, none the wiser, said demurely, "Thank you. I'm so glad I could share my heavenly voice with others. My gifted voice is available for hire at weddings and funerals. Just call my number in the church directory."

But this was not the case with Brenda. Congregants knew that when Brenda got the microphone, she would sing them to the third Heaven. Brenda was invited to sing at several churches during Sunday morning services. Preachers would get upset since some of their church members would follow Brenda to every church she attended. After church, she would eat Sunday dinners at various members' homes. It was clear she had no intention of losing weight, as evidenced by those meals converting over her hips all these years. And no one cared about her size. The old folks claimed that if she lost weight, she'd lose her voice. As Brenda ended the last note of "What a Fellowship," the grumpy usher opened the door and pointed for all to walk in.

"Yeahhhhhh! Glory!" Brenda shouted as she slowly walked back to her seat in the choir. Most of the congregation was standing. Doris and Mary remained seated with their arms crossed in protest to Brenda and the congregation's reaction. Some cried; others clapped their hands. Everyone knew that when Brenda said, "Yeah, Glory," she was not truly finished singing the song despite the final note. Knowing this cue, Defay Jones, the choir director, dragged the microphone to Brenda, who was already in the middle of singing the first verse again and clearly didn't need the microphone.

The sanctuary was tainted with mango-scented carpet freshener as if sprinkled on the well-worn burgundy rug that held evidence of mud, grease, and oil stains from congregants during Reverend M. B. Allison's tenure during the 1940s. Reverend Allison died thirty years ago. The pews' cushions—once a bright red—had suffered through many years of drink spills, food deposits, and moistures of every kind. Spider webs hung on the bottom of the stained-glass windows while the four daddy longlegs sat on the window sill as if remembering Booker Johnson.

Montgomery realized he had arrived too late for the wake and the funeral was just getting started, just as the second usher walked him to the fourth pew in the front and motioned him to sit in the empty space at the end. Suella Mathis and Erma Cowhune, two of the biggest gossips in Catticoro, South Carolina, gave him side-long glances that non-verbally stated, "Who the hell are you?" as he buttoned his suit jacket. They were nicknamed Hedda Hopper and Louella Parsons by the community since they knew everybody's business in town. It was rumored that they could even tell anyone's daily schedule: the time you ate, the time you shitted, who you were sleeping with, what stores you shopped in, and how often you came to church. They dubbed themselves as the only two holy women in the community; all the other women were on their way to hell. Their husbands died long ago, and they probably embraced death with open arms just to get away from those babbling biddies.

"Chile, is anybody clear on how Booker died?" whispered Suella.

"Honey, the word on the street is that Angelic killed him during an argument over another woman. Bella Lee told me that this is the second husband that Angelic killed.

Erma stated, "Girl, I ain't heard that. But that damn Angelic is nothing but a skank, trying to go around and take people's husbands. I hope the police get that whore. When my husband Alvin was still living, Angelic had the nerve to come to our house in a polyester dress that was too small for her wide ass and tell my husband she was selling encyclopedias. My dumbass husband had the nerve to invite her into our living room while I was in the kitchen cooking. He even bought two sets of encyclopedias from her, claiming he would give a set to the grandchildren. How 'bout those encyclopedias are still in the wrapping paper after 30 years."

Suella chimed, "Gurl, I told my sistas years ago that they betta hide their man if Angelic anywhere near them. And apparently, everyone didn't get that memo. My sources tol' me that Angelic killed her first husband by putting antifreeze in every food and drink she served him since she got tired of his womanizing and gambling. Three months later, he was gone."

Erma's eyes widened, "Hush yo' mouf! That was way back in 1981! Why am I just hearing about this?"

"You and I weren't on speaking terms then, Chile, remember? You accused me of sleeping with Alvin and stealing $10 out of your purse when I was last at your house. You cut off communication. I was offended that you'd think I'd do something so unholy." Suella pursed her lips as she looked at Erma, pretending as if she was over what had happened (even though she had slept with Erma's husband three times).

At that point, the people seated around Suella and Erma scowled since they were trying to enjoy the moment. Suella and Erma, sensing the people's displeasure, started singing and clapping their hands. Suella stated, "Gurl, we will talk later," Brenda and the choir started singing the final verse again. "Praise Him!" Suella shouted as she stood up. When the song ended for the second time, the church members took about fifteen minutes to *come out of the spirit*. Even Suella shook rather spasmodically when Reverend Allison looked at her, almost as if the look was a cue for her to demonstrate the convulsive behavior. Suella screamed as if riding a rollercoaster before collapsing by the pulpit. Two church nurses who were sisters helped her complete her fall.

The Reverend finally arose to the podium as the churchgoers' excitement calmed over Brenda's song.

"What a fellowship! What a joy, divine! That's what Booker is saying right now as he's entering Heaven! YES! YESSSSS!!!!" exclaimed the aging Reverend Countee Allison into the microphone as he was situating his notes and the Bible on the podium. "We are gathered here today to remember the life of Booker Johnson, a great man who was a public servant, a God-serving and family man. May God encourage your hearts, Sister Angelic, Brother Warren, and twins Tony and Lorraine," added Reverend Allison. "You are the wife and children who knew him best."

Angelic sat stone-faced in her wheelchair with her lips poked as if she just finished sucking a lemon. Agnes Johnson, Booker's mother, cried out, "Boo, whoo, whoo," pretending she needed solace from Arthur Johnson, Booker's father and her husband of 50 years. She pressed her eyelids together as hard as possible to produce a tear. Arthur sharply cut his eyes away, only for Agnes to silence her fake crying.

Reverend Allison continued, "Deacon Booker reminded me so much of my dad, the Reverend M. B. Allison. Deacon Booker was a man who cared about the poor and gave his time to read the Bible to the children. This was an upstanding man of valor who encountered many life troubles, including losing a troubled son, being falsely accused, and undergoing an upsetting divorce. But he kept his head held high."

Erma poured further contemptuousness on Booker, passing this note to Suella: *Why is the Reverend lying about Booker? Booker is in hell right now, being barbecued or rotisseried.* Suella had a knee-jerk reaction as she tried to stifle her laughter while putting her head in her hands.

"Now I can talk about Booker's goodness all day," the Reverend said, "but let us bow our heads and have a moment of silence in his honor as we reflect on our good experiences with Booker."

As Montgomery slowly bowed his head, he felt like someone was watching him. He looked over to the right only to have his eyes meet squarely with the eyes of Deacon Chuckie Downs. Montgomery broke his glance and slowly bowed his head. Just as the church became quiet, Chuckie screamed, "YOU ARE THE MAN WHO KILLED BOOKER!"

2

Transforming from Girl to Woman

During the fall of 1962, Bus #81 stopped by her tin roof house, the only house in the area with no neighbors. Dreama's white lace dress blew slightly in the wind, and her long locks neatly coiffed down her shoulders as the bus stopped. Booker glanced at Dreama as she walked gingerly to the back of the bus, where she sat by Sally Mae Ross. Booker was dating Carlette Thomas, who was seated right behind him. Carlette was a gap-toothed, dark-skinned girl with an afro who wore a brown-floral polyester dress with hints of orange and pink. She was jealous, particularly since she caught Booker lock-lipped with Sandra Hunter the week prior.

Booker's best friend, Bobby Anderson, sat opposite the aisle. He was a skinny boy dressed in mid-thigh green shorts and a blue T-shirt. Bobby was a follower of Booker. He idolized Booker because he was a fast-talking, charismatic charmer. Booker also knew how to be bidialectal, knowing how and when to speak Standard English or Black dialect. Bobby hoped that by association, he would catch some of Booker's popularity.

When the bus stopped at the front of Brelding High School, Carlette stole a kiss from Booker as she got off the bus while Bobby observed from his seat. Booker and Dreama locked eyes as Dreama walked down the bus's aisle. As she approached the first step, Booker said, "Aye, girl. Hold on a minute," while motioning the remaining students to get off the bus. Booker spoke to Dreama in a deeper voice—while noticing that he had the audience of his best friend—slowly dragging out, "Hey Mama. I'm Booker Johnson."

Coyly, Dreama responded, "I'm Dreama Miller."

"I'm in the twelfth grade. What grade are you in?" Booker shared while studying her.

"I'm in the tenth grade," Dreama mentioned.

"You a choice girl. I'm stoked by you already. I think it would be groovy if you and I went out and got to know each other," Booker said.

Dreama, having never before been approached by a boy, was nervous yet intrigued by Booker's boldness.

Booker went on, "You wanna go out with me?" Dreama subtly took a deep breath and coolly said, "I don't know about that. Everything is so sudden. I don't wanna be another girl you've been kissing on. I heard about you and Sandra. Plus, you're going out with Carlette now." She was trying to sound more mature.

"How 'bout I dump both of those girls, and you and I can just go out and get us a burger or something," Booker invited.

"My father would kill me if I went out with any boy right now," Dreama anxiously stated.

"Perhaps you can tell your dad that there is a school dance coming up, that you were interested in going, and that perhaps you could just meet me there and give me the first dance," Booker stated. The dance is tomorrow right here at the high school gym. I can pick you up at 6 p.m."

"Then it's a date!" Dreama exclaimed, chastising herself internally for her response. But maybe I better meet you at the dance since my father doesn't yet know who you are," Dreama reasoned.

The next evening, Dreama wore a long burgundy polyester dress with a turquoise and orange butterfly pattern, complementing her curvaceous figure. It was obvious that she was still developing; her nubile breasts were held hostage in her bullet bra. Her long, silky dark hair went well with her caramel complexion, and bright red lipstick accentuated her look. She was the youngest child who got anything she wanted out of her protective father, Wilson Miller. She was the only one of his children who looked exactly like her mother, Senora Miller, who passed away four years ago. She told her father that she wanted to stay after school to catch up on some studying with her girlfriends and then stay at the school to go to the dance. This idea seemed acceptable to her father.

"There's nothing like education. I wish your mother and I could have graduated from high school. But during our day, education was so hard to come by. We were only able to finish sixth grade. You can only go to the dance if Lee and Oscar go with you. You can never tell when the police or Ku Klux Klan may try to chase you," Wilson advised in a cautious tone.

"Daddy, I understand education is important. And I'm a big girl; I will be the only girl with her brothers watching over her. You know how Lee and Oscar try to control me when you are not around," Dreama stated in a cool voice that usually reminded Wilson that she was his little girl.

"No, they are going, and that's final. They go with you if you want to go to the dance."

"Fine." Dreama muttered as Wilson stood at the back door, calling, "Lee and Oscar! Come in the house now." Lee was the older of the two. He was of average height, lanky, light-skinned, and ashen with an oval face and unkempt afro, while Oscar was dark-skinned, tall, and solidly built with chiseled facial features. "Both of you get washed up and take Dreama back to the schoolhouse so she can study and go to the dance with her friends. Watch her closely and bring her back no later than 10:30," Wilson instructed.

"Dreama, you are not to dance with any boys tonight. We are going to stay right outside. If you need anything, just let Bo Jones know, and he'll come get us," Lee stated as if he were her father. Oscar added, "You just stay around your girlfriends and dance with them. We will tell Pops if you even look at any boy." Dreama hated to be treated as a child. But she felt as if her brothers would be true to the threat. She would just be there to have a good time with her girlfriends.

"Now go on and get out of here. I don't want any of my friends to see you walk me into the school," Dreama rasped as she exited the truck.

"But we are your older brothers," they said in unison.

"But yeah, you graduated ten years ago. Now go on; I can take care of myself."

Dreama could hear the blaring sounds of *Your Love Keeps Lifting Me Higher and Higher* just as she approached the admission desk. "That'll be 25 cents, Dreama," Tameka Littlejohn said stoically.

"But I don't have . . ." Dreama started to say before she saw two-quarters land on the table.

"The girl is with me, and that should cover the cost for both of us," Booker cooed to Tameka as she looked up at him.

"Does Carlette know you're with Dreama?" Tameka asked. Booker scowled at her wanting to say, "None of yo' damn business!" but decided to keep his cool.

Dreama's classmates were doing the Twist as Chubby Checker sang over the loudspeakers as Booker and Dreama walked into the gym. Booker softly said, "You look very nice tonight."

"Thank you. My mother made this dress for me."

"I'd like to get to know more about that dress later."

Dreama replied innocently, "Are you interested in knowing the steps in how she made it?"

Booker laughed, finally saying, "Hey, why don't we dance!"

The song *My Girl* hit the airwaves as they made their way to the dance floor.

Booker held Dreama very close to him. He placed his arm just above her waist as beads of sweat rolled down her face. She placed her head against his chest as they slowly danced. He sang the lyrics in her ear so poorly that she laughed. He snickered as he smiled at her, looking into her eyes and piercing her soul. Sensing that she was starting to weaken her defenses, Booker pressed his manhood against her pelvis. She did not know exactly how to respond to the feeling; she just knew her body was pleasantly responding.

This moment was instantly broken when Carlette got close to Booker's face. She pretended to be dancing with her girlfriends, hoping Booker would notice her presence. When the song ended, Booker told Dreama a joke in her ear, only for them to burst out laughing just as he released her from her arms. Carlette suspected that the joke was about her; she tapped her finger onto Booker's shoulder three times, to which Booker turned and said in an annoyed tone of voice, "What do you want?"

Carlette said, "I need to speak to you alone, please."

Booker casually responded after looking her up and down and then at Dreama up and down and said, "I don't need to speak with you because I think I have already spoken. Come on, Dreama; let's get out of this joint and get a burger from Route 66." Dreama shrugged her shoulders as she walked past Carlette, proud that she had been crowned the prize of the night by one of the most sought-after boys in school.

Booker walked Dreama to his Monte Carlo. He opened the door for her and gave a winning smile as she giggled to herself.

Booker and Dreama talked about their families, hobbies, and dreams en route to Route 66. Booker touted, "I don't like school. I like being a part-time bus driver, driving either in the mornings or afternoons. When I graduate, I'm just gonna work at Chev Mills. My dad works there and makes good money, so I'ma do the same."

Dreama added, "That sounds good. I'd like to go to school to be a nurse."

Booker stated, "Really?

You and I can play doctor and nurse if you become my girl tonight."

Dreama snickered as Booker smiled.

He placed his hand on her mid-thigh, only for her to grab and hold his hand. Dreama did so out of nervousness; she didn't know how to interact with boys, but she didn't want to come across as easy. As a compromise, Dreama inched her way to sit closer to him. Booker wrapped his right arm around her shoulder, only to move her shoulder left to encourage her to slide even closer to him. Dreama had heard rumors about Booker from the other teens in school, but she dismissed them since she was convinced she was learning about the real Booker. And nothing was going to stop her from claiming him as hers.

She looked at Booker's lips as he talked, though she didn't hear a word he said. She was mesmerized by his Old Spice cologne, even-shaped black afro with a pick at the crown, white teeth, full lips, and growing beard. His white platform shoes complemented his neatly creased green, polyester pants with a matching light-weighted coat and his white and green paisley shirt unbuttoned down to the third button. She saw a portion of his hairy chest. Just then, she snapped out of her trance when Booker said, "So you want a milkshake or something, Mama?"

"Oh, I was just looking over the marquee to decide," Dreama stated while glancing at the choices. "I'll take a chocolate milkshake," Booker ordered a cheeseburger and soda. The carhop took Booker's money and roller-skated back to the restaurant to submit the order.

"You are a smart girl. I like that."

"Thank you. What makes you think that?"

"You use big words. What did you say you were looking over?"

"The marquee. That's what the menu board is called."

"Oh, ok."

"I enjoy reading and learning new words."

"Well, the only words I am interested in hearing are more about how to make you mine."

"Booker, I don't know. You just treat all the girls this way," Dreama said shyly while smiling.

"Maybe I'll just have to figure it out," Booker added with a smile.

"Ok, I have a cheeseburger, soda, and milkshake." The carhop placed the items on the tray before the marquee while Booker reached for them and passed the milkshake to Dreama. Booker and Dreama drove back to the school since Dreama knew her brothers would be picking her up in forty-five minutes. Booker suggested, "Why don't we go somewhere with some privacy? Dreama was nervously surprised as she asked, "Where can we go; everyone is around?"

"Hey, why don't we go to bus 81?" Booker suggested. "I know the bus driver won't mind," Booker jokingly stated.

Softly, Dreama stated, "That is a great idea." As they drove to the buses' parking lot, Dreama looked down at Booker's crotch. Any curiosity she had about how the size of his penis was dispelled, for Booker gave a clothed display that left little to her imagination. Dreama was starting to feel apprehensive. Though she had never had sex, she knew what a penis looked like. After all, she has accidentally seen each of her brothers naked due to their small home and the bathroom they shared.

Dreama reflected on her Kleenex cleavage and experienced a moment of insecurity. She pondered whether to subtly transform her tissue-assisted B cups back into the A cups they were. Dreama grabbed her milkshake to have something occupy her hands in light of her becoming fidgety as Booker opened her passenger door.

"After you, sweet thang," Booker whispered. Dreama slowly exited the vehicle, excited but frightened at the thought of the coming moments. Booker and Dreama held hands as they walked onto the bus, saying nothing. Booker closed the doors using the bus door handles while Dreama sat in the middle of the sixth seat on the left. Booker said, "Well, we're finally alone."

"Yes, we are."

"Enjoying your shake?"

"I'm trying to. I haven't even tasted it yet."

Booker watched Dreama struggle to slurp the thick milkshake through the straw. She sure has some nice full lips, Booker thought as Dreama's jaw sunk in and out with effort.

"Here, let me help you." Booker leaned forward and slurped more of the milkshake than intended.

"You have some milkshake on the corners of your mouth," Dreama piped up.

"Help me out by getting it off." Booker coolly leaned forward to kiss Dreama. The sensation rushed through her body. She did not know what was happening, but she enjoyed every moment of it. She felt her temperature rising as Booker fondled her back as he put his tongue down her throat. Dreama subtly moaned with pleasure, which gave Booker the indication to go further. He laid Dreama down on the seat while kissing her neck and working his hands down to her waist. Dreama started to shake.

"Baby, don't worry. Just relax. Let Daddy Booker make you feel good," Dreama said, nodding with consent.

After 20 minutes, Booker ejaculated inside her. Dreama was enjoying her newfound womanhood as she held him.

After three minutes, Booker whispered with concern, "You ok, mama?"

Dreama softly cooed, "I couldn't be better." As Dreama envisioned a future with Booker, she glanced at her watch at 9:40 p.m. "I've got to get back in the gym. My brothers will be back to pick me up in twenty minutes."

Hurriedly, Dreama cleaned herself using the tissue in her bra and rushed to put her panties back on. She was resigned to using a towel left on the next seat by one of the basketball players. She quickly looked in the small mirror to ensure she had no visible evidence of her adventure with Booker.

"Meet me back at the gym. I don't want people to see us get off the bus together. You get off first," Booker whispered.

Thanks to the malfunctioning parking light that occasionally brightened the bus parking lot, darkness escorted Dreama to the back of the school's entrance, where she could enter unnoticed. At this point, the lights were dim while the teens were dancing their last dance. Dreama meandered around the crowd, anxious to find Booker, hoping to have one more dance during the last few minutes of the song before going outside again to run into her brothers.

And there he was by the bleachers talking to Carlette. She found herself getting flustered and began to increase her pace. She didn't know what she would do, but she was willing to do something. As she approached, she heard Booker say, "Carlette, it's over between us. I'm building a new life with Dreama." Dreama quickly shifted her body language as she came closer. "You see this, Carlette? Dreama is the girl of my dreams. Come on, Mama, let's leave this joint," he said, turning toward Dreama. Carlette's girlfriends immediately gathered around her and whisked her off to the bathroom as she sobbed.

The school's front doors opened, and the lights went up. The principal announced, "This concludes the school dance. Thank you for coming, but now everyone must leave. Get home safely."

Dreama envisioned running away with Booker as she walked closer to the doors, holding his hand. She saw her brothers in the distance, though she was certain they did not see her.

"Booker, my brothers are outside waiting for me," Dreama stated under her breath.

Booker knew others were observing him, so he shifted his natural vernacular.

"Oh, ok. They just protectin' they sister, huh?"

"They like to think so."

"How 'bout you an' me get together afta schoo' tomorrow?"

"Sure. I'll tell my father I'm staying after school for tutoring."

"Why? You are a grown woman. You're sixteen, right?"

"I am sixteen. My dad and brothers don't think I'm grown."

"Da law says you can drive, get married, and get housin'. Dat sounds grown to me."

"Oh, really. What are you trying to say?" Dreama joked.

"I'm just sayin', Mama." Booker snickered, squeezing her hand.

"I'll see you tomorrow."

"Yes, you will," Booker stated as he let go of her hand and winked at her.

Dreama quickly approached her girlfriends, whom she told to put up a united front as if they had been together throughout the dance, particularly since she was getting into her brother's view.

"Well, here comes Daddy's baby girl! Hurry up and get in this car so we can rush you home," Lee announced as she walked to the truck. Dreama rolled her eyes at her brothers and thought, "I left Daddy's house as a girl, and I'm returning as a woman: Daddy Booker's woman!"

3

Kicking Ass at the Church

Dreama threw up three times before her stomach started to settle. She didn't dare to tell her father, Wilson, that she was six weeks pregnant, but she knew she had to. Booker told her she must do it to prove she is a woman ready for the next change in her life. She wished her mother was still alive to guide her since her sisters had their own issues with the men in their lives.

Dreama was the youngest child of nine, the "Oops!" baby since Senora and Wilson's other eight children were in their late teens or older by the time Dreama came along. Senora was forty-seven and sickly throughout much of Dreama's life. Dreama had limited memories of her mother, for she died four years ago, just before Dreama turned twelve. As she stood in the mirror, rubbing her belly, she had flashbacks about her mother.

Senora was known to be a no-nonsense woman who spoke her mind at a moment's notice. She was short and known to carry a pocket knife. As a Native American and Black woman with a freckled caramel complexion, she loved to wear white and deep red lipstick. Her long hair was most often tied back in a ponytail. She was an excellent cook and a legendary fighter.

The town still talked about when Rhoda Bell and she fist-fought one another at Missionary Baptist Church. Rhoda Bell was known as "The

Homewrecker," a reputation spanned over forty years. No wife felt her husband was safe—especially in church—anytime Rhoda Bell came around, especially when her bullet bra aimed solely in the direction of the man she wanted. All she did to reel him in was bounce her breasts as she walked in his direction, batting her eyes and smiling with her gap-toothed grin, just to say, "Hi, I'm Rhoda, and anytime we can fellowship, call me." with a polite southern, seductive drawl. This line worked every time. The men instantly knew that the invitation was an entry into all things salacious. She was responsible for breaking up fifteen marriages.

On this particular Sunday, Senora was ushering. She saw Rhoda Bell snuggling up to Wilson and whispering in his ear after church service as they walked onto the church ramp. Six-year-old Dreama was holding her father's hand. Senora crept behind them and used the element of surprise by tapping Rhoda on her shoulder. The moment Rhoda turned around, Senora grabbed her by her blouse and quickly commenced beating her ass from the bottom of the church ramp to the church's lawn. No one stepped in to help during the two-minute fight, though churchgoers hollered for Senora to stop while cheering her on. Senora only had one thing in mind: "Beat this homewrecking bitch's ass for every woman whose husband she slept with." Senora's white cotton dress flew in the wind as she landed punch after punch, yet her matching pillbox white hat shook from left to right without falling off her head.

When the fight was over, Senora pushed herself up, smashing Rhoda's head in the ground, dusting herself off, and quietly told the bleeding and embarrassed Rhoda, "That ought to make you think twice before laying eyes on my husband again. Come on, Wilson and Dreama! We are leaving now." Wilson obediently tightened his grip on Dreama's hand and walked with Senora. Pastor M. B. Allison—trying to wield control—stepped forth, saying, "All right, y'all break it up! That's right, Mrs. Senora, get in your car."

Senora looked back at the pastor wide-eyed; even he knew that Senora was not beyond fighting a man if he crossed her.

Not making a move, he said forlornly, "Somebody help Sister Rhoda up." Rhoda covered her makeup-smeared face and whimpered as her sister Jennie valiantly tried to dust the mud and grass shavings off her lilac polyester dress. As Jennie was helping her up, she saw only brown and green on the back of her once lilac dress. She helped Rhoda hobble to the 1957 Ford Fairlane, forgetting that her left white shoe had landed in the ditch while her white brim hat had blown in front of the church door.

After that day, Rhoda was never seen again. Rumor had it that Rhoda Bell packed her belongings, moved out of state, and assumed a new identity. And not one woman missed her. One month later, the women's auxiliary group crowned Senora missionary of the year.

But now Dreama felt she just had her father. Wilson walked into his house unnoticed to find Dreama rubbing her stomach, looking in the mirror, and rehearsing what to say to him.

"Honey, I figured you were pregnant."

Dreama moved her arm quickly, startled that she was caught. "I've always known when yo' momma got pregnant with all nine of y'all. She had that look in her eye and rubbed her stomach the same way you're rubbing yours. It's just you and me in this house. We can get through this together. Who's the father?"

Dreama shuddered at the thought of having a conversation related to sex with her father. She closed her eyes to muster the strength to speak. "Booker Johnson, a boy about to graduate from high school. He wants to marry me. Daddy, I'm a grown woman, and I just don't want to hear . . ." Dreama's voice cracked.

"Well, you're sixteen now. The law says you can marry. Your mom's gone. I wish she could see you now," Wilson stated. "I'd like to meet the boy."

"Sure, Daddy. But you're not gonna run him off, are you?"

"What kind of question is that? I didn't run off your sisters' husbands. And I don't like most of 'em!" Dreama and Wilson stole a laugh.

"So, no, baby. What good is that gonna do? And you have my grand-child growing in you. Do you wanna marry this boy?"

"Yes, I do, Daddy."

"Then marry him. It would really look good to the church if he did the honorable thing by marrying you. It was the same reason why I married yo' mother."

"What! Daddy!!!" Dreama stated, obviously shocked.

"It is true. Me and yo' momma got married the same day her father Charlie was buried on December 29, 1929. She was three months pregnant with yo' oldest sista, Catherine. Her daddy didn't know, but her momma, Lula, did. She talked to me about my intentions with Senora two weeks before your grandpa died and said that I can't see your mother again unless I marry her since that was the honorable thing to do."

Dreama stood in awe over what she heard yet broke the silence by say-ing, "If it was good for Mom and you, then it's good for Booker and me." She was at peace, though she felt nervous about who would look after her father once she ran off with Booker.

Wilson softly grabbed Dreama by the hand and held her close. "You're still my baby girl, honey. I'll always be here for you." Dreama held her right ear very close to his upper chest. It reminded her of the girl she used to be.

"So, when are you gonna introduce the boy to me?" Wilson asked as he turned his head to reach for his pocket handkerchief to wipe his eyes.

"Let's say within the next three days. It'll take me that long to clean this house."

—〰—

Booker eased his car down the Millers' grass-gravel driveway. The tin roof could not camouflage the years of bruises it had endured as the rusted cracks with an iridescent smile greeted Booker. The roof covered the six-room house, held together with dilapidated wood and protruding nails. The wraparound porch consisted of curbed and broken wood pieces and missing flooring. The remnants of what used to be a banister had fallen into rot. Six rock pillars, each three feet long, kept the house stationary. The makeshift outhouse was in shabby condition, appearing like the four walls would come down simultaneously on cue with the next person who used it.

Booker checked his beard and his afro in the driver-side mirror. "Damn, you a good-looking man," Booker said aloud to himself as he shone a gap-toothed smile. He slowly opened the door just after placing his pick at the crown of his head. Booker's black platform shoes were spit-shined and matched his black and white plaid bell-bottom pants, white paisley shirt, and matching black and white jacket. Bargaining with time to strive to build more confidence, Booker sauntered towards the weather-worn wooden steps. He tapped on the door three times. Instantly, he heard creaking footsteps coming closer. He rehearsed whispering what he planned to say when the door was answered.

The rehearsal was interrupted when Dreama opened the door. "Hey, Booker. Don't you look handsome!" Booker playfully turned his head, pretending to be shy, before saying, "Thanks, Mama. You are looking like a million dollars, Sweet Thang." Dreama's chartreuse one-piece sleeveless, above-the-knee dress showcased her hourglass figure. Completing the look, compliments of her older sister Catherine, were white squared-toe high-heeled shoes.

"My family has been expecting you," Dreama proudly shared. "Come into the kitchen." She grabbed Booker by the hand while he reached for his kerchief to wipe the sweat off his brow.

The aroma of fried chicken, black-eyed peas, collard greens, and cornbread arrested Booker's nostrils. "Daddy," she said nervously, "This is Booker Johnson. Booker, meet my dad, Wilson Miller." Booker was visibly nervous as he stated, "How do you do, sir?" Dreama was surprised to hear him enunciate his words.

"Well, how ya doin' youn' man?" Without waiting for a response, Wilson pointed, "Have a seat close to the head of the table. Dinner will be ready in a minute. Cat, give me and the boy some sweet tea."

"Yes, Daddy," Catherine gingerly replied while Booker sat down at the dinner table next to Wilson, who sat at the head. Marigold cloth placemats with an array of dandelions and daisies sat orderly on the emerald plastic tablecloth to camouflage the cerulean-and-white card tables they would revert to once Booker left. The tandem dinner tables were two matching card tables hidden in plain sight.

Wilson looked Booker up and down quickly as the two sat, studying him. Booker discerned that Wilson knew something about him that Booker was trying to conceal. Once seated, Wilson initiated the conversation: "Aren't you Agnes Johnson's boy?"

"Yes, sir, I am."

"I figured so. You kinda favor your mother. So tell me about your future plans and how they include my daughter?"

"I am a young man who grew up in the church. My father is a deacon. My mother teaches Sunday school. I have three brothers and three sisters. I am the oldest. I sometimes drive the church bus to pick up the members. I am going to be a pastor one day. And Dreama will be my First Lady," Booker proudly stated. He had memorized his speech and recited it without stumbling over any words.

"Well, those are some lofty goals, young man. But what will you do for work before fulfilling your dream of becoming a pastor?" Wilson asked. Though he only had a sixth-grade education, Wilson was self-taught. He ensured that each of his children would graduate from high school and go to college or learn a trade.

Booker started to sweat. Finally, he stated, "Well, my dad works in a textile factory, and I will do the same. I figure Dreama can work or go to school."

Wilson nodded his head, pleased by Booker's response. He stated, "It's time for you to meet the rest of the family here. As he got up from his chair, Wilson placed his hand on the right side of his back, letting out, "Oh, my back!"

Dreama's siblings, who lived locally, came from the kitchen where

Mabel was completing the family meal and stared at Wilson. Oscar stated, "Daddy, you really need to have that examined by a doctor." Dreama exclaimed, "Get what examined?"

"Well, Dreama, I have this annoying dark spot on my back. It's been there for the past thirty years, I guess," Wilson shared as he lit a cigarette.

After dinner, Wilson told Booker it was nice to meet him. "I hope to see you again. You seem like a nice young man," he added, showing Booker to the door.

"It was nice to meet you and the family, Mr. Wilson. I better get back home," Booker turned and chimed over his shoulder immediately before leaving.

"Booker, I will walk you out," Dreama stated hesitantly in front of her father.

"So, what do you think your father thought about me?" Booker asked, anxiously waiting for an answer.

Dreama enthusiastically stated, "He thinks you are a nice guy and is happy for us. He told me so while we were in the kitchen."

"That's great to know. I enjoyed meeting him and your brothers and sisters. The food was great, too. Kinda tasted like my mother's cooking."

"That's nice! Tomorrow, I'll meet your family. I have to admit that I'm nervous," Dreama said, looking into his eyes for support.

"I told my family all about you. And they have been wanting to meet you. But I haven't told them that you're pregnant."

"Any reason why?"

"Well, I know my dad will lecture me on what I will do about taking care of you and the baby. I still live at home. I am 18 years old with a baby on the way and don't have a steady job. I am still a man, though."

"Well, don't worry, honey; things will work out just fine. I'll work up until the baby is born."

—⚏—

Booker and Dreama walked into Arthur and Agnes Johnson's house quietly. "Glenda, Eva has been sleeping with Doris' husband for at least five years. So when Eva found out, she said, 'My husband is in love with me; he would never cheat.' Since then, Eva has gained all that weight, and I can see why her husband is looking at other women," Agnes Johnson gossiped as Booker and Dreama made their way to the living room.

"Eva needs to stop putting on that heavy makeup. She looks like a Jezebel with all that mix-match makeup," Agnes added, rocking her flowered chair in the living room, enveloped by faux-wood brown walls with black stripes dividing the panels. A black and white floor model TV, a goldenrod couch, a few pictures of her children, and a hi-fi stand made the décor complete. The only additional sound came from the actors on *Days of Our Lives.* The living room was next to the kitchen with a white electric stove, refrigerator, faux-wood light cabinets, and a white kitchen sink. The open floor plan made the living room accessible only via the kitchen door.

Booker and Dreama carefully eased their way inside the kitchen, which smelled of fish grease. Agnes turned her back to them as she continued sharing the town's gossip with Glenda. Booker stood behind his mother. "Momma!"

"What Booker?! You see, I'm on the phone," Agnes snapped before turning to look at him with Dreama close behind.

"Glenda, I'll have to call you back. My son just walked in with a beautiful girl in a stunning geometric dress. I'll tell you all about her after I talk to her. Bye." Agnes placed the phone back on the red rotary phone's base.

"Booker, what are you doing at home already? You don't usually get home from school until 3:30. It's only 2:00," Agnes chastised.

"Momma, we had an early dismissal today. But never mind that. I brought Dreama over to meet you."

Agnes lit a cigarette and walked twice around Dreama. She said, "Uh huh," to express her approval of the parts of her body, hair, and clothing. Dreama silently suffered as Agnes exhaled a stream of smoke from her nostrils. "Well, you're very pretty!"

"Thank you, Mrs. Johnson," Dreama said nervously.

"Let me go get Arthur. He ate some greens that gave him terrible gas. I'm going to pass this cigarette to him to freshen the bathroom. In the meantime, have a seat. Booker, get the girl something to drink. I'll be back," Agnes assured.

"Momma, really? We have a guest."

"And the guest needs to know that we shit daily around here. I hope she does too," Agnes declared as she disappeared down the hall.

"I hope your mom likes me. She seems tough," Dreama pondered.

"She just says whatever she thinks. Don't mind her. She likes you; don't be nervous, babe. Wanna soda pop?"

"No, cold water is fine."

As Booker chopped ice from the ice bucket, Agnes returned with Arthur, who was drying his hands with a flimsy washrag. "Well, hello there. Welcome to our home. I'm Arthur Johnson, Booker's daddy. Sorry that I didn't greet you when you first got here. I didn't feel good earlier, but I feel pretty good now."

"Well, come on over and sit down. Let's talk since you're going to become a part of this family," Agnes pointed out.

"Momma, how do you know? You're just meeting her."

"I know you are the oldest of my seven children, and she is six weeks pregnant, so, obviously, I know the signs of pregnancy. I know you have been going out with her for some time. I know you love her, and she loves you. I know you will marry her since we taught you that if you get a girl pregnant, you are marrying her. Did I say anything wrong?"

"No, Momma, you didn't."

"No, Mrs. Johnson, you did not."

"Then let's not play with each other. We have to come up with a family plan since my first grandchild is coming. Let's talk about it over some fried fish. Wait until I tell Glenda the great news that I have a new daughter and a grandbaby on the way."

Booker thought, *I'm glad Mom likes Dreama. I broke up with Carlette. Now I have to end my relationship with Jimmy before anyone finds out about us.*

4

Breaking Up Is So
Hard to Do

Jimmy Anderson watched the last few seconds of the Warriors and Celtics basketball game on his floor-model RCA black-and-white television. "Bill Russell just blocked Wilt Chamberlain," said the host. As Jimmy grabbed his Pabst Blue Ribbon, he shouted, "Come on Wilt! Block his shot! Don't let the Celtics win this game!"

Jimmy was the father of Bobby Anderson, Booker's best friend. He was one of the few Blacks who owned a house with a detached garage that was converted into a one-bedroom apartment. Jimmy was known to be a 'man's man,' six feet tall and athletically built. Women were always impressed by the confidence he exuded in his walk. The former basketball player managed to pick up a few pounds during his marriage. He had still held onto his chiseled bone structure that complemented his caramel skin tone. Anytime he wanted to escape Beverly, he could usually be found at the apartment. His wife knew neither she nor their children were permitted to go near the apartment. It was Jimmy's 40th birthday, and he wanted to spend part of the day with Booker to have a conversation.

The Warriors called a timeout immediately after Walt fouled Bill. Jimmy stated, "I can't believe this shit, man! The game is too damn close." He took the last swig of beer as the basketball broadcast went to commercial.

"Three males were arrested at a local rest stop for engaging in homosexual acts in the men's restroom. Police won't state their names but share that they are married and hold prominent positions within the community. The men were charged with sodomy. They will have their day in court Monday," the White middle-aged newscaster revealed, wearing a drab gray oversized suit that did little to compliment his pasty face and sandy blond pompadour.

"So these dudes got caught fuckin'?! That's what those cats get for not doing the beat feet," Jimmy added as if he were a guest commentator.

As the news continued, Jimmy grabbed another beer and walked to the jalousie window, waiting for Booker. Gazing at the street, he thought of the first time he met Booker two years ago. He'd been waiting in the parking lot of Las Sega High School in his red Pontiac GTO to pick up his twelfth-grade son from basketball practice while listening to "Stop! In the Name of Love." From the gym doors sprang two sweaty boys, Bobby and Booker. Bobby's mid-thigh blue and white shorts held his 28-inch waist snuggly to the round curvature of his derriere. The stride in his walk accentuated each hip, forcing anyone to notice his developing confidence.

Booker took his sweaty shirt off as he walked with Jimmy to the car. His athletic frame, chiseled torso, gap tooth, and perfect afro made him appear more man than a teen, especially since his jock strap could not camouflage its struggle to keep his genitals from bursting free. The boys slapped each other playfully and laughed as they approached the car.

"Dad, this is Booker Johnson, forward for Brelding High. We were just talking about the game. Booker, this is my Dad, James Anderson," Bobby shared as the boys walked towards James' car. Bobby was a small forward who played for Brelding.

"Great game, Booker!" Jimmy excitedly shared. His excitement came from watching Booker walk toward him.

"Thanks, Mr. Anderson, Sir."

"Oh, please don't call me Sir," Jimmy smiled. "Mr. Anderson is just fine."

"Mr. Anderson, it is," Booker uttered.

"You scored sixteen points, five assists, and ten rebounds tonight. You faked out Ben Caldwell and dunked on Sammy Miller." Jimmy said, praising and summarizing Booker's athletic performance.

"Thank you; I study my opponent's strengths and weaknesses. Then, I prey on the weaknesses. Ben has a solid defense, although he lacks speed. And Sammy has great speed, though he needs to work on how to jump higher," Booker explained.

"Pops, what about how I played?" Bobby pressed.

"Bo, you play with heart, you dig? You have a love for the sport. You gave your all for the time you played, scoring four points. You need to practice more outside of school, and I'll need to talk to the coach about letting you on the court more," Jimmy reasoned. He turned back to Booker. "So Booker, you have a ride home? You are welcome to hang out at my place and have your ride pick you up from my house. We'll get you pizza or anything else you might want," Jimmy said, attempting to hide his rhapsodizing hero-worship.

"My pop's supposed to be coming to get me, but he is late or sometimes forgets. If he's not here within thirty-five minutes, then I can hitch a ride with somebody," Booker resolved.

"Well, five cars are left in the parking lot, including mine. What do you wanna do?"

Booker motioned with his right hand for Bobby to initiate opening his father's car door in tandem with Jimmy slowly sliding to the middle of the seat, telling Bobby, "You can drive us home, Bo." Bobby quickly bounced into the car, his leg hitting Jimmy's leg. Booker walked to the other side, throwing his shirt over his head before he got into the car. He carefully eased his way onto the seat's plastic covering as he casually closed the heavy door. Jimmy gapped his legs wider so his right-side buttock and outer thigh touched Booker's now-glistening left thigh.

The ride to Jimmy's house was filled with sing-a-longs to soul hits: *Chain of Fools*, *Try a Little Tenderness*, and *Don't Make Me Over*. During commercial breaks, Booker and Bobby were jonesing with each other while Jimmy laughed more at Booker's jokes than Bobby's. Jimmy absent-mindedly looked at Booker as he talked, not knowing a word he said. Bobby chimed in but kept his eyes on the road, driving the speed limit to avoid any attraction from a police officer, especially since they had to go around the White neighborhoods an additional ten miles to get to their home in the Black neighborhood. They could arrive home twenty-five minutes sooner if they could drive through the White neighborhoods.

Night descended on Jimmy's house, greeting the three guys as Bobby coasted the car up the sloped driveway. "Well, boys, we made it home," Jimmy stated as if he had rehearsed it. Booker got out of the car slowly, mesmerized by Jimmy's brick house and detached brick garage. The carefully manicured yard was surrounded by red-and-white rose bushes, begonias, trimmed shrubs of various colors, and a granny-smith apple tree surrounded by red mulch. "I didn't know Black people lived like this," Booker drawled.

Jimmy's wife, Beverly, greeted them at the door just as Jimmy fumbled with the keys. She wore face cream, had her hair in pink rollers, and was dressed in a lime-green polyester housecoat. "I was getting worried about y'all since you're usually home from games by now." Jimmy kissed her as he walked in and twirled her around. "Now, what do you think could happen to me, huh?" Jimmy playfully asked. Upon seeing Booker, Beverly managed to say mid-laugh, "Put me down, Jimmy. Why didn't you tell me a guest was coming? I look like a mess!"

"Beverly, this is Booker Johnson. Booker, this is my wife, Beverly Anderson," Jimmy formally shared. "He will be staying the night."

"Well, Booker, it is nice to meet you. Bobby has mentioned you a few times. Welcome to our home. Over time, I am sure I will get to know you better. And my husband and son should tell you that I look ten times better when the housecoat, hair rollers, and face cream come off," Beverly cajoled.

"I can tell by the pictures on the wall, Mrs. Anderson, that you are a beautiful woman," Booker complimented.

"Well, I like him already," she laughed. "Come in the kitchen and tell me more."

"Hey, Mom, what about me? How was your day?" Bobby asked, playfully feeling ignored.

"Baby, I'm sorry. My day was good. Come in the kitchen and tell Momma all about your day while she fixes your plate, feeds you, burps you, and then bathes you," Beverly teased as she kissed him.

"Ahhh, Mom, you slobbered and got cream on me," Bobby joked.

"Boy, you just get in the kitchen and eat. You have school in the morning."

As Beverly and Bobby walked towards the kitchen, Booker said, "I need to call my parents. Can I use the phone?"

"It is right on top of the table next to the lampstand. When you are finished, just come to the kitchen," Jimmy instructed.

Booker returned five minutes later with permission to stay at the Andersons' home. He was welcomed with the scent of pinto beans, fried chicken, and cornbread. The meal was complimented with sweet tea. Beverly bid the three guys goodnight once the meal was on the table. Bobby followed shortly after that to take a shower and go to bed. Jimmy and Booker were left talking about the basketball game and Jimmy's days of playing basketball in high school. By the time they made it upstairs, they were welcomed by the sounds of Bobby's low-frequency snoring and Beverly's rhythmic breathing.

Jimmy escorted Booker to the guest bedroom with a twin bed, a matching dresser, and a small black and white TV on a TV tray encased squarely by a wall. Moments later, Jimmy showed Booker the guest room. "You'll be sleeping in this room. You can put your dirty clothes in this bag. You can put these clothes on once you are finished. You can shower next door. The towel and soap are on the bed. I'll make sure everything is clean. By the way, sorry, but the bathroom door doesn't close all the way. I'll get it fixed in a few days. Take as long as you need. Let me know if you need anything. My home is your home," Jimmy gushed.

"Thanks, Mr. Anderson," Booker politely mouthed. I really like how this house feels," Booker commented.

"Well, maybe you can come by more often, and we can talk about what I did to get this house. I am a military man. We can talk about that as an option since you need to think about life after high school," Jimmy advised. "But it is late, so go ahead and shower. There is even a new pack of underwear next to the towel that I hope fits you, "Jimmy added slyly as he quickly stole a look at Booker's crotch. Booker boldly responded, "Thanks for everything," before closing the door to disrobe.

Booker turned on the radio as he disrobed in the teal-blue bathroom. Sam Cooke was crooning, with Booker dancing and lip-syncing to the lyrics. Wearing only white briefs, Jimmy looked through the three-inch gap in the bathroom door. He noticed Booker's green briefs were on top of his basketball uniform in the guestroom. He grabbed them and put them on his head in sexual pleasure, allowing Booker's aroma to overtake his olfactory senses.

Jimmy was a masculine man by societal and religious standards. While he masturbated, he thought back at his sexual experiences with Marc Petry 20 years ago. Jimmy's religious convictions instilled fear about acting out his sexual desires with men, though he had a few male-to-male sexual encounters in his youth. But there was something about Booker that brought it all back.

Jimmy's mind quickly focused on Booker when Booker slightly bent his knees while masturbating. Booker closed his eyes as he stroked faster. The moment Booker opened his mouth, Jimmy inhaled deeply, imagining that he was performing fellatio on Booker, working to get him to climax. The thought instantly caused Jimmy to ejaculate. He used his briefs to collect all of the seminal evidence. Seconds later, Booker released heavy semen, which was swallowed down the drain of the tub. Booker let out a sigh of relief before rinsing off again.

Jimmy quickly got his clothes out of the linen closet and tiptoed into the bedroom that Beverly and he shared.

The next morning, Jimmy dropped Bobby and Booker off at Brelding High School. "Booker, you left a book in the car," Jimmy called.

"Bobby, tell Dreama I'll be in shortly," Booker said.

Bobby nodded in the affirmative as he walked inside.

Booker walked back to the car and took the book from Jimmy. "Thanks, Mr. Anderson."

"Call me Jimmy. Classes don't start for another 20 minutes. Why don't you ride with me to the store?" Jimmy invited.

Booker, happy to be the focus of attention, got in.

The Coca-Cola commercial interrupted Jimmy's thoughts when he heard ratta-tat-tat on the vinyl door. Jimmy took another swig of his Pabst Blue Ribbon as he casually walked to the door. "Happy Birthday, Old Man!" Booker chortled as he brought the brown bag and Mary Jane, the perfect break for Jimmy to steal a kiss from Booker. "It's my birthday. What are you gonna do for me?" Jimmy asked as he gazed into Booker's eyes.

He nervously stated, "We are not having sex today. We have to talk."

Jimmy said, "What is it?"

"I am not going to have sex with you anymore. In fact, I'm not seeing you anymore," Booker stated, as if he was reading from a cue card, though his unzipped pants couldn't hide his interest.

"Are you jiving me? What do you mean? We have a good thing going on," Jimmy sounded bewildered.

"I am getting married and have a baby on the way. I have to focus on what society and my religious beliefs say I should do. I know we had a good time, and I will always love you for it, but I can't do this anymore. We can work on being friends. Of course, we can hang loose occasionally. My priorities have to change. I hope you understand."

Jimmy walked around his living room, caressing Booker's right hand and stating, "I'm married too. I met you when you were at your lowest point. Think about all of what I've done for you. I've gotten you a job, given you money, bought your school clothes, and helped you run away from home when you didn't get along with yo' parents. Look, I'm all you got. And now you wanna get married?"

Look, "I appreciate everything you have done for me, giving me so much and being the first man I've had sex with. You helped get me a job as a bus driver. You've been doing my schoolwork and helping me get to the next grade. But I can't let you control me just cuz you're helpin' me. We been fuckin' around since I was 16 and you were 36. I was a kid who needed help and guidance; you made me feel like the only way to pay you back was to have sex with you anytime and anywhere you wanted. I understood you were married, but now you act like I can't be married. And you know I need more support now than ever. Don't cut me off."

The broadcaster's breaking news announcement tapped Booker on the shoulder, stopping him mid-thought. "There were more than twenty men arrested today in New York for degeneracy, cruising for sex with men in the local rest stops. The FBI Director is reported as saying, 'We cannot allow these people with sexually deviant behaviors to overrun our country. I will use all my power to ensure the American public that these people are prosecuted to the fullest extent of the law.'"

"That is the shit I am talking about," Booker resumed his thought. Black people are already going through hell from White folks. What do you think would happen if people found out we were fucking? That's why I need to leave this shit alone and get married."

"I won't support it," Jimmy stated resolutely.

"What do you mean you won't still support me since I am getting married?

"I mean exactly that," Jimmy replied matter-of-factly. "You owe me. I got this apartment for you, bought you clothes for school, and fed you. I sheltered you when you would argue with your parents. I had you around my wife and family; Bobby and you are great friends. If you get married, you won't be free to leave or continue to meet me. So you can forget about getting additional support from me unless you don't get married. I need you."

Jimmy reached for Booker with a nervous boldness, hoping to use the last modicum of his manipulative, camouflaged desperation to maintain power. Booker recoiled as if a snake were springing upon him.

"It just means that I have to move on with my life. We live in a society where two males shouldn't be fucking. Plus, you're married. Did you hear about the recent arrest at the rest stop where sixty men were arrested?" Booker asked. "The Director of the FBI can't stand Black people, and even though he dresses in drag himself and enjoys boys, he certainly wants to out every male that wants to have sex with another male from time to time."

Booker continued, "I know you've done a lot for me; you got me a place to stay when I got tired of being around my parents. We've had good sex. But I'm 18 now, and I have a baby on the way. I can't keep this up. And I'll always keep this secret between us since I don't want Bobby disappointed."

"Well, we've been doing this for years, and no one suspects us. I don't understand where this is coming from. Don't you love me, Booker?"

Booker stated, "I really don't know what this is. I don't even know how I am supposed to feel about you. We can't hang out as much because I'm about to be a husband and a father."

Jimmy stood up and walked around in a circle; suddenly, his countenance changed. He looked at Booker square in his eyes and said, "Boy, you ain't nothing without me. And I promise you that I am cutting you off financially. I got you that job as a bus driver. I helped you out with your studies. I bought you clothes and food. I wrote you love letters that I asked that you keep since I wanted you to be with me forever. How many kids does your mother have, seven or eight and, you the oldest? They damn sure haven't taken care of you like I have. But I will ruin your life if you end what we have. You don't know how much power I carry."

"Oh, so, this is retaliation?" Booker asked.

Jimmy flatly stated, "Hell yeah. This is payback because you are rejecting me and what I want."

"So you mean to tell me that being with me is what you wanted? You just simply want to use me? You're the one who introduced me to having sex with a man two years ago. And though you are active in your church and have spoken against homosexuality, you've been with me all the time and shown me pictures and even made a real-to-reel video of us having sex and took Polaroids, too. I risked so much by being with you, and that's what you don't see. You made me keep the pictures and the reel-to-reel in my possession. And all you can say is you want to get back at me now just because I'm grown now, and I made a decision! But let me tell you this. You haven't seen the last of me," Booker warned. "You want to pay me back? I'm getting ready to pay you back."

"Get out of my house! I don't want to see you again!" Jimmy stated in a raised voice.

Booker walked slowly towards the door. He turned quickly and stated: "You will see me one more time and regret the day you fucked with me."

5

The Closet Without Doors

Beverly Anderson peeped out the window to see the burgundy Lincoln Continental ease its way to the curb of her house. "It is about time that girl got here. We are pressed for time getting to the wedding rehearsal," Beverly whispered as she closed the rose-patterned curtain.

That girl, Wanda Oates, was the bride who was marrying Kenneth. Wanda was a chocolate-skinned twenty-year-old woman with bright, bulging eyes and a wide smile. She was a burly figure with a deep voice and an afro three inches longer in the front and sides than in the back. The neighborhood community never thought she would get married due to her reputation as a manly-looking woman with the face and hairstyle of Mrs. Potato Head and the body of Fred Flintstone. She had faint facial hair; the neighborhood women gossiped about her not being a *real* woman since she did not wear heels and hardly wore dresses—although no one had the nerve to tell her that in person out of fear of how she fights like the man she looks like. She and Kenneth went to two sporting events in one month. On their second outing, she was in love with him. He was only interested in being around her because she knew sports, so he treated her like one of the guys. She knew he was far more handsome than she was pretty, even with donning the best of any cosmetic brand.

Kenneth was a sports enthusiast, and his chiseled six-foot-four frame showed it. Kenneth's dark chocolate skin, straight chalk-white teeth, and slanted eyes were hypnotizing to everyone he encountered. He met his match after Wanda took a trip to the south, where a root doctor gave her a small satchel of ingredients said to make any man fall in love with the satchel holder. The only direction she had to follow was to pepper the taste-less ingredients over his favorite dish. The next time he came to her house, she already had his plate of fried chicken thighs, rice with gravy, green peas, deep-dished apple pie, and sun-brewed sweet tea on the table. She carefully watched him voraciously eat as she casually nibbled on her plate of a small chicken thigh, a spoonful of rice, and green peas (though her rect-angular shape could not hide her secret penchant for eating heavy meals.) Immediately after taking that last morsel of that southern dinner, Kenneth burped and said, "Woman, this food was so good. I want to marry you." Two weeks later, he proposed. They were getting married the next day, and it was the town's gossip.

Wanda arrived at Beverly's house with the wedding decorations. Wanda was putting on the last makeup retouches since she sweated pro-fusely while driving to Beverly's house, even though the windows were rolled down. She checked her cracked compact, pursing her lips and cock-ing her head from side-to-side for a final look. Just as she started to open her car door, she noticed someone emerging from the forestry area across the street.

Booker was quite disheveled as the forest regurgitated him on his two-speed metallic blue bike and a small box. He wiped the sweat from his face and the dust from his clothes just before he picked up the small cardboard box. Satisfied with his effort, he dropped the bike on the shoulder of the road as he walked across the street to Anderson's red front door. Wanda remained in the car, befuddled over who this teenage boy was and why he would be at the home. She watched vigilantly, wondering how to plot her next move.

Booker set the box on the porch just before knocking violently on the door and then turning his body laterally. Beverly peered out the window, frightened that she could not immediately tell who was knocking. She sure wished she hadn't allowed Bobby to spend the weekend with his older brother Willie, who lived across town. But she reasoned within herself, knowing he was a graduating senior. Still, she would have felt more secure had he been in the house.

She could see Wanda leaning towards the passenger's seat, watching Booker as if she had eagle eyes. Booker knocked a second time for a solid fifteen seconds, causing Beverly to jump away from the window out of fear of being seen.

"Open this door, you selfish son-of-a-bitch!" Booker shouted. Growing impatient, Booker grabbed a red brick from the flower bed of daisies and threw it through Anderson's dining room window. Beverly screamed so loudly that Wanda drove her car up the driveway. Just as she turned off the ignition, Jimmy's Chevrolet Impala sped up the driveway, with Jimmy's eyes fixed on Booker, whose teenage insouciance made Jimmy angry.

Jimmy rushed out of the car, leaving the motor running. Quickly glancing at Wanda, he shrieked, "What the fuck happened to my window?"

Booker said, "Step one to pay back, you sorry ass asshole."

"To damage my window at my house? And your broke ass don't have the money to replace it. I am getting ready to call the police. Now, how is that for payback?!" Jimmy hollered.

Booker retorted, "What the fuck do you mean? My fingerprints are all in your house! And you know it. Do I need to name where? Surely you remember last week when I was over here."

"I remember that I should've never had you at my house, you fucking bum. You walked all the way here to try to get back at me. You don't know who you fucking with! And another thing . . ."

Just as Jimmy was about to say more, Beverly interrupted by opening the door and questioning, "Jimmy, is everything all right?" As she walked to the end of the porch, she said, "The neighbors have been calling to check on us due to this outside commotion." Upon seeing Booker, she sighed and said, "Oh, Booker. It is you. Had I known, I would've opened the door. I couldn't see your face as you knocked so hard. I haven't seen you in a week. But who threw the brick?" Beverly stated with relief. "And what is this talk about police and fingerprints, Jimmy? Booker has often been to our home and has caused no trouble. What is all this fuss about?"

"Your husband is threatening to call the police on me when I've been nothing but good to him. So good that our fingerprints are in the kitchen, on the porch, and even in your bedroom," Booker charged. Jimmy attempted to camouflage his nerves by saying, "Well, I won't call the police. You are like a son to me, so I brought you around my family."

"Just a second, Jimmy," Beverly mentioned curiously. Tell me more about these fingerprints in MY bedroom," Beverly uttered with suspicion.

"Now, now I think this whole thing can be resolved if only Booker and I talked . . ." Jimmy intervened.

"No, this will be resolved now in my presence as a family!" Beverly said matter-of-factly. And Booker, it's time that you complete your answer to my question."

"Your husband and I have been fucking around for the past two years. We fucked in every part of this house, including on your bed. If the son-of-a-bitch wants to call the police, he needs to tell them that," Booker revealed. Immediately, Wanda began to cough upon hearing this news; Booker, Jimmy, and Beverly had forgotten her presence. "Wanda, get out of the car, girl, and go in the house to get some water," Beverly commanded. "Jimmy, go see about Wanda and turn your car's engine off."

"Now, Booker, this accusation is a very strong one. I know that Jimmy and you have a mentor-mentee relationship. You are still a boy who may be trying to figure out his identity. My husband is a church leader who knows what the Bible says about homosexuality. And even though he uses expletives when he is angry, he is an upstanding man."

"How upstanding is it for him to seduce me, fuck me for years, and then try to manipulate me when I am trying to end this sexual relationship?" Booker chided.

Having overheard the dialogue while leading a shocked Wanda into the house, Jimmy realized his defeat and made a last-ditch effort to muster some courage. "You a lying ass! How dare you falsely accuse me. You must be going through a phase where you like men. You know I don't go for that punk-ass shit!" Jimmy spat out the words defensively.

"How the fuck is it a false accusation when I got the proof right here!" Booker squinted his eyes at Jimmy as he said, "Then you can see for yourself who is *upstanding*."

As Booker walked to the top of the porch to get the box, Beverly looked at Jimmy with disgust. "What am I going to see, Jimmy, when this boy presents this box?" Beverly spoke fiercely.

"Beverly, I have no idea what he has in that box. This boy is making trouble, and I have a good mind to beat his ass like his daddy should've done," Jimmy snarled after realizing that the surrounding neighbors stood outside their respective homes witnessing the whole kerfuffle.

"Well, guess no more!" Booker concluded as he handed Beverly the open box. Inside, you will find a treasure trove of all the evidence you need to find him guilty!"

Beverly shook her head back and forth as tears flooded her eyes upon seeing the first picture. As she continued to view each picture, she uttered, "No, no," and her head shook more vehemently. When she saw the picture of Booker and Jimmy's intimate moments, she screamed, "NO! NO! NO! NO! NO!" As she stepped from the door's threshold, Wanda threw her arms around Beverly and slowly whisked her into the house. Booker—in a triumphant voice—added, "Don't forget to watch the reel-to-reel if you really wanna see why your husband prefers me than you."

Jimmy was embarrassed when he realized that all eyes were on him. He childishly chortled, "There has got to be a total mistake of identity. That ain't me! Why did you come around this neighborhood causing trouble?

People who are homosexual have a mental illness, and clearly, you have a mental illness that caused you to act this way." Jimmy nodded his head while pausing for ten seconds to assess a response from the bewildered crowd.

"You need to stop acting like you're a victim and face the fact that you are no longer a closeted homosexual. You caused trouble the day you decided to marry Beverly, knowing you like dick," Booker charged.

"I am calling the police to have you arrested. Then we will see who will land in the newspapers tomorrow."

"Call them. I will give them all of the evidence, too. Do you think those are the only pictures I have? Remember, you taught me how to hold the camera to snap the picture of Deacon Jimmy Anderson."

"Jimmy! Get inside this house NOW!" Beverly screamed uncontrollably as she held the door open. And as for you, Booker, the police will be here any moment to arrest you for property damage." Beverly looked around and saw the neighbors walking towards her yard. "All of y'all can go home. You're just coming over to be nosey. I'm handling my household. Now go and handle yours. OUT!" she shrieked.

Booker ran across the street and disappeared into the forest with his bicycle, keeping him company. Just as he hopped on, he heard the police sirens wailing. He turned his bicycle around and peeked his head out to witness the exchange. Beverly was the first to greet the policemen, and Jimmy followed.

"Well, well, well, look at what happened here. Was there a protest in this pristine neighborhood, too?" said Officer Glen, a White male in his fifties, morbidly overweight. "Yeah, it looks like somebody broke a window in the name of equal rights," mentioned Officer Smith. Both officers laughed harder than they should have to arouse Beverly and Jimmy's anger. They did not respond to it, knowing that the officers would find any reason to pull out a baton to commence an all-out brawl. "So why did you call us?"

"A boy named Booker—Jimmy, what is Booker's last name? Johnson, isn't it?"

Jimmy hesitated as if he was trying to think before responding, "Williams."

"Booker Williams?" Beverly questioned while giving Jimmy the side-eye, knowing he was lying. Jimmy told her Booker's last name was Johnson when he first introduced Booker.

"Anyway, Officer, he came over and threw a brick through the window. I want him to pay for the damage."

"Where is he now?"

"He left through the woods."

"How do you know he did it? Did you see him throw the brick?

"Well, no, I did not. But I . . ."

"Then how do you think we are to arrest someone who you didn't see a brick thrown?"

Realizing they were not going to get any assistance from the policemen, Beverly shared, "You have his name. What other information do you need?"

"His address?"

Beverly looked at Jimmy, who responded, "I don't know."

"How old is he?"

"18"

"Is he a Negro?"

"Yes."

"Uh-huh. It's always the Negros who do this stupid shit. Then they call us to fix the problems in their community," Officer Smith boldly stated.

"Ma'am, we just don't have time to look into this matter. You people need to do better in your communities to resolve your own issues. Even now, you may have thrown a brick through your own window in the name of trying to get insurance money," Officer Glen advised.

"Thank you for your time," Beverly whispered, unable to hide her humiliation. She wasn't sure if it was Booker, Jimmy, or this fat cop who caused her to feel mortified.

"That's, thank you, SIR, for your time," Officer Glen *corrected.*

"Thank you, sir, for your time," Beverly repeated as she burned with greater indignation.

She stood in the driveway, ossified by the events of the day. The cops backed out of the driveway only to hit the metallic mailbox post. "It was a raggedy mailbox that needed replacing anyway! We just helped you get rid of the damn thing" the officers laughed heartily as they placed the gearshift in D and slowly drove off.

"I know how we can replace the mailbox," Jimmy mumbled nervously.

Beverly rolled her eyes and walked back towards the house. Jimmy cautiously went in behind her. The swing-and-slam of the door cued Beverly to break her silence.

"How dare you make me the laughingstock of this neighborhood! For the past twenty-two years, I have been covering for you, justifying to others why I know you aren't a homosexual. I still have the love letters you received from Marc Petry during the 2nd year we were married. I stood by you when you were working night shifts at Johnny's Textile Mill, claiming to be working overtime, only for me to find Tommy Cannes and you in the back seat of the car, steaming up the windows as I pulled over to pick you up. I came to your defense even when you were going to the gym with our daughter's boyfriend Lamont, only to find out from the gym's manager that y'all got caught sucking each other's dicks while being in the same shower. I had to pay that manager for a solid year not to tell anyone. To this day, our daughter does not know that her ex-boyfriend and her father like sucking dick. And then, on top of that, you lie about Booker's last name to protect him while you've done nothing throughout our marriage to protect me!"

Jimmy held his head down in undeniable guilt, especially since he was stung by Beverly's usage of descriptively vulgar language. He was not sure what to say or do since he could not refute any of the obvious evidence presented. He glanced up carefully, hoping she would not look back at him right before Beverly ordered, "Look at me!"

Beverly then hissed, "This is what you WILL DO! First, you will tell the children, then I am going to call Pastor Allison so that you can tell him too!" Beverly walked to the wall-mounted rotary phone to dial Willie Anderson's phone. Willie was the oldest child of three and homophobic; Martha was the only daughter who was indifferent about anything; Bobby saw Booker as a best friend, though all they talked about was sports and girls. Jimmy was fearful of how Willie might react and what he might say. Willie had a reputation for going to the streets, corralling other homophobic men to taunt as part of his one-man crusade against all things gay. He was also concerned about what Bobby might think since Booker, and he had a great relationship.

Jimmy forlornly asked as Beverly picked up the receiver, "Please do not do that. I want us to work on our marriage. That would ruin our pristine reputation. You know that people look up to us for marital counseling. We have a perfect marriage," he stated pathetically.

"Our marriage has never been perfect, Jim. It takes two to make it work, and doing that makes the two people work towards perfecting it. The joke has been on you for so long, Jim, that now the joke is on me. I am going to call the Pastor myself, then I'm calling the children."

Beverly placed the wide-rimmed glasses on her dejected face before opening the large telephone book. She looked under C for Churches and then found the information. Pronouncing each syllable, Beverly said in a weary voice, "Reverend M. B. Allison, Saint Elijah Baptist Church 555-78 . . ." Jimmy was tempted to snatch the phone book away but figured doing so would be another admission of guilt.

"Thank you for calling Saint Elijah Baptist Church, where we serve a miracle-working God. This is Reverend Countee Allison. How may I be of service?" the young Reverend melodiously spoke.

Surprised that the younger Reverend Allison answered the phone, Beverly didn't bother to exchange pleasantries even though she wanted to speak to Reverend M. B. Allison. She exclaimed, "My husband has a homosexual spirit, and I want a divorce!"

"Wha . . . what? Please, Sister. Tell me who you are."

"This is Beverly Anderson, Deacon Jimmy Anderson's soon-to-be ex-wife. Is your father available?"

"No, Pastor Allison has taken ill today and asked me to serve in his capacity. I am happy to help. Why do you feel that way, and why do you want to go that route?" the younger Reverend stated quietly to avoid being overheard by passersby.

"He likes to have sex with males, and I have proof!" Beverly stated robotically.

"Let's not be hasty, Mrs. Anderson. Perhaps there is another route you can consider."

"Well, too many men have been involved in this marriage for years, which has put this marriage *asunder* a long time ago. As soon as the courthouse opens Monday morning, I will see an attorney about putting this marriage asunder legally," Beverly retorted. "And another thing, he. . ."

The Reverend saw his secretary walking into his office. "Sister Rosa Lee, cancel my remaining appointments for the day," Reverend Allison mouthed to his secretary, placing the palm of his hand on the receiver while Beverly continued ranting. When he released his hand from the receiver, Beverly was in the middle of her accusations: ". . . so I didn't say anything to him even though those letters described the kind of sex he and Marc had. I kept parading around others at the church as if we were in love. And that took so much energy. Furthermore, we were counseling other couples, yet not even following the advice we gave."

"Mrs. Anderson, before you do anything, I will come over to pray for the two of you and give some spiritual counseling."

"I respect your willingness to try to help Reverend. But I didn't call to get counseling; I called to expose him for his sin. He is the one who needs prayer and deliverance. He no longer deserves to be a Deacon. Sit him down immediately!"

"Sister, let's talk about this when I arrive. In the meantime, stay away from him until I get there."

"He hasn't touched me in over twenty years, so it is natural for us to stay away from one another. When you get over here, I have more to say!" Reverend Allison's head snapped back quickly as he held the phone away from his ear once he heard the click.

6

Clobber Him

"I appreciate you coming, Reverend Allison. I am sorry to hear that Pastor Allison has taken ill. I hope it is nothing serious," Beverly shared with concern.

"Pastor Allison is coming along. The doctors have run a variety of tests and reported that he is experiencing high blood pressure induced by stress. He will be taking medication daily. Just continue to pray for him," the young Allison posited.

"Would you like some coffee or tea?"

"Don't go through the trouble."

"Well, I have to admit that you seem a little too young to speak on marital concerns and family, considering you have only been at the church for a year or so. And are you even thirty yet?"

"I courted my wife, Vanessa, for two years prior to marrying her. We have had our share of ups and downs in the relationship. I was a pastor in Texas prior to coming here to be back under my father's ministry. Plus, I have a master's degree in pastoral counseling," Reverend Allison carefully articulated as if he were interviewing for a counseling position. "And I am 35 years old and have been married for fifteen years, and we have four children aged nine to fourteen. Enough about me. What seems to be the problem?"

Satisfied with the cursory review of his verbalized credentials, Beverly poignantly voiced, "My husband is a closeted homosexual Deacon who needs to be relieved from his duties. And Rev, you know what the Bible says about homosexuals. All of them are going to hell! Even the leading psychologists say they have a mental illness," Beverly hissed. "I can't be bothered with this anymore. I want a divorce!"

Reverend Allison asked, "How long have you held this perception?"

Beverly adamantly stated, "As I told you over the phone, it's been twenty years, and we've been married for twenty-two years. I didn't want to break up our marriage because of the children. Now that the children are grown, I need a man who loves me for me. James and I have not had sex since year two of the marriage, and I need to be touched. I am getting older, and I cannot waste time with a man who also wants a man." With a sigh of resignation, Beverly looked at Jimmy, who sat gloomily at the kitchen table, and murmured, "Tell him yourself, Jimmy. Tell him the reason you haven't touched me in 20 years. Tell him about your fetish for a teenage boy; tell him about the two of you having sex in MY house. Tell him!" Beverly stopped herself after recognizing her voice was cracking.

"Well, Rev," Jimmy voiced with a drawl. "I only had a fling with a man who happens to be eighteen. He likes women, too. He got a girl pregnant and was getting ready to marry her. I guess I got caught up with having one too many drinks since I had never been with a man before then, and I . . ." Jimmy stopped mid-sentence, noticing that Beverly nodded her head from left to right, facepalming as she whimpered.

The Reverend emphatically shared, "I completely understand your sentiment, Beverly. We have to be guided by the Good Book and determine the best course of action. You have been married for too long to allow anything to interfere with the marriage. With prayer and pastoral counseling, your marriage can survive. For the Bible says . . ."

Jimmy noticed Beverly looking pensive while the Reverend continued speaking. He interrupted, saying, "But she wants me to tell the children about this incident. It would tear the family apart." He appealed to Beverly,

"Most couples look at our marriage as a model. I know I haven't been perfect and have been neglecting you all these years. I see the error of my ways crystal clear. I need another chance."

"The Bible says we should forgive, Sister," the Reverend posited.

"What does the Bible say about a woman who has given up her life to a man who gives his body to another man? What does it say about how to overcome this pain? What does it say about what to do when he goes out and meets another man to have sex with? Oh, I've been such a fool! I didn't know he was a homosexual," Beverly said, her voice shaking.

"Sometimes the truth is harder to face than a lie. Have you thought about what role you play in this matter?" Reverend Allison mentioned quizzically.

"Role? What role?" Beverly said curiously.

Refusing to have a conversation around banalities, the Reverend coolly shared: "You say you didn't know he was a homosexual. Yet, for the past twenty years, you say you have been covering for his sexuality. You have evidence that dates back to year two of your marriage that he enjoys having sex with men. Ask yourself: Why did you stay in the marriage with this knowledge? If it did not bother you in year two, why did it bother you in year twenty-two? Are you a masochist whereby you enjoy this pain you say you are experiencing? And since his sexuality is not new to you, then clarify why you say you've been a fool?"

Beverly pursed her lips together and hoarsely forced this response: "I guess I need to reflect on those questions. But why can't you see that I am the victim in this?"

"I am not taking sides, Sister Anderson. And I haven't even gotten to Brother Anderson yet. I strive to guide your thinking to look at additional facets surrounding this matter."

"I protected him out of the love I have for him. I thought I could change him," Beverly said, looking defeated. "Isn't that always why the woman stays? I have children, I have financial concerns . . ."

"And the love sounds like it is still there." The Reverend glanced at this watch surreptitiously before adding, "Now, what do the two of you think about us meeting twice a week for a month to plan a course of action? For starters, I will give you the number of one of my dad's dearest friends, Dr. Ruthie Gunther, who can provide resources that may help. Don't tell anyone about this matter, including your children. I can meet with you one-on-one, Brother Anderson, then with you, Sister Anderson, then bring the two of you together. And it is best to say nothing about this to anyone. How does that sound?"

"This is a marvelous idea. Beverly, I am willing to make this work, and I hope you are too," Jimmy said with a forced enthusiasm.

"I don't even know what to think now. I know I won't say anything about it. I also know you will sleep in the guest bedroom and not share the master bathroom with me. I don't know what you may be carrying. I don't care how much penicillin you might've already taken."

"Whatever, Beverly. I just need time for us to work this out together," Jimmy said in exasperation.

"Well, Brother and Sister, it sounds like we have a plan. I'll pray for you both. And Jimmy, I'll have Sister Rosa Lee call you to schedule a time to counsel you one day next week. Let me pray over both of you."

As the Reverend prayed over Beverly and Jimmy, Jimmy's thoughts were on how to see Booker again while trying to keep Beverly from divorcing him.

7

The Pastor Wants My Man

Dreama's back was against the aluminum locker, and Booker stood close to her, whispering jokes just before the bell rang for his English class. "Booker Johnson, please report to the office," Ms. Nancy announced over the intercom. She was the school's secretary, often called Nancy the Nasal. She knew how to move her lips, but her voice box was apparently in her nostrils. Booker gave Dreama a quick kiss before rushing to the office.

"Your father is on the phone. Please limit your call to three minutes," Nancy announced to Booker without looking at him. "Use the phone in the back corner and press down on the flashing light button."

"Hello, Dad. I'm surprised you called me at school since I know you're working."

"This is Jimmy. This was the only means I could think of to contact you." Jimmy's voice gave evidence that he missed Booker.

"I've got three minutes. What do you want?" Booker whispered sharply.

"I just want to see you so we can talk. We can move past what happened."

"I told you that I don't want to do that anymore with you, so if that is what it is about, then I am just cool with keeping my distance from you," Booker whispered out of fear of being overheard.

"That's cool. I just want things to be peaceful between us. How about I pick you up after your bus route ends? We can go to the Soda Shack."

"Ok. See you then," Booker sighed.

"Thanks for agreeing to meet me again. I've been really missing . . ."

"Look, I have to get to class, and you know they tap these phones," Booker interrupted as Ms. Nancy glared at him, saying, "You have to get off the phone at this time." As Booker placed the phone back on the receiver, he wondered whether he had made the right decision. "You need to get back to class at this time. I am sure your English teacher wants you in class," Ms. Nancy charged.

"Yes, Ma'am," Booker said respectfully. He thought, "I wish this bitch would blow her nose."

Jimmy arrived at the bus lot and waited for Booker's bus to pull in. He consciously wore fitting brown bell bottoms with a brown and tan shirt with circular patterns, which is the same outfit he had on when he initially met Booker. He was nervous about seeing him. Jimmy reflected on his counseling sessions with Reverend Allison, playing back each word that was said.

"So, tell me about your feelings for Booker?"

"I think I love him as one who wants to be in a relationship with him, while I also want to be married to my wife."

"What do you love about him?"

"He's attractive, passionate, witty, and makes me feel wanted."

"Tell me more about the passion and desire of feeling wanted. Are you not getting this from home?"

"We have good sex. The chemistry between us binds us together. And I haven't gotten this from Beverly at all."

"Does the good sex with Booker impact your ability to experience good sex with Beverly?"

"I desire to have sex with men that impact my ability to give Beverly the kind of sex she deserves. I just want to be married to her and fulfill all of my duties as a husband except to have sex with her."

"Beverly deserves all of you. You must've had an active sexual relationship at one time since you have three children."

"Well, we did. But even then, I'd have to pull out the porn magazines and admire men's penises to get an erection prior to having sex with her. I didn't even feel emotionally connected to her and imagined having sex with a man. The visual images aroused my curiosity about having sex with a man."

"Well, in order to rekindle your marriage to Beverly, you need to speak with Booker. Search within yourself over whether you forgive him. You can share that you will not see him again and that you'll pray for him. Call the school. They will conclude that you are his dad. Arrange to pick him up at a location of your choosing. Then drive him to the Soda Shack, where I will meet both of you. I will be there for support and to perhaps provide spiritual advice to Booker. Perhaps you and Beverly could explore how to love and make love again."

Booker snatched open the passenger door of Jimmy's car, breaking Jimmy's thought process. Jimmy looked around, realizing he was oblivious to Booker's bus pulling up to the parking lot. Booker stood in the door's opening as he spoke with another bus driver about an abbreviated schedule for the next day. Jimmy could only see Booker's mid-torso, which showcased his button-down shirt and bell-bottom jeans. Jimmy wanted to reach out and touch him. Jimmy murmured as Booker closed the door, "It is good to see you. Let's go to the Soda Shack and talk."

"Thanks. I can't stay out long since I have to pick up Dreama at six," Booker reported, a little nervous himself.

The five-mile ride was completed in silence since Jimmy did not want to say anything that might upset Booker. Booker looked straight ahead, not even noticing what Jimmy was wearing. Booker did not want to relive the events from weeks prior or be asked how he planned to reimburse the Andersons for replacing the broken window. When Jimmy turned off the car ignition, Booker managed to say, "The food smells good."

Jimmy replied, "So you have been here before?" "No, my dad hardly takes us out for dinner since there are too many children to feed in the house."

Upon walking into the Soda Shack, Booker was enamored by its cleanliness. The red leather seating booths were carefully covered in clear plastic, and the faux marble floor smelled faintly of Pine-Sol. The aluminum napkin dispensers accentuated the red and yellow ketchup and mustard containers on the white countertops. "This place is happening," Booker managed to say.

"Let's grab this booth and sit down," Jimmy said as he pointed left.

"Welcome to the Soda Shack. What will you boys have?" Maybelline, the large, gap-toothed, dark-skinned waitress said.

"Give me a cheese sandwich and Fanta Grape," Jimmy decided.

"And I'll take a cheeseburger with fries and a Tab," Booker ordered.

"Give it about ten minutes for your order to be ready," Maybelline said.

"So, we didn't talk the whole ride here. Why did you call me?" Booker questioned.

"I just wanted to say that what happened between us has . . ." Jimmy stopped himself mid-sentence, looking ahead.

"Come on over," motioned Jimmy.

"Who are you talking to, Cat?" Booker murmured.

"Booker, meet Reverend Countee Allison. Booker, meet the Reverend," Jimmy nervously vocalized.

Booker, looking bewildered, loudly whispered, "Why is he joining us at this table?"

"I just figured we needed a person on hand who won't take sides for what words we may say," Jimmy mumbled.

Booker's countenance changed as the Reverend sat down, saying, "Hey, Booker. What's happening?" Booker slowly rose and got in Jimmy's face right before Reverend Allison excitedly asked Booker, "You're one of the star basketball players for Brelding High, right? I knew I recognized you. Man, the last game you played was epic! You scored the last three-pointer that caused Brelding High to win the game. Are you about to show me how it was done? Come on and get up and give us the play-by-play man." The Reverend's voice became elevated, drawing attention from other customers. Whereby one of them said, "Yeah, I was there, and that boy can play!" Booker's visage gradually became a bright smile.

"Now I'm Nathan Lee playing defense against you," The Reverend squatted his knees to assume the position. Booker was hyped over the attention he was getting and moved to the aisle. He pantomimed, bouncing the basketball down the sidelines, and quickly spun around the Reverend just before the imaginary three-point line to raise his lanky arms to make the shot. "Final score 55-54! And Brelding wins the game!" Reverend Allison exclaimed with a guttural gasp. The customers cheered as if they were vicariously experiencing the game. Reverend Allison and Booker embraced each other before taking their seats in the booth with Jimmy.

"Man, you have skills. You must've played ball when you were younger." Booker concluded.

"Yeah, I played a couple of sports in my day. And I was quicker and more handsome than you," Reverend Allison boasted.

"We have to play together on the court some time to see if you still have it," Booker challenged. "And you'll never be as handsome as me," Booker laughed.

"We can do that whenever you're ready. There is a court behind my church."

"Sounds like a plan. Man, it felt good to relive that moment!"

"Yeah, you're good. But let's talk about why we are here."

"Ok, talk, Reverend," Booker said.

"Just know that everything we talk about is between us. I keep everything in confidence."

"I understand."

"So, let's just make this a conversation, Brother, so we can work together on moving forward. Cool?"

"That's cool with me."

"Me too."

"Here you are, boys," Maybelline chirped as she placed the food on the table. "And here is some water for you, Reverend. Who knew you could still play ball, Reverend, with all that grown man weight."

"This grown man's weight is the reason I'm going to have just this water."

"Well, if you change your mind, call me. Y'all enjoy."

"Let's say a prayer over the food, gentlemen," the Reverend beseeched.

The jukebox played Sam Cooke's *A Change is Gonna Come* as the Reverend recited a twenty-second prayer over the food and the conversation's outcome.

"All right, Jimmy, why don't you tell Booker what you've shared with me during our counseling sessions?" the Reverend entreated.

"So, what have you been telling this man about us?" Booker stuttered.

"No need to be a nervous young man. In light of what Jimmy shared, it is better to bring your faults to one another and talk about them openly. I am just here to offer guidance. I understand you are about to get married. Congratulations," the Reverend redirected.

"Yeah, I'm about to marry a great girl. She's smart, sweet, pretty . . ."

"I imagine that you want to build a family with her."

"I do."

"That is admirable. I understand how you feel about your soon-to-be wife. Do you have any feelings for anyone else?"

Feeling like the Reverend was seeing through his soul, Booker replied, "I don't have feelings for anyone else."

"How do you feel about Jimmy?"

"Jimmy has been a good friend and guide to me overall. But I felt like he used me and then manipulated me."

"Oh yeah. Explain more about how he used you?"

"Jimmy knows I'm the oldest of seven kids; my parents focus more on my younger brothers and sisters. They let me do what I wanted, which was how I could hang out with Jimmy without them even knowing who he was. He knew I needed a male figure in my life. He introduced me to sex with a man and taught me how to do it. He bought me things I needed, and everything was cool until he wanted to act like my father and threaten me and shit."

"Let's find another way of expressing our words, young brother."

"Sorry, Reverend. I'm starting to feel like this is a waste of time since what's done is done. I'm a changed man and had my experience with a man, and I just don't want to do it anymore. Jimmy, you used sex to try to keep me bound to you and what YOU wanted."

"We weren't a waste of time, Booker, and yeah, it hurt to hear you don't have feelings for me. And you are an eighteen-year-old man! In this state, you can marry at sixteen. If you're old enough to choose to marry, then you're old enough to know and decide to have sex with a man. Stop this bullshit of playing as if you are a victim when you know damn well that you were curious about it and saw me as an opportunity to explore your curiosity. Hell, I was used. As payment for sex with you, I bought you clothes, shoes, and food, got you a job, picked you up from school, introduced you to my family, and more."

"You only gave me those things to manipulate me into remaining your puppet. You were fine when I did not have an original thought since I always did what you wanted. When I shared that I could no longer have sex with you, you threatened revenge. You wanted me to be fine with you being married and having children, yet you wanted to threaten me for wanting the same thing. I'm sorry for throwing the brick through your window, but don't threaten me, and do not expect me to react."

Maybelline sauntered to the booth before saying, "You boys have hardly touched your food. Is everything alright?"

"Everything is great. We just got caught up in conversation. Can we have two bags to carry out the food and the check, please?" the Reverend asked quickly, wondering if Maybelline had overheard any parts of the conversation. "Coming right up," Maybelline said quickly as she sashayed away.

"Jimmy, is this information true?"

"Well, yeah, it is, but I . . ."

"Booker, do you have anything to add?"

"I am hurt that Jimmy did not support me in making an adult decision. I regret everything we've ever done since you expect me to be under your control. I just want the best for you. I am marrying and planning on having children with or without your support."

"Apparently, this relationship is not healthy. Jimmy and Booker, it is suggested that today is the start of you staying separated from one another, not harboring any unforgiveness. Work on strengthening your relationships at home. In this day and age, the two of you have taken risks that could have gotten you killed. You know that one of the leading crimes today is men having sex with men. Do you want to get arrested? It is bad enough that we are fighting for civil rights. You don't need to take on another fight when these people will make sure you will lose."

"It is not something that just goes away, Reverend," Jimmy said.

"Well, let's not get into it here. We can have counseling sessions to discuss it further. You will no longer serve as a deacon until further notice. I have to communicate my decision to the deacon board. I won't give them any details on why. Now, I have to get back to the church. Booker, why don't I give you a ride back home? Jimmy, I will see you Wednesday at 4 p.m. for our counseling session."

"I've been a faithful deacon, Rev. I don't think this is fair, especially since no one knows."

"Booker, Beverly, Wanda, the police, your neighbors, you, and I know. My decision stands."

"Here's your check and bags, boys," Maybelline chirped.

"We will bag up this food. Here is the money; keep the change," the Reverend declared.

Maybelline's eyes widened as she said, "Thank YOU!"

When the three of them got to the parking lot, Jimmy said, "Thanks, Rev, for coming out to talk to us. And Booker, I'll see you around."

Booker threw up his clenched fist to signify peace and Black unity as he looked at Jimmy while getting into the Reverend's Thunderbird. Secretly jealous, Jimmy stood outside his car, watching the Thunderbird disappear from the parking lot.

Jimmy drove in silence for miles, thinking about his role as a deacon, who is a Black bisexual man who has adult children, who has a wife who exposed him, who loves Booker but can't envision a life with him because he is trying to overcome homosexuality as a *mental illness*. He is a man who derides men, who engage in same-sex behaviors to cover up his desire for the same, who doesn't even get a compliment on his outfit from Booker, but he compliments the Reverend. He wondered what the Reverend and Booker were talking about; he became obsessed over the thought that Booker and the Reverend were forming a sexual relationship. After all, they were closer in age. "The *Reverend* ain't fooling nobody; he wants *my* man," Jimmy spoke aloud. "I saw the way you were looking at him and hugging him and shit," Jimmy yakked to himself.

Absent-mindedly, Jimmy pulled his car in the driveway. "Beverly must've gone to the store," he rambled after not seeing her car in the driveway. Feeling dejected, he walked slowly past the window that now held boarded pieces of wood. Upon opening the front door, he exclaimed: "What the FUCK? No, no, this can't be! No, no, this is not happening to me!" Beverly's red handwritten message on the kitchen stove foreshadowed the events to come.

Dear James,

I filed for a legal separation today and moved all of the contents out. Your clothes and other belongings are in the back shed since I am putting the house up for sale tomorrow. And note that while this home is in both of our names, this house became solely mine when you decided to commit adultery for the umpteenth time. I already told the children, your mother, and my mother. Go live your life with Booker since he has made you a happier man than I ever could. The children and I will keep this information private since your choice has been an embarrassment to the family. I will not masquerade as if I am happy with our marriage at the expense of being neglected. I deserved to be loved as the woman I am. I am staying at my mother's. I have tried to stay with you for better or worse. Know that I plan to make my life better and yours worse, for I am taking everything you have except your name, which I will gladly give back!

With No Regrets,
Beverly Madison (formerly Beverly Anderson)

Jimmy wept so hard his tears soaked the red-stained letter. He vowed, "I am going to really fuck up Booker's life six times greater than the way he fucked up mine." Jimmy searched the house for any kind of paper. He finally found a brown paper bag and a pen in the kitchen drawer. He wrote so long on both sides of the bag that the pen ran out of ink.

Jimmy then walked through the back door to get to the brick shed. "At least the ditzy bitch made my shit easy to find," Jimmy huffed while wiping his eyes while opening the black case that housed his .357 Magnum. He checked the chamber to ensure there were six rounds before leaving the shed to go to the post office and then to the church to execute his plan.

"I am sorry, but Reverend Allison has not returned yet. I know you have called three times, Brother Anderson. All I can do is leave him a message," Sister Rosa Lee heaved.

"I told you it is an emergency and that I must see him now. I have been calling from a payphone. Do you not know where he is?" Jimmy stammered.

"He should be back within 30 minutes since he has a meeting with the trustees at six p.m.," Rosa Lee stuttered nervously.

"I will come to the church then and wait."

"Suit yourself, Brother Anderson. You can wait in the sanctuary when you arrive."

Jimmy hung up the phone without saying another word and sped to Saint Elijah Baptist Church.

"So the Reverend is not back yet, huh?" Jimmy grumbled as he drove into the parking lot, where he noticed that Sister Rosa Lee's lime green Ford Thunderbird was the only car present. "By now, he and Booker are probably fucking," Jimmy reasoned as he got out of his car. Jimmy looked at his reflection in the glass as he closed the door, not recognizing the man he was becoming. He mustered the courage to walk inside the Reverend's office, where Sister Rosa Lee did not bother to exchange pleasantries. Curtly, she said, "Like I told you over the phone, you can wait in the sanctuary. And another thing, if he is not back within thirty minutes, you will be leaving since I will be leaving then, too. Now, if you will excuse me, I have work to do." Sister Rosa Lee pointed in the direction of the sanctuary as a non-verbal way of telling him to get out. Jimmy angrily made a swift exit as he placed his hand in his pocket.

Jimmy fumed while he entered the sanctuary, "Now I've been rejected by the church, Beverly, and Booker. My children have disowned me. My mother will side with Beverly. I will have an ugly divorce. She will take everything I got. My neighbors have spread what they witnessed. I can't handle this stress. Lord, this pressure is too much. Please forgive me for what I am about to do."

Jimmy raised the gun under his chin, closed his eyes, and pulled the trigger. Rosa Lee let out a shrill scream since the bang startled her. Upon seeing Jimmy's brain matter and blood spatter on the first three pews, she dialed the operator to have her call the police. She managed to give them the address before passing out on the phone.

The Reverend arrived, noticing a news crew, ambulances, police officers, and neighbors swarming around the parking lot. He rushed out of his car, leaving the engine running, asking, "What happened? What is going on?"

"Please stay back and let us do our work," the White freckled-face policeman kindly stated.

"I am the pastor of this church. Please tell me something so I can contact the necessary families." The news crew and neighbors quickly swarmed around the Reverend, some nearly tripping over the microphone cords as they pointed the microphone at him. There was a cacophony of questions, accusations, name-calling, and shouting. The Reverend managed to hear:

"Sir, can you tell us whether this was an attack?"

"Why did someone bring a gun to church?"

"What kind of nigger would bring a gun in church? If he wanted to be shot, he just needed to go to any White neighborhood."

"Well, we do need somebody to recognize these niggers," the lead officer snarled.

The Reverend was enraged hearing Black people referred to as such, but he managed to maintain a calm demeanor. "Where are they?"

"Oh, I can't take this! Why, Lord, why?!" the Reverend heard. He ran past the policemen and news crew to see Sister Rosa Lee screaming while she was rolled out on a gurney. "Rosa Lee, are you hurt? Quickly tell me what happened," the Reverend demanded as she was being rolled into the ambulance.

"Jimmy shot himself in the head, and now he is dead. Sister Rosa Lee managed to say through her tears. The Reverend stood in shock, whispering, "I just saw this man." Just then, the ambulance workers were seen zipping Jimmy's body in a black body bag. "Just a moment," the tall, lanky veteran policeman directed.

"Pastor, can you identify this body? Perhaps he was one of your parishioners." The Reverend nodded in the affirmative. The kind police officer unzipped the body bag, exposing only the portion of Jimmy's face that had not been damaged. "Yes, that is James Anderson. I will call his wife and mother."

8

Punishment Too
Much to Bear

The *For Sale* sign camouflaged the true purpose of why people were gathered together. Unbeknownst to Jimmy, his last visit to the home Beverly and he once shared became the location of his funeral service. Beverly stood stoically at Jimmy's closed pine casket, waiting for the funeral services to end. Wanda, Willie, Martha, Bobby, Beverly, Beverly's mother, and Reverend Allison were the only ones in attendance. Beverly decided to have the services at night to minimize the likelihood that her neighbors would realize what had happened. Jimmy's death was not announced in the newspaper. His death did not make the news; the limited circumstances of his death were not up to the news outlets' tabloid standards since they could not get an interview from the Reverend or Beverly. Besides, it was seen as just another Black man who is dead. Beverly did not have an announcement or a eulogy to deliver; she even had the funeral the day after he died. Beverly did not want to deal with a bevy of people celebrating Jimmy's life. Sister Rosa Lee was convalescing at home, wishing she was kinder to Jimmy in her last words to him, yet she had nothing to say to anyone at this time.

No one shed a tear. The empty home had six folding black chairs with the chalk written words: *Property of Joe's Funeral Servicing Home.* Jimmy's mother had a nervous breakdown and was in no mental condition to attend, especially since she lived nearly 800 miles away. She was not overly fond of Beverly and believed that she concocted lies about *her* son and only child being homosexual. When she was told about his death, she became convinced Beverly was involved.

The Reverend discerned that the attendees were only there out of duty. He started the service with a prayer, and then he shared condolences from his wife, Vanessa, since she could not attend because she was eight months pregnant. He sang a song, gave a ten-minute speech about how great of a man Jimmy was, and said a prayer. The service lasted all of fifteen minutes. When the Reverend said, "Amen," the attendees quickly went to the car to wait on Beverly, leaving Beverly and the Reverend behind.

"Thank you, Reverend, for officiating this service," Beverly stated dryly. "I hope Jimmy made it to Heaven despite killing himself and being a homosexual. You know that Judas killed himself and that the Bible says Sodom and Gomorrah were destroyed because of all those homosexuals that lived there. If Booker dared to show up here, I would've told him ten reasons why he needs to repent, especially since he is partially responsible for Jimmy's death."

"Sister Beverly, you are not the judge of Jimmy. And besides, the destruction of Sodom and Gomorrah was not due to homosexuality. Without getting into those details, please remember that the Bible says to work out your own salvation with fear and trembling. Jimmy had his struggles. Perhaps you're a woman who never had any spiritual struggles and doesn't need God's grace as much as others. Remember, Beverly, all of us have skeletons in our closet. If we spend time trying to unlock the closet of others, then we shouldn't be surprised when karma unlocks our doors to expose parts of us that we do not want anyone to see," the Reverend insisted.

Beverly, realizing she could neither gainsay nor resist the Reverend's response, changed the subject. "My children and I are moving to California next week. I have a buyer for this house. The funeral home already has the instructions for Jimmy's body, and they will come for his body and the chairs within an hour. Thank you for attempting to counsel Jimmy and me. This funeral was all the closure I needed."

"I'll stay with the body until they arrive and will lock up before leaving. May the Lord watch between you and me while we are absent from one another. May God keep your family and you," the Reverend shared solemnly as he looked deeply into her eyes.

Beverly turned on the ball of her foot and marched out of the house like a zombie. The Reverend took his time folding the chairs and stacking them by the door while watching Wanda back the car out of the driveway. He witnessed Beverly in the front seat mouthing something to her children, who sat in the back. When he felt certain they were gone, the Reverend elevated his voice, saying, "Booker, you can come out now."

A shaken Booker emerged from the hidden room that only Jimmy and he knew existed. "It was a good service, Reverend. Quick and to the point."

"He was a good man who had his faults like all humans. I am going to leave you alone with him. You only have about twenty minutes since the funeral home will pick up his body today. Just meet me outside when you are ready. It'll be a good idea if you are lying in the backseat of my car when they arrive," the Reverend conveyed as he walked out of the front door.

Booker nodded in the affirmative.

The sound of the *click* prompted Booker to retrieve a letter from his pocket as he walked to the casket.

"Well, I never thought it would come to this. When I got the news, I was stunned and forced to weep in my pillow since I knew I could tell no one what had happened. Jimmy, I can't tell you how I will deal with you being gone. Hopefully, this letter I wrote will help you understand my feelings wherever you are," Booker sputtered.

Jimmy,

I am so sorry for what happened. I couldn't see my life without you. I looked up to you, wanting to be like you: married, with children, active in church, business-minded. How could you not understand that? You backed me into a corner when you threatened to end our relationship. I am asking myself: Is it my fault? What does Bobby think about me? Will I be arrested? I appreciate everything you did for me. The Reverend is a nice man. Thanks for introducing us. I hope to see you again in eternity. I love you.

Booker

Booker wiped a tear from his face as he folded the letter and slid it into the crevice of the casket. He tapped on the casket once before shutting off the lights and closing the door. Just as soon as Booker was in the back seat of the Reverend's car, the funeral home hearse pulled into the driveway.

"I hate that it had to end like this. But he made his choice," Booker said.

"Yes, he did. And life goes on. Now that Dad has made me Pastor, I need a deacon and a replacement for Beverly on the Prayer Team. You can be his replacement."

"Does it pay? I need money."

"I'll pay you personally each week and train you. Would your bride like to serve on the Prayer Team?" The Reverend smiled with encouragement.

"Getting paid each week? I'll absolutely do it. And my bride will do what I say. Consider her a part of the Prayer Team."

"Good. I will have Sister Tiffany train her. Meanwhile, you and I will spend much time together, getting to know each other in different ways. Again, you'll be paid regularly in cash."

"Then count me in. I am ready to go and start my new life as a husband, deacon, and father, leaving this chapter behind," Booker confessed. The Reverend looked straight ahead and replied, "I am glad you and I are starting a working relationship."

9

Mama Doing Damage Control

"Booker, Sister Wanda told me that something went down at Jimmy Anderson's house, and all of a sudden, Jimmy is dead. Boy, what happened? Never mind what was said in the news. You know more information than the police. And you need to tell me," Agnes Johnson questioned as she washed clothes.

"Mama, Beverly didn't like the bond Jimmy and I had. He was a good mentor. We had a minor disagreement, and we resolved it. That's all that happened. You know how nosey Wanda is. Whatever she told you, I am sure it is a lie." Booker knew his mother did not believe him; inwardly, he admitted he couldn't blame her.

"Uh-huh." Agnes pursed her lips, realizing that he was lying. "Well, Wanda wouldn't tell me all of what she witnessed out of respect for Beverly. All she said is that you were there, and you were involved."

"I had nothing to do with any of that Mama."

"Me and your daddy trusted Jimmy to be a mentor to you since he was a deacon in the church and a righteous man. Beverly was a fine Sunday-school teacher. She and Jimmy were the model of a perfect marriage."

"Ma, I know they were. Whatever happened between them was between them."

"Booker, I have seven kids and I KNOW all of them, and I'm through talking about this.

Besides, I know what I'll do to fix this." Agnes was through talking about this since she had already pressed Beverly and Wanda for all the information she needed. They gave her all the parts of the scorching tea, including the tea bag, water, sugar, lemon, and teacup.

Booker gained confidence that his mother believed his lie. Agnes was never one to reveal the *true* sources of her information.

Two days after Jimmy died, Agnes received a letter from Jimmy addressed to Booker. "This is my house, so I have the right to open *all* mail," Agnes justified her curiosity to herself. "And why would he write a letter on a paper bag when I know they have money?" she questioned as she pulled the letter out of the envelope. She put her bifocals on and read the whole letter, only to reread the parts that told her everything she needed to know so she would never forget them.

Booker,

My life is fucked up after you came to my house making a fucking scene like you a bitch! Wanda and Beverly were shocked by your behavior . . . My wife is leaving me, my kids don't want *nothing* to do with me, and now I'm alone. You and I had a good thing going, having sex regularly and confessing our feelings together. I gave you far more attention than your parents could. And to pay me back, you destroyed my life! The church would never forgive me once they find out that I had an ongoing sexual relationship with an eighteen-year-old man, especially once your gossipy mother finds out . . . I hope this makes you feel good. By the time you get this, I'll be gone for good!

Signed, Jimmy.

"I don't appreciate Jimmy thinking that I'm a gossiping woman. I can't help it that people come to me for counseling. Hell, if yo' ass would've come to me for counseling, I could've helped you," Agnes defended her transgression aloud as if she were talking to Jimmy in person. This letter prompted her to call Beverly moments before she would have her phone disconnected. She then called Wanda to ask how she and her new husband were doing. She successfully reeled the woman into telling her all of what happened. When she hung up, she promptly destroyed the envelope and the letter.

Booker was relieved that Agnes did not press him further. He quickly changed the subject since he didn't want her to change her mind. "Dreama and I have decided to get married Tuesday at the courthouse. We just need to live here until the baby is born, if that's okay."

"Booker, it's past time that Dreama and you married. This house is crowded. But you and Dreama can stay here until the baby is born. Dreama needs to be trained by me on how to take care of you."

"Ahhh Ma, I take care of myself now."

"You say that. Who still feeds you? Who still gives you housing? Whose car are you driving? Who gives you money when you are short on cash?"

"Mama, you just have an answer for everything, don't you?"

"I haven't lived this long for nothing. There are just some things I just know. Ain't it time for you to pick up Dreama from her daddy's house?"

"Oh, thanks, Ma! I am about to be late. Can I take your car?"

"Sure you can, especially since you take care of yourself now."

"Ok, Ma. I get that I still have some growing to do."

"And I am going to help you grow starting *now*! While y'all are out, go to the grocery store and get the things on this list. I have to cook since your daddy will be off work in two hours. Dreama can help me in the kitchen. We can have some girl-talk about the wedding and her pregnancy."

"Ok, Ma. I'm gonna need some money."

"Money for what? You will pay for the groceries, my gas, and for feeding you and Dreama."

"Welcome to being an adult," Agnes said, handing him a few bills. "Now, get going!"

When she saw Booker backing the car out of the driveway, she whispered, "I'm so glad Booker is getting married so that people won't think he is a homosexual. Since I heard about what happened between him and Jimmy, I'm sure somebody else has. I've got to get on the phone to tell others that Jimmy attempted to abuse my son and killed himself out of embarrassment that others may find out."

—m—

It was a sunny fall day at the Daunting, South Carolina courthouse. Booker and Dreama kissed before the judge while Arthur, Agnes, and Wilson served as witnesses of the wedding. Reverend Allison came for moral support. Booker's mother cried as Wilson held himself tightly as if he felt the presence of Dreama's mother and embraced her again for the first time in four years. The parents were very excited about the event.

Wilson's embrace quickly weakened as he fell to the floor. Dreama screamed: "Daddy, Daddy!" Booker knelt down to fan Wilson's face as he started to sweat profusely. Agnes and Arthur grabbed Wilson by each hand, petting it. The courthouse clerk called the operator to get an ambulance for Wilson. The doctors quickly saw him as he went into the emergency room.

After he regained consciousness, one doctor came into his hospital room to explain his problem.

"Mr. Wilson, I am sorry to inform you, but the black sore on your back came back cancerous. You have two options: One, we can provide you with medication in hopes of slowing it down, or two, you can opt to have surgery to have that sore removed. And it looks as if you've been a heavy smoker for some time. So, the medication would only work within a limited timeframe. I will step out and let you talk it over with your family," Dr. Clonigan reported.

The following week, the surgery was performed at 9:00 a.m. at Bundry

Memorial Hospital. When the surgeon cut the wound open, he recognized it was melanoma. The cancer had swiftly spread throughout Wilson's body. The surgeon saw no point in continuing with the surgery. The surgeon told Wilson's children, "Your father has cancer throughout his body, and he is not going to live longer than five days. When we opened him up, the cancer had already spread throughout his body. We closed the wound back up. I'm sorry that there's nothing we can do. I will leave it up to you to tell him unless you want me to tell him."

"Thank you, Doctor," Oscar spoke on behalf of the family. "We will discuss it and let you know."

All the family members agreed that it was best not to tell Wilson that he was dying and that they were going to put on their best face to keep things as normal as possible and spend the last five days with him. When he awoke, Wilson stated, "I feel odd, and I don't know why." Wilson started talking about how he wanted to spend time with his grandchildren and how he was excited about Booker marrying Dreama. He talked about wanting to go back to school to get his high school diploma even though he was 59 years old. The family listened to everything he had to say.

Wilson died three days later, and his funeral was held three days afterward with hardly any fanfare. Wilson's children and their spouses were present. While they had a headstone for Senora, they did not have one for Wilson. In fact, they didn't even bury Wilson beside Senora. They provided a metallic memorial grave marker with the intention of getting him a headstone. The wind eventually rewarded their intentions by blowing the grave marker away, only for no one to remember exactly where Wilson was buried. The passing of her father saddened Dreama, but her sadness was overcome with Booker by her side and their baby growing inside her.

10

Because I Said So

"Bart, I will tear yo' lil stupid ass up if you don' get over here and sa' down!" Booker told his four-year-old son Bartholomew Johnson, who was crying silently and walking around in circles at Arthur and Agnes Johnson's three-bedroom, one-bath, brick home. "Booker, he ain't doing nuttin' but walking around in circles. Leave him be," Agnes pleaded.

"Mama, that's why I wanted a girl. He is sorry and dumb. I need to beat his ass again." Booker retorted. Bart was walking in circles to avoid sitting down due to the beating he received just five minutes prior due to getting dirty after tripping over his shoelaces in the yard.

"He is just a child, Booker. Can you please be patient with him?" Dreama Johnson said tepidly.

"Don't you fuckin' tell me what to do, woman! That's his problem now, walking like a sissy. Yo' ass ain't no help since you try to take up for him." Booker stated. Their second child, Warren, cried as he awakened from his nap. "I'll go see my baby boy since he's the only *real son* I have."

As Dreama looked helplessly at Booker walking down the hall, she took Bart in her arms. "Daddy didn't mean to beat you. Just be careful next time, ok?" Bart remained silently stoic, for he learned early that if he were to open his mouth, he would likely be beaten again. Dreama also learned that if she had said anything more about this matter to Bart, she would have encountered Booker's wrath. Booker had become increasingly aggressive towards her since their marriage four years ago. He couldn't stand the sight of her.

Dreama studied Bart, realizing that the older he got, the more he looked exactly like her. She chalked up Booker's behavior to the fact that he recently lost his job as a cab driver, plus his mama wanted him out of the house. He was twenty-two and the oldest of seven children. Booker and Dreama were sleeping on the recliner and parts of the living room floor. And the two additional children, along with the remaining six children, made the space too small. Dreama worked at SignUp Convenient Store, half a mile from the Johnson's home. She obeyed Booker by bringing her weekly paycheck to him.

"Todd and Melvina! If y'all don't stop fighting, I am going to fight you! As a matter of fact, I'm coming to break up this fight now," Agnes yelled after hearing them argue.

"Todd broke the head of my doll, Momma," Melvina alleged. "That raggedy doll's head was already off," Todd charged. Agnes got off the phone and only walked down the hall to see what they were arguing about. "Todd put some glue on that doll's head. That doll has been passed down for five years and has got to last at least two more years. Fix it!"

She peeped her head in the bathroom. "Who just came out of this bathroom? David, I know it was you! Get in here, flush this toilet, clean this tub, and throw your dirty clothes in the washing machine! You are too old to be doing this shit!" Agnes ordered. David quickly got into the bathroom to perform the chores.

Agnes continued walking down the hall, seeing crayon messages written on the wall, finger paintings on doors, dried food in the corner, and crevices on the floor.

Agnes dragged her husband Arthur out of bed, though he needed the nap after working a 16-hour shift. "Arthur, I can't take this! Booker and his family have been here for four years now. Booker claimed he was saving money but asked me for $10 every week. They need a place of their own. We have $1500 saved. I say we help them find a place."

"Well, he needs to leave the nest. We have six other mouths to feed. Let's bring him in to talk to him about it."

"I'm bringing his wife Dreama in, too. They are one now. She will hear the same message Booker hears. I don't want any misunderstandings. Booker and Agnes, come to my room now!" Agnes yelled down the hall. "Yvonne, get in there and wash those dishes. Doug and Samantha, before y'all think about going outside, get to the table and do your homework. I'll check it later."

Booker and Dreama stood before Arthur and Agnes, bringing Warren for good measure since all household members pampered him. Before the bedroom door could close completely, Agnes affirmed, "Booker, you're twenty-two, and Dreama, you're nineteen. It is past time for both of you to get full-time jobs and get your own place. Arthur, you will talk to your supervisor about getting Booker and Dreama hired at Chev Mills. I'll ask Glenda about hiring them at Walker Dee Brens' Factory. Tomorrow, I will talk to Mr. Dodd, who owns all those single-wide trailers a mile from here. Glenda's daughter lives there, saying the rent is $100 a month. In two weeks, y'all will be out of here."

"Mama, I am scared to leave. This home is all I know. Can't we stay another six months? I promise that Dreama and I will work, save, and then move," Booker pleaded.

"Your request is denied. You got four years of free food, rent, babysitting, and washing. And you want another six months of that? I don't. I'm scared you'll never grow up if I don't put you out, so you will be out in two weeks. Now, get out of my room and help Arthur cut grass. Dreama, you're gonna help me get dinner ready."

Booker opened the door swiftly, then stormed out of the house to the backyard shed, cursing under his breath. Agnes went after him, "Booker, I know you don't have an attitude about what I said. I know you are trying to get adjusted to being an adult; thinking that and going around cussing and raising your voice around here is a part of it. When you get your own place, you do as much of that as you like. Meanwhile, you have ONE more time to disrespect me! And another thing, let me tell you what, you have ONE more week of STAYING AT MY HOUSE! ONE week from today, you, your wife, and chaps are out! Why? Because now I have an attitude. Your wife and you take turns sleeping on my good recliner, which I got from the flea market, and my recliner hasn't been the same. My soap operas haven't been the same. I feel like I'm experiencing *As the World Turns* as this recliner turns me as I sit in it. Do you understand everything I said?"

"Yes."

"Yes, WHAT?"

"Yes, ma'am."

"Well, that's good. I'm glad we could have a conversation in which we were both clear about the expectations. You have been served your eviction notice. I'm going to cook dinner."

Booker had long known that when he had pissed Agnes off, it was best to acquiesce to her demands at the expense of public embarrassment, including the subject talked about all over town. She had no respect for people when it came to gossip, including her children.

Dreama was in deep thought while she sat on the red faux leather couch, accentuated with two asparagus and orange pillows with triangle-and-square geometric shapes. She looked at her pin, which said, "For one year of good service" as a cotton manufacturer at Chev Mills Factory. Booker dropped her off at home as he planned to drink with some fellows Dreama didn't know.

"We've been in this trailer for a year now. Wow, how time flies!" She still relished in her marital vows to love, honor, and obey him. For the past ten months, she brought her paycheck home to him, cooked and cleaned, cared for the children, and made his family her family. He responded in thanks by drinking more, arguing with her over petty matters, and paying bills late. Though she had four brothers and four sisters, she only stayed in contact with her brother Fred, who lived twenty minutes away, and sister Mabel, who moved with their sister Catherine to Washington, DC after leaving high school. Even though Dreama was the youngest, Mabel was her father's favorite.

"Girl, I got accepted into Skinston College on a scholarship. That's just two miles away from you, isn't it?" Mabel enthusiastically stated over the phone.

"Well, that is good news. I can stand to hear some good news right now," Dreama said pensively.

"Why do you say that? You have a happy marriage, a man in the church, two handsome boys, and you're working. What else do you want?"

"That's just it. We have been attending Reverend Allison's church. You know his daddy, Pastor Allison, died two or three years ago. Booker was recently named a deacon. Booker and he are very close, which is good, I guess. Booker has been coming home late and always fighting with me. Bart is four, and Warren is two. He is even calling Bart a *sissy* all the time. He spends more time with Warren; I spend more time with Bart. He does act like a girl, but I believe it is a phase. I am confident it will all work out. But you didn't call to hear me talk about that. Tell me more about your good news."

"Well, I know we haven't talked since your marriage. And, of course, I am in support of your marriage working out. At least you are married! I am still waiting for the right man to ask for my hand in marriage. Every marriage has its problems."

"Right," Dreama replied dryly. "Get to telling me more about your acceptance into college. I want to go to nursing school, but Booker says I can't. I am glad that someone in the family is going to college."

"Well, to go to Skinton, I'd have to move back to South Carolina. I wondered if I could stay with Booker and you and help with the bills while in school."

"It would be nice to have you here. I hear Booker pulling up in the driveway now. Let me talk to Booker and let you know tomorrow," Dreama concluded as she quickly hung up the aquamarine blue rotary phone and got a broom to be found cleaning the living room.

Booker instantly noticed Dreama's long hair swaying from left to right as she swept the floor. He grabbed from behind and kissed her on the cheek as she dropped the broom in shock. "I'm so glad you're my wife."

Dreama turned to him, smiling, "I am glad to be Mrs. Dreama Johnson and the mother of our two children," as she kissed him on the lips. "You're back so soon. Did you forget something?" Dreama asked, pleased with Booker's kindness.

"No, I just decided to come back home since I'm tired."

"Oh, okay. Mabel called me about thirty minutes ago," Dreama posited since Booker was in a good mood.

"What did she want?"

"She got accepted into Skinton University on a scholarship. It covers her tuition but not her room and board. She needs other family support. She wants to know if she can stay with us."

"If she is ok with sleeping on the pullout bed in the living room, I am fine with it. I would even take her to and from school. She would have to babysit the boys and give us $25 monthly for bills," Booker affirmed coolly.

"Oh, Booker, thank you. I will tell her she can move in with us next week."

"This woman really takes pride in her work here. She is a team player and gives her all. She has had glowing reviews during her time here at Chev Mills. It is a pleasure to be her supervisor. This month's employee-of-the-month award and $25 cash bonus goes to none other than Mrs. Dreama Johnson," Daniel Boonson announced, wearing a wrinkled white shirt that matched his countenance and a blue necktie with khaki pants. Her colleagues clapped vociferously. Dreama gushed like a school-girl as Daniel extended the award and check to her. Ralph Custon—a light-skinned, pink-lipped, short-afroed, gangly man hugged her tightly as he congratulated her. Dreama eased Ralph away from her and shook his hand.

"You deserve this for everything you do for this team," Belinda Andrews added. Dreama demurely said, "Thank you," so often that she was almost emotionally overcome. She had never experienced any recognition for her efforts, professionally or personally.

"All right, all right, let's not embarrass the young lady. Because all of you are valued employees and have made the most cotton production out of all the other departments, you can go home for the rest of the day with pay," Daniel Boonson announced. Everyone cheered.

Ralph opined, "Dreama is the reason why we exceeded other departments. Let's cheer for Dreama. Dreama! Dreama! Dreama!" The department encircled Dreama, chanting, "Dreama! Dreama! Dreama!" Inconspicuously, Booker eyed the series of events, fuming she was getting so much attention, especially from Ralph Custon.

"Now, before you all go," Daniel uttered to quiet the group, "we have overtime opportunities for those who have already been trained on our ZXY machine. Dreama, Linda, Ralph, Andy, Candy, and Charles, you may sign up if you want to work overtime hours for the next four weeks. You and the others may sign up for the ZXY training next month. Be careful going home. Have a great day!"

Booker went to the locker Dreama and he shared to grab his keys and lunchbox while hangers-on flanked Dreama to congratulate her and request her to train them on the ZXY since they knew the others who had been trained on it frequently asked Dreama questions about its usage. Booker silently walked to his car to wait for Dreama without saying a word to anyone. Five minutes later, Dreama walked out with Linda and Candy. Ralph caught up with her, saying, "Dreama, you dropped this check by your locker. I would've cashed it if I weren't an honest man."

Ralph handed the check to Dreama as she said, "Oh, thanks so much, Ralph! I definitely can't afford to give away $25. My husband would've killed me if I didn't bring that check home." Ralph laughed to ease the nervous energy he felt from Dreama. Dreama managed to snicker.

"Oh there, I see Booker is waiting for you. I am sure he will be happy to share this good news. Maybe one of the ladies could announce your award during the announcements on Sunday at church. I am certainly going to tell my wife."

Dreama rushed away from him as she said, "Yes, Booker is here, and I do not wish for it to be shared with anyone at this time." Booker's eyes reddened, and veins appeared on his forehead as he witnessed the exchange.

Ralph watched Dreama walk ahead of him before getting to his white Ford pickup truck. Courteously, he waved at Booker. Booker waved back nonchalantly.

"Honey, I am sorry to be late. I looked for you at the locker. Linda told me she saw you walking out of the door. Are you ok?" Dreama asked timidly.

Booker drove out of the parking lot, breathing heavily and watching the Chev Mills Textile Plant diminish in his rearview mirror. Dreama softly grabbed his arm as she beseeched, "Booker, tell me what's wrong."

Booker backhanded Dreama so hard that her head hit the glass. Dreama shrieked, "Booker, please not again! I promise to be a good girl! What did I do?!"

Booker hit Dreama repeatedly, landing each punch on the side of her head. "You know damn well what is wrong, you stupid bitch! I saw how you let Ralph hug you and how he slipped his number on a piece of paper and gave it to you. You ain't nothing but a whore!" Booker yelled.

Dreama looked down at the floorboard before pleading softly, "Booker, I pushed Ralph back and shook his hand. I am not interested in Ralph. And he didn't give me his number; he found our $25 check and gave it to me. Let me take it out of my purse and show you."

"Bitch, don't correct me! You looked like you were liking the attention he was giving you." Booker got his right arm in formation to hit Dreama again. "Please don't, Booker. My head is hurting me."

Dreama was looking out of the window, feeling hopeless after she placed the check in the middle of the seat. Booker picked it up, happy to have the extra money.

"You can work overtime this month. I will take you to work and pick you up," Booker smirked.

"Booker, if it will make you angry that Ralph is working with me, then I can tell Daniel to separate us."

"Don't you tell that slave driver about us! And if anybody asks you about the bruises on your face, tell them you fell. Just know that I'm keeping an eye out on y'all."

Dreama did not respond. They rode in deafening silence. She replayed the day's events in her mind to assess what could've gone wrong. She knew that Booker received his last warning for taking extended lunch breaks off-site, clocking into work at the same time as Dreama only to go back out to his car and leave for an hour. She never asked him questions since he was the man of the house. She did not want to deal with his anger.

"Are you going to pick up Mabel? I am kindly asking since she is out of class and you just passed the University."

"I'm dropping you off at the trailer so you can prepare dinner for Mabel, the boys, and me. Get the boys from the neighbor's house. Then I'm going to get Mabel," Booker aggressively instructed.

"I will do just that. I'd like to see the University campus at least once. It is just that Mabel has been with us three years, and I don't ever ride with you to pick her up," Dreama commented timidly.

"You complain too damn much. You know that? You asked if she could stay with us. I told you she could. She pays me her portion of the rent and babysits the boys. You just need to . . ." Booker's voice escalated.

"Ok. No problem. Please forget that I mentioned it," Dreama softly interrupted.

"What would you like for dinner?"

"JUST FIX FOOD, BITCH!" Booker hollered as they pulled into the driveway.

Dreama opened the door carefully. The moment she applied pressure to her right foot to stand after it landed on the gravel, Booker put the car in reverse, causing Dreama to fall face-first to the ground. Booker was about to continue to back the car until he saw Susie, their next-door neighbor, and Bart and Warren run out of Susie's trailer. Bart ran ahead of Susie, and she ran back to retrieve a crying Warren, who had stood with toy army men in his hand once he saw Dreama on the ground.

Booker quickly put his car in park and ran over to Dreama, kneeling just in time to ask her within earshot, "Dreama, are you ok? I told you about wearing those shoes to work since they attract grease. Let me help you up," Booker mentioned gingerly as he grabbed her left arm. "Girl, you have to watch your step," Susie ordered as she grabbed Dreama's right arm.

Bart looked at Booker suspiciously as he piped, "Mama, please say you're ok."

"You know I'm a tough cookie, son," she whispered as she stood up completely. "I just scuffed my knees—nothing a little peroxide couldn't take care of. I'll clean these shoes to give them away so this won't happen again. Now, y'all stop making a fuss over me. Susie, thanks for your help. I'll get the boys in the house and make dinner. Booker, I'll see you when you get back," Dreama commented to absolve Booker from any wrong-doing, no matter what Susie and the boys may have witnessed. She also wanted to avert the terrific friction that could have followed her unsatisfactory response.

Satisfied with Dreama's response, Booker said, "Darling, would you make my favorite dinner: fish sticks, macaroni and cheese, and green peas?"

"Absolutely! And Susie, thanks for your help! The boys will be over at the same time tomorrow."

"Ok, Dreama. They enjoy playing outside with my kids since they are out of school for the summer. Just let me know if you need anything,"

Susie waved as she ran back to her trailer the moment she heard her phone ring.

Booker backed out of the driveway with seven-year-old Bart, watching the car eventually disappear. "I hope he does not come back," Bart growled before walking into the trailer.

"Mama, I saw everything that happened. He would have run over you had we not run out to help you. He doesn't seem like a happy man," Bart said as if he were the man of the house. Dreama shuffled through the frozen foods in the freezer to find the box of fish sticks.

"Well, I'm just trying to figure out what to do, Bart," Dreama jabbered.

"Where is your mama, Mama? Can we go stay with her?" Warren asked.

"My mama died before y'all were born. I don't have a mother now."

"Where is your daddy?"

"He is dead, too." Warren played with his army men in the living room, leaving Bart and Dreama in the kitchen.

"I just hope we aren't stuck, Mama." Bart made his wrist limp before adding, "We have to do something." Dreama recognized that he was imitating her movements when she was speaking animatedly.

"I'm just waiting until your Aunt Mabel graduates from college next year. Perhaps she and I could move in together. And don't do your wrist like that. Boys don't do that."

Dreama spoke to Bart as an adult since she didn't have *relationships* with other adults. She knew that she could not even speak to the Sisters on her Prayer Team about the inner workings of the household, though they spoke weekly. Booker even forbade her from interacting with her other siblings.

Bart was embarrassed. He was reminded of the times Booker's brothers often derided him for engaging in activities assigned to girls. He had no male relatives who would play with him, so he often played with girls or alone. To get the focus off his effeminate behavior, he said, "We do everything we can to please him; he seems angry all the time."

"What do you mean *we* do everything to please him?" Dreama questioned.

"One time when you were at work, Daddy took me to y'all bed, and we played a game."

"Tell me more about this game, Bart," Dreama said, flummoxed by Bart's words as she opened the box of off-brand macaroni and cheese.

"When I get in the tub to bathe, he washes me and tells me he loves me."

"Well, it is nice for him to tell you he loves you since he hardly says it. And you do have some challenges washing your back. Is there more to this game?" Dreama questioned inquisitively.

"He said, 'Don't you love me?' I said, 'Yes.' Then he dries me off and tells me to prove my love by playing the game he calls *Putting the Worm into the Apple*. He says, my mouth is the apple, and his pee-pee is the worm. He told me that I could never tell anybody about our secret game or else he would have to hurt me for disobeying him. Please don't tell him I told you, Mama, 'cause I don't want him to hurt me."

Dreama turned her head away from Bart for five seconds, tears welling up in her eyes. Then she took Bart in her arms. "Bart, how long have Daddy and you been playing this game?"

"Since I turned five."

"Where else have you played this game?"

"In the car and the bathroom."

Dreama thought, "Booker has not had sex with me in two years. Has he been getting an ejaculation from other means?" She knows that Bart is a perceptive child. She didn't want to show any emotions that would cause him to ask questions. "Bart, don't tell your father you had this conversation about this game with me. This will be our secret."

"I really don't like this game, Mama. I do it since it is the only time he is nice to me. He told me he loved me. The game stops him from calling me *sissy* and *punk*. He said I would grow to like the game more," Bart remarked.

"I will figure out how to get your Daddy interested in a different game that will cause him to lose interest in playing that game with you anymore.

You take your brother to wash up for dinner. Your daddy will be back with your aunt shortly."

Gingerly, Bart took Warren's hand as they walked to the bathroom. She heard Bart didactically mention, "Warren, today I am going to show you how to wash your hands." Watching her two boys walk down the short hallway made her smile. Her mind turned to what Bart told her. She cried over the thought that her son was sexually abused by a man she was powerless over. She knew that her son could have an overactive imagination. Perhaps it's not true, she thought. If it is true, she must do something, but what? She took one look at the mac and cheese and began to gag.

11

My Husband and My Sister

It was 10 p.m. It had been four hours since Booker left to pick up Mabel. Dreama placed Booker's dinner on the stove in aluminum foil and went to bed since she had to work a double shift in the morning. She knew that each Thursday, Mabel had another late-tutoring session; if so, perhaps Booker went to his mother's house. Rather than question their whereabouts, Dreama was thankful that the boys and she were experiencing peace. She had her weekly Thursday evening call with the sisters on her team to pray over prayer requests, which ranged from addictions to financial blessings and from automobile requests to finding a husband. It was one of the few times she could have a moment to herself with the boys asleep, Booker who knows where, and Mabel in tutoring. She was grateful that Sister Tiffany led all of the prayers, for Dreama knew she needed someone—anyone—to pray for her.

Unbeknownst to Dreama, Booker picked up Mabel at 6:15 p.m.

"I'm so glad to see you, babe," Mabel cooed jovially as she kissed Booker squarely on the lips, getting into the car.

"Aye, Mama, not where all these people can see us. And close the door all the way," Booker cautioned as he looked around cursorily to assess if there were witnesses.

"Bookie baby, I'm sorry. I'll be more careful. You know how I get when I am around you," Mabel responded bubbly as Booker drove away.

"Come slide closer to me so I can throw my arm around you."

Without hesitation, Mabel scooted left as she examined Booker's shirt being buttoned, subtly exposing his hairy chest.

"I'm so glad to see you too with yo' sexy self, and Big Duke is glad to see you too," Booker went on, grabbing his penis. "Why don't you give him a warm welcome to show him how glad you are to see him?"

"He enjoyed my last performance. I am happy to give him an encore."

"Well, quit talking and get to performing while I drive us over to my man's spot. And don't stop until we get there."

Mabel followed Booker's orders to the letter with a non-stop, 45-minute fellatio performance that left Booker's jeans highly salivated. "We are here. You know what to do when we get inside," Mabel nodded compliantly.

Booker parked his black Monte Carlo at the back of the One-Night Motel in a town called Seedy, which was the best adjective to describe the motel. It was an hour away from town and sat on open land. The motel was valiantly holding the foundations' crack together. It was known to the frequent patrons that all of the rooms smelled of cigarette smoke and foot odor. The duvets held cigarette holes, memorializing who last used them. This motel protected the identities of every customer, for it did not require identification, just a fake name and some cash. Countee, Booker, and Mabel's room 435 became a temporary home-away-from-home most Thursday evenings with Countee footing all expenses from Sunday-service donations.

Booker knocked softly, knowing that if he knocked one decibel louder, he could interrupt the activities he heard on both sides of him.

"Were y'all held up in traffic?" Reverend Allison asked as he opened and hid behind the door, which acted as an article of clothing that hid his complete nakedness.

"Don't worry about all that. You know why we're here. So let's not waste time talking, Countee."

Mabel took off her red-and-black plaid pinafore dress in a strip tease as Booker took off his clothes. She threw her white laced panties and white bullet bra on Countee's face as he watched her in admiration, which revealed the voluptuously round-and-caramelized twins. Mabel marched slowly in her white-chunky-heeled boot, collapsing backward on the bed which held evidentiary memories of those who came before. Her legs gapped open, giving a full view of a perfectly manicured vagina as she began to pleasure herself. Booker motioned for Countee to dim the lights. Booker lightly slapped his penis on Mabel's face, instructing her, "Continue where you left off." Countee proceeded to perform cunnilingus on Mabel while watching Mabel swallow Booker's penis while her head bobbed up and down as he stood over her. At the sound of a gag reflex, Countee shifted Mabel to lie at the top of the bed on her stomach, where Booker entered her passionately. He grunted once he was completely inside her. She hid her face underneath the pillow, whispering salacious secrets to the mattress. Booker said, "You feel so good that I wanna leave Dreama and marry you."

"I say 'Yes, Booker. Yes.'" Mabel said loud enough for Booker and Countee to hear.

Countee surreptitiously kissed Booker's neck before deeply kissing him as he gave harder and faster thrusts. "I'm about to cum," he grunted as his lips moved from Countee. "I love you, Booker," he heard from the pillow. He released inside Mabel as she rotated her hips with pleasure to ensure her vagina swallowed the ejaculation completely. When Booker pulled out, Countee slid inside Mabel for round two. Mabel kept her face inside the pillow, moaning with every stroke. Booker caressed his penis as he watched Countee perform. After five minutes, Countee pulled out after Booker motioned that he wanted another round with Mabel. The synchronously rhythmic action caused Booker to climax once more, announced this time by subtle grunts and heavier breathing as he pulled out partially, adding seminal memories onto the duvet. Countee's ejaculation made its way onto Mabel's left upper thigh seconds later as the clock struck 10 p.m.

12

Abusing to Empower

Dreama awakened to find Booker grabbing his car keys. "I already sent the boys to Susie's. I will take Mabel to the university and then pick you up so we can go to work. She's already in the car. Be ready when I get back," Booker said dryly as he turned his back away from Dreama.

Dreama softly replied, "Ok. I'll be ready when you return," as Booker walked swiftly down the hall.

Dreama yawned and shuddered at the thought of working another 16-hour day. "I do it for my family," she thought aloud as she put on her arctic-blue housecoat. Walking closer to the kitchen, she saw Booker's dinner sitting on the stove untouched.

"How is it that Booker had me make his favorite dinner, only for him to not eat it? Perhaps he didn't feel like reheating it in the oven. And he and Mabel came home late last night. I have to get a better handle on knowing Mabel's schedule," Dreama reasoned. She put the food in the refrigerator and quickly got dressed in her olive-green slacks and matching blouse. She knew the consequences if Booker had to wait on her versus her waiting on him. Dreama decided to wear her long black hair down and cherry lipstick with a light foundation. She decided to wait on the outside steps so he did not have to wait.

Booker depressed the car's horn twice at the top of the driveway to announce his pending arrival. Dreama quickly walked to the car so that Booker could not initiate an argument over her being thirty seconds late getting in.

"Good Morning, Booker. Did you rest well?"

Booker did not acknowledge her question, yet she continued.

"I waited up for you last night, but I got sleepy. Did you spend some time at your mother's house?"

"All you need to know is that I was out."

"I made your favorite dinner, as you asked me to. I can reheat it and serve it to you tonight."

"We can see."

Dreama discerned that Booker just wasn't in a conversational mood. They rode in silence until they parked at Chev Mills.

"You are working 16 hours today, so I'll get off at 3 p.m. and pick you up at 11 p.m."

"No problem."

Dreama ran inside, grabbed her timecard, and rushed to the time clock to punch in at 7:00 a.m., just before it changed to 7:01 a.m. "I just made it," Dreama said to herself.

Booker could not find his timecard after looking for it three times. "Ask Mr. Boonson to come over here before you start your shift," he instructed Dreama. I cannot find my timecard, and it is already 7:08 a.m." Dreama nodded and asked Mr. Boonson to assist Booker in finding his timecard.

"Hi, Mr. Boonson. I can't seem to find my time card. Will you please assist?"

"Booker, I am sorry, but we will have to terminate you. We have documentation of you being repeatedly late, clocking in and leaving the parking lot for at least 40 minutes, and taking longer breaks than what has been allotted. We have written you up twice. Your productivity is the lowest in our department. You can file for unemployment. Dreama can get your things. All the best to you!" Mr. Boonson turned his back and walked away.

Booker hung his head low as he walked back to the car. "I couldn't have been that bad. These White folk are always trying to get over on a brother." Booker convinced himself that all he needed was a little pint of gin from the liquor store to lift his spirits. After making the purchase, Booker drove to the visitor's parking lot of Skinton Elementary School, drinking little by little. "I have a wife I don't want; I don't have a job; I have a kid that's a sissy," Booker lamented as he took a swig. "I have to take control of this since I'm a man. *I'm a MAN!*" Booker yelled.

Booker put all the weight of his left foot on the accelerator of his car, speeding to get home. He honked the horn to let Susie know he was home so the boys could come home. He walked into the trailer and waited in his lounge chair for the boys to come home. All physical evidence of his drinking was strewn in chunks of broken glass across parts of Danxerk Street.

"Daddy, Daddy, you came home early?" Warren said, confused.

"Yeah, son. I did just so I could take you to get some ice cream after your nap," Booker replied lovingly. "Was your brother behind you?"

"He was helping Ms. Susie wash dishes," Warren reported.

"Well, get in the bed and take a nap," Booker directed.

Warren was sound asleep when Booker watched Susie thank Bart for helping her grease her hair and clean her kitchen. She gave him $5. Bart was so happy with his newfound wealth that he skipped to the trailer, holding his hand across his chest as if he were trying to cover his cleavage. Bart's happiness was short-lived the moment he entered the portal of the trailer's door.

"Come over and sit on my lap and tell me about what you did to get $5," Booker plotted.

Bart was so nervous as he walked, especially when Booker opened his legs. Bart climbed up Booker's knee. "So when I got to Susie's, she said, 'My back has been bothering me, Bart. Can you help me with cleaning my kitchen? And so, I . . .'" Bart stopped mid-sentence when Booker brought him closer to his chest.

"I watched you run back home, skipping and having your hand across your chest like you are growing titties. Since you want to be a girl, I will treat you like one. We are going to play our game, but this time, we're going to try something new. And if you ever tell anybody about this, I will fucking kill you, you faggot!" Booker whispered. "Now, take off all your clothes in front of me." Shaken with tears welled in his eyes, Bart complied until his superhero briefs were around his ankles. "It is time I will show you what boys do to girls."

13

The Scandalous Prayer Request

"Today's scripture will be read by Deacon Booker Johnson," Associate Pastor Pat Greene announced as he led the order of church services. "Say Amen, church! I know this is a Wednesday night service. God is still worthy! Say Amen!" Reverend Allison exclaimed from the pulpit in support of Booker. Booker, seated with his arm around Dreama and Bart and Warren beside her, emerged from the front pew. Booker gave her a kiss on the forehead. He felt presidential in his light-blue fitting suit with a dark blue woven shirt accessorized by a thin dark blue and light blue necktie. Dreama wore a dark-blue polyester sleeveless dress with a light-blue thin belt around her waist. The children were dressed like twins in matching light-and-dark blue plaid suits, white shirts, and clip-on dark blue neckties. It was Mabel's first time going to Dreama's church. For the past three years, she used Sunday as a day of rest and Wednesday night as a day to study. She only came to church since Dreama pressured her. She wore a light-blue A-line dress with a light-and-dark blue square pattern.

Booker smiled at the congregants as he arrived at the podium where Pat was standing. "Did y'all see that? We are so glad to see a husband that loves his wife. This godly man clearly loves his wife as Christ loves the church! We need more men to be like Deacon Johnson. He is absolutely godly. Hallelujah!" The congregants clapped their hands profusely, some saying "Amen," "Glory to God," "I'm looking for a husband like you," or "Do you have a brother?"

Pat Greene stepped aside as Booker stood erect before the podium, basking in the churchgoers' applause lines. Booker immediately elevated his voice to sound educated and *holy*: "Giving honor to God who is the head of my life, our dynamic leader Pastor Allison, Associate Pastor Greene, my beautiful family, deacons, trustees, members, saints, and friends: We praise God for whom all blessings flow! Let's go to the gospel of Ephesians 6, where I will start by reading verses 1-3. When you have it, say Amen!"

"Amen!" the congregants stated.

"Amen, Pastor Johnson," a female voice exclaimed. Some congregants laughed softly.

"And the Word of God says: 'Children, obey your parents in the Lord: for this right. Honor thy father and mother, which is the first commandment with promise; that it may be well with thee, and thou mayest live long on the earth," Booker exclaimed. He added, "If you want to live long, you've got to obey your parents. I obeyed my parents! I expect my children to obey me! Amen."

"Let's move to verses 22-23: Wives, submit yourselves unto your own husbands, as unto the Lord. For the husband is the head of the wife, even as Christ is the head of the church, and he is the Savior of the body. Wives, you have a responsibility to the husband. You are to follow the lead of the husband. That is the order! May the Lord add a blessing to this Word," Booker enthusiastically said.

The congregants received Booker as a voice from Heaven as he slowly returned to his seat. He threw his arm around Dreama as she took a handkerchief from her eyes to dab them, and then she scurried to the ladies' room. Onlookers concluded that Booker's words must've so moved her that she needed some brief time alone.

"Mama, I need you NOW; oh I need you now," Dreama sobbed as she sat on the toilet in the first stall. "I have experienced nothing but loss with this man. I lost my siblings, lost my independence, lost my identity, lost my strength, lost my voice, lost my peace, and lost control. I cook, clean, dress the kids, and give him my paycheck so he can pay the bills. He hollers, fusses, and cusses every day! I suspect he is doing something sexual with my son. He has even created a wedge between Mabel and me, and she and I have to have stolen conversations when he is not around. I just don't know how much more I can take, Mama. I wish I could be half as strong as you."

Dreama leaned forward, put her hands on her face, and thought about Senora and the strength she exuded, wishing she could channel her.

She started to snicker, thinking about the time her mother got unwanted guests out of her house. Don, Wilson's cousin, was visiting. He called over his friends August, Chris, Louis, Kitty, Valerie, and Tameka to come over, although he didn't ask Wilson's permission. When they arrived, Dreama and Senora were cooking in the kitchen. Wilson set up a card table and chair on the porch. The moment Senora heard unfamiliar voices, she went to the screen door. "Chile, walk with me to the door. The food will be all right for a few moments unattended," Senora directed. When they got to the door, Senora motioned for Dreama to stay while she went out on the porch.

"Don, who in the hell are all these people you brought to my house?!" Senora confronted.

"Ah, Mama, you ain't gotta address him like that. We are just about to play cards," Kitty complained.

"Bitch, I ain't yo' mama. For if I were yo' mama, yo' ass wouldn't be dressed like a whore. I bet if you walked butt-ass naked down Highway 18, not one car would stop unless it was after they ran over you." Senora retorted. Kitty rolled her eyes as she took a swig from her flask.

"Senora, leave my guests alone. Wilson, who is the boss around here, you or Senora?" Don challenged. "Deal the cards." Wilson remained quiet while dealing with the cards.

"When I come back, I'm going to be the dealer! And all I'm going to deal are six BANGS!" Senora promised. Senora quickly stomped to her bed and reached under her pillow for her snub-nose revolver. Just as she had it in her hand, she heard the hum of cars starting. Only Don and Wilson were present when she got on the porch, with the empty glasses of liquor and the ash-laden ashtray.

"Don, you brought those whores to my house and nearly got shot for trying to show your ass. Now I am showing you and yo' ass to the door. You've got five minutes to pack your shit and go, with the clock starting now. If you ain't out of here in five minutes, I'll have SIX reasons to open the windows and doors of my house to make all the gun smoke clear. OUT!" Don was out in three minutes with a partially unzipped suitcase with dress shirts, socks, and underwear dangling outside. Dreama snickered to herself like she did when she witnessed the event.

Dreama's trance was broken when she heard Esther James and Dionne Candly enter the bathroom to discuss recipes. Dreama quietly whispered, "I have to muster the strength to get through this somehow, Mama, with the help of the Lord." Encouraged by this confession, Dreama arose, checked herself in the mirror, and quickly got back to the sanctuary. She provided a pageantry smile as she walked by congregants, just as Booker taught her to do.

"My daddy, the great M. B. Allison, told me right before he died to remember to pray and cease not. I'm grateful that he had the strength to pray over me just as he passed the mantle for me to be the Pastor of this great church," Reverend Allison revealed. Congregants clapped, said "Amen," and nodded their heads as he continued speaking. "My beautiful wife, Vanessa," the Reverend paused with non-verbal expectation for applause. "She and I pray fervently for all of you. We thank you for the love and support you consistently show us. Just stand up and show the church just how beautiful you are." The congregants slapped profusely as Vanessa stood and modeled her navy blue, polka dot sleeveless dress, white pearls, and white pillow box hat, complemented by her white chunky-heeled mule sandals.

She felt like Miss. Congeniality. "That girl looks good; she is one biscuit away from bursting out of that dress," Dreama heard Beulah Murphy say louder than she intended. Dreama was taught to respect her elders, so she clapped all the more in support of Vanessa, knowing that pregnancy brings extra pounds.

"Before the choir comes to render a selection, we have come to the part of our service where we invite you to submit your prayer requests. Because we value the privacy of all, you may take the prayer-request slips and write your requests on them; you do not have to give any identifying information. We keep it all confidential. Our dynamic prayer team—led by my lovely wife, Vanessa—will intercede on your behalf. Ushers will come around and gather them and place them in the prayer box. Amen!" Upon hearing her name, Vanessa thought, "I may be over the prayer team, but I need prayer for my marriage. Every Thursday at 6 p.m., he claims he will do ministry work only to come home around 1 a.m.! He hasn't touched me in months. Well, maybe I'm overthinking it."

"Amen!" the congregants replied in unison.

"Let us have one song selection by the choir."

As the choir sang "How Great Thou Art," Mabel asked Dreama for an ink pen. Dreama passed her a pen that dispensed green ink. Dreama was pleased to look down the row later and see Mabel write something on her prayer request slip. Dreama had the boys scribble their prayer requests while she and Booker collaborated openly on writing that they pray together for spiritual growth. All prayer requests were provided to Sister Tiffany, who eventually signaled to Reverend Allison that the task was complete.

"Thank you for your submissions. All of us need prayer," Reverend Allison shared solemnly. "Aren't we blessed to have a dynamic choir!" Reverend Allison exclaimed. The congregants responded affirmatively. "We are also blessed to have a dynamic Prayer Team! My wife, Vanessa, is doing a great job guiding it. The team will gather together Sunday morning for one hour before service intercedes mightily on your behalf! Keep your prayer requests coming! God answers prayer!"

"Yassss, he does!" "Glory to the Most High!!!" "Won't he, though?" various congregants replied.

"Let's take a moment to recognize those praying and interceding for you. When I call your name, please stand: Sister Tiffany, Sister Geneva, Sister Rose, Sister Grace, Sister Constance, and Sister Dreama! We thank God for your service."

Upon hearing Dreama's name called, Mabel gasped and drifted off to think about what she had written on the prayer request slip: *I am in love with my sister's husband and three months pregnant. I need to tell my sister. Please pray that I receive direction on what to do.* Mabel's gasp quickly turned into her choking on air. She coughed repeatedly while Reverend Allison proceeded with the service. The head usher quickly escorted her out of the sanctuary to the nearest water fountain.

14

Who's the Daddy?

Dreama was cooking breakfast for her family just before Booker could take Mabel to the university. As Booker went outside to warm the car, Dreama rushed from the kitchen to the bathroom, where Mabel was throwing up violently. She pushed the door open and saw Mabel on her knees over the toilet.

"Girl, I don't need to tell you that you are pregnant."

"Yes, I am three months along, according to the doctor." Mabel laid her head down on a towel she had thrown over the toilet cover.

"Uh-huh. I knew you were pregnant two months ago, especially when I saw you craving dill pickles, potato chips, and ice cream. I was just waiting to see when you would say something." Dreama looked at her in curiosity.

"I was just nervous about what you might say, especially since I am contributing very little but receiving so much."

"Girl, you're older than I am. What you do is your business. Who is the father, and why have we not met him? When are y'all getting married? You know if Mama was living, she'd have y'all married today."

"You're right. We have to talk about that later since I have to get to class." Mabel dropped her eye contact with Dreama and looked away.

Dreama remembered that she had breakfast cooking on the stove. "You get to class. I have to get these boys ready for school and be ready for work. I'll clean up this mess."

"It'll only take a minute." She smiled and rubbed Mabel's back for a moment.

Mabel managed to speak despite her retching.

"Go on, go on," Dreama insisted. "Plus, Booker wouldn't like it if you kept him waiting. I will see you later this evening."

"I know, but it'll just take a minute," Mabel said, pushing herself up from the floor and leaning on the sink.

"Girl, if you don't get out of here!" Dreama teased.

"Okay, okay. I just gotta brush my teeth. She finished straightening herself and walked through the kitchen. See you later, Dreama. Have a good day, boys!"

Dreama gave a quick wave at Mabel and turned back to her children. "Come on to the table to eat your breakfast! We have to rush this morning since your bus will be here in 20 minutes."

As she was preparing the boys' breakfast, Dreama thought about the situation. *I will have to work overtime to afford to care for Mabel and her child. She has two more semesters to go before completing her sociology degree. She will be the first in the family. We should be able to make it with what I am bringing and Booker's unemployment check, but I keep seeing disconnect notices for lights and gas. I'm glad I put in a prayer request for a financial blessing so that we, as a Prayer Team, can pray about it on Thursday.*

—⟊—

"So, Booker, what are we going to do? Dreama knows I am pregnant but doesn't know you are the father. She wants the family to meet the father, and she's asking about when we are getting married. Oh, this is so stressful!" Mabel confessed.

"She's such a nosey bitch! But today is Thursday, and we have our weekly session with Countee. Don't worry, I know how to relax you," Booker grinned.

"And besides, I will arrange for a friend to *meet the family*. When the time comes, you will just go along with what I say," Booker stated coolly. "He can act as if he is the father until we figure out something else."

"Anything you say. You know, I can't wait until our love child arrives. I was thinking Constance if she is a girl or maybe Connor if he is a boy."

"Love child? You are just having a baby. That baby wasn't conceived out of love. You had to pull your weight for living at my house. Since you couldn't pay rent in cash, you paid it by giving up some ass when I wanted it. And like clockwork, you've given it up to me and Reverend Allison most Thursdays. And don't worry about child support. Countee will send you money to pay for my child support."

"But Booker, I love you. I only have sex with Countee because *you* want me to. I want only you. You promised me that you would leave Dreama and marry me. What about me and the baby?"

"I don't feel the same way. The way you give it up to Countee, how do you really know what you feel? And what about you and the baby? You can do whatever you want with the baby. Just don't go around saying it is mine. It could be Countee's kid—have you thought about that possibility? You can go at any time," Booker stated nonchalantly. As soon as Booker expressed his last word, he parked the car in the visitor's parking lot at the university.

Mabel stared at him, amazed at his indifference. "Before I go to class, I need to tell you one more thing," Mabel said with a worried face.

"You will be late to class if you don't leave now. I'll pick you up this evening. You may go now. Whatever it is, it will wait."

Mabel was shaken to hear this news; she looked forlornly at Booker, wishing he would reassure her. He only looked forward and motioned his right hand for her to leave. She exited the car and watched as Booker drove off. She walked shamefully towards Skipper Building, where her class was. Upon entering, she pondered Booker's words: "But today is Thursday, and we have our weekly session with Countee." Her guilty conscience guided her to the payphone, where she called St. Elijah Baptist Church.

"Reverend Allison is not here today. May I take a message?" Rosa Lee stated mechanically.

"It is Mabel Miller, Dreama Johnson's sister. I was a guest at your church Wednesday. It is an emergency! I need to speak with him *now!* Please contact him wherever he is and have him call me at . . ."

"Ma'am, are you there?"

"Yes, I am. I just don't have a way for him to call me. I'll have to keep calling back."

Mabel hung up the phone.

—m—

"Sisters, I rejoice in the Lord that we are gathered here in one place to pray for each of these prayer requests. We are grateful to have a full team tonight because we have to intercede mightily for our brothers and sisters in Christ!" Vanessa Allison stated reverently.

"Let me add that we should pray over Reverend Allison this Thursday as he goes with his team to do ministerial work in the community and beyond. He was a bit agitated when he left the house today. Now, Sister Tiffany, lead the ladies into our next steps," Vanessa directed.

"Thank you, First Lady. We will pray for Reverend Allison in addition to the other prayer requests. Now, you know the routine. We are going to distribute these anonymous prayer requests. Some of you will have two; some will have three. You are to read the prayer request aloud to the group and then lead the prayer over those slips. Anyone is allowed to say an additional prayer aloud regarding the request after the lead person has prayed," Sister Tiffany instructed.

"Sister Grace, lead us in prayer," Sister Tiffany voiced.

After the prayer, the members of the Prayer Team had their slips. Dreama got three prayer-request slips: one for a woman seeking to learn about her purpose in life, one for help with raising five children alone since her husband died unexpectedly, and one for a new job.

As the group sat down in the chairs, which were arranged in a semi-circle, Sister Tiffany initiated, "We have a prayer request for a husband and wife to obtain a better understanding of the Bible and a prayer request for a young, married mother to receive a scholarship to go to college." The Prayer Team prayed with Sister Tiffany. As they prayed, Dreama thought, "I wish I had these kinds of problems." After Sister Tiffany finished praying, Sister Grace added, "And may they teach their children about the Bible and raise them in the nurture of the Lord. We know we have so many disobedient children today as a result of godless parents."

"Amen!" "I know that's right!" "Help them, Lord!" were the responses.

"Next is Sister Rose," Sister Tiffany announced.

"I have two prayer requests: A family needs help buying a home." Sister Rose then hesitated as she reviewed the second prayer request.

"So, what is the second prayer request for Sister Rose?"

Sister Rose was slightly sanctimonious when she replied, "A woman is pregnant by her sister's husband and doesn't know what to do!"

"My, my, my!" one of the prayer-team members shouted.

"Chile, these people are going to hell!" another one shouted.

"It can't be happening in this church," Sister Tiffany said in astonishment.

"What? The devil is busy!" Sister Grace said. They were murmuring to each other until Dreama jumped up and asked hastily, "May I see that prayer request? I want to be sure we know exactly what we are praying for." Sister Grace passed it swiftly to Dreama as if releasing a demon-possessed note from her hand.

Instantly, Dreama recognized by the green-inked handwriting that the prayer request was from Mabel. She was seething with fiery anger, plotting in her mind to kill her and the unborn child. Working diligently to show a detachment from this prayer request, she says calmly, "I'll pray over this prayer request."

"But Sister Dreama, this prayer request was assigned to me."

"I said, 'I'LL pray over THIS prayer request.' I will give you one of my prayer requests in exchange." Dreama instantly realized she was quite sharp-tongued in her response to Sister Rose.

Vanessa softly stated, "It is ok if Dreama prays over this prayer request. We do not need any strife to hinder the prayer request. Dreama, is there something you'd like to say?"

"My heart goes out to this wife and sister. My apologies, Sister Rose, if my response was out of line. I admit I was a bit passionate since the devil is busy! I just felt led to pray first."

Sister Rose said, "It is all right. I'll pray after you."

Dreama mechanically prayed that the Lord would make a means of escape for the sister and that forgiveness would abound. She also prayed that He would transform the husband's heart to love his wife again.

Sister Rose added, "May the baby be healthy since it has nothing to do with this matter. "Continuing on, saints . . . Sister Grace, it is your turn to share what is on your prayer-request slips."

Dreama zoned out during the rest of the prayers. She decided she would help the Lord make a means of escape for her sister, but she knew she would never forgive her.

Reverend Allison paced the motel floor, playing in his head, explaining the reasons why Mabel tried to contact him. The alcohol just wasn't enough to calm his nerves. *This stupid bitch needs to think. Why would she be calling me repeatedly, knowing that no one can make a connection between me and her,* Reverend Allison thought to himself. He wasn't in an amorous mood; hence, he was completely clothed. When he paced towards the door, he looked out of the window surreptitiously. "At least they pulled up right on time," he whispered as Booker and Mabel walked across the parking lot.

The Reverend left the door slightly ajar using the door latch and sat on the bed. Upon seeing Mabel, he quickly stood up and slapped her so viciously that she stumbled over the pine table and chairs, causing them to hit the wall with a thud. "Hey man, we can't make any loud noises to draw unwanted attention. What the hell is wrong with you?" Booker reacted as he closed the door. Mabel looked at the Reverend wide-eyed, shocked that he had hit her.

"My secretary told me you called the church multiple times today asking for me. Why would you do that knowing that I have a wife and kids? Don't ever do that again, you stupid bitch! Do you know that your calls could have drawn suspicion? I have a great name in this community," Reverend Allison admonished as he sat down on the faded bedspread.

"I needed someone to listen to me. Booker, I tried to talk to you this morning, but you were dismissive. And Countee, you were not at church all day. I am desperate," Mabel pleaded as she sat at the same table she tumbled over.

"Vanessa asked me why I was flustered just before I left the house. I told her the devil was busy, so she wouldn't keep pressing me." Mabel mouthed, "I'm sorry, but I needed to tell you what happened in case it gets out."

"Mabel, what do you need to say?" Booker asked curiously as he made himself a drink.

"At Wednesday night service, I put in a prayer request saying that I am pregnant by my sister's husband, with whom I am in love. I need guidance on how to tell my sister. I didn't realize that Dreama was on the Prayer Team until you announced it," Mabel stated in a trembling voice.

"What the fuck? You are more stupid than I thought. I can't believe this shit," the Reverend stifled his voice. "Do you know how this could play out? You ain't married; you ain't got a boyfriend. People will ask who the father is. Now the whole Prayer Team knows that somebody who has been to the church is pregnant by a married man who happens to be married to her sister. FUCK!!!"

Booker calmly said, "I have a plan to fix this. Mabel, call your sister Catherine in Washington, DC, and tell her you will move in with her. I will arrange for you to take the bus in the morning."

"I am about to be in my last semester of college. Can't I just stay until then? You said you could find a guy who would act like he is the father. I can't go back to DC without some kind of education."

"No, you cannot stay. The less people know, the less they have to talk about. Then, there would be pressure from the community on you to get married, and there would be one more mouth to feed. We just don't have the room in a two-bedroom trailer. Call your sister now, and don't talk long since that call is expensive."

Mabel sat on the bed near Booker and reached for the yellow rotary phone. She took a deep breath, buying time to absorb her new reality. Catherine answered the phone on the first ring.

Booker and Countee poured another round of drinks as a pre-celebration of their plan for Mabel to leave town. Booker whispered, "When she's gone, we can find a replacement to keep her mouth shut. We got a good thing going on."

Countee replied in a hushed tone, "Everybody would've benefitted if she would've kept her fucking mouth shut. Bitches don't know how to enjoy the dick and not tell anybody."

"We need to work on getting a replacement for Mabel, though."

"I want to introduce you to Bernard, a long-time friend. He is trustworthy, married, keeps his mouth closed, has a side chick that he nicknames *Flossie,* and a married dude that he fucks around with. They obey him. His chick can be Mabel's replacement. I can talk to him about it."

"He sounds like the right one to connect with. Set it up," Booker concluded.

The two men heard the phone being placed on the receiver. "What did she say?" Booker asked.

"She welcomes me to her home and will assist in raising the child," Mabel stated dejectedly. "I will let her know when my bus will arrive in DC so she can pick me up."

"It is good that you will have some help. I ain't working right now, so I may send something when I can. You need to pack your stuff tonight. I'll take you to the university so you can tell them you are withdrawing, then I'll drop you off at the bus station," Booker told her.

"I completely understand now" was all that Mabel could say as she held back tears.

"Good. Take this $30. Five dollars of it goes to the long-distance phone call. The rest is for you to get snacks along the way. If Dreama asks why you're leaving, tell her the pregnancy is too much for you right now with going to school. Now, go to the lobby, pay for the long-distance phone call, and wait for me in the car. I need to talk to Countee about something personal," Booker directed. Countee went to the bathroom in preparation for what would soon follow.

Still crying, Mabel quietly left the hotel room and headed to the lobby.

"This is who?" Dreama asked harshly.

"This is your sister, Mabel."

"Why are you calling me, knowing that you will see me within 30 minutes after Booker picks you up from school?"

"I just needed for us to talk. And I don't have much time."

"Well, I'm here. Get to talking."

"I am pregnant by your husband. I am so sorry. I didn't realize . . ."

Dreama zoned out when she heard those words again while Mabel continued talking. Dreama refocused on the conversation when Mabel said, "I hope you can understand and will forgive me."

"You come into my home, pay no bills, eat my food, borrow my clothes, hardly babysit my children, use my gas to go back and forth to school, and the thanks I get is that yo' ass fuck my husband AND get pregnant by him?! Bitch, I'll never forgive you. I don't want to see you or your child at any point in my life! I will have yo' shit packed and sitting by the door. Don't bother saying goodbye in the morning because I just did."

"Click." Mabel did not have to question whether it was a bad telephone connection. She knew that she had just experienced a lifetime disconnection with her sister.

15

Teaching How to Fight

Dreama awoke to a quiet home. She took sleeping pills after her conversation with Mabel, and she did not want Booker's entrance turning on lights, rummaging through drawers, and talking on the phone to disturb her sleep since it was going to be another 16-hour workday.

The boys stood outside with Susie's children, waiting for the bus. All traces of Mabel had disappeared, and Booker, too, was gone.

Dreama stood by the window watching her boys play. "Bart plays like a girl," she whispered aloud as Bart skipped after he snatched Rhonda's scarf from her neck. He twirled around three times, pretending the scarf was his hair. By the end of the third twirl, the bus was arriving. "I just don't know what to do about that boy," she wondered out loud.

While getting ready for work, she replayed what was stated during the prayer meeting and what Mabel said over the phone. Booker and Mabel's affair caused a permanent wedge between Mabel and Dreama. She was disappointed in Booker as a father, deacon, husband, and man. She remembered her vows to love, honor, obey, and submit to Booker since she believed the Bible said that. She figured the best way to address this matter with Booker was not to address it at all since Mabel would be gone. Booker honked the horn twice, prompting Dreama to exit the trailer.

Booker arrived at Chev Mills's parking lot at the end of Dreama's shift. Bart and Warren were asleep in the back seat. When he switched off the ignition, he saw Ralph Custon and Dreama cavorting and laughing as they descended the black metallic steps.

"Dreama, I did not know you could be so funny. It was great to work with you for 16 hours. We will do it again tomorrow. Get home safely," Ralph looked her squarely in the eyes, feeling a wave of magnetic energy ignite his nervous energy.

"Thanks for all your help and kind words this evening. I'm looking forward to working with you tomorrow," Dreama responded.

Dreama correctly sensed that Ralph was watching her walk toward the parking lot. She widened her gait to draw attention to the curvature of her hips. She added a bit of bounce to her step, causing her hair to bounce and swing in the light wind. She was glad to get some sort of positive attention from a man. For the first time in a long time, she smiled.

When she saw Booker, her smile instantly inverted, as indignation was written all over his face. Upon entering the car, Dreama whispered, "Hi, Booker; I hope you had a good day. I thought we could develop a plan to get you back to work."

"How about you work on being less of a whore and MORE OF A WIFE!" Booker's voice escalated as he pulled out of the parking lot. "I saw how you were all up in Ralph's face, laughing and then twisting as you walked away from him. So NO! I am not doing better! I was wrongly fired! And now I have to witness you wanting Angelica's husband, Ralph?"

Booker's loud voice awakened Bart and Warren, but they had been taught never to intervene in adult matters.

"Booker, I do not have any desire for Ralph. I worked 16 hours to help *our* family. Can we not have this conversation around the boys? Whatever is bothering you, we can address it together."

"DON'T FUCKING TELL ME THAT LIE! YOU BEEN EYEING RALPH AND DRESSING FOR HIM. AND I WILL SAY WHAT I WANT TO SAY ABOUT IT NOW! YOU JUST DON'T WANT THE

BOYS TO SEE YOU FOR THE WHORE YOU ARE," Booker ranted as he drove 65 in a 25-mph zone.

"Booker, I do not have eyes for Ralph. I was assigned to work with him and Margie. What would you like me to do about it, Booker? Shall I quit my job so we have zero income?" Dreama calmly stated, looking out the passenger window.

"WOMAN, YOU ARE FULL OF LIES. I SEE WHY THE BIBLE TALKS ABOUT Y'ALL BEING EVIL. YOU JUST LIKE JEZEBEL! JUST KNOW IF I SEE RALPH AROUND YOU TOMORROW, I WILL BLOW YOUR BRAINS OUT!" Dreama turned to find Booker's .357 Magnum cocked to her head. "SAY ONE MORE WORD AND YOU'RE DONE!!"

"If you're going to kill me, Booker, do so. Just not in front of the boys."

Booker resorted to hitting Dreama across the face so hard that one of her incisors became loose, and her gums bled. Dreama said nothing as blood trickled from her lips onto her clothes.

Bart held Warren close to him as he thought about everything he witnessed and experienced with Booker. "I hate this man!" Bart thought. "Why can't he just die?"

—⁂—

Dreama was so nervous while lying in bed with Booker that she did not fall asleep until 5 a.m. When the alarm rang at 6:30 a.m., she jumped straight up in horror. Relieved that it was just the alarm and more relieved that Booker was gone, Dreama found comfort in lying in bed. "Just five more minutes is all I need."

Those five minutes turned into two hours. "Oh my goodness, the boys missed the bus, and I am late for work. Where is Booker?" Dreama got to the kitchen and saw Booker's note: "Walk the boys to school, then call a cab to get to work."

"This home would be far more peaceful without you! I don't care where you are or what you are doing!" Dreama said under her breath as if she were practicing saying it to Booker. She called her supervisor, who told her she would arrive as soon as possible. She decided to take her time with the tasks of the day. After getting the boys up, she had them wash up while she prepared breakfast. Bart was allowed to turn on the TV to watch his favorite show, *Wonder Woman*. At the time he turned it on, Diana Prince was being chased by two men. Successfully, she hid behind a truck while the men ran past it. She emerged, and then the music signaled her transformation from Diana Prince into Wonder Woman. Diana extended her arms out, spun once, and her bun fell to her shoulders. She spun again, only for the bright light to appear, and spun two more times to complete the transformation. Her red-white-and-blue costume, hair, and makeup were perfect. She caught up with the men and threw them around like ragdolls into boxes. Her magic lasso forced them to tell the truth about why they wanted to capture Diana. Bart was so fascinated that he imitated the spin, calling himself Wonder Woman, *then* took an imaginary lasso and roped it around two imaginary criminals.

"Bart, boys, don't act like that. Boys act like Superman and Incredible Hulk and Captain America," Dreama went through a list of superhero names.

"I'm a boy who likes *Wonder Woman*. What's wrong with that?"

"The Bible says there's everything wrong with that."

"That I spin around and call myself *Wonder Woman*? Where is that in the Bible, Mama?"

"Just show me your homework so I can look at it," Dreama deflected, not wanting to get into a conversation about it.

"I didn't have any homework," Warren said.

"Then take out all your notebooks so we can be sure together."

"Oh, I do have math homework."

"Get to it now."

"Here is all of my homework, Mama," Bart stated enthusiastically.

"My goodness! You are so smart. You got all of the answers correct.

Plus, you got an award for learning your times tables. Why didn't you tell me about this?"

"You work all the time, and Dad is not interested."

"I always want to know about your grades, son. I believe in both of you! Keep striving to make the best grades. It will help you get into college someday. How is school going?"

"It is good for me. My favorite class is PE," Warren chimed.

"We need to do something about that. You have the ability to make better grades, Warren. I think I need to meet with your teacher about what we can do to improve them. How is school for you, Bart?"

"It's ok. I have two boys that pick on me, calling me names like *sissy, faggot,* and *punk.* Or saying, 'You play like a girl.' One guy acted like he wanted to fight me, but I just ignored them since I learned in Sunday School to turn the other cheek," Bart said.

"Well, if they hit you, you hit them back."

"I'm not sure if I know how to fight, Mama."

Dreama grabbed a stuffed animal. "What are the boys' names?"

"George and Patrick."

"This stuffed animal is George. Anytime you walk by George, you say nothing. Don't even respond if he calls you names. Be prepared to fight him if he hits you first. You have to be a thinker when you fight back. You can be angry yet be in control at the same time. Now, when George hits you, you need to think instantly about what makes you angry. What makes you angry?"

"Dad, with all of the things he does to me and you. I am tired of him calling me names like *sissy, sorry ass, stupid,* and saying that he wishes I was a girl."

Dreama was thrown off for about ten seconds before resuming. "Ok, let's not say the a-word. That's a bad word."

"Ok, Mama."

"Now, back to the fighting lesson. You need to think about all the anger you feel and be determined to beat his ass so badly that he will never start a fight with you again. Aim to knock him down first and then hit his head and chest with your fists as hard as possible. The word will get out that no one at school will start a fight with you," Dreama prophesied.

"Hey, punk! What would you do if I hit you?" Dreama said as she put the stuffed animal near Bart's face.

"If you hit me, then I will hit you back."

Dreama's stuffed animal hit Bart across the face. Warren watched intently. Bart knocked the stuffed animal out of Dreama's hand and swung on its face and chest so many times that the plastic eyes were dangling and the neck was partially severed. Dreama had to project her voice to get Bart to stop.

"You are certainly ready now. And know this, you better not come home with yo' ass beat, or else I will beat yo' ass."

"Yes, ma'am. I understand."

"Good. Now, y'all get ready for school."

Suddenly, Bart looked around, "Where is Daddy? Isn't he driving us?"

"He had to step out. I will walk you to school."

Bart walked behind Dreama and Warren, holding his head low, thinking about how his father touched him, how he treated his mother, and how there was peace when his daddy was not around.

Dreama gave both of the boys a kiss on the cheek upon their arrival at school. She went so far as to walk them to the door, which she had not done since the season began. "Make this a great day! Dreama said, blowing them kisses. She was trying to hold back tears. Always remember, Mama loves you," she added, but they both were out of sight.

Warren rushed in after seeing Peter, a classmate. Bart walked inside, only to watch his mother walk away, sobbing in her hands. "She must be crying because of something my dad did," he thought, walking to Ms. Lucky's class.

"Today, let us start our morning by going outside for recess. Line up!" Bart quickly puts his things down, and George and Patrick knock them down and kick them across other desks. "What are you gonna do, you little fairy?" George teased. "Yeah, is your mommy gonna come kiss you on the cheek so she can put some makeup on your face, punk?" Patrick questioned as the three boys were standing in line. "Don't bother me," Bart charged just before Ms. Lucky said, "We're going to walk quietly to the playground."

"You run like a little sissy! My Daddy said, 'Sissies are going to hell,'" George said.

"I ought to come and beat the punk out of you," Patrick added.

"If you hit me, I will hit you back," Bart promised.

"Oh yeah!"

The taunting from the boys got three other kids to notice. Bart walked around the corner of the building unseen. He heard one of them say, "The punk is probably running away to cry. Ha ha!" The truth was that Bart felt like he needed a bit more strength to handle both boys. He instantly thought about Diana Prince and the lessons his mother gave him. "I wonder what would happen if I spin around four times?" Bart thought. Looking around to ensure no one was watching, Bart spun four times, playing the *Wonder Woman*-themed music in his head. Confident that he had changed into Wonder Boy, he ran back into the presence of George and Patrick, who were on the side of the playground, away from the teacher's view.

"Oh, the little fairy is back. And you look like you skipped your way here. I wonder what would happen if I pushed you to the ground," George questioned.

"I'd then come and beat your face in just because you're a sissy," Patrick added.

"I wouldn't try that if I were you," Bart advised.

George immediately ran towards Bart with a raised fist. Bart quickly grabbed his wrist, twisted his arm, pushed him to the ground, and beat him so badly that it took four boys to get him off of him.

"WHAT DO YOU HAVE TO SAY, PATRICK, BECAUSE YOU WILL BE NEXT IF YOU EVER CALL ME OUT BY MY NAME OR ATTEMPT TO HIT ME," Bart yelled as he got up in Patrick's face as the four boys whisked him away. Patrick was shaken and amazed by what he saw. "I can't believe that a sissy beat up my best friend," he murmured softly to himself. "You said WHAT?" Bart asked.

"I ain't said nothing. Get up, George, and let's go."

The other boys around Bart were having sidebar conversations.

"Did you see how George went to hit Bart, but Bart blocked it and took him to the ground?"

"Yeah, Bart is super strong. George got all scuffed up. He won't mess with Bart anymore," Eugene McClain shared.

"Patrick betta not say anything to Bart. He *don't* want what George got."

By this time, Ms. Lucky had appeared, coughing lightly since the dust was still settling. "What happened here? I thought I heard some noise."

"We were just racing Ms. Lucky and then talking about the winner," one of the boys lied. "Well, it is time for us to go back to class. Everyone, line up!"

Eugene Washington caught up to Bart. "That was some fight. I think you are a cool boy. Can we be friends?"

"He is so cute," Bart thought. "Yeah, we can be friends."

"Great! Let's sit together in the cafeteria today with two of my other friends."

"Ok, we can do that."

Bart basked in the glow of having won that fight and making a new friend as he whisked himself away from the other students to transform from Wonder Boy into Bartholomew Johnson.

16

Throwing Dirt without a Shovel

"The boys are growing so fast. Bart is twelve, and Warren is ten. Bart makes good grades in school and likes to write poetry. He reads the Bible every day, constantly asking me questions about it. He knows the scriptures better than I do. And he has an advanced vocabulary. Chile, I have to look up some of the words he uses. Warren likes to play sports. He is very good at basketball and football," Dreama happily shared with her sister, Catherine.

"Girl, I hope someday I can meet them. Ever since you got married, you have become distant from the family. Your boys don't even know you have brothers and sisters that love you. If Mama were living, she would not be having that."

"Chile, I know. I will work to do better. I'd let you speak to the boys, but I put them to bed at 8 p.m. since they have school in the morning."

"Maybe next time you call, I can speak with them. How's Booker?"

"He's all right."

"What does 'He's all right' mean? Girl, speak your message and make it plain."

"We've been having marital problems. I am so tired of him abusing me and Bart. I fear that he will kill me, and then my boys will not have a mother. He is a jealous man. Any man that looks at me swears I provoked him to look at me. I'm working all these hours and giving my check to him to pay the bills. He is just irrational. I want out. The best and only thing he has done was give me my boys."

"How is he abusing Bart and you?"

Dreama got quiet after realizing she shared more with Catherine than she intended.

"Ok, we can talk about it another time," Dreama answered.

"Why don't you pack your stuff and come to DC to live with me? I am fearful that things will get worse before they get better! I can pay for the bus tickets," Catherine insisted.

"I have to think about that. I just don't know what to do."

"You sound just like Mabel. She is raising that boy by herself, if you wanna call it that. She left your house and came straight to mine. The boy is smart but doesn't know how to socialize with kids or his mother. Her lazy ass just wants to sit in front of the TV with her fig newtons, black coffee, and soap operas. What that boy needs is a father. He's acting like a little lady with no man around this house. I guess I'm glad I never married. After all, Mama told me on her deathbed to take care of all of y'all."

"What is the boy's name?"

"Lee."

"That bitch had the nerve to give the little bastard Booker's middle name," Dreama thought.

"Who is this boy's Daddy, Dream?" Catherine asked in a serious tone. "He needs to be supporting him. I am getting him clothes from flea markets and clothing donation centers. And I need some help."

"Why are you asking me? I don't know."

"Well, he looks a lot like Booker."

"You've only seen Booker twice, so how can you be sure?"

"I just know that one day, Mabel was at your house and going to school. The next day, I was picking her up from the bus station. When

I was helping her unpack, she went to the bathroom, only for me to find pictures of her and Booker. They looked like they were in love."

"Well, I took those pictures of them. They were my models for my photography project."

"Oh, ok. Sounds like you should've taken pictures of other models."

"They were the only ones available."

"Uh-huh. When I asked Mabel who Lee's daddy is, you know what that heifer told me?"

"What?"

"Jesus!" Dreama and Catherine laughed for a while.

"I told her that there is nothing virginal about her for Jesus to even think about doing an immaculate conception with her."

After laughing at the joke for a while, Catherine said, "Dreama, Booker is the father, isn't he?"

"Yes, I'm afraid he is," Dreama nervously confessed.

"Uh-huh. I know it hurts. But Mabel is your sister; Booker is the problem. As gorgeous as you are, you can find a much better man. Mabel needs to know that you have forgiven her."

"I don't know about that, Cat. After all, I've done for her. Right now, I cannot forgive her. It was why I threw her out. I have enough marital problems without her adding to them. Lee is my stepson and nephew. Booker is his father and uncle. Bart and Warren are his brothers and cousins. Girl, these dynamics are too much."

"What's done is done. Your sister will always be your sister. Booker will not always be your husband. You better think about how to mend your relationship with Mabel. All of her siblings are behind her except you."

"Thanks so much, Sis, for taking my call and offering to stay with the boys and me. But I need to go. I hear Booker pulling in the driveway, and I want to pretend like I am asleep."

"That's no way to live, Girl. You must guard your peace; otherwise, it will impact your mind. Call me anytime. The times I called you, Booker answered so rudely that I quit calling. I'll tell our other brothers and sisters that you called. We love you, Dreama."

"Tell them I love them too," Dreama replied, fighting back tears.

—m—

Dreama's alarm clock blared in her ear. "Thank God it is Friday," she said as she stretched and turned the blanket back. When she got to the bathroom, she gasped when she saw this message written with her red lipstick on the large bathroom mirror:

YOU ARE A DEADBEAT WIFE, A SORRY MOTHER, AND A WHORE. YOU NEED TO BE MORE LIKE MABEL. YOU DON'T THINK I KNOW WHAT YOU BEEN DOING? YOU BEEN SEEING RALPH CUSTON BEHIND MY BACK. THAT'S WHY YOU WANT TO KEEP WORKING OVERTIME SO YOU CAN WORK WITH HIM AND FUCK DURING YOUR BREAKS. WHEN I COME AND PICK UP YOUR CHECK DURING YOUR LUNCH, I SMELL YOU ALL OVER. IF I SMELL ANY PART OF A MAN ON YOU, I'M BEATING YOUR ASS ON THE SPOT.

"Why does this man create havoc? He is terrifying me!"

Dreama left the bathroom to go to her closet to pick out her work clothes. The moment she opened the door, she saw another message from Booker written in black on the back of a brown paper bag:

I HAD A DREAM LAST NIGHT THAT YOU WERE FUCKING JEREMY BROWN, RALPH CUSTON, AND THOMAS MOORE. I'M A HOLY MAN, AND I KNOW THAT IT'S HEAVEN'S WAY OF TELLING ME YOU ARE CHEATING ON ME. SUNDAY, YOU ARE GOING TO THE

ALTAR FOR PRAYER. AND BART IS GROWING UP AND ACTING LIKE YOU. THAT LITTLE SISSY IS GOING TO THE ALTAR TOO. THE BIBLE SAYS GOD HATES GAYS AND WILL JUDGE THE ADULTERER. KEEP UP THIS BEHAVIOR, AND BOTH OF YOU WILL GO TO HELL WHILE WARREN AND I WILL BE IN HEAVEN HAVING FORGOTTEN ABOUT BOTH OF Y'ALL.

Dreama's mind was racing so fast that she became dizzy. She took some aspirin just before going to the boys' room to wake them up. Bart was on the top bunk; Warren was on the bottom. She turned Bart's bed back only to see dried blood on the bedsheet with Bart's underwear on the bedpost and Booker's tee shirt and underwear on the floor.

"Bart, Bart. What happened last night? Bart, wake up," Dreama shook her firstborn son three times.

Bart sat up on the bed with the blanket draped below his torso. "Daddy woke me up and told me to take three pills because he felt I had a headache. I took the pills and went back to sleep very fast. I woke up with no clothes on, and Daddy didn't have any on either. Oh, Mama, I don't know how long I can deal with him. He treats me so badly and calls me names," Bart cried so hard as he spoke that it made Dreama cry.

"Mama, I didn't sleep good last night, and Daddy didn't give me any pills," Warren whined. "Daddy and Booker kept rocking the bed, and I don't know why." Warren started to cry when he saw Bart and Dreama crying.

"Don't y'all cry, boys. Bart, I am so sorry that Daddy did this to you. I will speak with him so that it won't happen anymore." Dreama heard her empty words as if they came from a voice other than hers. She put her arm around Bart, realizing that neither she nor Booker had ever told Bart they loved him. She decided not to tell him since she felt he was confused about love. With that epiphany, she thought about love only to choke back her own cries. Booker's ideas about love were simply horrific. She couldn't even go there in her mind.

"Get up and get ready for school. Bart, take your bath first; make sure you wash real good. Warren, you can pick out your clothes for school. Things are going to get better. We will go to church Sunday and pray about it." Even Dreama realized she didn't sound convincing.

17

Sexual Sins in the Church

Reverend Allison, Booker, and Apostle Bernard Daniels met in the church's office during Sunday School. "Bernard, I'm glad to have you here, man."

"Now, Countee Allison, you know that I couldn't miss your anniversary as Pastor of this church. I appreciate you having me. Just let me know what I need to do to help the church, and you celebrate."

"Our church needs money, and you can help raise it. We can divide the money immediately after service and just before we go to the dining hall to eat with the congregation. Now, I want you to meet Deacon Booker Johnson. We get together every Thursday evening to enjoy one another's company. He's a good guy, private, and respected."

"You're a handsome man. Handsome enough to join you on Thursday *and do whatever y'all do on Thursday.*"

The three men laughed.

"Thanks. We can make it happen," Booker stated coolly as he physically assessed Bernard.

"Glad that it was easy. Where is Ivan Burns?"

"Y'all help yourself to some orange juice and grapes." Reverend Allison walked to the door to check on where Ivan was, only to find Ivan almost knocking on the door. "Come on in, Ivan."

Ivan has been the church's minister of music for thirty years. He was deemed a musical child prodigy, and Reverend M. B. Allison made him the minister of music when Ivan was just sixteen years old. When Ivan played the Hammond B-3, people would fall onto the floor, jump up and down, and cry joyfully. Nora Burns, Ivan's mother, was a single parent who touted herself as a self-taught opera singer and pianist who valiantly attempted to take credit for Ivan's musical prowess, which obviously surpassed hers. She was nicknamed *Nora Desmond* since she would sing for anyone anywhere, only to stop mid-song. She was convinced that imaginary paparazzi were after her to take more pictures. She would even pose, turning her head right or left, with her grossly widened eyes, and smile like a jack-o-lantern. Ivan took four lessons from the late David Banister and has played independently for various churches ever since. Churches spoke in hushed tones about his flamboyant and effeminate appearance, as evidenced by his flowing clothes, feminized language, and not-so-subtle makeup. Ivan's long Jheri curl and endomorph body completed the appearance. Churchgoers in the neighborhood knew that if they were to have a good church service, then Ivan needed to play. Most of them concluded that his father was absent, so he took on the traits of his mother.

Ivan sashayed into the office, saying, "Hello, boys. Why are we gathered together in a foursome?" Ivan asked in a southern drawl as he sat and crossed his legs. Booker could not stand the sight of him. Not only was he jealous of Ivan's talent, but Ivan's feminine inclinations turned his stomach.

"Well, we need you to help us in today's service as part of the business at hand," Reverend Allison refocused the conversation. "Now I will introduce you, Bernard. Is there anything in particular you want me to say as part of the introduction?"

"You've known me for a long time and all my titles. Just be sure to say all of them," Bernard touted. "Your congregation loves titles. You brought me here to help you raise money after getting people emotionally charged to give," Bernard asserted.

"Absolutely. You have a way of holding church services that bless the people and bless yourself—sometimes spiritually and financially! Ivan, have Brenda Matthews sing an upbeat song. She will get the crowd excited."

"Then just tell me what all you want me to do after she sings, and I'll make it happen. Of course, you have to pay me well. I have even brought *Flossie* to be a visitor to help in the service flow."

"I'm expecting a raise for my efforts too—in cash or *ass*," Ivan flirted. The three men ignored him, trying hard not to grimace.

"Let's talk about the terms of how we all are going to be paid today because this church has quite some bills. We'll make the plan to get the show started," Reverend Allison quickly interjected. And there is something you can do for Deacon Booker, too, during the service."

"I'll do whatever is needed. You know the trustees will be counting the money in the back. You have to come up with a plan to get the money so each of us can get our cut."

"Don't worry. I'll tell them that I'll make the deposit and then later tell them that somebody hit me over the head and took the deposit," Countee shared. "Now let's go! It's time to get paid."

Reverend Allison and Apostle Bernard Daniels walked out onto the pulpit as the choir sang *Hallelujah* with Brenda Matthews leading. Brenda summoned the spirit of all of the Clark Sisters—the original singers of the song—and sang every part with such emotion that the congregants were standing and clapping their hands. The two men fell to their knees to pray before joining the attendees in worship. When Apostle Daniels started jumping and dancing, some of the congregants started doing the same. When Brenda growled after the song, the congregants jumped and danced in the aisles. Booker and Dreama acted in good spirits, clapping and smiling. Bart stood up, too, fascinated by how Brenda sang, and Apostle Daniels jumped. He attempted to imitate how he moved his feet. Warren sat indifferently since he hated being at church. When the song ended, the pianist played softly.

"Everybody say 'YES'!"

"YES!"

"Say it again!"

"YES!"

"One mo' time!"

"YES!"

"Celebrating being your Pastor for the past 17 years has been a real joy. Thank you for celebrating my beautiful wife, Vanessa, and me. This is the best church in all the land."

The congregants gave a standing ovation, cheering as if the pastor's three-sentence statements were personally direct to each of them. The Reverend motioned for the congregants to sit down.

"To help celebrate my pastoral anniversary, I asked this great man of God, our Apostle, to lead today's services to the next level. You all know that when Apostle Matthews comes to our church, our church is set on fire! Amen! But Apostle is just one of his titles. He is actually The Reverend, Doctor, Judge, Professor, Prophet, and Apostle Daniels. We look forward to what this man will do in this service today! Come on up, Apostle, and let the Lord use you!"

An electric current ran through the crowd as they anticipated Apostle Daniels's gifts. The congregants clapped vehemently as he rose to the podium.

"Praise be to God for allowing us to join together to worship! Thank God for Reverend Allison, your great leader, who invited me to come to celebrate his pastoral anniversary. As you remain standing and the musician plays softly, the spirit of prophecy is upon me. Continue to lift your voices unto the Lord as He speaks to me."

The congregants obeyed the command, waiting anxiously to hear who would receive a prophecy. The apostle came down from the pulpit and walked about the crowd, selecting various people who knew to go to the altar to receive what *thus saith the Lord.* Dreama and Bart completed the selection.

The apostle prophesied jobs, cars, homes, strong marriages, checks in the mail, promotions, or surprise money to each selected person. Ralph Custon and his wife, Angelic, prophesied that their twins would receive college scholarships when they graduate high school next year. Ralph's auto-mechanic business would flourish so much that Ralph would have to quit working at Chev Mills to manage his business full-time. The apostle had this *spiritual insight* into the Custon news since the church secretary told Sister Josephine, who told Agnes Johnson, who told Booker, who told the apostle that the Custon twins received scholarships, but Angelic wanted to keep it a secret for another two weeks when her parents would come to town. The reactions ranged from shouting, dancing, and crying as the person returned to their seat. Dreama and Bart were left standing.

"How many of you know that God chastises those he loves?"

"Yes!"

"Amen!"

"Glory!"

"Ephesians 5:5 says, 'For this ye know, that no whoremonger, nor unclean person, nor covetous man, who is an idolater, hath any inheritance in the kingdom of Christ and of God.' We want every saved person to inherit the kingdom of God. So we have to cast out some whoremongering spirits today!"

The congregation's reactions ranged from "Amen, Apostle," "Get that unclear spirit out," and "Tell who it is, Apostle."

"To the two of you, God loves you but does not love your sin. Sister Johnson, I see in the spirit that YOU are an ADULTERER!" Apostle Matthews stated charismatically.

"Call it out, Apostle!!!" a female congregant shouted.

"I see three men; somebody say three!"

"Three."

"You have been sleeping with three men while your husband is at home reading Bible stories with his children." The congregants gasped and murmured. Sister Tiffany had the usher pass a note to Sister Grace that said, "She is off the Prayer Team effective immediately. She is probably the reason why some of our prayers have not been answered. We will talk more later." Sister Grace nodded her head in agreement.

Dreama was dumbfounded. She couldn't believe that this apostle would tell this lie. Her face flushed hot; her heart rate increased, and she started shaking. The church nurses gathered around Dreama as the apostle placed his right hand on her forehead while speaking into the microphone with her left hand.

"I am going to cast out that demonic spirit now! IN THE NAME OF JESUS, I COMMAND YOU TO COME OUT *NOW!*"

The apostle pushed Dreama's head back, causing her to fall to the floor. The nurses broke her fall by catching and guiding her to the floor. Dreama screamed and cried so angrily and loudly that the congregants were instantly convinced of the apostle's power. The nurses covered her legs and fanned her, petting her shoulder as she lay there.

"What did you do to my Mama?" Bart questioned in a low-pitched voice as he put both of his hands on his hips.

"Little boy, do you love the Lord?"

"Yes, I read my Bible daily; I believe in Jesus Christ, and I sing in the children's choir," Bart said proudly.

"How old are you?"

"Twelve."

"You don't question adults. And from what I heard about your father, he is a righteous man teaching you well."

Bart felt Booker's eyes on his back. He was still unmoved by the apostle's words as he looked at his mother, lying as if dead while her eyes were closed.

"I delivered your mother from being a whoremonger. That is a sexual spirit. You have a sexual spirit, too. You are a homosexual! God sends all homosexuals to hell. Even twelve-year-old boys can go to hell. You don't understand this now, but you will thank God in the future for using me to deliver you from being a sissy! You're a sissy who won't be singing for the children's choir no mo' until that demon is permanently cast out!" The apostle dropped the microphone to the floor, forcibly placed both hands on Bart's head, and then started speaking in French—though the congregants thought he was speaking in tongues. "*Tu es un mauvais enfant. Comment osez-vous essayer de m'embarrasser. Tu seras toujours homosexuel et ta mère est une pute menteuse*! Demon, come *OUT NOW!*" He repeated three French sentences, which in English means, *You are a bad child. How dare you try to embarrass me. You will always be gay, and your mother is a lying whore!*

The congregants were shouting; cacophony filled the room. Bart was walking backward as the apostle gently pushed him. The apostle realized instantly that Bart was very strong for his age. When he did not fall back after three of the apostle's attempts to make him appear *slain in the Spirit*, he said, "There are several demons in this boy. Reverend Allison and Deacon Johnson, I need your holy ghost power to lay hands on this boy. Everybody needs to keep PRAYING HARDER for THESE DEMONS to come OUT!" The whole church pointed in Bart's direction. Even Ivan stopped playing the organ to point in Bart's direction.

Reverend Allison and Booker were on each side of him, with Apostle Daniels in front of him. "When we put our holy hands on you, all those demons will flee. IN THE NAME OF JESUS, **Tombe par terre, espèce d'idiot**!!" The churchgoers were amazed to hear Apostle Daniels speaking in tongues—or so they thought. In French, he had said, "Fall to the ground, you idiot."

All three men laid hands on Bart. When Bart gave resistance, Booker tripped Bart, causing him to fall to the floor. "You are to stay on this floor with your eyes closed until the church nurses come and get you," Booker instructed as Bart's head hit the floor.

"Give God glory, church!"

The church went into a dancing, shouting, and hollering frenzy.

Bart obeyed the directive when he noticed a woman dancing inches from his head. Ivan played so hard that his linebacker shoulders bounced up and down. He swung his Jheri Curl from left to right as Brenda sang the reprise of *Hallelujah*. He stopped playing to swoop his hair back from draping over his left eye and engaged the choir in foot stomping and hand clapping while he stood up and played the tambourine.

"Parents, if you even think your child has a homosexual spirit, bring him to the altar so he can be delivered! Now is the time! You see how the power of God has been moving in this place!"

Bart thought that Glen Harris, Sebastian Rouse, and Kurt Kenton's parents should have brought them to the altar, as his suspicions were matched by the gossip of a few of his classmates. And Ivan Burns' momma was dead, so his momma couldn't bring him. But no one else came.

"Well, we thank God that there was only one homosexual in this church." Ivan screamed, "AMEN, Apostle!" as he swung his head from left to right.

The church nurses were given the cue to help Dreama and Bart come off the floor. They were about to place some smelling salts by Dreama's nose when, just then, Dreama jerked off the floor. Bart quickly got up to accompany her back to their seats. Dreama vowed that she would address this latest embarrassment with Booker.

Bart's hatred for Booker grew deeper. He was starting to understand that Booker was using the Bible to manipulate and then convict him. Bart thought, *Children are to obey their parents in the Lord. I obey everything my dad says. The only time he says he loves me is during sex. I have sex with him out of obedience, though I find it gross. Now, I am told that God hates homosexuals. I obeyed my dad in doing a homosexual act. Now, God must hate me. But what does that say about my father?"*

Apostle Bernard then called out a 14-year-old girl who was pregnant and told her mother to stand beside her at the altar. The boy who made her pregnant and the girl's father remained seated with the congregants.

"You are a little girl and pregnant. You're not even old enough to get married. That makes you a whoremonger. And as for the mother, what have you been teaching your child about the word of God? She was to remain a virgin until she got married. Both of you need deliverance," Apostle Bernard charged. The girl started to wail from embarrassment. As the Apostle laid hands on the girl and her mother, congregants were moved by what they perceived as his holy ghost power.

Bart wondered, as he witnessed what was happening, why the boy and the girl's dad weren't up there.

As Apostle Bernard shared, Bart snapped out of his thoughts, "It is time to give. I want every person under the sound of my voice to sow a seed to bless your Pastor. The spirit tells me that a woman in a white dress has $1000 in her pocket right now. She is sowing that seed on behalf of something she expects God to do. While the musician continues to play softly, I will be led by the spirit to point her out."

Apostle Bernard stepped off the pulpit and walked among the congregation. People were anticipating even greater *power* being demonstrated. When he got to the third to the last row of the center pews, he pointed and said, "You! Come out to the aisle and meet me."

The woman chanted silently, "My soul says yes! Yes!"

"I need the church nurses to encircle this woman now." The nurses quickly answered the summons.

"I have never met you. Your name is Flossie Byers. You are the CEO of your own sewing business. You don't have any children. You have been living a holy life. You are pure. You are visiting this church in South Carolina, although you live in Virginia. You have a sister named Sue Ellen who is sick in her body. If you sow the $1000 you have in your purse, I can decree and declare to God that she will be healed within one week! When you get the news that your sister is HEALED, YOU ARE TO SEND A TELEGRAM TO THE CHURCH! Hallelujah!!"

Flossie jumped up and down in excitement. She trembled as she said, "Yes, I will, Apostle!"

"Now saints, witness my prophetic power. Sister, have we met before?"

"No."

"WHAT is your name?"

"Flossie Byers"

"What is your occupation?"

"CEO of a sewing business in Virginia."

"Why are you in South Carolina?"

"To help care for my ailing sister?"

"Exactly how much money do you have in your purse?"

"$1000"

"Do you wish to sow a seed today?"

"Yes, because I am believing in God for a miracle."

"Trustee Carter, come over and get this seed while we praise God!"

The congregation was ecstatic. Some jumped up and down, some hollered, and some cried. Dreama cried, but not for the reasons others did. Booker raised his hands to the sky.

"Now, church," The congregants calmed down. "We are going to continue in the spirit of giving as the spirit gives me a prophecy for others of you. If you love your pastor, you'll freely give. We need to celebrate him on this day. Now, we will form three lines—in the name of the Father, the Son, and the Holy Ghost, representing $1000, $500, and $100. If you want to be blessed abundantly, sow a seed of $1000. If you don't have $1000 right now, then you can make a vow to sow the seed in payments. Even if you have to borrow it, sow it! Sow your rent payment! Sow your light bill! Sow your gas bill! Everyone under the sound of my voice should be in one of the three lines. And I'll add that if you sow $1000, I'll give you my anointed cloth that I have here, plus give you a prophecy from on high." Most of the congregants were moved by this prosperity preaching and made an emotional decision to receive a prophecy.

Ivan stumbled from the organ to be the first person in the line, and then twenty people stood in line, giving $1000, and got a prophecy. Ivan was so attracted to the smell and voice of the apostle that he had to ask God for forgiveness for his lustful thoughts. The attraction increased when the apostle laid hands on him to prophesy increased talent and a love life with a mate. Booker and Reverend Allison stood behind Ivan to catch him as he fell back. The moment the men touched the back of him, Ivan became a dead weight that neither man could hold. Ivan fell to the ground with a thud, hurting his lower back. He lay there for a while before rolling on his side to get up.

Everybody in the church got in one of the lines with dollars in hand, including James Hayes, his wife Darlene, and their three-year-old son, Curtis, the youngest of nine. James and Darlene gave $30 in $1 bills in an envelope. Upon seeing the thick envelope, Apostle Bernard became excited. These out-of-town visitors were shocked when Apostle Bernard prophesied, "God is going to bless you with another child!" Darlene thought to herself, *I already have nine, and my tubes are tied. But whatever the Lord says . . .*

Dreama felt so alone since everyone received prophecies of goodness while she and her son received prophecies with the intent to misinform, embarrass, and condemn. She couldn't endure pretending as if she was in the spirit. She felt that everyone she considered family—Agnes, members of the Prayer Team, Booker's siblings and spouses, and her children—all saw her differently as a woman she was not. Yet even she saw Bart as the gay boy he is, and she loved him.

18

Raining on Her Parade

The gray clouds in the sky gave an ominous warning that thunder and lightning threatened to make their majestic appearance as the family was riding back from church. Booker stared straight ahead as he drove home, and no one said anything.

Dreama broke the silence: "Booker, why did you have the Apostle tell a bald-faced lie to the whole congregation? Only you could have been involved in setting this up. I have been nothing but the best wife I could be to you. Why Booker? Why?" Dreama questioned as she was building her confidence in confronting him.

"Daddy, the preacher said I have a sexual problem. Why did he say bad stuff to me? Why did he try to push me to the ground? Why did you trip me?" Bart asked, puzzled. Warren echoed, "Daddy, I think you accidentally tripped him."

"You and your Momma have different sexual problems, and the apostle prayed for both of you. There is nothing wrong with prayer. And the apostle has a holy gift. I can't help but think that the Most High revealed what I know and what he learned about you. He was just following what God told him to say."

"Even if that were the case, Booker, why didn't you step in to do something to save Bart and me from being embarrassed? Everybody at the church thinks I'm cheating on you with three men. I have *never* cheated on you at all."

"You are more FOCUSED ON your embarrassment THAN THE TRUTH," Booker's voice escalated.

"What needs to happen for you to know the TRUTH Booker? I go to work and come home every day. You know all of my whereabouts, but I don't know yours."

"YOU AIN'T NOTHING BUT A CONNIVING 'HO!!! I AIN'T GOT TO GET NO MORE PROOF BECAUSE I KNOW YOU FUCKING AROUND ON ME WITH THE MEN. AND YOU DON'T NEED TO KNOW MY WHEREABOUTS. JUST KNOW THAT I AM NOT HOME OFTEN TO GET AWAY FROM YOU AND THAT FAGGOT ASS BART!!!"

Bart curled in the corner of the backseat and cried silently. Warren remained stone-faced as if his mind was elsewhere.

"What do you think would happen if I told the church that you are the father of my sister's son; if I told them that you don't read the Bible at all to the children; if I told them you beat me; if I told them you aren't working; if you aren't paying any bills; if you aren't. . ."

Booker punched her in her head so hard that the passenger window cracked.

Bart cried loudly and punched the air repeatedly, imagining that he was fighting his father.

"GET THE FUCK OUT OF MY CAR, AND WALK YO' ASS HOME!!! I HATE BEING MARRIED TO YOU. EVERYTHING YOU SAID IS A LIE, AND THE TRUTH AIN'T IN YOU!!!! YOU ARE ON YOUR WAY TO HELL. GET OUT!"

Just as Dreama got out of the car, the sky released an amalgamation of thunder, hail, and rain. She held her head down as the weather beat her from the crown to the soles of her feet. Booker drove alongside her slowly, taunting her for a mile and signaling cars to go past him. Dreama did not look at Booker; she took her hair out of a ponytail so that it could act as an umbrella against her bleeding head. Bart and Warren cried as hard as the sky did.

"I'M TIRED OF YO' ASS AND I WANT A DIVORCE. BART AND WARREN, WHO DO Y'ALL WANT TO STAY WITH: ME OR YOUR MOMMA?"

In unison, the boys said, "With momma."

Shocked, Booker said, "Well, it's fair that one of you stays with me and the other stays with her. And since you look just like your momma, Bart, you can stay with her, and Warren can stay with me."

"Booker, I think we need a divorce too. Let's talk about who gets Warren," Dreama softly spoke as she walked. Bart felt dejected that neither parent wanted to talk about who got him.

After yelling his last expletive, Booker commanded, "GET IN SO WE CAN TALK ABOUT IT THEN!" Just as Dreama slowly opened the door handle, Booker sped off, causing Dreama to be dragged two feet before falling to the ground. Bart and Warren looked back sorrowfully in the window until Dreama disappeared from sight. "Y'ALL BETTA SIT DOWN AND SHUT UP!" Booker turned up the gospel radio to tune out the crying. He started singing along to *There's Not a Friend Like the Lowly Jesus*.

As Booker pulled into the driveway, the thunder struck two trees simultaneously in front of the trailer with such force that they split into four. Bart thought, "God, you missed hitting Daddy," as he watched the rain beat on the trailer and the car. Warren's face held the dried tears in place as he slept.

"All right, boys. It is time to run out of the car and get inside."

Bart pushed the seat forward and ran swiftly into the house. Booker covered Warren and himself with a tarpaulin. Warren went inside as Booker got the taped envelope from the door.

Bart changed clothes, climbed to his top bunk, and opened the Bible I Samuel 25 to the story of Nabal and Abigail, where Nabal was an evil man married to Abigail whose life's focus was to do good. Nabal treated David and his men so evilly that David vowed to get revenge. Abigail thwarted David's plans by bringing him bread and interacting with him kindly. When Abigail told her husband about the kindness she demonstrated, Nabal had a stroke. Ten days later, he died. Shortly after that, David married Abigail. Bart was still crying, thinking about where Dreama was. Booker escorted Warren to his bed for a nap after he changed into dry clothes. Warren fell asleep instantly.

"Boy, you are going to go crazy for always reading that Bible."

Bart looked up at Booker with such contempt that he was willing to risk getting beaten if it meant one less beating for Dreama. He continued to read his Bible and thought, "God, this man is Nabal all over again. I hope he has a stroke and dies. Then I hope Mom marries a man who loves her and treats her right. Protect mom and keep her safe." Bart lay on the bed and coddled the Bible, crying himself to sleep.

—⁂—

Dreama cried profusely as she trembled in the rain. Cars passed her, some splashing rain on her, some honking the horn, and some asking if she needed a ride. She flatly ignored them all. Her mind was on how alone she felt.

"I CAN'T TAKE THIS, LORD! I CAN'T!" Dreama wailed as she fell to her knees on the shoulder of the road.

A white Ford pickup truck slowly drove past Dreama. The driver put on the hazard lights and backed up closer to Dreama. The male driver got out with an umbrella and threw his trench coat around Dreama while covering her with the umbrella.

"Come in the car, Dreama," Ralph Custon softly said.

Dreama looked up at him and nodded her head three times before getting up.

Ralph opened the truck's passenger door, patiently waiting for a soaking-wet Dreama to get in before closing the door.

"Why were you walking on this road? This road is too curvy for anyone to be walking it. You could've gotten yourself killed," Ralph shared his concern. "I recognized you by your hair and dress. I was on my way to my auto shop. Again, why Dreama, why?"

"Booker and I must've missed each other after church today. He probably thought I caught a ride with Sister Tiffany," Dreama stated as Ralph attempted to decipher the tears and raindrops on her face.

"Dreama, you and I both know that is not true. If that were the case, you would not be soaking wet, walking on a dangerous road. I need you to tell me what is actually going on. Something tells me that things did not go well between Booker and you after the Apostle prophesied over your son's life and yours."

Dreama confessed everything she had been going through with Booker.

"I'm so sorry you have been going through so much with Booker. Would you like to get some counseling from Reverend Allison?"

"No. Reverend Allison and Booker are very close friends, and he influences him. I will have to figure out what to do."

"Well, I am happy to help you with that. In the meantime, we have to get you out of those wet clothes. Let's stop by this thrift store right here and get you something."

Ralph pulled the truck in the back parking space. "I'll ask if they have a warming space inside the store while you remain under the heat in the truck." Dreama nodded in agreement. Five minutes later, the White, blond female manager and Ralph escorted Dreama into a heated room via the docking entrance. "You sit here and warm up while I get you some clothes, hon. Your dress size looks like a size five, and your shoe size looks like a size four. We also have some underwear still in a packet that we will give you. I'll be right back, hon."

Dreama sobbed. Ralph gave her the unused handkerchief from his pocket.

"Why are you crying, Dreama?"

"For years, I have never had anyone do anything to help me. I centered my life on doing whatever Booker wanted. I tried to raise my kids the right way, the best I could. I am moved by your act of kindness, especially after all I experienced today. The apostle did not hear from God that I am a whore. I have been a faithful wife to Booker, obeyed him, submitted to him, gave up my family for him, gave up my dreams for him, gave up my identity for him, and what has it yielded me? A life of misery! And I am tired! Bart wants his father's love, and ever since he was five years old, Booker has raped him. Now that he is twelve, he is called out for being a homosexual who is going to hell. I am at a loss as to what to do!"

"He's a deacon, Dreama. He knows that these things are wrong. If you don't make a change, then the circumstances you're experiencing will permanently change you. Think about what kind of help you need. I could contact social services, but they will likely take your children, inspect your backgrounds, arrest Booker and you, and whatever else."

"Oh no! Please don't do that! Oh, maybe I should not have told you what was going on!" Dreama panicked as she thought about Booker's retribution.

"You needed to tell someone, or else it would constantly eat at you. I will not tell anyone, including Angelic. When you're ready to make a move, let me know, and I will help you. You are a beautiful woman who does not deserve this treatment. I will pray for Booker and your children. We can talk more later. Here comes the manager."

The White lady approached with several material garments folded over her arms.

"Now I got you this olive green dress with these beige shoes and this red-and-white striped dress with white shoes. You like these?"

"I like the red-and-white dress."

"Well, it is yours. You people are so nice; don't worry about paying. The bathroom is right over there. If you give me your wet clothes, I can throw them in the dryer."

"That would be so nice. Thank you so much."

When Dreama emerged in her new clothes, she felt like a princess. She looked at herself in the mirror, spun around, and smiled.

"It looks really good on you, Dreama. You look like a ray of sunshine that matches the weather outside right now," Ralph said with a smile.

"Thank you. I am glad the sun is back out."

"So let's get your other clothes from the dryer and get you something to eat. I can drop you off near your home and meet Gordon Carter at my auto shop since he wants to drop his car off around 4 p.m."

"Gordon Carter, the head trustee at the church who collected the seed money today?"

"Yes. What made you ask?"

"Just clarifying. I never knew his first name. In fact, I know very little about him."

"I've known him and his family for years. He's a good man. Now, let's get going since it is already 2 p.m. The last one to the truck is a rotten egg."

Dreama sprinted out of the store so swiftly that Ralph would've been embarrassed if others had witnessed her outrun him.

"We don't have to guess who the rotten egg is, do we?" Dreama laughed as she stood by the truck's passenger door.

"You just got a head start," Ralph laughed as he opened the door.

As Ralph walked in front of the truck to the driver's side, Dreama thought, "Angelic is so lucky to have a husband like Ralph."

"Barbeque King is a good spot on the other side of town. Is that good for you?"

"Absolutely. I haven't had a good barbeque in some time." Dreama thought, "There's nothing but White people on that side of town, so we won't have to be bothered by running into church folk."

After placing an order with the waitress, Ralph and Dreama sat in the booth, talking about hobbies, goals, and dreams while laughing about television episodes of Sanford and Son, Good Times, and The Jeffersons. When she brought water and bread, Ralph pensively said, "Things are going to work out for you. We just have to believe it will. Grab my hands, and let's pray over the food."

Dreama felt a person's presence as Ralph prayed. When he said, "Amen," Dreama looked up and saw Agnes and Sister Tiffany. "What are *you two* doing here?" Agnes asked.

"It is not what it looks like," Dreama explained.

"Uh-huh! And does your wife know that you are on a date with Booker's wife?" Sister Tiffany inquired as her church hat shook from left to right. "We can't even enjoy a dinner with our church families without having whoremongers in our midst."

"This goes to show that the Apostle's word was correct! We caught you in the act!"

"We do not owe you any explanation for this! Dreama, let's go," Ralph said quietly, motioning with his head towards the door.

Ralph and Dreama quickly got up from the table. As they exited through the door, they saw other church members in the distance. "Of all the times I go to a restaurant, I go to the one where some of my church members decided to attend," Dreama thought. Agnes and Sister Tiffany rushed back to their tables and interrupted the grace that had just started. "Chile, we just saw Ralph Custon and Dreama Johnson on a date! And they looked like they were in love!" Agnes loudly shared with the church group. Everyone stopped eating to ask for the details.

19

Breaking Point

It was 3:45 p.m. Booker's car was in the driveway. Against Dreama's advice, Ralph said, "Don't worry. I will explain to Booker what happened. I know your marriage is being challenged, and I won't share what you have told me. It will be okay." Dreama opened the door to find Booker sitting in the lounge chair, placing coins in coin wrappers. Ralph walked behind her.

"Hi, Booker," Dreama said nervously. I have Ralph Custon here. He was so kind to bring me home when he saw me walking on the road. I told him you probably just concluded that one of the ladies was bringing me home since I met with the prayer team after church today. When I realized I may have missed you, I opted to walk home. Ralph saw me, and I caught a ride with him."

Booker smiled, "Darling, you know I wondered what happened to you. Ralph, thanks so much for picking up Dreama. I don't know how I can thank you. I was so worried. The boys just cried themselves to sleep, wondering where you were. Ralph, how much do I owe you?" Booker walked to the living room table to get his wallet.

Glancing at the papers on the kitchen table, Dreama noticed a disconnection notice for the lights and gas. She also noticed the wet envelope and note from the landlord, Mr. Dodd, saying, "You are two months behind in rent. I have been here twice. Call me today." Ralph also noticed the bills as he gave a cursory look around the trailer.

"Don't worry about it, Booker. It was my Christian duty. I just wanted to talk to you in person to explain what happened and answer your questions."

"Well, thank you very much! Dreama is safe; that is all that matters. Dreama, how about some refreshments for Ralph?"

"No, thank you, Booker. I have to get to my auto-mechanic shop to meet Gordon about his car. I better be going."

"So soon? How's Angelic?"

"She's doing good. We are about to send our twins to college soon. She is out now with them at an amusement park. I'll tell her you asked about her."

"Please do. May your family be blessed for caring for my wife," Booker stated, smiling falsely through his teeth.

"Absolutely. Enjoy your day."

Booker looked surreptitiously out the window to ensure Ralph was on the road. Satisfied, he looked at Dreama indignantly. His anger was interrupted by the ringing of the phone.

"Hello."

"Booker, yo' 'ho ass wife was caught snuggling up with Ralph Custon at the Barbeque King on the White side of town. Did you know she was wearing a new dress and some new shoes? Evidently, not only is Dreama seeing Ralph, but he is also buying clothes for her. Can you believe that?" Agnes mused.

"Mama, where did you get this information?" Booker's eyes foretold what would come as Dreama was in the kitchen, placing a greased skillet on the stove to preheat while she was mixing cornbread.

"I saw it with my own eyes. I and other members of the Mother Board were eating our dinner and discussing scripture when I saw Dreama come out of the bathroom. I got up and went to their table, and when I got there, they were holding hands."

"Oh, is that right, Mama?"

"Chile, that apostle's words proved right. Y'all to talk about this since the laying of hands didn't work."

"Dreama and I will talk about this," Booker promised.

"Well, call me immediately after you do. I have to call one of the girls from church."

Click. Booker gently placed the phone on the receiver. He removed his left white sock and placed six rolls of ten-dollar quarters into it. He slowly turned his head to Dreama, who was heating a lightly greased skillet by the gas stove. She was making the boys cornbread.

"So, you want to throw it up in my face and deliberately embarrass me in front of my mom and the ladies I grew up with?" Booker gritted his teeth, carrying the white sock, and walked slowly toward Dreama.

"Booker, don't do this."

"Don't do what? YOU ARE THE SLUT WHO THE APOSTLE CALLED OUT IN CHURCH. EVERYBODY IN TOWN KNOWS IT. AND THEN YOU WANT TO PARADE AROUND WITH THAT GREASY RALPH CUSTON IN PUBLIC. WOMAN, YOU ARE REALLY BOLD. YOU ARE GOING TO QUIT THAT JOB TOMORROW, SO YOU WON'T HAVE AN EXCUSE TO SEE RALPH."

Dreama turned to the oven, put on stove gloves, and took out the heated skillet that lightly popped grease. "Booker, I need peace today. I am not quitting my job. The boys need shelter, clothes, and food."

"OH YOU TRYING TO DEFY ME WHEN I AM THE MAN OF THIS HOUSE? I'M STILL PAYING THE BILLS AROUND HERE."

"How can you pay the bills, Booker, when disconnection notices are everywhere? The landlord has not received rent in months. I bring my check home to you and work overtime, which is more than enough to pay the bills. WHEN was the LAST time YOU contributed anything to this home, Booker?"

The words prompted Booker to swing at Dreama swiftly, but he missed. Dreama's gloved hands swiftly grabbed the heated skillet and promptly whacked Booker *upside his head,* knocking him to the floor. Dreama held onto that skillet and hit him across the shoulder twice as she bent over him. Bart ran to the kitchen as Booker grabbed Dreama's neck, yanking her to the floor as she dropped the skillet. Bart jumped in the foray and punched Booker in the face. Booker managed to get up swiftly. He jacked Bart up, screaming, "FAGGOT, DON'T YOU KNOW I'LL KILL YOU?"

The words hurt Bart more than his father's reaction to the hit. "YOU MUST BE A FAGGOT TOO SINCE YOU TAUGHT ME HOW TO PLAY WITH YOUR DICK SINCE I WAS FIVE!" After saying these words, he instantly started to cry. Booker was stunned by those words.

"YOU AIN'T KILLING NOBODY, Booker," Dreama raised her voice. "If you touch him, then I am going to whack your ass, and I won't stop until you're dead. That's my son!"

Booker slowly released Bart and went to sit in his lounge chair. Dreama went to Bart. "Son, are you ok? I'm sorry that Mama didn't protect you before from Daddy. I don't know what kind of scars that may have left on you. From here on out, he will not touch you again, and he will not touch me again."

Booker cried upon seeing the exchange between Dreama and Bart, stunned that they defended themselves against him. That hurt him more than the double-team blows on his face and shoulder. "Bart, come help me clean this kitchen," Dreama commanded gently.

Bart quickly picked up the skillet and chairs. He washed the skillet out and placed it on the stove. Dreama prepared the cornbread mixture, though she didn't have an egg or milk, and placed it in the skillet and then into the oven.

"You and your brother go outside and play while I get dinner ready."

Bart walked towards the bedroom entrance to find Warren shaken by what he witnessed. "Come on, Warren. We can go outside and play. Everything's okay now, little bro."

Dreama looked at the mounting bills. Then she looked in the refrigerator and freezer, where she was met with an empty ice tray, a stick of butter, and baking soda. She looked in the cabinet only to find two cans of corn and two cans of peas. "My kids can't live like this," Dreama muttered.

"What did you say? I didn't hear you," Booker spoke softly, attempting to get Dreama to say something. Dreama looked at him for five seconds as she washed out the tin aluminum pot that would later contain a mixture of corn, peas, and butter.

"Y'all come wash up for dinner," Dreama called from the single-pane window.

Bart and Warren quickly ran into the trailer and followed the directive. They made their way to the kitchen table. Dreama set a thin plastic plate in front of each of the boys, dividing some of the corn-and-peas concoction and cornbread. "You boys say your blessing and eat," Dreama charged. "There is some left in the pot if y'all want more."

"What are you and Daddy gonna eat?" Warren asked.

"Me and your daddy have already eaten. All of the food is for the two of you," Dreama lied.

Dreama guarded the kitchen to ensure Booker would not take the remaining food. Booker stared absent-mindedly in complete silence as he sat in his lounge chair.

As Bart and Warren finished the last morsel of food, Dreama thought, *My kids don't have to live like this. They are growing out of their shoes and clothes. I'm going to find a way to make sure they don't do without. No matter what it takes.*

20

Image Means Everything

Dreama decided to get up earlier than usual on Thursday morning to start her day. Besides, she had become a light sleeper since she was listening out for what Booker may attempt to do to Bart or her. She kept a rusty knife by her bed hidden in her makeup bag. At 6 a.m., Booker was already gone; she didn't even care. She dressed for work, wearing a fitting work uniform and some makeup. She even wore her hair down. "Today is a new day," Dreama said as she kissed herself in the mirror. She awakened Bart and Warren, directed them to handle all hygiene matters, and told them to get dressed. She walked them to Susie's when she knew she was about to feed her children.

"Hey, girl. Good morning to you."

Bart and Warren spoke to Susie as they were greeted by Susie's children, Melvin and Kelvin. "I got a new Atari system. Wanna play Pac-Man?" Each boy talked about who would go first as they walked to Melvin and Kelvin's shared room.

"Hey, Dreama. How's your morning?"

"Girl, I have a new attitude, and I am going to have a great day."

"That's a good attitude, especially with what I heard you went through at that church."

"I figured you and the whole neighbor heard something about it."

"Would your boys like to have some breakfast?"

"Well, they are growing boys. If you are sure, it is not a problem…"

"Chile, no. They can eat some grits, eggs, and bacon with my kids while we have a conversation. I'll fix them a plate, and we can go outside to talk. Bart and Warren, come to the table to eat," Susie called.

Susie and Dreama walked outside beyond the steps to ensure their respective children did not overhear. Dreama was direct: "I'm sure Agnes is the ringleader behind this foolishness. I ain't got time to be cheating on Booker since I work all the time."

"Girl, I hate to tell you. I know the real Reverend Allison and Deacon Booker, and that's why I just stopped going to that church," Susie shared as she pursed her lips.

"I haven't had any *real* interaction with the Reverend to really know him. And I wish I just had my boys and not Booker," Dreama confided. "I live in misery with the *real* Booker every day! But Chile, what do you *really* know about the Reverend?"

"Girl, there's too much to tell you. Just know that the Reverend is the reason you have never met the fathers of my three kids."

"I've only known of your twins Melvin and Kelvin. Who is the third child?"

"That's my oldest, Todd. He is 25 now. In fact, Melvin and Kelvin hardly know him. Todd doesn't speak to me."

"What does this have to do with the Reverend?"

"The kids' father's name is Joe. I met Joe at the church as a teenager. After graduating from high school, we wanted to get married. The Reverend counseled us and then married us, and then we had Todd. Joe never worked, but he always had money. I worked three jobs and dealt with any physical and verbal abuse he dished out. The Reverend beat me over the head with scriptures that tell what a wife should do and disregarded what a husband should do. I obeyed Joe. Joe taught Todd that I was a bad mother and that all women have evil within them." Susie heaved a deep sigh, remembering her sorrows before she continued.

"When Joe started using drugs, the Reverend funded his habit in exchange for sex. I figured that he was doing this because I was working so much and was too tired to give him sex. I didn't work as much on my third job so that I could be home. I thought it worked. We had sex, and I got pregnant with the twins. As time went on, Joe started experimenting with harder drugs while teaching Todd how to smoke marijuana while I was working. He stole from the children and me so much. Joe sexually abused Todd in his drug-induced stupor. Todd was very young and looked up to his dad, so it was an act of love as best as he could understand. He did anything he could to satisfy him. Todd would witness Joe calling me names, abusing me, and telling me about what the Reverend said about women being gossipers, quarrelsome, and emotional during his Sunday sermons. Todd began to hate me as a result." Susie teared up, and Dreama was speechless and stunned by the parallels between Susie and herself. The experiences were so similar that Dreama wondered if this abuse would go on in every woman's home.

"Anyway, as Todd was developing as a young teenager . . . Susie wiped her face, blew her nose, and went on. The Reverend took notice of Todd, who was maturing physically. When Joe wanted more money to buy drugs, the Reverend told him to bring Todd to a dumpy hotel about an hour north from here. It was the start of the Reverend having sex with my husband *and* my son regularly. The Reverend paid them both. I left the church, and Joe moved the twins and me into my trailer. Todd chose to be with him. Joe's drug habit worsened. That's when Joe and Todd went and robbed different stores in the area for money. The Reverend then no longer wanted to maintain a sexual relationship with either Todd or Joe. When Joe and Todd went to Virginia and robbed the food market, they both went to prison."

"Chile, NO! Does the Reverend's wife, Vanessa, know about this?"

"Girl, she acts like she's in denial when she knows damn well her husband does not want her for sex. She just wants to have the M-R-S in front of her name. She's a miserable woman who is all about public image. She wants to fool everyone into thinking she and her husband have a perfect marriage. As a matter of fact, she has been confiding in her best friend, Michelle Askew, about what's really going on in her marriage. Michelle, Vanessa, and I went to high school together. Vanessa and I didn't interact much, but Michelle and Vanessa were best friends. Michelle moved to Texas to marry her boyfriend after high school. Vanessa doesn't know that Michelle tells me everything. Anyway, Vanessa told Michelle she is very suspicious of her husband's activities while away from the house every Thursday, *saying he's doing ministry work.* She smells a combination of floral scents and an Old Spice Smell every time she washes his clothes, knowing that it's not her perfume and that he doesn't wear cologne."

"Well, Booker goes with the Reverend each Thursday to do the ministry work. I never questioned it since he brings home church programs or other artifacts. The Reverend probably hugs a number of people and gets that scent on him," Dreama reasoned.

"Vanessa told Michelle that she's wondering exactly what kind of ministry work he does every Thursday. She even told her that Reverend hadn't had sex with her since the birth of their fourth child, and that baby is now six years old. She hasn't been able to lose that baby weight like she did after she had the first three. You see, Vanessa always wears heavy makeup and clothes that are too small to appeal to her husband visually. That girl is getting bigger by the minute because she is depressed. She even told Michelle that she wears makeup to bed and sexy lingerie every night, but her husband gives her no attention and no compliments. You'd never know she wears makeup privately since y'all church teaches that makeup is Jezebel's paint. Anyway, Vanessa is no dummy; she likes being referred to as First Lady and the attention she gets from it. This charade, however, is getting to her since she knows her husband ain't shit. And girl, you have a lot to learn about the Reverend *and* your husband," Susie retorted.

"What do you mean?" Dreama looked startled. "I really don't know the Reverend, and I just go along with Booker to keep the peace. Vanessa presides over the Prayer Team and has always been kind to me. She doesn't give me vibes that anything is wrong. Girl, I'm so surprised by all this news."

"Vanessa knows how much image means to her husband. And besides, her parents told her she should not marry him when he proposed. They died in a car accident ten years later. She lived her life wanting to prove them wrong. Her husband helped ruin my marriage, and slowly, he will ruin yours," Susie predicted.

"Girl, I'm so sorry your marriage didn't work out, and you don't have a relationship with Todd. I can only imagine the financial strain it has put on you. Poor Vanessa. I wish there was something I could do to help both of you."

"Chile, don't be sorry! My kids and I have peace. And forget about trying to help us when we have to do things that help ourselves. What you can do to help yourself is to re-evaluate what happiness looks like to you. Find out who you are since your identity has been wrapped into what the church and Booker say it should be. I work from home, and the moment my kids get on the school bus, I'm paid in cash daily. If you know what's good for you, you better pay attention to how your husband doesn't work but still has money."

"Honey, Booker is given a small salary for his role at the church. What skills do you have to do that work at home? I need a job like that."

Susie looked at Dreama pensively for ten seconds. Decidedly, she stated, "I'll tell you what. One, you need to stop being a naive bitch. Open your eyes, girl! You don't even know Booker's role in determining how much he is being paid at the church. Two, you need to hang around after our kids get on the bus so I can show you how I make my money. I need to make a call for my 8 a.m. appointment to bring his brother. But you have to agree that you will engage in the kind of work I do and say nothing about it to anyone."

"I don't even have anybody to tell. Besides, I need to do this for my kids."

"Good. Once the money starts flowing in, you want to keep it to yourself. Now call your boss and tell him you will be three hours late for work today. Wear a dress and high heels. I'll get your kids to the bus."

Dreama left feeling excited about this work opportunity and thought, *Whatever this job entails, I am gonna do it for my kids.*

—⟋⟍⟍—

Dreama watched bus #181 pick up and transport all four children to Buckdry Junior High School. Dreama found Susie's door ajar as she walked in. Susie was looking in her compact to apply lipstick that matched her low-cut, red terry cloth mid-thigh dress. Susie was ten years older than Dreama, yet her knee injury did not allow her to wear high heels anymore. "Now that the children are gone, it's time for us to get to work. First, we need to change your whole outfit and your shoes." Dreama's long white, flowing dress with white wedge shoes was not the outfit Susie had in mind.

"What is wrong with my outfit?"

"Nothing, if you go to a holiness church where they wear no makeup and white dresses past the floor. You'd fit right in."

"Well, girl, what kind of dress do I need to wear?"

"I am glad you asked. You look like a size four or five and like you are wearing a size five shoe. I have just the outfit for you. I will be right back."

"How did you get a dress in my size when you looked like a size twelve with a size eight shoe?"

"I have several girls working for me, and there are times I have to provide for them," Susie said casually as she brought a strapless, dark lime green Bardot midi dress with matching lime green four-inch shoes and a petit tube floral mini dress with red patent leather, four-inch heels.

"Hmmm. Put on the lime-green dress. It complements your skin tone. And take that red lipstick off and put on some lip gloss. The out-of-town customers will be here any minute. To the customers, your name is Sally Anne. Your job is to give them what they want. After the job is done, they pay you in front of me. Then you pay me my fee of 20%." Dreama moved quickly. The moment she approved of her new look, she heard a faint tap at the door and the voices of two men. She didn't see a car in Susie's driveway and wondered how they arrived.

"Girl, meet these two gentlemen in the living room." Dreama sauntered down the hallway slowly, nervous about interacting with strangers. Upon arriving, Susie quickly looked at Dreama and said, "*Sally Anne*, this is Marshall and Winston. Boys, she is one of my new girls working for me a few days during the week. Both of the men were seated."

"Very nice to meet you, Sally Anne," Marshall asserted as he stood. "Today, lime-green is my favorite color. You are absolutely a sexy fox," Marshall cooed as he visually examined *Sally Anne*. She noticed his towering figure, demonstrating his past as a former football player who still worked out in the gym. His fitted jeans and long-sleeved light blue dress shirt gave an unintentional silhouette of his body frame. His dark skin, low haircut, and gap tooth made Dreama quiver within as she extended her hand as a hand-shaking jester. Marshall wrapped his arms around her waist and pulled her close. Dreama gasped as the teachings of church and desire warred within her while she took on the persona of *Sally Anne*. The moment Winston cast his eyes at *Sally Anne's* figure while Marshall held her, he shook his head in approval. He even gapped his legs open, giving clear evidence that his genitals approved too.

"She needs to loosen up a bit. Maybe a little refreshment will help her relax. Let's all have a drink. What will it be, a gin and tonic or a bourbon on the rocks?"

During the next twenty minutes, the foursome had drinks, joked, laughed, and listened to Millie Jackson's album as they played strip poker under dimmed lights. Winston was left wearing only his briefs; Marshall only had on an undershirt and briefs. Susie had on her skirt, displaying her bare breasts to foreshadow the soon-to-be salacious activities. Dreama was wearing only her one-piece dress, singing along to Millie Jackson as they played cards. Winston said, "The losers of this hand have to take off three pieces of clothes." All agreed. "It's on you, Susie."

"Well, I have a straight," Susie asserted confidently.

"I have a flush. Ha Ha!" Winston trumped.

"I just have four of a kind," *Sally Anne* shared coolly.

"Looks like all y'all asses gotta drop some drawers 'cause I have a straight flush!" Marshall presented with a hardy laugh.

Everyone laughed as the losers completely disrobed in front of Marshall.

"*Sally Anne*, what do you really know about what Millie is saying?" Marshall asked with his right hand dangling over his crotch.

"I can do everything she describes," *Sally Anne* touted as her black-laced panties dropped to the floor. Her high-heeled shoes were the only items she still had on.

"Oh yeah? Come over and give me a workout for $75."

"Since this is the 1970s and things are as expensive as they are, you need to pay for inflation, taxes, and fees that total $100, and you have to pay upfront."

Susie thought to herself, "That's a quick-witted bitch! I'll have to tell her that $20 belongs to me."

Marshall stood up fully erect, his heavy manhood nearly forcing its way out of his briefs. "Here is your $100; you'll get a tip if you can take all this meat to the base."

"Then I need to get to work, starting on the tip," *Sally Anne* observed as she descended to her knees. Winston was stroking his dick, watching *Sally Anne* perform. Susie proceeded to perform on Winston. No matter how hard Susie worked, Winston was completely distracted by watching Marshall and *Sally Anne*. The acrobatic feats *Sally Anne* performed on Marshall yielded three back-to-back ejaculations. Winston landed two via masturbating as he watched the live porn, much to Susie's chagrin.

"I need to see you at least twice a week, *Sally Anne*. That was just the experience I needed," a breathy Marshall confessed. "Yeah, I wanna see you twice a week too . . ." Winston admitted.

"Oh, you can see me twice a week," Susie replied, even though Winston was referring to *Sally Anne*.

"We can meet on Tuesdays and Thursdays at the same time. We can skip strip poker and go right into the stripping," *Sally Anne* concluded.

Marshall and Winston exited Susie's trailer from the back door. The woods enveloped the men as they escaped back to their vehicles, which were waiting for them on the other side.

"Girl, you made me proud. Now that you made $80, you need to buy your own dresses."

"He gave me $100." Dreama couldn't help but smile.

"And my fee is 20% for arranging it; now hand me my $20," Susie insisted.

"Here you go! We are doing this twice a week, right?" Dreama handed over two tens to Susie's open palm.

"Absolutely."

"Thanks for the opportunity and for being there for me." Dreama was beyond pleased to make so much money at once.

"I was once just like you until I reclaimed my independence. I am a very secure woman. Yes, I know that my customers will desire you more than me. You're a younger woman and beautiful. I have my freedom and am trying to help my Black sisters experience it. Now go off to work."

"I'll have to talk to my supervisor about shifting my work hours so that I can make all of this fit," Dreama said, feeling confident she could pull this off.

"You're a smart girl. Get on out so I can prepare for my next customer. And I want my dress back. Keep in mind that we still hardly know each other. You know what I mean?"

"You only know me as *Sally Anne*," Dreama laughed as she walked out the door.

Once alone, Dreama counted the money twice, thrilled that she could hold money in her hands for the first time since she'd been married. "I will take my kids out to dinner today, buy them school clothes, get a few groceries, and save some so that someday I can leave that man."

21

The Affair in the Pastor's Office

"Hey, Dreama. It is good to see you. I was a little worried about you after what happened at church," Ralph Custon mentioned as he hugged Dreama. "How are things going?"

"Things are going, Ralph! I just have a new attitude to work hard and provide for my kids," Dreama commented as she punched the time clock to start her shift. Ralph nodded to the right, suggesting that Dreama walk with him to continue the conversation.

"I understand that. My wife and I were talking about how inappropriate it was for your son and you to be put on public display. I am so, so sorry. It was so embarrassing. My wife made an appointment to speak to Reverend Allison about it. Let me know how I can help if needed."

"Your wife doesn't really know me. Well, for that matter, no one at the church knows me. Why does she want to help me?" Dreama felt suspicious.

Ralph put his hand on her shoulder to reassure her his wife had only good intentions. "She doesn't have to know you in order to help you. She felt that she needed to speak up as a woman and a mother. You must've felt embarrassed for Bart and you being called out like that."

"Booker has ripped every emotion I have to the point where I have none left to know what embarrassment means. I should be ashamed for saying this, but I don't even know what to feel for Bart. I haven't spoken to him about his feelings, though he seems to be doing just fine," Dreama stated more than she intended.

"I can understand how the recent events may make you feel a sense of loss. No one really has the right words to say. I am happy to offer my friendship and help."

"As a matter of fact, Ralph, you can help me. I need to apply for food stamps and housing assistance, but I don't know how. I have to be strong for my kids."

"It's none of my business, but are you seeking to leave Booker?"

"I seek to get as far away from him as possible. My kids and I need peace."

"Booker seems like such a gentleman. The church reveres him much the same as they do for Reverend Allison. I know he was angry about what he heard, as evidenced by me finding you on the road. He is human. Are you willing to perhaps try counseling first or forgive him and try to move forward together? Today, Black families are starting to break up. The children need their mothers and fathers to stay together in one unit. In the years I have known Booker, he has been active in the church, a community pillar, and seems to know the Bible."

"I appreciate what you shared, Ralph, but you think you know Booker based on what you have seen on the outside. I KNOW him for his works." Dreama turned away, offended by Ralph's words.

"Dreama, I am sorry. I guess I should have done more listening than talking."

Dreama turned swiftly to face Ralph. "No apology is needed. Ralph, I need a friend that I can trust. I'm sorry that I asked you for help. I'm sorry that my mother-in-law saw us at the restaurant together. You have been the kindest person. At some point, I have to thank your wife for being understanding.

"Yeah, I guess you do. I have been thinking about how to tell my wife about that."

"Oh no! You haven't told her?"

"No, I didn't. She is a very jealous woman, and I just didn't want her to think . . ."

"I need you to think, Ralph. By the time the news gets back to Angelic, she would likely be upset since YOU didn't tell HER first."

"I will talk to her immediately when I get home. Don't you worry about it." Ralph knitted his eyebrows as a worried look crept over his face.

"Oh Ralph, I am sorry for putting this on you," Dreama said sincerely.

Ralph quickly hugged her. "Dreama, you are not putting anything on me. Just know that Angelic and I want to help you. I will let you know the outcome of her visit with the Reverend. She will definitely share her displeasure about what happened with Bart and you."

"It's nice to know somebody is advocating for me. I feel like I'm stifled in advocating for myself."

"Well, think about how you need me to help you. Meanwhile, we better get to work before the *plantation* manager comes here."

"Yes, suh, Master," Dreama snickered as she got to her workstation.

—⁕—

Angelic wore a jean dress that innocuously accentuated her hourglass figure. After exchanging spiritual pleasantries with the church secretary, she sauntered gracefully towards Reverend Allison's office. Knocking on the door lightly, she was greeted by Reverend Allison. Seconds later, she heard, "Come in, Sister Angelic. It is refreshing to see you. Have a seat here," the Reverend directed as he examined Angelic's body frame as she walked. The moment she sat and crossed her legs. "So before we start this meeting, let's pray," the Reverend stated solemnly. After the short prayer, the Reverend offered, "Let me get you something to drink."

"But really, I don't have much time and . . ."

"Deacon Booker, bring Mrs. Custon a ginger ale," the Reverend called.

"Right away, Rev," Booker chimed as he continued to stay out of view. Booker knew about the Reverend's request before Angelic entered; he was just stirring quaaludes into her drink.

"Why is Deacon Booker here? I told your secretary I needed a private conversation with only you."

"I understood the request. Since I knew the matter was regarding what happened in church recently, I figured Deacon Booker should be here as head of his household to hear everything said and share information with you."

"With me? He does not have any information to share with me."

"Oh, I beg to differ," Booker chimed on cue as he brought refreshments on a silver tray. He handed the ginger ale to Mrs. Custon and the orange soda to the Reverend before taking the water for himself.

"Well, I'm totally dissatisfied with how you allowed Apostle Daniels to call out Sister Dreama and YOUR son Bart in front of the whole congregation," Angelic maintained.

"You don't know my wife or son like I do."

"I don't have to know them to know that they didn't deserve to be treated like they were. The whole church community knows that your son is peculiar. It did not take an apostle to receive a divine message to point out the obvious. And your wife has been a faithful member of this church, not even speaking to other people unless she has received your non-verbal permission. What you did, Reverend, was in poor taste, and you need to determine how to fix this! And another thing . . ." Angelic started to cough lightly.

"Drink your ginger ale, Sister Angelic," Booker stated as he lightly patted her on her back and held her hand. He lifted the glass to her lips as she drank."

"Well, I don't know where that coughing spell came from. Maybe I swallowed some air or something. That ginger ale really hit the spot. Thank you, Booker."

"It's my pleasure, Angelic. Now take a minute to breathe and relax," Booker shared as he moved to sit in the lounge chair across from her with his legs gapped open. Angelic batted her eyes twice after looking at the bulge in Booker's light gray khaki pants.

"Angelic, I do not control God's movement. I just walk in it. I have known Apostle Daniels for a long time; he is an upstanding man. You cannot deny that we had a good church service. Now, Booker, what is your response to what Angelic shared?"

"It was not good for you to even bring up my son Angelic, considering he is a boy. He's not trying to hide who he is. He will grow out of it and one day marry and have kids. Focus on the adults and what's going on in your household."

"My household? My husband respects me to the utmost. We are God-fearing people. You are just trying to avoid the issue at hand. Get to telling why you, as a Reverend, allowed a peaceful woman and her son to be humiliated in front of a church congregation. Don't you understand that people all around town are discussing it?" Angelic started rubbing her temples gently.

"There is talk about Ralph and your marriage. It is not as peaceful as you make it out to be.

"What do you mean? If you have something to say, just say it. While no marriage is perfect, Ralph is an excellent provider, hardworking, faithful to me as his wife, and certainly faithful to this church. Why are you making this matter about Ralph?" With these words, the Reverend and Booker looked at Angelic intently. "Oh, my head feels like it is swimming. I feel lightheaded," Angelic shared as she slouched back in her chair.

"Come over to the couch and lie down. Relax. You have a lot on your mind right now." Booker coolly concluded. "You must be stressed that you know what I have known for some time. Your husband and my wife not only work together, but they are having an affair. The Apostle told me he saw it in the spirit. Also, congregation members saw them on a date a few days ago. They went shopping too. I know that from Dreama's new dress when she finally came home."

"Oh, I need something to drink. Will you fix me another ginger ale? Is it me, or is it hot in here?"

"The temperature is just fine here. Maybe you could take off your jacket and maybe your shoes so you can relax while we talk," Booker casually posited. One ginger ale coming right up."

The Reverend placed a damped handkerchief against Angelic's forehead as she lay on the couch, panting lightly. Booker quickly emerged with the laced ginger ale in his left hand, positioned just below his belt buckle, drawing attention to his unzipped pants and frontal print.

"Here you are. This drink should make you feel better."

Angelic propped herself up slightly so she could consume the beverage without choking. She did so ravenously.

"Feeling better?" Booker asked while standing over her inconspicuously at full attention.

"Yes, I noticed that Ralph wasn't coming home at what he normally does, and he works all the time at the plant and then goes to his mechanic shop. He has not touched me in months. I couldn't figure out what was going on. I tried to talk to him about my concerns, but he insisted there was nothing different in our relationship. When I try to initiate sex, he turns me away or acts like he is too tired. I don't think he is attracted to me anymore," Angelic cried as she said the words aloud.

Booker kneeled down and caressed her face as the Reverend watched in anticipation. "You're a beautiful woman with many talents. Any man in his right mind would be pleased to give you much attention and all the sex you wanted and needed."

Angelic's chest rose up and down, picking up momentum as Booker spoke. She grabbed Booker's hand, pulling him closer to her. "Booker, I feel better. I feel so good that I could kiss you."

"Then why don't you?" The moment their lips touched, Booker was determined to give her the best sex she ever had. The Reverend knew he had to be a spectator instead of a participant to do so. He also knew that she had just become a part of the Thursday-night sex rotation starring Booker, Reverend Allison, and Angelic.

22

Drag Queen with a Five O'clock Shadow

It was Saturday morning. Neither Booker, Dreama, nor Warren was home. Booker drove to eat breakfast with Warren at Shoney's. Dreama was at Susie's, servicing her client. Bart awakened, realizing his prayer to be a girl was still unanswered. He reflected on the physical fights with boys who teased him and the verbal responses he gave to community members and church folk alike. Dreama taught him to stand up for himself, no matter the cost. He felt that he did not have anything to lose. He silently struggled to make sense of his love of reading the Bible, singing in the children's choir, and being taught, thus becoming a gay boy. He reasoned that all he needed to do was become a girl, and all of this outward and inward fighting would go away. But no matter how much of Dreama's makeup he put on or how many of her dresses and high heels he tried on, it just didn't happen.

Bart wanted to get out of the trailer for fresh air. He knew that Booker and Dreama forbade him and Warren from being outside without permission. But he felt bold. He walked half a mile when he saw Glen playing outside with a man in hair rollers staring at him through the window.

"Bart, what are you doing walking on this street? You know better than that. Your parents would kill you."

"I'll be back home before they know about it."

"Well, you wanna come inside and listen to some Michael Jackson records?"

"Is it ok with your mom?"

"My mom is working today, so she won't be back for a few hours."

"Who is babysitting you?"

"It's my mom's friend. His name is Peter, but he prefers to be called Shirley."

"Oh, ok. I guess I'll come in."

Glen gave Bart a tour of the three-bedroom brick house as they talked about what had been happening at school.

Shirley emerged with curls in his permed hair, high shorts that revealed his scrawny legs, and a midriff shirt. "What's your name, cutie?" Shirley asked in a high-pitched voice that attempted to camouflage his natural manly voice.

Bart became very nervous. He heard about predators in the area who kidnapped children and turned them into sex slaves. "I'm Bart, and I'm in middle school." Though Bart volunteered more information than was asked, he wanted to nonverbally state that there is an age difference between him and Shirley.

"Well, you look like you can pass for eighteen. How do you know Glen?"

"He is a friend from school."

"How *close* of a friend?"

Glen interrupted the line of questioning by asking, "Bart, do you want to walk with me to the kitchen to fix a bologna sandwich?" Bart followed Glen to the kitchen. Shirley watched the boys walk away before quickly disappearing into his guest bedroom.

In a hushed tone, Bart asked, "Is he your uncle? I felt like he was looking through me."

"He dresses in women's clothes. My mom met him at a drag show when she and her girlfriends went to Atlanta last month. They shared their life stories. The next thing I knew, she invited him here, and he has been here ever since."

"What is drag?"

"Something like a man who dresses like a woman with wigs and makeup and moves his lips during a song in front of people. And they get money from the audience."

"Why is he dressed in drag now when no people are around?"

"I guess he just likes to be dressed like that all the time."

"How well do you get along with him?"

"Well, since my dad is not around, he has taught me things like driving, fixing my toys, riding a ten-speed bike, and shaving. He also taught me how to cook and about the birds and the bees."

"I hope he has not taught you about the birds and bees as my dad taught me. It is not a good feeling."

"What do you mean that it is not a good feeling? It was a good feeling when Glen taught me about it. He just talked to me about how a boy treats a girl."

"What did he say? Maybe I want to learn."

"Well, I can tell you after we eat this bologna sandwich. Shirley is going to work at some club shortly."

Bart nervously felt like he had a connection with Glen, yet he was still afraid of admitting that he hated the person he'd become because he felt everyone else hated him. He was eerily afraid of Shirley since he had never seen a man look like a manly woman. Glen broke his train of thought and said, "I'm sorry about what you experienced at church and what you have been going through at school. Are you doing ok?"

"I'm not doing ok. I have been fighting boys after school who call me names. Parents have told my mom that they don't want me around their children anymore. My dad calls me names every day. The only friend I feel like I have is my mom. I am forced to face these people every day—if not at school, then it is at church. If it is not at church, it is out in the community. I have tried to kill myself by slitting my wrists and taking pills. I even thought about how to take the longest knife we have to cut myself in the chest."

Glen looked at Bart with compassion and placed his hand over his. "I need to use your bathroom," Bart said tearfully. You remember where it is, right? It's the first door on the left."

Bart quickly went into the bathroom and silently cried. Looking into the mirror, he whispered, "God, why doesn't anyone love me? I'm tired of fighting. I just want to be loved for who I am. I want someone just to love me by name. You said, 'Honor your father and mother.' I have obeyed everything my parents say. I have sex with my dad out of obedience, and then he calls me names in public and private. I work hard to get good grades in school. I am respectful to my elders. I share my toys with my brother. I don't know what else to do. Help me, God, to take my life because I am just tired."

Seconds after his prayer, Shirley knocked on the door three times. "It is quiet in there. I haven't heard the toilet flush, so you must be in there having a relationship with a bottle of lotion. Open this door. I need my compact!"

Bart quickly washed his face to remove any evidence that he had been crying. When he opened the door, Shirley greeted him with "Ta-da!" Shirley wore an aqua-green sequin dress with a red feather boa, tan stockings, red high-heeled shoes, and gaudy costume jewelry. His big blonde wig and thick makeup did an ill job of covering his five o'clock shadow that completed his look. "So . . . what do you think?" Shirley asked, posing with one arm raised on the door's portal and the other on his hip.

"Uh, I don't know what to say," Bart said, struggling to determine if that was the response Shirley was looking for. Glen stifled his laughter.

"I know I have you speechless. Even a boy like you recognizes a true queen. And this queen has to go to work to make her dough, so get out of this bathroom."

Bart quickly moved past Shirley, dismantling his arm in the process. "Little boy, I ain't been in a fight all year. Don't think I won't even whoop yo' ass."

"If you touch me, you will feel like 100 men beat yo' ass," Bart swiftly responded, though he shocked himself while doing so.

"I don't have time for this. A girl has to go to work. And Glen, you know yo' momma don't want no company here while she is gone. So you need to tell your friend to leave, else I'll tell yo' momma."

"You ain't gonna tell her shit. If you tell her, then I will tell her you've been stealing her makeup while she's been at work. The moment she gets the information, the faster yo' ass will be out on the street. Now get yo' ass to work before Bart and I get to working ten knots upside yo' bitch ass head," Glen said adamantly.

The taxi announced its arrival by honking twice. Shirley scurried out of the house and passed the boys, clearly pissed that Glen had told her the truth. Shirley's matted wig waved one curl that bounced while he was storming to the taxi.

He only lived with Ms. Leila Harris because Shirley was evicted from the motel he was overstaying in. It just so happened that Ms. Harris and her girlfriends went to a drag show where he performed. The tips he received from shows weren't even up to half the cost of the weekly stay at the cheap weekly hotel. He was four weeks behind. The moment Shirley lip-synced "And I am Telling You, I'm Not Going," he thought it could be applied to what was referred to as the "Cheaply Weekly" motel staff. Ms. Harris and her girlfriends gave her a total of $50 after observing the audience's inattention to his performance, which yielded no money. He instantly decided to appeal to Ms. Harris' emotions by sharing what he was going through. She told him to just ride by with her and her girlfriends to South Carolina so that they could work out a plan. When they drove him to the motel to get his things, they saw the police gathered around room 200 and the manager speaking with the lead officer. "What in the world are the police doing here?" Leila asked rhetorically.

"Honey, the police are probably breaking up a domestic fight. Who knows? Gurl, just park right here; I'll go get my things," Shirley stated apprehensively.

"Chile, don't be long. While you doing that, we're going across the street to Joe's Convenient Store to get gas and use the bathroom. Just walk to the car when you finish," Leila hurriedly stated. "We gotta get home. I have to get to work tomorrow."

Shirley breathed a sigh of relief once he saw Ms. Harris' car drive off since room 200 held his things. The police were called due to Shirley breaking into the hotel room after being locked out multiple times and being bold enough to tell management he was not leaving since he had rights. Even when management booked the room for paying customers, Shirley would pack their things and take them to the front desk with a note saying, "Room 200 is occupied; please assign them to another room." Management called the police to arrest him.

Shirley moved to the left hallway past room 148, where he would be unnoticed. He saw the housekeeping cart between rooms 146 and 148. While the housekeeper was making the bed in room 146, Shirley went into room 148 and took the suitcases he found. He whisked his way across the street to avoid contact with the police.

Since he lived with Ms. Harris, Shirley taught Glen how to treat girls at the expense of Shirley telling him how handsome he was.

"I'm glad that ugly hag is gone. Since he has been here these last few months, he has been trying to get my mom to do things she ordinarily wouldn't do," Glen shared. "Mom has been giving him money and letting him wear her clothes. She's even been trying to bring him to church to sing in the choir, even though he sings like a broken-down chain smoker."

The boys laughed. "I guess one good thing about him staying here is that he is the closest thing to a man living in this house. My mom says she is working out where I can live with my dad in North Carolina sometime soon."

"What do you mean, Glen?"

"Yeah, I am moving, but I just don't know the details."

"Wow, I wish you didn't have to go. I just want a friend."

Glen pressed himself against Bart and held him. "I know what it is like to be you because I am you. I know I have lots of girls who like me at school and church. I know how to make it look like I am interested in them. I know our church teaches that homosexuality is deemed the number one sin that will cast people to hell. I don't believe that. I believe love is love no matter who you love."

"I can't say that I knew love. I know sex with my dad, and I cannot stand it. I never felt loved by my dad. I know my mom loves me, but she will fight for my younger brother more than she'll fight for me. I have yet to find someone to love me by name. I have never heard anyone say, 'I love you, Bart, just for the person you are. I don't know if I ever will."

"All I can say is that in holding you, one day I can love you by name. We just have to keep our friendship a secret and go out with girls together. Even after I move, I promise to find you someday."

23

Doing Things Differently

"Do you want breakfast?" Dreama asked as she was stirring the pot of grits.

"No, I don't. You ain't gonna try to poison me. Feed it to your new man, Ralph Custon.`"

Dreama rolled her eyes and decided she would not entertain Booker's allegations today. She was already in a bit of a funk since Booker had not left as he usually did this typical morning. She had to figure out how to get to Susie's since she had three out-of-town clients lined up. It was just another day in hell, and every day he was around. Lately, Dreama has been standing her ground with Booker; he no longer held such blind control over her. He decided to test just how much control she had when he saw Bart walking out of his room in his underwear, clearly having just awakened.

"I'm hungry, Ma. The food smells good."

"You just get in that bathroom, wash your face, and brush your teeth. Then get your brother up. Breakfast will be ready in a moment. And put some clothes on," Dreama charged as she stirred the grits on simmer. "Bart, I'm going over to Susie's to ask for some sugar and butter," Dreama announced as Bart was about to go into the bathroom. She said it for Booker to also hear and also a means of asking Susie to reschedule her appointments.

"OK, Mom. I'll be out in a jiffy."

Dreama turned off the gas stove just before exiting. When Booker held the door click, he put down his newspaper and stood in front of the bathroom door that was permanently off the track. Bart attempted to close the door completely, but it was too heavy. The crack gave Booker just enough visual entertainment as Bart stood by the sink and began to wash what he considered were the essentials: face, armpits, and lower torso. Booker undressed and slowly pulled the door back, just enough to slide in. Bart looked at him in amazement mid-wash.

"I used to wash you as a baby. You are growing up so fast. How about Daddy washing you one more time, huh? I know what your body looks like, and we're so used to each other that you ought to feel at ease."

"I don't want you to touch me anymore. I am old enough to bathe myself. I need you to leave so I can bathe myself privately," Bart sternly said. "Get OUT!"

Booker quickly moved behind Bart and choked him with his elbow with his left arm, grabbing Bart's penis with his right. "Don't you ever say that to me again, faggot. I'm just giving you what you always wanted. You're gonna do as I SAY, or else I'll kill you."

Bart swiftly elbowed his father so hard that he stumbled backward into the bathtub. "At this point, if you touch me again, *I'll KILL YOU*. You no longer have any power over me! I've gotten to a point where I hate you and hate being in this trailer because it is hell every day you are here. Touch me again and see what happens! God, I wish I was part of another family!"

Angelic took long drags of the Virginia Slim immediately after Booker and she released their third orgasm within two hours of sweaty sex. The Reverend knew that Booker had more permanent plans for Angelic that he could not be a part of sexually. He was satisfied with being an observer, getting just as many ejaculations as they did. Angelic and Booker lay in one full-sized bed while the Reverend lay in the other, sound asleep.

"Booker, you have really changed my life. I know we've been secretly seeing each other for nearly a year, but I'm tired of sneaking around and pretending. Ralph is a good provider, working at Chev Mills and his auto-repair shop. I don't love Ralph anymore, especially since you convinced me he is seeing Dreama. I'm in love with you. We need to do something to take our love further."

"Yeah, I haven't loved Dreama in quite some time. I'm just ready to divorce her and perhaps marry you. Is that something you wanted to hear?" Booker replied, lightly tickling Angelic.

"Stop it, Booker. You know that's my funny bone," Angelic whispered as she laughed softly. "I'd be happy to be your wife, to honor and obey you like you deserve."

"I like the sound of that. Dreama has been costing me so much money throughout these years that I'm just trying to rebound financially. I just work for the church and do side hustles to make ends meet. Plus, I have Bart and Warren. I'll bring Warren with me and leave Bart with his mother. Your children are grown. That's a lot to bring into a new marriage."

"Well, if I divorce Ralph, we would have to split assets, including his repair shop. Plus, he has three life insurance policies, and I am the beneficiary. Ralph will give me everything I want in the divorce, so his loss is our gain. And Warren is such a boy, with his cute "self." Angelic thought it wise to keep her opinion about Bart to herself; after all, he was still Booker's son. She was glad that Bart would remain with Dreama.

Booker was mesmerized by the thought of how much money he would gain just for marrying Angelic. "What do you mean *if you divorce Ralph*? You mean *when*! He and Dreama can have each other as long as I got you. Give me one year."

"We've got each other, Booker. And next year, I look forward to becoming Angelic Bains-Johnson." With these words, Booker and Angelic kissed passionately, initiating another round of sex while the Reverend slept.

24

Calling That Spirit Out

"Girl, I am moving out of this horse town and going to make some real money in Vegas," Susie said joyfully as she drank a shot of bourbon. "You have made some good money for me, but it is time for me to move on." Susie and Dreama stood together at the window in Susie's living room. Dreama wasn't thrilled with Susie's plan to leave town. "Susie, with all I have been through, you have been like a big sister to me. I would not have been able to keep up my household without you. I just feel like I'm losing hold of everything," Dreama said, whimpering.

"Don't you even bring that attitude to me," Susie scolded while lighting a cigarette. You have to find your own way now. Dreama, your problem is allowing yourself to depend on others. I have my opinions about that husband of yours. But know that you are still in the trailer with him because you are afraid of life without him. He is all you have known. His church is all you know."

"Before I met Booker, so much happened in my life. He was a savior to me at the right time."

Susie blew smoke into Dreama's face and raised her eyebrows. "Now you call him a superhero who saved yo' ass? Bitch, please. You don't even have a driver's license— nor a car. You take a taxi to work each day, which costs you money. You go to a church that secretly and constantly judges you. Your so-called husband alienated you from your family to where you don't even have a relationship with any of your siblings. You even created a dependency on me using my home to fuck, drink, and smoke." She stubbed the cigarette into an empty beer can and continued with her lecture. "At my home, you can be the real you, only to go back to your home miserable. Misery has become your normal state. You need to take charge of your life. You won't have me to depend upon after next week."

"Thanks for caring about me enough to tell me the truth." Dreama felt grateful despite the thought that she was losing her best friend. "I just haven't had anybody to take the time to teach me how to get a license. I am afraid of change since I don't have a support system," Dreama revealed.

"Well, Bitch, change out of that orphan-Annie outfit into the black bra-and-panties set I got for you as a parting gift. Chester and Bruce will be here in ten minutes. Since they are married, you know they don't have much time. And neither do you."

Dreama headed to the bedroom to change but stopped and called out over her shoulder, "What do you mean I don't have much time?"

"You're wasting time staring at a fairy tale that does not have a happy ending the way it is currently going. You have little time to change it."

A few minutes flew by as Dreama tried to calm herself. "I'll come up with a plan to change my life and work towards goals. Right now, I have to make it about giving Bruce a happy ending," she smiled at Susie, wanting to lighten the mood.

Both women laughed. "Come here, girl, and give me a hug." Susie opened her arms for Dreama and held her tightly. "I wish I could stay to see you make changes. Just promise that you will stay in touch."

Dreama pulled out of the moment, sincerely smiling at Susie. "Thanks for everything."

"Yeah, yeah. Get dressed. And assume the position since the guys will be here any minute."

—m—

Glen and Bart spent much of their time together outside the public eye, but enough for Shirley to see that the boys loved each other. They looked forward to their alone time in school, church, or the woods. They also expressed attraction for girls at school and church. The gossip around the church was that maybe Bart was evolving out of his *homosexual* phase.

And it had been months since Booker attempted to have sex with Bart. Bart was now just as tall as Booker and physically stronger. Booker was away from home more often, juggling Angelic, maintaining face with the church, and keeping his Thursday night trysts with the Reverend and the selected women of the night.

On a particular Thursday, Booker stated, "You know that every church around us is preaching against homosexuality. We need to bring in somebody to teach the church one Sunday so that we won't look like we endorse it. Third Missionary Church, and our church is the only one that hasn't said a word about it."

"You do have a point about that," the Reverend said softly as he snuggled against Booker. "I will have my secretary make a call and invite someone to teach the topic during Wednesday night Bible study."

"That sounds good. And make sure he is married, has kids, is good-looking, and manly," Booker reasoned. We want to put his picture on a flier so those factors alone bring the community in. If necessary, we can work with him on inflating his credentials because the community loves a man who sounds educated."

"Whatever you want. I have the right person who fits that description. We will have him as a guest teacher in two weeks."

"Just don't have Ivan there on that day. I suspect I can give you a list of others."

"And what about Bart? He ain't exactly a straight boy."

"Bart is showing that he likes girls now. That was just a phase he went through. And besides, he's a kid."

"Ok, but I really thought that *Cinderfella* was trying to turn into Cinderella."

The men shared a laugh as they pulled the covers over themselves. Booker coddled Countee in his arms.

"We have definitely had a few women and men in this room over the years," Booker recalled as he stared at the ceiling.

"Yeah, we have. I think I was your first man in this hotel, and Mabel was the first lady," the Countee said fondly. "Have you ever heard anything more about Mabel or the kid she had?"

"Why did you ask me that? I don't keep up with her nor the kid." Booker quipped as his hold on Countee loosened.

"Booker, you know I just asked since I have been sending money to Mabel on your behalf every month for several years," Countee reasoned.

"And I thank you for it. You've been really good to me all these years, Count. Sorry if it sounds like I snapped at you. Forgive me?" Booker playfully asked as he planted a kiss on Countee's forehead.

—m—

Brenda sang a rousing rendition of *What a Friend We Have in Jesus* acapella to a crowd of over 150 people who came to hear Bishop C. J. Davidson teach about *How Homosexuals Can Be Delivered.* Reverend Allison rose immediately.

"YES! WHAT A FRIEND WE HAVE in JESUS! How many of you know that Jesus is a healer, a way-maker, a forgiver?"

The church erupted in hollering out and clapping in agreement. "Say so, Pastor!"

"Won't He Be a Friend?" Brenda shouted.

"Yes, Sister Brenda. He is also a deliverer of all kinds of sin, including witchcraft, whoremongering, lying, cheating, stealing, and homosexuality. Can I get an AMEN?!"

"AMEN, Pastor! A—MEN!"

"Now ladies, y'all look so good tonight in your long dresses, no makeup, flat shoes, and hair done. Y'all look like true holiness, especially my beautiful wife, Vanessa. Honey, stand up and let your husband show you off."

Vanessa obeyed Reverend Allison, stood up, and carefully spun around once as she waved daintily to the congregation. Each of their adult children clapped robotically as they sat erect.

"She is the most beautiful woman in the world. And she's understanding. She is my wife till death do us part," the Reverend stated passionately. "My first lady is kind to all and a great mother." Vanessa blushed coyly as if on cue. "My wife gives me the freedom to engage in ministry in the church, out of town, in the prisons, and the hospitals, knowing that I am always accountable to her." Vanessa looked around at her children and gave a rehearsed smile to camouflage her unhappiness with being married to the Reverend.

"Now, every member with a spouse, children, and love in your home, stand up and give God glory," the Reverend commanded. "I see you, Brother Booker and Sister Dreama; I see you, Brother Coleman and Sister Betty; and I even see you at the back, Brother Ralph and Sister Angelic. These men lead their families through Jesus Christ! We need more men like these in the church." Dreama and Booker occasionally had brief conversations around Bart and Warren, but they didn't speak largely because Booker spent much of his time away from home. Still, they managed to be at church each Sunday and Wednesday. She went to try to instill values in Bart and Warren while he went because he could count on the congregants to do or say something that reinforced his ego. Ralph was working double shifts four days a week. Angelic timed her evenings with Booker around Ralph's schedule. Following Booker's directive, she keeps up the facade of her marriage by going with Ralph, who has no clue that she is in love with Booker. Ralph was too tired to work a double tonight but attended church with Angelic.

"Say it again, Pastor!"

"That's right, Pastor!"

"Now, what God can't stand is the sin of homosexuality. He loves the person but hates the sin!"

"That's what the Bible says, preacher!"

"So tonight, I invited Bishop C. J. Davidson, a Bible scholar from Creed Seminary who has won many awards for his work in ministry and philanthropy. He is the Bishop of The Greater Mount Genesis Church of God. Let's praise God as this great teacher comes forth."

The congregants clapped vehemently as Reverend Allison sat beside his wife.

"Thanks to you, Good Reverend, and your lovely wife for inviting me to come," Bishop C. J. Davidson enthusiastically said. "Now we are going to make this an interactive teaching whereby you can ask questions during teaching segments. While every question can't be answered, the Reverend, his trained leaders, or I will address it. Amen?"

"Amen!"

After the Bishop led the prayer, he opened with, "We have a growing homosexual problem in this world. Psychologists are still calling it a sickness, while God calls it a sin. There is a new disease called AIDS that is only impacting gay men in New York City. It is spreading. Don't you know that it is God's judgment against gays? It reminds me of Sodom and Gomorrah."

Twenty minutes were spent discussing Sodom and Gomorrah and how God wanted Adam and Eve to be fruitful and multiply. He peppered his teaching, calling homosexuality an abomination worthy of hell.

The Reverend, Booker, and other men gave the most *amens*.

"Before we continue, I'll take a few questions."

Congregants asked questions ranging from how to best protect their children from homosexuals and what to do if there is a suspicion that their child may demonstrate homosexual tendencies. Bart asked himself, "But I know God loves me just as the gay boy I am. How can they interpret the scriptures without emphasizing God's love for all?" He mustered resolve to stand to ask the church leaders questions, not caring about the consequences.

"Yes, young man. What would you like to ask?"

"We do not know the full circumstances why God rained fire and brimstone on the people of Sodom and Gomorrah. We do know that by the time the angels arrived, God already decided to destroy the cities. We do know that they mistreated the people in their towns, but you focused on homosexuality based on the men's desire to have sex with the angels who visited Lot. And how did the men of that land live among a population? They had to have women that they impregnated who later had babies. I have not heard you discuss how these supposed homosexual men managed to have marriages and children with women. Additionally, Ezekiel 16:49 says of this matter, *Behold, this was the iniquity of thy sister Sodom, pride, fullness of bread, and abundance of idleness was in her and her daughters, neither did she strengthen the hand of the poor and needy.* So, will you share how you arrived at the notion that it was God's position to destroy Sodom and Gomorrah solely because there were homosexuals in the land?" Bart remained poised and calm as he heard murmuring among the congregants. Booker shifted in his seat while the Reverend wiped his brow.

"Thank you for your question, young man. You see, the men sought to have sex with the male angels, and it upset God to where He decided to destroy Sodom and Gomorrah. That was the primary reason. It didn't matter that these men may have had families and marriages with their wives. They wanted to commit a gang rape of two male angels. And the church, if you are a male and you have a sexual desire for any male, then you too will be destroyed like Sodom and Gomorrah." Bishop C. J. Davidson attempted to camouflage his nervousness by adding, "Let me make this statement: Your question sounds like you are trying to defend homosexuals. I am discerning that you have a homosexual spirit."

"You just taught that the only way to rid homosexuals is for God to cast fire and brimstone on every town where homosexuals live. I am not trying to defend anyone; I only seek to gain a rightful division of what the scriptures say versus what we want them to mean and what we may have been taught to make them mean. And since you are quoting from the Bible, I want to add that I Clement 6:1—from The Lost Books of the Bible—it says, *By hospitality and godliness was Lot saved out of Sodom, when all the country round about was destroyed by fire and brimstone.* And like Lot, Rahab, known as a harlot, had *therefore being hospitable, received them, and hid them under the stalks…* according to I Clement 6:6. So help me understand how your argument in light of this scripture supports the destruction of Sodom and Gomorrah due to homosexuality?"

C.J. swallowed hard, maintaining his composure. "Son, we are living in the last days, and your way of thinking reflects that. Paul told Timothy that men would be lovers of themselves. The Word is there in black and white. Get it in your heart and head, young MAN. I have been studying the Bible for the past 40 years. Read the Bible for yourself first before challenging my teaching," the Bishop stated in a raised voice in his effort to trump Bart.

"You may have been studying the Bible for 40 years, but how long have you understood what you've been studying? It is clear that you can read the *text*, but your understanding is clearly out of *context*. And if you got the gift of discerning that I have a homosexual spirit, then where are the people that can pray, lay hands, and cast it out? Where in the Bible has a homosexual been delivered? And I don't follow Paul or Timothy; I am a follower of Jesus. What about the eunuchs in the Bible? Also, you took a letter from Paul to Timothy that we were using to gauge righteousness when Paul did not intend to have the letter in what we now know as the Bible. Men love themselves when they are talking about their selfish gain without regard to women, people with low incomes, and children. And since you want to quote the Bible, explain to me how David can say of Jonathan that your love for me surpassed the love of women according to II Samuel 1:26?"

In growing frustration, Bishop C. J. Davidson shuffled Bible pages and examined his notes, striving valiantly to find an answer in the presence of bewildered congregants who remained quiet. He began resenting the Reverend for putting him in this position. Booker sat opposite Bart. He was seething, mentally plotting how to get Bart to hush.

"We have to study to show ourselves approved. You need to study your Bible, young man, and let the Word of God deliver you. You are in bondage and not engaged in God's ways. I need all of the church's elders to come together and gather around this boy. *Whose son is he?"* he bellowed.

"He is my son," Dreama boldly stood up and shared. Booker looked wide-eyed but said nothing.

"I can tell he is a problem child. Elders, I was there when you tried years ago to remove that sexual demon out of this boy. But in order to be delivered, you've got to want to be delivered. Amen?"

Six congregants stated, "Amen," three of whom stood to ask Bishop C. J. Davidson questions.

"This boy doesn't want to be delivered; he is justifying being a homosexual. I see it in the spirit that you are a devil." The congregants looked at Bart, who stood stoically. Dreama was worried about what was coming next, while Booker silently vowed to deal with Bart when they got home.

"Why didn't you answer my questions, Bishop Davidson? And you think I'm a problem child for what? I'm just asking you questions, but you are not giving me biblically supported answers. Again, why did David say of Jonathan that his love for him surpassed that of women?"

"David wasn't a homosexual, and neither was Jonathan. David was a man after God's own heart. He had several wives, and Jonathan had a wife too. And they had children. David was just talking about spiritual love."

"What kind of love do a man and woman have if it is not based on spiritual love?"

"I think we need to have other people ask questions centered on what the Bible says. So you just need to pray to God to deliver you from homosexuality so that someday you will marry and have children as part of God's order. But I am going to give you grace. Next question?"

"I'm not finished," Bart boldly stated. "First of all, why should I compete for your grace when I have God's? Secondly, there are eunuchs in the Bible who were castrated or who were born in such a way. Who made them that way? And what can they do to marry and have children as part of God's order since that is what you are teaching? How do you explain God's order when there are some people born with both male and female parts?

The Bible says that God created us in His image. Since there are males and females among us, God must be male and female. You need to answer my questions before we go to the next question."

"YOU have now disrespected me as the Bishop. I am going to have God deal with you—with your reprobate mind! Saints and friends continue to pray for this boy since he is twisting the Bible. And I'm afraid we are going over time. Reverend, how about we resume this teaching on another night since I want to respect the saints' time."

"And it's time YOU answered my questions. I've got one more for you. What does a boy do when he has been sexually abused by the same father who put him before the altar to get delivered from homosexuality?"

The congregants quickly spoke among themselves in hushed tones.

Befuddled, the Reverend stated, "Did our hearts not burn for this great teaching we experienced tonight? We cannot receive all the teaching this great man has in store during one Bible study. Bishop, I want us to pray for covering over your family and you, as well as pray for all of the homosexuals in the land. Let us all stand and join hands as we bow our heads and pray."

The congregants obeyed silently, hoping the Bishop would answer Bart's questions. No one grabbed Bart's hand as he stood with his eyes wide open, contemplating what a contradictory situation he had revealed.

25

The Pastor's Wife Investigates

"Why did your punk-ass son challenge the Bishop on his teaching? What that kid did tonight will cause our church to be the laughingstock of this community if something isn't done," the Reverend angrily stated to Booker and Bishop C. J. Davidson. "Bishop, you and I have been friends for a long time. So I know you won't be offended when I ask, 'What the hell were you thinking when you decided to open the floor for questions and answers?' You could hardly handle any of the questions that boy asked."

"It has been my style everywhere! I have been a guest preacher, and it's worked fine before," the Bishop quipped. "I have never been challenged. And why didn't you step in to interrupt the line of questioning from a kid?"

Booker chimed in, "Now, now, boys. Let's not fight among ourselves over this. I will deal with Bart when I get home. He won't be coming back to this church anymore."

"Whatever you do, just don't cause it to be linked to the church."

"Don't worry about it. I got it covered."

"Speaking of covered, where is my fee for attending your church to-night?" Bishop asked expectantly.

"The way you made me look tonight, you don't deserve a damn dime," the Reverend stated harshly. "My secretary must've forgotten to bring it. Booker, fix the Bishop a drink while I catch her. Y'all talk. Excuse me."

The Reverend walked from his back office to the sanctuary, where he spotted Ms. Rosa Lee laughing with Ruby Laston. "Ms. Lee, do you have a moment?"

Ms. Lee walked with a bounce towards the Reverend, but not before saying, "Ruby, you know that was a good joke. I'll call you later this evening."

"OK, girl. I have to get home and cook my chitlins. Rev, may God bless you and Sister Rosa so they can get home safe."

"Be blessed, Sister Ruby!" the Reverend said robotically.

"Hey, Reverend. What can I do to help you?"

"I need you to give me the check for Bishop Davidson's services. You didn't leave it on my desk."

"Reverend, I just don't know how to tell you this, but just to be straight up, you should know— The church just doesn't have the money. We were barely able to pay the church's bills this month. I know the Board granted you a raise, and you were giving a pastor's appreciation service recently, but coupled with the cost of the Thursday night ministry, costs for you and those who accompany you, the church's budget is stretched too thin. If I simply produced the check, knowing it would not clear the bank, it would not look good. I tried to tell you earlier today, but we kept missing each other."

"Damn, I thought we had at least $200 to pay him."

"Our account has a grand total of $10 in it right now."

"We have a church of 200 members. I can't believe that they are not paying their tithes and offerings," the baffled Reverend stated solemnly.

"Well, it's no secret, Rev, that some members just don't have money like that to spare. But most of the members pay their tithes and offerings faithfully. The free spending of the church's money hits much closer to home, Rev," Rosa expressed as she looked at him side-eyed.

Feeling that Rosa took a dig at him, the Reverend calmly said, "I think we just need an audit of the books. In the meantime, I need you to help me devise a way to pay the Bishop."

"I have $100 in my pocket for my telephone and light bill if you want."

"No, no, Rosa. I'll pay the Bishop from my pocket. Go home. I'll see you in the morning."

"Now, Rev, I'm your confidential secretary, just as I was with your father. You receive a handsome salary, plus you get a discretionary fund. The church pays for your mortgage, all household expenses, and the car insurance on all three vehicles. Additionally, Booker receives a weekly stipend for serving as a deacon and armor bearer. I get a full-time salary as well. The church receives tithes and offerings consistently. The problem is the hefty spending. I am just telling you this in love."

"Yeah, I know Rosa. It is like since I was hit over the head and robbed of thousands of dollars on my way to the bank years ago, we haven't been able to bounce back. I will figure out how to get us on a better financial plan. I just don't want to think about it right now."

"You _better_ think about it and then do something about it. The church can't sustain itself as long as there are no clear checks and balances regarding how much money is coming in and how much is going out."

"Good night, Rosa."

"Okay. I can tell when I've gotten on your nerves, but you know I'm right. Good night," Rosa said as she shrugged her shoulders as she walked out of the sanctuary.

The Reverend pulled out various denominations of money from his left pocket, counting slowly to assess whether he had $200. "I should've taken that $100 from Rosa since it looks like I have $140." The Reverend mumbled a rhetorical prayer as he reached into his right pocket and pulled out three $20s. "I really shouldn't pay this guy who couldn't even handle the arguments of a 15-year-old boy." The Reverend walked hesitantly towards his office as he turned off the lights in the sanctuary.

While pacing back and forth in her kitchen, Vanessa was on the phone with her Texan friend, Michelle. "Gurl, I have grown exhausted with being married to Countee. I raised our kids alone while he is always away from home, especially on Thursdays. I can't tell you the last time we had sex. These bills are piling up. I discovered that the mortgage hadn't been paid in two months. He forbids me to work, saying, 'A woman's place is in the home to take care of the house and kids.' We live in a fine home and drive new cars. But right now, I'd give anything not to be a part of the church," Vanessa said, obviously exasperated.

"My heart goes out to you for all you have been dealing with for years, Vanessa; anytime you want to come to Texas to get away, just let me know. You know my husband won't mind. Countee has never been good with money, always wanting to buy stuff to impress people. Now, he has you living beyond your means. It's not that much ministry in the world, Chile."

"I know. Countee couldn't keep his hands off me when we first got married. Now, he has to be in the presence of church members to acknowledge me or give me a peck on the cheek. He may be a good Pastor right now, but he sure could be a better husband and father. He's spending more time with Booker Johnson than with me. And it doesn't sit well with me." Vanessa tapped her fingernails on the countertop, a habit she had when she was nervous. Anger felt like the better emotion, and it wasn't too difficult for her to indulge in her temper. She was close to exploding on her husband.

Meanwhile, Michelle was making much sense. "You know something is not right with that, Vanessa. I didn't interact with Booker much in high school since I was a grade ahead of him. But I overheard my mother talk on the phone about some drama between Booker, an older man, and Countee years ago, something about Booker being the cause of a divorce. Anyway, I couldn't understand it, and if she were living, I'd ask her about it. But you can make sense of it by doing some investigative work to find out what your husband is really doing with money and what he is doing on Thursdays so that you will be at peace. And I have some ideas."

Vanessa sucked in her breath. This was something she wasn't sure she wanted to hear. "Girl, I don't believe Countee is involved in any wrongdoing. And I'm willing to prove it to myself. What ideas do you have?

"Just spit it out quick 'fore I change my mind about hearin' any of your ideas," Vanessa snapped.

"If you follow what I tell you to the letter, you'll get all the information you need," Michelle confidently added. "And Countee wouldn't ever know. Every girl needs to keep most of her secrets to herself. And since you can't come here, I'll fly there next week to help you."

Vanessa was apprehensive about executing the plan but felt rebuilding her relationship with Countee was necessary.

26

Stay Out of Adult Business

After the church drama, Dreama didn't know what to think and decided to confide in her sister, Catherine. Booker was still at the church, but she and the boys had silently walked home. As soon as she entered the trailer, she reached for the phone.

"Catherine, I have to admit that Bart's questions to Bishop Davidson tonight caused me to rethink my feelings on homosexuality." "Booker taught him to be like that since the boy was five. He's a teenager now; he has a girlfriend named Evelyn, but I still haven't met her," Dreama confided.

"Chile, somebody needs to stand up to all those so-called religious leaders at that church! What was the reaction of that sorry-ass husband of yours?" Catherine piped.

"He hasn't gotten home yet. Knowing Booker, I'm sure he didn't appreciate Bart challenging the Bishop. Booker would see it as Bart trying to embarrass him. I told Bart to watch TV in my bedroom until Booker comes home, but I'm afraid of the fireworks once he gets back."

"Uh-huh. I haven't seen the boys since they were babies. And with you allowing that husband keeping you away from your brothers and sisters during the years y'all been married is a damn shame! You had to sneak and call me when you told me you stood up more to Booker. But I don't see that happening," Catherine groused.

"There is no peace in this house, and Booker and I hardly talk. He angrily throws things around when he is here, leaving a mess. He curses and calls Bart and me names. I told Bart to say nothing to him and concentrate on making good grades in school. And Booker's actions scare Warren. I'm so afraid of what it's doing to him," Dreama rasped.

"It's high time that I visited you. How about I come tomorrow?" "I want you to pack your bags and bring the boys along, too! Y'all can live with me!" Catherine commanded.

"Thanks for the offer, but it's not that simple, Girl. And you know it wouldn't work since Mabel and *her child* are still in the house with you."

"Like I don't know that? Mabel *and her child* are still part of *your* family, so I don't know why you think you can abandon the family the way you have. Mabel is your sister, and her child is your nephew and stepson. I know it's a messed-up situation. When Booker leaves you for good, who will you have to support you? Your marriage to Booker has been over for years. If Momma were here, you know she'd be highly disappointed in the decisions you've been making. She didn't raise you to be meek like this," Catherine chided. "Like I said, I'm coming to visit you next week whether Booker likes it or not! I'll stay at a hotel near the University.

"When Momma died, I felt like all my brothers and sisters abandoned me, and I grew up alone," Dreama defended herself. "Booker's family once gave me family stability when we first got married. Catherine, I know we only talk once every two or three months, but I feel like y'all don't know me, and I don't know y'all."

"Well, what I know is that Momma told me before she died that she wanted me to look after all of you since I'm the eldest. I never got married nor had kids since I took Momma's dying wish seriously. That's why I'm visiting you the day after tomorrow to check on Momma's baby girl. Now, I'm getting off this damn phone since I have things to do. You got things to do too: Dump Booker and forgive Mabel!"

"I get it, Catherine," Dreama said, staring out the kitchen window. I have to get off this phone since Booker just pulled into the driveway. And I need to tell Bart to get out of my bedroom."

"You need to tell Booker to get out of your house!"

With the sound of the click, Dreama breathed a sigh of relief that her sister would be coming to visit. Yet, while agonizing over that, Booker was about to walk through the door.

"BART, GET YO' BITCH ASS OUT HERE RIGHT FUCKING NOW!" Booker exclaimed. Dreama stood by the olive-green gas stove with her arms crossed.

Bart appeared immediately before Booker and asked, "Why are you screaming at the top of your lungs?"

"I'M SCREAMING SINCE YOU KNOW DAMN WELL YOU MADE ME LOOK SO FUCKIN' BAD TONIGHT. WHY DID YOU CHALLENGE THE BISHOP ASKING HIM QUESTIONS ABOUT HOMOSEXUALITY? YOUR QUESTIONS MADE HIM VERY UNCOMFORTABLE AND SUSPICIOUS! YOU DISRESPECTED ME AND THE BISHOP!!! AND NOW I'M SO EMBARRASSED EVEN TO BE CALLED YO' DADDY SINCE YOU TURNED OUT TO BE A SMART-ASS FAGGOT!" AND YOU GOT THE NERVE TO ASK THE BISHOP WHAT TO DO IF YOUR FATHER HAD SEX WITH YOU AND THEN TOLD YOU TO GET TO THE ALTAR?"

Bart kept his hate-filled eyes on Booker as he said, "You know that I have read the Bible from Genesis to Revelation three times. He invited people to ask questions, so I asked questions about homosexuality since you taught me how to be one when I was five. Now that I am a teenager, you don't want to take responsibility for your role in influencing my sexual identity. I am trying to change it and need biblical answers on how to do so. If that makes me disrespectful to the Bishop and you, you need to own your role and think why you are embarrassed."

"SON OF A BITCH! YOU MUST BE SMELLING YOURSELF. JUST BECAUSE WE ARE THE SAME HEIGHT DON'T MEAN

THAT I WON'T BEAT YOUR ASS LIKE A MAN FOR TALKING TO ME LIKE YOU HAVE LOST YO' DAMN MIND!" Booker roared into Bart's face as he walked around him like an angry tiger. "YOU ARE GOING TO LEARN THAT I AM THE HEAD OF THIS HOUSE AND YOU WILL GO AND OPENLY APOLOGIZE TO THE CHURCH FOR THE DISRESPECT YOU'VE SHOWN, YOU FUCKIN' SISSY."

Booker stepped so close to Bart's face that Booker's breath gave evidence that he had been drinking. Bart clarified his position: "I will NOT apologize to anyone for asking questions! At this point—and hear me well—I DON'T GIVE A FUCK WHAT YOU WANT ME TO DO. I'VE HAD YEARS OF PHYSICAL, VERBAL, MENTAL, AND SEXUAL ABUSE. I'VE DECIDED TODAY THAT I DON'T GIVE A SHIT ABOUT WHAT ANYBODY THINKS OF ME, ESPECIALLY YOU. JUST AS YOU DON'T WISH YOU WERE MY FATHER, I DON'T WISH TO BE YOUR SON!! YOU ARE AN EVIL, MANIPULATING DRUNK WHO SPENDS MORE TIME TERRORIZING EVERYONE IN THIS HOME THAN CONTRIBUTING A DIME TO HELP MOM PAY BILLS."

Those words stung Booker so hard that he slapped Bart with all his limited strength, causing Bart to crash into the table, splitting it into pieces before landing on the floor. Bart quickly got up and whacked Booker across the head, causing him to stumble. Bart was more concerned about what Booker might try to do to Dreama.

Booker screamed, threw, and kicked objects as he headed toward Dreama. Unfazed by the action, Dreama looked straight ahead with her arms crossed. Bart, holding a wooden table leg, walked up to Booker.

"BOOKER JOHNSON, I DON'T GIVE A FUCK WHAT YOU DO TO ME. BUT I WILL MURDER YOU IF YOU FUCK WITH MY MOTHER!!" Bart charged. Without uttering a word, Booker turned swiftly and punched Bart in his right eye, knocking him back to the floor.

"I SHOULD'VE MADE YO' MOMMA ABORT YOU!!! I NEVER WANTED YOU!!!" Booker screamed! "I'VE HAD ENOUGH OF YOU

DREAMA AND YOUR BITCH-ASS SON. I'M TAKING ME AND MY SON WARREN TO MY MOMMA'S HOUSE, NEVER TO RETURN TO THIS HELLHOLE." Booker stormed to the bedroom to get Warren, packed a few items, dragged Warren behind him, and rushed out the door.

Dreama allowed Bart to sleep in her bed while she replayed the events of the night before. He awakened to bacon, eggs, and toast. She reflected on Catherine's words about Booker leaving her as she feverishly cleaned the single-wide trailer thoroughly in preparation for her sister's visit. Dreama thought, "I don't want Catherine to see Bart with a black eye. I'll just have him walk to Ms. Harris' house. He likes spending time with Glen anyway. He can catch the bus with him to school. It's Glen's last week before he has to go live with his dad."

The next day, anticipating Catherine's arrival, she gave her home a thorough check for cleanliness. She even planted a few flowers in front of the trailer as part of the beautification process. As she filled her garden pitcher, she recognized Catherine's Ford Country Squire rolling into her driveway. "Let me hurry up and get outside to water these plants before they come in," Dreama thought.

Dreama got to her flowers without being seen. She wanted to appear that she wasn't sitting around waiting for her to pull up. Catherine turned off her car and slowly exited. Dreama turned her back. Almost on cue, she just poured water on the flowers and hummed a tune.

"Girl, stop acting like you're so busy watering flowers that you didn't even hear me, and come give your oldest sister a big hug," Catherine entreated.

"Oh, my goodness! It's my big sister!" Suddenly overwhelmed by the drama of the situation, Dreama dropped the garden pitcher to run to her sister. She sobbed as she hugged her tightly even though Catherine had let go.

"Girl, you can let go now. You wouldn't need to hug me like this if you made it your business to see me more often."

"I know. I know," Dreama babbled as she dried her eyes and released

Catherine. "It is just that you look so much like Mama. I miss her so much."

"We all miss her, Dreama. She would be disappointed over what our family has become. We do not stay in contact as we should. I decided to do something about it. I brought someone who might help."

"I don't see anybody out here or in your car. Catherine, who are you calling on, Jesus?"

"Girl, don't get all funny on me!"

Looking at the corner of the trailer, Catherine said, "Y'all can come on out."

Mabel nervously emerged first, followed by Lee, the spitting image of Booker. Mabel stopped within five feet of Dreama. Lee stood behind her.

"Y'all haven't seen each other in thirteen years. Now, this is the part where y'all two sisters throw your arms around one another and express how happy you are to see one another," Catherine cued.

Mabel stammered, "Dreama, I'm sorry for what happened. I can't change it. I just want us to try to get a fresh start. This is my son—your nephew—Lee. Lee, come meet your aunt Dreama." Lee hesitantly took steps towards Dreama's right side, not sure what kind of greeting he would receive.

Dreama stared at Mabel with intense hatred, and Mabel began to shake subtly. Speaking to Catherine while continuing to stare at Mabel, Dreama said coldly, "I don't give a FUCK that you are my oldest sister. Don't you ever bring THIS BITCH back over to my house EVER again! I told her years ago that she and I can NEVER have a relationship because out of all the men that live in this area, she decided to FUCK my husband."

"Dreama, I am sensitive to your feelings, but you have to realize that a boy is present. If you want to talk about this, we can leave him in the car and go inside to talk about it," Catherine reasoned.

"That boy needs to know what kind of momma he has. Step over here, Lee!" Dreama said with authority.

Lee took just enough steps to stand in front of Mabel, not sure what he thought about the open adult conversation he had just heard.

"Lee, I'm Dreama. I'm your aunt. Do you know who your daddy is, boy?"

"I never met him. Momma told me he sends money every month and lives out of state," Lee said shyly, not sure if he gave Dreama too much information.

"Well, your daddy is my husband, meaning that your momma had sex with her sister's husband while living in her sister's house, eating her sister's food, while her sister was going to work every day financing her college education. And since your daddy is my husband and your momma is my sister, that means I'm your stepmother and your aunt, and the two children I have are your brothers and your cousins," Dreama smirked.

"Dreama, is all of that really necessary? I brought all of us together to establish peace as a family," Catherine beseeched.

"I don't have a family with any of you! I will have greater peace the moment all THREE of you leave my house for good. Don't bother contacting me for anything!" Dreama charged as she opened the trailer's door.

Catherine grabbed the door with a commanding force so that Dreama would not have a chance to slam it in their faces. "Let me make something clear to you, *sister*! You are busy cutting off the very family who you're too stupid to know that you need right now. That husband of yours is the one that you need to cut off after all the hell he has put you through. He has manipulated your mind into thinking that his family is your family when I KNOW they don't give a damn about you. You are still defending that man! Mabel came to tell you that she is sorry for what happened and just to get her sister back. Lee is already here, so nothing can be done about that. He didn't choose to be here. You had no right to talk to him the way you did! I'm trying to build a relationship with you. Get a good look at the three of us now because you won't see us again!"

Dreama stared blankly as Catherine, Mabel, and Lee entered the car without looking back at Dreama. Dreama heard the car's engine reverberate while Catherine put it in reverse and gunned out of the driveway. The next time she saw the car, it disappeared down the hill.

27

I Fell Down the Steps

Bart was really annoyed when he arrived at Brelding High School since kids on the school bus asked him, "What happened to your eye?" And over and over, he told them that he fell head first onto the ground, and his eye landed on a large rock. Bart couldn't bring himself to tell them that he lost his first fight against his father. He didn't want to ruin his reputation as the only kid in class who had never lost a fight.

He quickly went to the bathroom without being noticed. He knew he had three minutes before the bell rang. When Principal Cherry announced, "Students, you have 30 seconds to get to class," Bart scurried inside Ms. Kirby's biology class, wiping his right eye injury with a tan paper towel. He was glad that Ms. Kirby assigned his desk at the front on the end closest to the door. The bell rang seconds after he sat down.

"Okay, tenth-graders. Take out your homework assignment, and Kenny will collect it. After you give your homework to Kenny, you are to begin your five-minute warm-up exercise posted on the chalkboard, which is related to what we learned about the parts of a frog. Bart, step outside, please."

Bart quickly went into the hallway, grateful that no one was walking in the hallways.

Ms. Kirby walked behind the science table and repeated her instructions as she walked to the door. "You have five minutes to work quietly on this task," Ms. Kirby reported as she closed the door. She peered through the glass window to ensure all students were focused.

Once satisfied, she turned to Bart, saying, "Now, why are you covering your eye with a coarse, brown paper towel from the boys' bathroom?" Bart didn't think it was any of her concern as to where he got the towel until she said it *like that*. It prompted Bart to move the paper towel from his eye quickly.

"Bart, that does not look good. Tell me *exactly* what happened, Bart."

"Ms. Kirby, I fell and landed headfirst onto the rock," Bart said in a monotone voice.

"I want a closer look at your eye, Bart," Ms. Kirby said, turning Bart's head without his permission.

"Bart, that was *some rock* that your eye landed on," Ms. Kirby stated in disbelief.

"Well, that's what happened. Do you think it'll clear up on its own?" Bart asked, showing some concern.

"I think you need to go to the guidance counselor's office. I am going to write you a pass. You wait right here." Bart contemplated grabbing his books since he did not know when to return to class. Before he made a decision, Ms. Kirby reappeared.

"Here is your pass to the guidance counselor's office. His name is Mr. Branson. You are to give him this sealed envelope as well regarding another matter. You can make up for the work you missed today," Ms. Kirby chirped.

"Thanks, Ms. Kirby," Bart quietly said.

"No problem. You're one of the most special students in my class. I just want to do what I can to help you. Mr. Branson is a good person who also wants to help."

"Thanks again, Ms. Kirby. His office is . . .?"

"Down the hall, past the main office on the right."

"Can you watch my things?"

"I'll hold them in my secure closet. I'll see you later."

Bart walked into Mr. Branson's office nervously, uncertain why he was there.

"Hi, young man. I'm Mr. Branson. Why don't you have a seat?" he said absent-mindedly.

Mr. Branso's brown-and-blue plaid jacket—circa 1950—contrasted with his red pin-striped pants, wrinkled white-collared shirt, and penny loafers. His freckled face winced the moment he sat down. As he quickly got comfortable, he ran his fingers across the top of his comb over thinning hair and put on his large-framed glasses. "So, what's your name, and what brings you in?"

"I'm Bartholomew Johnson. Ms. Kirby suggested I see you. Here's my pass and an envelope Ms. Kirby asked me to give you."

"Let me see what we have here," Mr. Bronson said as he quickly read Ms. Kirby's note, which read:

HE WALKED INTO MY CLASSROOM WITH A BLACK EYE. PLEASE ASK HIM WHAT HAPPENED! IT LOOKS LIKE HE WAS IN A TERRIBLE FIGHT. AND DOESN'T WANT TO REPORT IT. —THANKS, DEBRA KIRBY

Mr. Bronson adjusted his glasses as he looked at Bart. "You look exactly like a basketball star who attended Breldring maybe fifteen or seventeen years ago. His name was Booker Johnson. Are you any kin to him?" Mr. Bronson asked in an attempt to make small talk.

"He is my father," Bart said dryly.

"I knew it! Ha. Ha. Ha. You walk just like him and have that same gapped tooth that he had in the '60s," Bart's indifferent response communicated that Mr. Bronson should get to the business at hand.

"So you have a black eye, huh? Tell me about how it happened."

Bart's blackeye was now in the spotlight and under scrutiny. Bart thought, *Apparently, no one believes that I fell. I have too many people asking me the same questions over and over.*

"My dad hit me yesterday," he confessed reluctantly.

"Oh my. What were the circumstances under which the two of you fought? What is an accident?"

"He just hit me."

"Uh-huh. Bart, make yourself very comfortable. I need to make a call. You want some chips or something?"

"No, I am just fine, thank you. Am I able to go back to class?"

"It's better to wait until I return here to give you further instructions."

Bart sat motionless as Mr. Bronson walked out of his office, not sure what to think or feel about what was happening around him. He casually walked to Mr. Bronson's office window and examined his family's photos. "We have never taken a family picture," Bart whispered. "They look so happy. I wish I were part of a loving family."

As he set the photo back on the windowsill, Bart was alarmed when he saw the white police officer and a white woman in a black polyester suit jacket with her picture on a badge accompanying Mr. Bronson into his office.

"Bart, this is Officer Greg Bramdt and Ms. Christie Mullinax with the Office of Social Services. You are not in any trouble. I called these fine people in to help you. We are just going to talk about the next steps. Ms. Mullinax, would you like to share some information with Bart?" Mr. Bronson prompted.

"It is a pleasure to meet you, Bart. And thank you, Mr. Bronson, for giving my office a call. Bart, I see that you have a terrific black eye. Will you share what happened that caused the black eye?" Ms. Mullinax shared in a soothing tone.

"My dad got angry at me for asking an adult some questions, and so he punched me in the eye."

"Where were the questions asked?" Ms. Mullinax inquired motherly.

"At St. Elijah Baptist Church in Catticoro," Bart responded calmly.

"Hmmm. Mr. Bronson and Officer Bramdt, may I speak with Bart privately?"

"Absolutely. You can remain in this office. We will be just outside this door if you need us," Mr. Bronson said, motioning for Officer Bramdt to stand. "Officer, may I offer you some coffee while we wait?" Mr. Bronson could be heard saying as they exited his office.

"Thanks for being accommodating, gentlemen," Ms. Mullinax commented, not sure if they heard her.

"Now— let's get back to this gentleman who I understand is very handsome, very smart, loves to read, and enjoys church," Ms. Mullinax forced a smile. Bart smiled just enough to show hints of his front teeth. He relished the compliment since he did not receive much positive reinforcement at home.

"And apparently, you're trying to hide a beautiful smile. I'd like to know what else this handsome young man is hiding. My office seeks to get you the best assistance, so I need you to be honest with every question I ask you. You don't have to be afraid; no one can harm you now," Ms. Mullinax reassured. "Do you have any questions?"

"Not at the moment, but I may ask some questions along the way."

"Good. Let's get started. Now you may see me take notes on my clipboard for my records."

"No problem at all. What would you like to know?"

Ms. Mullinax started the conversation about growing up in rural South Carolina, giving descriptive information about being abused by both of her parents and being homeless. She maintained a determination to survive. Helping children survive abuse was why she chose to get into the field of social work. She answered Bart's questions to his satisfaction. Bart felt compelled to share the years of sexual and mental abuse as well as what happened to his eye. The details made Ms. Mullinax teary-eyed, but she was determined not to cry in front of him.

After Bart shared his story, Ms. Mullinax remained composed, stating, "I am so sorry you went through all of this. Was your brother physically, mentally, and/or sexually abused?"

"My brother is the favorite of the family. He witnesses my mother and me being abused, but he was never abused," Bart commented.

"Well, he was abused since he was present. It is never right for a child to witness abuse or be abused. Here's where my office can help. I will need to interview your brother and then speak with my supervisor. You may go back to class unless you have questions," Ms. Mullinax chimed.

"I don't have any. Thank you for listening. You're like my only friend," Bart commented solemnly as he walked out.

"I am your friend, Bart, and I am going to work to make sure you are abused no more," Ms. Mullinax whispered as she took a Kleenex from her purse.

—⁂—

Vanessa honked the horn of her white Cutlass Supreme three times to get Michelle's attention as she pulled into the no-parking zone just outside baggage claim at Catticoro Airport. Michelle looked exasperated as she juggled three suitcases and her purse. Taking the hint that Michelle expected some help, Vanessa ran up to her.

"Girl, why you bring all this luggage? You only staying at the hotel for three days." Vanessa appeared hassled as she grabbed two of the suitcases.

"Can I get a 'Welcome Home' or 'I'm so glad to see you, dear friend' before getting the second degree? I mean, I did come on this trip to help you," Michelle teased as they approached the trunk of the car.

"Where are my manners? Of course, I'm glad to see you," Vanessa said with a smile as she put down the baggage and reached out to hug Michelle. "Now, just get in the car before somebody tries to give me a ticket."

As soon as Michelle closed the passenger door, Vanessa released a breathy sigh. Immediately after that, she said nervously, "Girl, I don't know if I can go through with this. I just feel like I'm trying to discover faults with Countee," Vanessa complained.

"Honey, your husband hasn't had sex with you in years; he is always away from the house; he parades you out every Sunday as the spotlight is on him; he makes you stay at home while you don't know how bills are being paid; he comes home very late every Thursday; he doesn't compliment you; your identity is all tied up in him. Chile, do I need to go on?" Michelle questioned, sucking her teeth. "Now, Bitch, you want me to coach you on how to investigate his ass or not? I am only here today and tomorrow. I fly back Friday."

"You so hellbent on finding out shit on him when I know my husband may have his faults, but lying ain't one of them. Go ahead and coach me, then watch me prove you wrong," Vanessa retorted adamantly.

"Fine. You'll thank me later," Michelle added as they pulled up to the hotel. "Help me get my bags up. We will have to move quickly while Countee is away. Our next stop will be your house."

28

Mounting Problems

"Angelic, I have been trying for months to get you to talk to me about what's going on. I've been playing it in my head over what it could be, and I just don't know what it is," Ralph said passionately, turning her back to him while she made herself breakfast on the gas stove.

Ralph gently grabbed her by the elbow and spun her around to face him. "Tell me what it is. I can fix it if you just tell me, darling."

"Don't ever do that again, Ralph. You or I could've gotten burned."

"Okay, okay. I'm sorry. But at least you are looking at me. Honey, what's going on?"

"Ralph, we are just at a crossroads where I'm at a place where I want out of this marriage. I'm not emotionally connected to you anymore. Ever since I found out about Dreama and you going out on a date together, it just made me second-guess our marriage."

"You found out because I explained everything that happened. I told you that she was walking in the rain. I picked her up, took her to get fresh clothes, and got something to eat. Come on, Angelic. You know there is nothing between Dreama and me."

"Then the church gossip started," Angelic stated dramatically. "Different people are feeding me news about how the two of you looked when you got caught holding hands. It's no telling what all you do with her while at work."

"Angelic, you mean to tell me you've been holding on to this? How else could I have handled it?"

"By dropping her off at her home so that she could be with her husband!"

Ralph nodded his head in disbelief. "So that explains why you don't respond when I attempt to make love to you. It explains why you don't clean the house; you don't prepare dinner for me or come home late. You forget that I work double shifts and at the garage to provide for you—giving you the best life I could provide. You've been spending more money lately, but I don't see what it's been spent on. But you haven't heard me complain. If you don't want me anymore, just say so. I don't have time to waste if you have already permanently checked out of the marriage," Ralph stated absolutely.

She looked away from Ralph. "I want a divorce," Angelic stated flatly.

"I don't know what happened that makes you just want to throw away our marriage. It's evident that you don't want to fight for the marriage. Just know that you'll get your divorce. But you won't get my business and house since I inherited them directly from my parents before marrying you. Our children are grown, so you figure out how you will tell them. And I will figure out why you really want a divorce all of a sudden; we were happy once upon a time, and I did nothing to change that. I have nothing else to say about this matter. I am going to work." Ralph looked at Angelic with such disappointment that Angelic shuddered just before closing the front door.

"Why are you in my home? I just sent my son to school, and I'm on my way to work," Dreama said hurriedly.

"As I told you, Mrs. Johnson, we are with the Department of Social Services. While my colleague here, Mike Smith, goes through each part of your home to check your cabinets and your children's bedroom, I just need to ask you a few questions based on some allegations of child abuse," Christie Mullinax poignantly stated.

"Well, whatever it is, make it quick. My ride will be here any minute," Dreama rushed, looking in her compact.

"Please verify your children's names and ages."

"Bart and Warren Johnson ages 15 and 12. And excuse me, but how did you come across this allegation of abuse? I don't abuse my kids."

"Just know, ma'am, that we are following up and protecting the confidentiality of all involved. How do you discipline your children, ma'am?"

"I talk to my children about the error of their ways, and that's it," Dreama answered curtly.

"Where's your husband, ma'am?"

"He is at his mother's house, exactly one mile from here on Maxland Street."

"Where does your husband work?"

"When you speak with him, then you ask him. You'll usually find him at St. Elijah Baptist Church."

"Are you and your husband separated? If so, do the children live with you or him?"

"Bart lives with me, and Warren lives with Booker," Dreama shared as she looked out the window to see an orange Volkswagen pulling into the driveway behind Ms. Mullinax's car. The driver gave two honks to announce his arrival.

"Okay, Mrs. Johnson. That wraps up this interview for now. If you have additional information to share, just call me. I'll leave my business card on the table. Mike, let's go speak with Booker Johnson and see what we can learn from him."

As Ms. Mullinax and Mr. Smith walked to the car, Dreama thought, "I wonder if I should call that sorry-ass man to warn him of their arrival." Once the cab driver honked again, Dreama made her decision.

Ms. Mullinax sat motionless, looking after Dreama, who left with her cab driver as he backed out of the driveway. Mike broke her train of thought when he asked, "Why are we still sitting here?"

"That woman tried to demonstrate a modicum of strength in talking with me. But from one woman to another, I know that she is carrying so much pain—the pain of knowing her son is abused, the pain from whatever she is experiencing from her husband. I just feel like I'm in a tough position since I believe her when she says she's not abusing her son. If we continue the investigation, both boys will be taken into foster care. It would carry greater trauma for her."

"You have a duty to protect the children," Mike shared emphatically.

"She was being abused, and Bart was abused. They are the only source of comfort to each other right now."

Ms. Mullinax's red Ford Festiva let out a gentle hum as the ignition started the vehicle after the second try. "Let us go to the church and see this Booker Johnson."

"I'm sorry, but Reverend Allison is unavailable. Yes, I know it is your third call this week. But as soon as he comes in, I'll give him the message," Rosa smiled.

"Good job, Rosa! Thanks for covering me," Reverend Allison spoke with relief as he stood in front of her.

"Reverend, it is the third time this week that the loan company has called. They said you are three payments behind. You need to return their call," Rosa stated in a motherly tone.

"It's a total misunderstanding," Reverend Allison brushed it off. "I need to check the mail."

"It just happened that I checked the mail today," Rosa told him. "For months, you've been checking the mail. The mailman handed the mail to me just as I came to work. I couldn't help but notice that the mortgage payments on the church were behind. Countee, I need you to tell me what's going on. How is it that we have a trustee board that counts the tithes and offerings and makes the deposits to the bank four times a month, yet we are behind in our mortgage?"

"I will speak to Brother Gordon Carter on the Trustee Board to get all this worked out. Now, Rosa, why don't you go home and take off the rest of this week?" the Reverend said nervously, pulling a chair out from his desk.

"Countee, I have worked as your father's confidential secretary for twenty-five years. He never hid anything from me. He knew he had to have at least one person he could trust to help him maintain oversight over church affairs. It was me. He and I worked out problems surrounding the congregation, your father, your mother, church gossip, church problems, and so much more. You need somebody to help you work out your problems," Rosa advised. "I was that somebody to your father after your mother died in 1972."

"Sister Rosa, you are blowing this out of proportion." The Reverend sensed that Rosa knew more than what she was revealing but was too afraid to inquire. "I just need time to sort things out. The church's finances and my finances will bounce back in order. Now, go home and enjoy the rest of the week."

"OK, I will." Rosa took her sweater off the back of the chair and began to leave. "But do know, Reverend, that it is very hard to be faithful to someone who refuses to let you know who they are," she stated ominously. "Have a good day, Reverend." Rosa didn't wait for a response as she quickly exited to the parking lot.

"Where are the keys to this file cabinet?" Michelle asked pointedly.

"Girl, only Countee has those keys. Besides, why do we need to go through the file cabinet when all he keeps in there are notes on counseling sessions with church members?" Vanessa shared dismissively.

"And how many times since your marriage have you seen him open it?"

"I don't know. Maybe once or twice."

"So he only opens it when you are not around?"

"I never thought about that."

"Well, I am going to open this file cabinet, and we are going to see for ourselves what's inside?"

"But Countee will know the lock has been tampered with."

"Not with the paperclip I am going to use to pop the lockout. I'll pop it back in once we've finished looking."

Michelle contorted the paperclip, inserting a sharp point into the lock with her left hand while jiggling the lock with her right. Ten seconds later, the lock popped out.

"Ta-da. See how simple that was. Now let's open this first drawer," Michelle instructed, observing that Countee had hanging folders labeled from A to Z. "I will look through files A through L, and Vanessa, you look through files M through Z. Now be careful not to place any paper out of order. If something is suspicious, just write it down on a small notepad."

Michelle took out her assigned files and spread them across the office table while Vanessa stood by the file cabinet to review them one by one.

"Girl, I didn't know that the Chamberlains were having marital problems. According to these notes, Denise has been telling George that he's got to get two jobs if he expects them to remain married. George took out a second mortgage on the house to give Denise all she wants, but she wants more. He said he is frustrated since he is getting further into debt," Michelle peeped.

"Those must be some old notes since Denise filed for divorce two years ago. George then had a heart attack and is now in a nursing home. You know it was a 20-year age difference between them," Vanessa chimed monotonously.

"Well, I guess that was a piece of drama I didn't hear about even though I'm in Texas," Michelle surmised. "What have you found so far?"

"I came across past-due bills, some of which are in my name. That's puzzling. I haven't worked a day during our marriage since Countee thought my place was at home, so I wouldn't go out and create debt knowing that I do not have the means of paying it back," Vanessa laughed softly.

Michelle peered over Vanessa's shoulders to see bills from two personal loans, three store charges, and a car loan. "You know what Countee did, right?"

"I think so."

"I don't need you to think Vanessa. Tell me exactly what these bills are proof of," Michelle commanded so that Vanessa would not try to deny the truth nor position herself to tell a lie, given the evidence.

"Countee used my social security number to obtain goods," Vanessa said, unable to believe what she saw.

"Yes, he did. And the balances are exorbitant. Look at the interest rates on all these bills! It will take you at least seven years to pay the bills off," Michelle sighed. "Hand me my handbag."

"What do you need out of your handbag? You already have a pen and a notepad," Vanessa asked Michelle as she handed her the pink-creased handbag.

"I need my disposable camera to take pictures of these documents. Keep looking while I take these pictures."

"One-Night Hotel, Seedy . . . room 435 . . . Don Seymore . . . cash," Vanessa thought aloud. "He has never taken me to this hotel. And who is Don Seymore? What the fuck?"

"Hand me that file, girl, so I can see what the hell is going on!" Vanessa charged. In flipping through each receipt, Michelle softly mentioned, "The dates of these receipts all fall on a Thursday, dating back almost twelve years. And he told you that he was going to do what every Thursday? Is a man named Don paying for the hotel?"

"Missionary work around the town."

"Missionary work, huh?"

"I gave this man my virginity, helped him build his church, and gave him five kids, even though my parents told me not to marry him. I played the role of a docile wife and served him in every regard. I AM on the verge of losing it, Michelle!"

Michelle quickly threw her arms around Vanessa, coddling her as she cried softly, "What am I going to do?"

"I know you are hurt. I need you not to do anything different to make him think everything is normal. Are you listening?"

"Yes, girl. I'm listening," Vanessa mumbled as she dabbed her eyes and wiped her nose with Michelle's tissue.

"Now let's put these files back and then grab some lunch. The next phase of our plan is to get to the One-Night Hotel before Countee does, and I have the perfect device we will plant once he arrives. Leave a note on the counter telling Countee you will volunteer at the city mission. It is so large that it's not like he could really check."

29

Red Flags

"What do you mean the Board won't give me a raise, Brother Carter? I need a cost-of-living raise to take care of my family. Y'all gave to my father every three years during the 25 years he was Pastor," Countee whined.

"The reality, Countee, is that your father understood the principle of accountability. Your father built a relationship with the Trustee Board whereby every dime that came in or went out of the church was accounted for. Your father was given a salary and a discretionary fund account. He lived within that budget to take care of his household. The Trustee Board monitored the cost of living and gave your father raises accordingly. And your father held quarterly budget meetings so the church members could see an accounting of where the contributions were going," the elder replied.

"You have to realize that we live in a different time now," Countee hastily replied.

"I'm not finished, young man," Gordon interrupted. "You started out embracing accountability, but as the church grew, you appointed people not qualified to sit on the Trustee Board. Then you changed the by-laws—bypassing protocol—to give you greater access to most of the church's bank accounts. You can't access the other two accounts because your father made me the sole authorized signer. From those accounts, I have been paying the church's monthly bills. And that's not what those accounts are for. So with all the money spent on Pastor's anniversary, Pastor's birthday, Pastor's appreciation, and the free-spending on cars and clothes far exceeding your salary, consider that your cost-of-living raise."

"After all I have done for this church, I deserve to be celebrated. I am the leader of the church. You know that the oil flows from the top down to the people," the Reverend appealed.

"Ahhh, you really need to think about what you've done to this church's finances. Your father was accountable to Bishop Tidwell and to the Trustee Board. We were his critical partners who loved him enough to tell him when he was right and wrong. He embraced it. He had a passion for the community. Since you have been pastor, you have not done one thing for the community. Yet you want these same community members to raise $10,000 for you while some of them don't have jobs or know how to read? You don't have one person that you are accountable to. And like a spoiled child, you want to do everything you want and then call upon others to help get you out of trouble. It's time you review your financial habits. Your wife can get a job, call in a big-time Bishop to help you raise money, and sell some of the excessive cars you have. Do what you have to do," Gordon concluded.

The brief pause was disturbed when Booker walked into the Reverend's office. "Hey, Brother Gordon. My apologies if I interrupted a meeting," Booker carefully mentioned. "Oh no, Brother Booker, I was just leaving. You, gentlemen, have a great day!" Gordon stated matter-of-factly.

As Booker closed the door, he asked, "Why was Gordon here?"

"I asked him to meet with me regarding an update on the church's finances," Countee casually pointed out.

"Gotcha. He looked annoyed for some reason."

"Maybe you're reading too much into it."

"Maybe so. But hey, we're all set tonight, right? Angelic is going to meet us there. Why don't you call one of our other usuals so I can enjoy Angelic while you enjoy the other girl?" Angelic has grown to be comfortable with you watching us, but I don't want her asking no questions on why you have to watch every Thursday. Besides, I think I will propose to her tonight," Booker mentioned absent-mindedly.

"It is too soon to do that, Booker. You haven't filed for divorce from Dreama; she hasn't filed for divorce from Ralph. Neither of you knows how long the divorce proceedings will take. Plus, what is going to become of the Thursday night sessions? You need to think this through," Countee advised.

"Maybe I do. You know that I'm the marrying type, family man. It's been a few days, and already I'm sick of living with my momma. The house is too crowded. I need a plan, and Angelic is it," Booker reasoned as he looked out the window, his hands on his hips. "Maybe once I'm engaged again, I'll stop doing this Thursday night thing," he said as if daydreaming.

"But what about us? I have been by your side for almost 20 years."

"We will still be tight, but my sexual interests have shifted. It's nothing against you. I am just trying to regroup my life." Countee was mumbling about their special bond when he noticed Booker was preoccupied.

Booker squinted his eyes when he saw a White woman and a White man exiting a car that blocked him in. The White man walked around Booker's vehicle once and wrote down the license plate number.

"Who the fuck are these people? I'm going outside to find out what's going on?" Booker charged.

"Don't be so damn haughty," Countee warned as he walked outside to calm Booker.

"Can I help you people with something? I noticed how you were admiring my car. Are you looking for something?" Booker postured.

The White woman spoke up quickly, "I'm looking for you, Booker Johnson. I am Christie Mullinax, and this is my colleague, Mike Smith. We are with the Department of Social Service. We are here to ask you a few questions as part of our investigation of alleged child abuse."

"Wha . . . What? I bet it was my ex-wife that made up that shit about me. What do you want to know?" Booker asked indignantly.

"Hi, Ms. Mullinax and Mr. Smith. I'm Reverend Countee Allison. Won't you come in?"

Mike and Christie looked at each other in bewilderment at the contrasting behaviors of Booker and Countee.

"Why, thank you!" Christie quickly spoke as she followed the lead of the Reverend into a conference room.

"Can I get you some water or juice?" the Reverend asked in an ingratiating tone.

"No, no. We just need to speak with Booker Johnson briefly."

"Whatever you want to ask or say, you can ask or say in front of him," Booker projected.

"All right, there are allegations of child abuse involving you and your son Bart. Reportedly, you gave him a black eye," Christie smugly stated as she attempted to sound objective.

"There has never been any form of abuse in my home. And tell me, who is making up these lies about me?" Booker stated intimidatingly.

Unfazed, Christie commented, "Booker, it is my job to find out if these are lies; I really hope they are. What I know so far is that your 15-year-old son is walking around with a black eye, telling people that he fell. So I need to know, how did he get that black eye?"

"I don't have to answer any of these questions. I am a good father to my children. I will not be a party to these false allegations," Booker stated as he stood up to signal that their meeting was over. Countee stood up three seconds later in solidarity.

Christie looked glossy-eyed at Mike, Countee, and Booker. Slowly standing, she looked squarely into Booker's eyes. "You live with your mother, right? I think the last time I checked, she was off Route 4. Now, do I have to show up at your mother's house to explain my purpose in making sure that her grandson is protected?"

"Just who is your supervisor?" Countee smirked.

"You have absolutely nothing to do with this, sir."

"I cannot stand to witness this kind of exchange when I know Booker

Johnson's character. What is your supervisor's name and phone number?" Countee's voice escalated.

When neither Christie nor Mike answered within ten seconds, Countee quickly picked up the green rotary phone receiver and dialed 411. "Hello, Information? Get me the telephone number of the Department of Social Services, Catticoro."

As Countee wrote down the number, Christie shared, "My supervisor's name is James Reed, and he will gladly inform you that I am just doing my job. I'll gladly wait right here."

"You will gladly wait in the sanctuary while I speak with James. I will call you when you may return," Countee directed. Christie and Mike walked out confidently to the sanctuary.

Countee was relieved to hear James is Christie's supervisor. James was Countee's former classmate and had even visited the church several times.

"Hi, James, It's Countee Allison. How have you been, my man? How are Samantha and the kids?"

Countee and James discussed politics, family life, and social justice causes. "Now, Countee, it is good to hear from you, but you didn't call me just to talk about random topics. What's on your mind?"

"Christie Mullinax and Mike Smith came to my church and berated one of my revered parishioners, Booker Johnson. He serves the community, is a faithful family man, and gives to charity. She practically accused him of abusing his son. Their approach made me so uncomfortable that I asked them to wait in the sanctuary while I spoke with you."

"Is that right? Christie is a lead social worker. She knows the protocol for asking questions," James shared.

"Why would she come to the church looking for Booker when it is clearly not his residence? Also, Booker's son went to school with a black eye. Booker does not know if he got in a fight on the bus or fell as he got off. I need you to have Christie and Mike close this senseless case. Christie didn't follow protocol."

"Didn't you say that Christie and Mike are at your church right now?"

"Yes, they are. Would you like them to come to the phone?"

"Absolutely."

Countee looked at Booker with a half-smile as he walked to open his office door. "Christie and Mike, James would like to speak with you."

"Hi, James."

"Christie, why are you at that church?"

"I was just seeking to interview Booker Johnson about the child abuse allegations."

"Why did you not follow policy and contact him by mail or phone to inform him of the allegation? The next step was to interview him at his home."

"I was told he was not home, so I came to the church. James, the premise is that I didn't want to delay the matter. What good was it to go to his home when I got a lead that said he was at church?"

"Who do you think you are, a private investigator? You are a social worker who does not get an opportunity to bend the Department's policies and procedures. You are supposed to be mentoring Mike, and already you are teaching him the wrong steps. You are both now off the case."

"What do you mean we are off the case?"

"Exactly that! Now, Mike and you are to come directly to my office to discuss the next steps. Goodbye!"

Christie slammed the phone on the receiver as she looked at the smiling Countee. She slowly turned from Countee and looked at Booker with a stare that made him feel she was seeing through him. "You may think you have won. But karma is chasing after you. When it catches you, I will be right there to see its final effect," Christie prophesied. Mike followed Christie out. When both car doors closed, Booker broke the silence. "Thanks for getting me out of that situation. She would've found it was false anyway."

"Booker, with all the shit I have going on at my house and this church, I don't ever want you to put me in that kind of position again. I never ask you about what's going on in your house, but whatever it is, keep it away from the church. I have a reputation to uphold," Countee admonished.

"You don't have to worry about that at all, man. Dreama knows that I am divorcing her. She probably made that shit up just to stall the divorce."

"If you're going to divorce her, then there is no need to ask her about the child abuse allegations. I've dealt with your stress all these years so that you wouldn't have to. Now, your sexual interest has shifted. You would not be where you are if it had not been for me." Countee's voice went from anger to hurt by Booker's change of heart. He heaved a deep sigh before continuing. "But I'll be mature about it. All of this stress makes me want to make a few calls to see who can join me tonight."

"With you having a wife and me having a wife, what we were doing could only go so far. We can be the best of friends." Booker tried to reassure him. "Make your calls while I use the other phone to call Angelic," he said emphatically as he walked into Rosa's office, reflecting on the child abuse allegation.

I've got to come up with a plan to get Bart out of this town. I won't even have his homosexual ass around Angelic and me. He'd ruin my marriage and image, Booker concluded as he dialed the telephone.

30

Investigation in Pursuit

"This place is a dump. With the Reverend always trying to be flashy, I'm surprised he'd come to a place like this," Michelle frowned as she looked at the dingy motel. "Well, something or someone has him coming here every Thursday," Vanessa said curiously. "And look at how these girls are dressed. Titties are out, and skirts at an all-time high."

"Look, girl, that man just gave that girl with the red stiletto boots a fat wad of bills, and she is following him into room 605. Chile, I need to show off my thick thighs and get paid for giving these men a pleasant surprise." Vanessa and Michelle laughed heartily.

"What time do you think Countee will be here? Maybe his money is going towards some of these women."

"He usually leaves the house around 6 p.m. Since it took us an hour to get here, I guess he will show up around 7," Vanessa deduced.

"Well, it's 5:00 now, and we need information from the clerk. We need to look the part," Michelle whispered.

"You mean for us to dress like these girls? I don't know how to dress like that. And besides, these men may hit on us."

"And if they do, let them, especially if they're flashing $100 bills," Michelle hollered as she gyrated her hips.

"Girl, you crazy! That's why I love you ass."

"I love you too, girl. Now, let's get to the sex shop that we passed and get the outfit we need to charm that hotel clerk. I think it's called Adult Costumes and Toys."

Nervously, Vanessa walked into the sex shop. She was so afraid that someone would recognize her even behind the sunglasses and low-brimmed round hat. As she walked, she was enamored with the various shapes and sizes of dildos. "I could use one of these since I haven't had maintenance on my pussy in a long time," Vanessa thought as she examined the brown, veiny, twelve-inch toy with an eight-inch girth.

The adult store had a cacophony of subtle sounds permeating the store that came from the private booths in the back. Vanessa felt like she was in a sex education class as she handled the anatomic plastic gear for both men and women.

"Girl, come over here and tell me which outfit you like the best," Michelle called out from two aisles down.

"Chile, don't be calling for me like that. I am not trying to draw attention," Vanessa hissed.

"Ain't nobody caring about yo' ass being in here. They want the same thing you want. So get over it. Now, which of these outfits do you like best on me?" Michelle asked. One outfit was a black patent-leather, dominatrix strapless blouse with ruby-red pastie hearts and tassels. The three-inch skirt was accessorized with an extending baton and six-inch patent-leather string-up boots. The second outfit was an A-line, black polyester cocktail dress complimented with a pink-and-white checkered petticoat and pink four-inch patent-leather pumps.

"The black dress shows off more of your curves. I like that one on you best."

"I do, too. Now we have to find you an outfit."

"Girl, what are you going to do with that outfit after tonight?"

"I'm taking it back to Texas and putting it on for my husband. I hope that'll help him get that dick up again since I'm not letting this dress go to waste."

Vanessa and Michelle laughed as they walked to the next aisle of dresses. "Oh! This dress is perfect for you, Vanessa!" The sleeveless, white body dress was made of polyester blend, and the five-inch white patent-leather heels completed the ensemble. "Girl, I am too big to be wearing a bodysuit. You forgot that I had five kids."

"Chile, all you need is a good corset. You have the titties and ass. I'm getting myself a corset, too, since I have to cram all this body into my outfit. So don't you worry. Let's look at the makeup and then get out of here. We have to get dressed and get information from the clerk about this Don Seymore before Countee arrives."

31

Halloween in July

"I can't believe it, Daniel! Chev Mills is closing down in three weeks?" Ralph Custon asked in disbelief.

"That's right, Ralph, on July 31st," Daniel Boonson said sympathetically as the crowd of workers murmured.

"But listen, you have some options. Chev Mills is moving to Dallas, Texas. You can uproot your family and move there. We can offer up to $400 in moving costs. I plan on continuing to be a supervisor at the Dallas location."

"That is nowhere near enough money to move, and you know it. Why didn't Chev Mills give us at least a two-month notice so that we could have time to explore all of our options? Many of us have families we have to support," Ben Southernland responded.

"I know it is tough news for all of you. We just didn't know how else to let you know. Now, some of you are eligible for retirement. I suggest you speak with human resources. For the others of you, you qualify to receive unemployment benefits through the unemployment office. Please know we are not granting time off during these next three weeks. So, with that said, let's get back to work. You are welcome if you want to see me during your break."

Dreama caught up with Ralph as he was walking to his workstation. "Ralph, this is really terrible news," She commented as she patted him on the back.

"It *is* bad news for all of us. Just another thing to add to the list of bad news I have been receiving."

"Ralph, look at me. What are you talking about?"

"Dreama, Angelic and I are getting a divorce. She asked for it, and I'm not fighting for us to stay together when she has it fixed in her mind that you and I have had a secret relationship for all these years."

"Oh no, Ralph! The times I've run into her at church, she and I make small talk. I would've never guessed that y'all had marital problems."

"Well, I was blindsided that she wanted the divorce. So, I guess we had marital problems that she didn't let me know about. She has been going somewhere every Thursday. I haven't tried to figure out where, but that's when I noticed that she started changing."

"Wow! This must be the season for bad news."

"Why do you say that, Dreama?"

"Booker told me he wants a divorce. He left with Warren while I was left with Bart. He left me with past-due bills, although I gave him my paycheck, which should've covered all the bills. To add insult to injury, Social Services came to my home this morning with allegations of child abuse. I anticipate they will be investigating further. When they find out that I don't have a job after three weeks, they will wonder how I can take care of a child. At least your kids are grown, Ralph."

"I'm sorry to hear this news. We have to believe that divorce is the best option for both of our situations. I will just have to work more hours at the shop. I have some friends who may help you get a job as a teacher's aide in the school system."

"Thank Ralph. But transportation will be an issue since I don't have a driver's license or a car."

"That's right. You know, I'll do what I can to help."

"Damn, here comes Daniel! Let's go ahead and get our machines set up so they won't try to dock our time even though we have been working double shifts for the past nine months."

"Thanks, Dreama, for listening. I will keep you posted. Be sure to do the same."

"I will."

—w—

Michelle drove directly across the street from Adult Costumes and Toys to the food market. She parked next to the shopping cart corral. "Girl, why are we here? You need to get some gum or something?" Vanessa asked naively.

"After we change into these outfits, we are going to buy some gum. Then we are going to catch a cab to drop us off at the One-Night Motel," Michelle divulged. "Now, let's go."

As Michelle and Vanessa entered the ladies' bathroom, a forty-something-year-old Black woman rushed past them to enter stall two. She almost missed the commode as she fell to her knees, upchucking. Michelle silently admired her silver-sequined short dress with matching shoes.

"I don't know what's going on with her, but we are letting nothing stop our mission. Go to the first stall and get dressed. I will get dressed by the sink," Michelle insisted. "We don't have much time."

Five minutes later, the Black woman emerged from stall two, looking back to inspect whether she had left any evidence of regurgitation. She walked carefully to the sink beside Michelle. As she turned on the water, Michelle said, "You doing ok? You almost knocked us down as you were coming here."

"I'm ok. My stomach was a little upset."

"Oh, from something you ate earlier?"

"Yeah, but I'm not able to keep some food down. It is the same feeling I had in all four of my pregnancies. I sure hope I'm not pregnant."

"I'm glad you're feeling better. I'm Tiffany," Michelle lied. "That's

Valerie, a girlfriend of mine." Vanessa waved as she sat on the toilet to put on her heels.

"I'm Fern. Nice to meet you."

"You too. Why would you be concerned about being pregnant?"

"One, I'm in my 40s; two, it would be the fourth child whose father is not in his or her life because I've been a prostitute for 20 years. Three, selling sex is all I know about making a living. I came into the food market to get some stockings only to have gotten sick as I walked down aisle 9."

"I respect you for being straight up. You work a corner in this area?"

"I primarily work within a two-mile radius. Thursday is particularly festive, and the girls can make the most money. I don't think I ever saw you girls on the block. Y'all working the streets tonight?"

"It is our first time being on these streets. We just want to see the clientele before deciding what to do next."

"Where are y'all heading to now," Fern asked.

"We're headed over to the area where the One-Night Hotel is."

"Oh, I'm headed there too. Y'all can ride with me."

"That sounds like a plan. Fern, why don't we walk together to get your stockings? I'll get a few things while Valerie dresses. I'll meet you on aisle nine as soon as I finish applying my lipstick."

"Ok, Tiffany. Thanks."

As soon as Michelle heard the click-clack of Fern's shoes faint in the distance, she told Vanessa, "Take our clothes and toiletries to the car. Place them in the trunk, and then come back into the food market to look for Fern and me. I don't want her to know we have a car to drive. We can take a cab back. I'll go catch Fern now."

Fern talked nonstop as Michelle and Vanessa sat crammed in her red 1972 AMC Pacer. They sat on top of books, boxes, and multiple McDonald's bags as Fern smoked two cigarettes while puttering the two-mile trek to

One-Night Motel. Michelle didn't wait for the car's ignition to be turned off when Fern parked behind the dumpster before quickly opening her door. After coughing three times, she folded the back seat to let Vanessa out. Vanessa cleared her throat before spitting phlegm onto the neighboring grass. As Fern took one more drag of her cigarette, Michelle boldly said, "Look, girl, thanks for the ride and conversation. But we got to go. We know that while we work the streets, we will act like we don't know each other. Make that money, honey!"

"So you know the code among us working girls? Well, here's another tip: the married men pay more," Fern offered.

"Well, here's a tip from me: You don't need to smoke if you're pregnant. And why would you want to meet a man smelling like a perfumed cigarette? If he goes down to taste your goody box, he's not going to want to taste menthol and flowers. Get it together, girl! Bye!"

Vanessa stifled laughter as Michelle grabbed her hand to walk as fast as they could to circle the building and leave Fern behind as they headed toward the motel. It was 6:45 p.m. They started to feel themselves glistening against their leather undergarments. "I hope the inside of this motel has air conditioning because it's freakin' hot," Michelle quipped. As they got closer, men of various backgrounds gave them catcalls and shouted how much they were willing to pay. Vanessa cautioned Michelle to ignore them as she grabbed the makeshift front door.

Upon entering the motel lobby, the flowery wallpaper was peeling, failing to camouflage the original paint circa 1925. The red, yellow, and black checkered carpet held remnants of every patron who had ever marched to the lobby. A mango scent from an aerosol can didn't quite mask the smell of feet, cigarettes, and lingering morning breath. Six dried-up donuts from the morning were still sitting on the check-in counter.

"Welcome to One-Night Motel, ladies! Don't y'all look stunning tonight. What can I do to serve you?" Jethro Boyine said with a bit of cheer. The motel was owned by Jethro, who inherited it from his father. Jethro was tight-fisted and wanted to keep more money in his pockets than invest in repairs and upkeep. Jethro was dressed in overalls and an off-white T-shirt with waterproof black boots. His look was completed with the remaining dyed black hair horizontally swooping from the side across his head. His false teeth were too big for his mouth, giving him a perpetual smile. The look was his way of convincing women he was only 45 when he was actually 20 years older.

"Oh, my! I didn't know we'd walk in and be greeted by a hardworking, cute man. That smile is gorgeous. Suga, what's your name? You just might get two for the price of one!" Michelle complimented, batting her eyes.

The senior's nervous laughter revealed that a woman hadn't given him that kind of attention in some time. "My name is Jethro, and I can still make the two of you feel like you won the jackpot with my magic tongue." Jethro wagged his tongue rapidly, nearly causing Vanessa to throw up in the back of her throat.

"You even look like you have a lot of talent. But we are about business. We know you can roll out the welcome mat for us as part of your wonderful customer service," Michelle softly mentioned.

"Jethro sounds so manly," Michelle seductively continued as she stepped closer. "And I just know that a man like you will tell me more about your fine work here. We're new girls here, just trying to make a few dollars. I guess since you've worked here a while, you know the patrons that come in and out of this motel, and maybe you can tell us about some guys who are some of your regulars. We only want to meet consistent men." Michelle caressed his overalls lightly, then snapped her fingers, adding, "Who knows? Maybe afterward, we could come back to say *thank you* in your back office."

Jethro, in nervous excitement, could only utter, "Wow . . . that would be real nice. You know how to make a man quiver. Well, we have five guys who are weekly regulars. I can't tell you their names, but they get the same weekly rooms: 106, 210, 435, 518, and 525. All of our rooms are only accessible from the outside."

"We just want to be visible to the guys who check in to 210 and 435. We can consider two for now and maybe the other three next week."

By the time Michelle finished rubbing Jethro's thigh as she told him about her fantasies, Jethro gave her the keys to 210 and 435 so that she and Vanessa could wait for the men. "Now, Jethro, this is our little secret. We want the men to be pleasantly surprised. And remember to let the hotel phone ring twice to signal that the men are coming."

Michelle whispered as she blew him a kiss. Jethro, vowing to secrecy, zipped his lips with his finger as Vanessa and Michelle walked out.

"Bitch, you owe me for the rest of your life. My hands nearly flinched each time I touched any part of him. I would take a shower, but I'm scared the bathtub is dirtier than Jethro is," Michelle stated to Vanessa in disgust.

"You know, I don't have that kind of boldness to approach men like that. You were doing such a great job that I felt I shouldn't interfere," Vanessa reasoned.

"Well, you can do a great job of jacking that man off when we finish our business in 435."

The scent of mildew, cigarettes, and old socks greeted Vanessa and Michelle as they opened the door. "Girl, it wouldn't surprise me if Countee was fucking Fern because this room smells exactly like her car," Michelle teased.

"Never mind that. It's 7 p.m. Now, where do you think we should place the tape recorders?" Vanessa asked.

"We will press record and turn the volume up first. Then we can place them behind the nightstand and get out of here."

The moment the task was complete, the phone rang twice.

32

Neglecting Responsibility

Bart was hungry and dialed the phone in search of Booker. "Grandma, there's no food here, and I'm hungry. Did you cook today?" Bart asked as he opened the olive-green refrigerator door and looked at the baking soda and ketchup.

"Who told you to stay with your mother when you know that she's an indecent woman? Your daddy told me that when he asked where you and your brother wanted to stay, you chose to stay with your mother while your brother is here with me," Agnes Johnson said slowly, taking a drag of her cigarette.

"My daddy didn't ask me anything, Grandma. He left me here without allowing Warren or me to make a choice. He made that choice for both of us," Bart responded respectfully as he closed the refrigerator door.

"Well, are you calling your daddy a liar?"

"I don't call my father names, Grandma. I'm just telling you what happened. I just need some food."

"Where's your momma?"

"She is working a double shift."

"First of all, she should've left you something to eat. Second, I got just enough to feed my household. Third, even if I did have some food, I won't let you have any. I ain't having no sissies in my house since that's a spirit. It'll turn into a house of homosexuals. And I don't have a problem forsaking family who engage in that sin. For the wages of that sin is death. It's probably something your momma did in her past that made you gay. That's why I've spoken to everyone who attends the church about how your mother and you need to leave the church. Both of you have spirits that need to be cast out."

"Ok, Grandma," Bart said, hoping to change the subject. "Can I speak to my dad?"

"He ain't here. You oughta know by now that he is doing the Lord's work since it's Thursday. And since you don't have any food, it might be time for you to fast and read your Bible to get closer to Jesus. Now I'm getting off this phone since I'm waiting for another call. Bye!"

Bart heard the click from the phone's receiver and realized no one loved him. As he walked around in the small living room, he reflected on the sexual, verbal, physical, and mental abuse from Booker, the favoritism he and Dreama gave to Warren, the embarrassment of having the church judge him, and the neglect his mother rewarded him for staying with her. Bart sat in the dark and started to cry silently.

God, why did you bring me into this family? I just wish you gave me a family that loves me as I am. All I know is abuse. I am a gay boy who doesn't want to be gay. I don't know what it is like to be loved by anyone. Glen was my only friend, and he moved to be with his dad. I am fighting every day not to be the ugly things my father said I'd be. I really don't like my father. I am trying not to be too bitter and unforgiving. But God, it is so hard. I just wish you'd take my life or just allow me to take my own. I'm so tired. Bart cried even harder, fantasizing about the ways to kill himself.

His thoughts were interrupted when he heard three knocks on the door. When he heard three more knocks, he took a white T-shirt to wipe his face before saying, in the manliest voice he could muster, "Who is it?"

"It's your Paw-Paw. Open this door, boy!" Arthur Johnson exclaimed.

Bart realized that he must have inadvertently locked the front door after coming home from school since no one in the neighborhood had locked their doors.

"Hey, Paw-Paw. Come on in," Bart said hesitantly. He wanted to ask why he came over but held his tongue.

"Your grandma told me you called and wanted something to eat. After she told me that you were not allowed to come over, I got you something to eat from Whirly King before I went over to your uncle John's house to play cards," Arthur shared.

"Paw-Paw, you got me my favorite burger with all the fixings," Bart gushed.

"Don't forget your fries and chocolate shake. I wanted to make sure you get enough to eat."

"This is plenty, Paw-Paw. Thanks for thinking of me in light of all that's happened between my dad and mom."

"I know your dad is a piece of work. I've got to let him figure all of this out. So I'm staying out of whatever he and your mother decide. You just enjoy your food. I've got to get to John's. Why don't you be productive and clean this place?"

"Thanks, Paw-Paw. I'll clean it really well after I eat. I appreciate you stopping by."

"Ok. I'll be checking on you," Arthur stated with good intentions.

Knowing that Arthur was fishing for words to say, Bart replied, "I'll be okay, Paw-Paw."

Bart looked out the window to see Arthur back in his car out of the driveway, and he took a second bite of the burger. "God, today I have to believe that you love me despite what I have been through. You made way for me to have food today. I have to believe that I am going to survive this. It's just me and you."

—⚍—

Countee, Angelic, and Booker pulled up to the back of One-Night Motel into a parking space just a few spaces away from where Fern dropped off

Vanessa and Michelle. "Y'all head up to 435 while I go to the front desk. I'm sure I'll find a girl to join me tonight." Countee wasn't in an amorous mood. He was deeply thinking about the number of outstanding bills he had not paid and the years he had financially supported Booker.

"Well, howdy, Mr. Seymore! You're looking a little down tonight. But I'm sure one of these girls will quickly cheer you up," Jethro heartily stated. "Here's your key to 435. When you meet up with a double surprise, you'll be grinning from ear to ear."

Concluding that Jethro was trying to find something to discuss, Countee dryly replied, "I'm just fine. Just a little tired from working today."

Countee paid the cash and placed the receipt in his left jeans pocket. Realizing that if he was going to meet a woman tonight, he had to have his attitude and money instantly ready. Mustering up mental courage, Countee confidently walked out of the lobby with his hands in his pocket. The moment the door closed behind him, Countee walked in front of a light-skinned, slim woman wearing a high-thigh lime-green skirt with an off-white sleeveless blouse. Her knee-high white boots complimented hints of the white eyeshadow and lipstick that brought out her light-brown eyes.

"Damn, you sexy. What's the cost to get you to spend some time with me tonight?" Countee asked plainspokenly.

"It depends on what you want me to do," the woman negotiated.

"Why don't you join me in 435, where you and I can work out a deal?"

"We can walk to room 435, but the deal has to be agreed upon prior to me walking in."

"I like how you think. Consider it agreed." The two walked down the broken sidewalk under the motel's flashing neon sign.

Michelle and Vanessa stationed themselves at the front of the hotel to blend well with the other women seeking to be hired. They half-heartedly talked to two men as they observed and overheard much verbal exchange between Countee and the mystery woman. Vanessa was burning to call out Countee and began to walk toward him, but Michelle grabbed her hand.

"Bitch, don't be stupid. Our plan is working just fine. There will be plenty of time to confront his trifling ass," Michelle prophesied. We will wait about two minutes to follow behind them with these two men in tow." Michelle casually turned to the men and said, "I'm sorry we jetted off like that. My girlfriend thought she saw one of our other girlfriends and wanted to catch her before she walked off with her suitor. Now you said you want us to be your company tonight?"

"Yeah, we can go to our room and have a few drinks, chat a little, do some adult things, then we pay you, and you leave," the taller, darker-skinned man replied.

"Well, let's talk more about it," Vanessa suggested, "as we walk in that direction," Vanessa pointed as she saw Countee and the secret woman walk up the first flight of stairs.

"That's the same direction as our room. Now let's get the chatting going, mama," the shorter, dark-skinned man motioned.

Vanessa led the foursome, who walked to the backside of the Motel, watching Countee and his evening date approach room 435. Vanessa nodded as she glanced at the lips of her would-be date. She was too preoccupied with watching Countee and the woman enter the room to notice another man and woman entering shortly thereafter. The man's silhouette reminded her of someone, but she just couldn't be sure.

Vanessa took over the conversation, saying, "Girl, I think I just need you to take me home. I am not feeling good. Come on, let's go."

"But Sexy Mama, I got just what you need to relax you," the taller man managed to say as he pulled out some quaaludes.

"You heard the lady. We are going home. Maybe next time, guys."

"Ahh damn! These bitches ain't shit. Wasting our time when we could've been . . ." the taller man to the shorter as they walked away.

Michelle and Vanessa went in opposite directions to sit and talk in the car. "Girl, I'm glad you said something. How can that man be so good-looking, but his breath smells like cow manure?" Michelle pondered aloud.

"Never mind him. Did you see Countee and that whore go into 435?"

"Yeah, Chile, 'fraid I did."

"Did you see another man and a woman also go into 435?"

"No, I didn't. What kind of question is that?"

"I know what I saw. You don't think they're having an orgy, do you?"

"We need to stay right here for a good hour, and then we will have all of our answers. Remember, we have to get the recorder and be sure you beat Countee home. And I have just the plan to get it," Michelle plotted.

33

Five-Finger Discount

Angelic and Booker shared a cigarette as they sat naked in the full-sized bed. Countee and the anonymous woman held each other fast asleep in the other. The anonymous woman was more pleased with Countee's money than his sexual performance. Glad that it was over, the woman reasoned that Countee's extra $50 paid for her to stay a little while longer.

"I told Ralph that I want a divorce. He told me I stand to gain nothing from it since he inherited the automobile shop from his parents prior to our marriage. Our children are grown so that I won't get alimony. Ralph took out a second mortgage on the house less than a year ago, so we won't get much after selling the house," Angelic said while wondering if divorcing Ralph was even a viable option.

"I left Dreama. I took Warren, and now we're living with my mother temporarily. I will have to go to court to gain custody of Warren. Countee has a friend who is a judge who will help me with the paperwork to do an involuntary termination of parental rights. I'll then have to take Bart to some address. Then, after that, we can start our life off with one child in the house," Booker thought out loud. "Dreama doesn't have any assets, so I'll be coming into the marriage with limited income."

"So what can we do to have some money? I want us to live well."

"You told me you have some life insurance policies on him, right?" Booker remembered.

"Yes, they were taken out when we first got married."

"How much are they worth?"

"A total of $450,000."

"How much do you want us to get married?" Booker asked.

"I want to be your wife from now until I take my last breath."

"We are working hard to divorce our current spouses. We are not trying to go broke in the process. We need to create a plan to get that $450,000," Booker appealed.

"He'd have to die in order for me to get money. And I don't know if he's even thinking about the insurance policy."

"He may decide to change the beneficiary if he remembers y'all having the policy. Don't you think your hurt and happiness are worth at least $450,000?"

Understanding the unspoken words, Angelic replied softly, "Yes, I do, Booker. I will do anything you say just to be your wife."

"Then we have to develop a plan that guarantees that Ralph Custon will be dead within a short time. Don't file for divorce; act like you want to work things out with him. Go to counseling; you can even get Countee to give you marital counseling," Booker spoke just before kissing Angelic passionately as a precursor to round two.

The sounds of pecking and moaning awakened Countee and his evening date. Countee, refreshed after his mediocre sexual performance, followed suit, determined to give his anonymous lover an orgasmic experience.

Thirty minutes into the sexual foray, Booker and Countee were in an unspoken contest over who could satisfy his partner as judged by the sounds each woman made. The contest was interrupted when a loud blaring alarm screeched throughout the Motel. "Everyone is to exit their rooms at this time and stand in the parking lot," Jethro announced. "The fire department is on the way."

The Motel guests scurried out of their rooms, feeling quite uncomfortable seeing that they were scantily clad. The moment Countee, Booker, Angelic, and the secret woman descended down the fifth floor, Vanessa entered room 435 to retrieve both recorders as Michelle blocked the door. "Let's grab a taxi and get the hell out of here before the fire department arrives. I don't want to be around if they start asking who pulled the fire alarm," Michelle stammered to Vanessa as they started to keep pace with the remaining guests.

The taxi pulled up to the food market as its manager locked the store. "Girl, let's get out of these clothes and throw them away quickly. My feet are hurting in my heels," Michelle nearly screamed to an audience in a nearby parking lot. "Chile, may I never wear an outfit like this again," Vanessa promised.

The ladies quickly changed clothes and removed all traces of makeup. "I am turning this cassette over to hear everything that went on in that room," Vanessa proceeded.

"We make a great investigative team!" Michelle hollered.

"Yeah, we do! I dressed in a way I never thought I would."

The moment Vanessa hit the play button, she heard Countee and the woman make conversation about their sexual interests and the cost of services. Countee attempted to state *his name,* but the vixen made it clear that she was just interested in knowing how much money he was paying for services. Outside of the salacious sounds, she heard very little else. When she played the second recorder, she was shocked that the silhouette of the man she saw was Booker and that Angelic was his woman of the night. The cassette tape thread became entangled in the recorder right when Angelic was talking about Ralph. Vanessa and Michelle inadvertently damaged the tape in their efforts to untangle it.

Breaking the silence, Michelle asked sensitively, "How do you feel about all you heard?"

Vanessa had turned to stone. "It confirmed what I knew. He hasn't made love to me in years. He had to have been getting sex from somewhere. And I see that he has been spending money on whores and motels. She looked up at the stars and spoke in a robotic voice. "I certainly plan to bring him down gradually. And can you believe—Booker and Angelic? They have a plan for something. Whatever it is, it has nothing to do with me."

34

Excess Baggage

Dreama couldn't believe that Booker wanted to talk in person about his proposal for the legal separation. She canceled her 9 a.m. gentleman's appointment to avoid Booker and the man seeing one another. Since Bart didn't know, but one of Dreama's brothers, Dreama was going just to say that he was Bart's uncle. It's been a month since she lost her job at Chev Mills; her unemployment check was not helping to make ends meet. Her side hustle as a prostitute interfered with her ability to raise Bart or even be involved in feeding or clothing him.

Dreama reflected on how her family and work dynamics had changed. She realized she had no family or friends to call; she had given up everything for Booker, only for him to file for a legal separation.

The three knocks on the door interrupted her thoughts. Her home just so happened to be spotless as she opened the door to let Booker inside. "What brings you here, Booker?" Dreama asked to avoid making small talk. She wrestled with trying to be strong against her deep depression.

"I want full custody of the boys, and I want you to pay child support. You can see the boys once a month. And you can keep all the trailer's contents," Booker offered.

"Booker, you can have custody of the boys. I won't be paying child support. I am not contesting the separation and won't contest the divorce. The way the people have been treating me at the church is driving me to run out of state to start over," Dreama sighed. "Anything else?"

"No, Dreama. That's it."

"Fine. I'll wait until I receive the legal papers. When do you want Bart? He's sleeping right now."

"I'll get him Monday. Make sure all of his stuff is packed. You can tell him whatever you want about why he's coming with me."

—ɯ—

Bart noticed that Booker drove past Arthur and Agnes' house. "Where are we going?"

"You'll know when we get there," Booker snapped.

Bart fell asleep only to awaken four hours later in northeastern South Carolina, watching Booker turn into the driveway of a large ranch brick house with black shutters and burgundy columns on two acres of land.

"Well, get out," Booker expressed as he opened the driver's door.

"Whose house is this?" Bart asked.

Ignoring Bart, Booker walked a few steps ahead, arriving on the porch. Just as Booker was about to knock, a 16-year-old boy flung open the front door. "Hi, my name is Matthew. I am your new friend," he said to Bart as he extended his hand. The moment Bart went to shake hands, Matthew shook his hand so vehemently that Bart felt like his right shoulder had popped out of its socket.

"Oh, Matthew, I see you have met our guest," Rodney Connor hastily shared. "I am the Director of Sentajo Group Home. And you must be Bart. You are very handsome." Moving past Bart, Rodney charismatically stated, "And you must be Booker. Countee told me you were coming by. I understand you have some papers you want us to sign. We have some papers for you to sign, too. Come right this way to my office." Rodney and Booker walked down the hallway as Bart looked around.

The home boasted hardwood pine floors. The yellow suede couch, olive-green plastic loveseat, and twelve mismatched chairs gave evidence that the furniture was donated. The walls were off-white, with a sprinkling of dirty handprints scattered throughout. Bart observed various pictures on the walls of boys aged 13-21 and the families that adopted them. The wall was named the Adoption Hall of Fame.

The aroma of the food brought Bart to the kitchen. Booker had driven from Catticoro to Nowville, South Carolina, for four straight hours, not stopping for gas, not feeding Bart, and not talking to Bart.

"Hey there. Are you a new resident of this house?" Asked the cook.

"No. I am just here with my dad. I guess he is in the back visiting with Rodney."

"We don't have any visitors. It is odd to have someone just come here to visit. We just see kids come and go."

"Oh, the kids don't stay here permanently?" Bart asked.

"Some kids are adopted while a few kids graduate from high school and then get their own place. By the way, I'm Sean. What's your name?"

"I'm Bart."

"Nice to meet you, Bart. Tell me about yourself."

"I like to read, write, play board games, run, and play some sports. Tell me about you."

"I'm 17; I like to cook and talk to people. My mom died four years ago, and I was placed in this home since my dad's alcoholism drove him to abuse me. He doesn't come to visit me. The only family I have is my Aunt Jo and Uncle Leroy. They come to visit me."

Bart felt sorry for him and instantly felt a connection.

"My parents are separated. I live with my father, though I prefer to stay with my mother. My dad has been abusive to me. I won't have anyone to visit me," Bart stated cautiously.

"Maybe you can come with me to Aunt Jo and Uncle Leroy's house. They have a daughter named Jaime, and they would treat you like family," Sean added, admiring Bart.

"Just let me know. It'll be good to get into a different environment," Bart commented.

In awkward silence, Sean and Bart looked at each other for about ten seconds.

"What are you cooking?" Bart casually changed the subject to relieve his discomfort as he heard his stomach growl.

"I am making sloppy joes for all the boys. There is enough food for you, too," Sean offered.

"Thanks so much. I'd love to have one," Bart graciously stated. "Where is your bathroom? I'd like to wash my hands."

"Down passed Rodney's office on the right-hand side," Sean directed as he divided the sloppy joe across thirteen buns."

Bart slowly walked to the bathroom, stopping to view the wall pictures and awards. Standing just outside Rodney's office, he admired the artwork by two of the boys. He started to resume his walk but stopped short when he heard Rodney and Booker talking.

"So I see you have the court papers that terminate your parental rights to Bart and make him a ward of the state. Let's check them out," Rodney requested.

"Umm Hmm. Bart has experienced sexual abuse, physical abuse, and neglect. And the judge honored your request to terminate your rights," Rodney added. "Is there more to this story?"

"Well, I don't know if Countee explained it to you, but all those experiences came from his mother. And I just think it has impacted his state of mind. He is beyond what I can do to help him. This group home would give him the help he needs," Booker reasoned.

Satisfied with Booker's answer, Rodney continued, "Let's talk more about the services we will provide for kids like Bart."

A flurry of emotions encapsulated Bart. He thought of making a loud scene, cursing Booker, throwing objects, and pleading to go anywhere else. He resorted to whimpering and wailing, finally falling on his knees to the floor.

"Did you hear something?" Rodney asked.

"I'm not sure," Booker stated uncertainty. He walked to the door to find Bart balled up on the floor.

"Get up off the floor, Bart! There's no need to make a scene," Booker's voice projected, not realizing temporarily that he was in the group home. Booker told Rodney, instantly bringing his voice calmer, "Give me about five minutes with Bart. Do you have a more private place where we could talk?"

"Sure. There is the bedroom that Bart will be sleeping in. For now, he will have his own room. It's next door to my office on the right," Rodney pointed.

Once the door was closed, Bart said quietly but threateningly, "What did I just overhear?"

In a condescending drawl, Booker said, "You've known for as long as you can remember that you are the child neither Dreama nor I wanted. I'm not sorry for saying so. You have caused me so much grief and stress that I couldn't wait until you turned 18 to get you out of my house. So this is your new home where these people can tolerate your way of speaking like White people and your constant Bible reading. When they discover that you are nothing but a sad sissy, they will have their way with you."

Bart looked at Booker intently, "For someone who raised me in the church and served as a deacon, you have condemned me for being gay, for being a Bible reader, for wanting to go to college, for just being me. I have put up with your abuse, your lies, your camouflage, your favoritism, and your tyranny. I cried about you dropping me off here, but now I choose to cry no more today. I have to believe that God has a larger plan for me. He loves me even though you don't."

"I don't wish to see you again. You'll become nothing! You won't even get into college. Whatever happens with you, know that no one will call me to come to your rescue. Get a good look at me now. It'll be the last time you see me."

Bart turned his back to Booker before he spoke. "I've had enough of seeing you," he said quietly. "Since you don't want to be in my presence, I suggest you drive back to Catticoro before it gets dark."

Booker turned around slowly, instantly reflecting on how his words had very little effect on Bart. He'd suspected Bart would be pleading and begging him to stay. He turned and walked away without speaking another word. Sean, who had been lurking in the hallway, walked in carefully. "Bart, I heard everything. I am sorry."

35

Just When You Thought You Got Away with It

For the past ten months, Vanessa kept a watchful eye on Countee's every move, saying nothing. She had even been cooking his favorite meals, cheering him on vociferously as he preached, speaking very highly of him publicly, and giving him massages. She was resolute in not having sex with him, saying that her desire for sex shifted, perhaps due to a medical reason to be confirmed by a doctor. Countee was quite content with such. And he was relieved that Vanessa was still uninformed about his shenanigans.

Thanks to Michelle, Vanessa planted tape recorders daily in Countee's car and his office at the church. Her timing in retrieving the cassettes and replacing the tape recorder with new ones was quite strategic. She had been putting love notes in his car at church, only to make the switch subtly. She then went into the church to state her purpose: "Honey, I wanted to deliver your lunch to you today. You work so hard for the family that I want to do my part to acknowledge your efforts. Is there anything else I can do for you, dear?" Countee's stomach and ego were fed tasty morsels of self-aggrandizement with each ounce of servitude Vanessa provided.

Samantha Andrick, Vanessa's attorney, would then listen to the cassette tapes, building a solid divorce case brick by brick. Teetering on the boundaries of the law, Samantha filed a legal separation after helping Vanessa establish another residence to which she moved items little by little. By no means was she giving the home to Countee. In fact, she planned to sell the house and keep all of the proceeds, especially since she knew that Countee did not want any of his proclivities for whores, embezzlement, and tax evasion to be showcased in court. Her attorney's next course of action was to file a dispute with Vanessa's creditors, noting that Vanessa did not authorize the opening of the financial accounts.

But the time was not yet. Vanessa continued to be subservient to Countee, counting down the day she would publicly expose his house of secrecy, without regard on whose heads the bricks may fall, Booker's least of all. She sensed Booker was somehow involved but was not sure how. She still wished Michelle she could've unraveled the damaged cassette tape to listen to what he said in the hotel.

Being none the wiser, Booker was too busy basking in the glow of his uncontested divorce from Dreama. He had his mother to thank for that. Agnes Johnson called each woman who was on the church's roster for the past ten years—whether a current or a former member—and spoke of factual and fictitious information about Booker as an upstanding, godly man whose wife engaged in drugs, alcohol, orgies, rubber checks, cheating, and parental abandonment. Even if the person taking the call didn't remember Agnes, she made the narrative so salacious that it held the caller's attention long enough to keep listening. Dreama was the target of Agnes' vitriol. The in-town gossip drove Dreama to move to Georgia to start life as an anonymous woman with no money and no family.

Angelic's pending divorce was far less of a public spectacle. Only Tony and Lorraine—Ralph and Angelic's adult children—and Agnes, Booker, and Warren knew. Agnes is less convincing when she tries to spread a rumor that Ralph and Dreama are secretly dating after she sees them when Ralph is well-known as a good man. Even Angelic didn't believe the rumor; she just became bored with Ralph the moment she had her first sexual encounter with Booker. She wants Ralph to fight for the marriage, but Ralph remains polite while having a short conversation with Angelic. She was annoyed with him but kept her distance. She had a driving reason for visiting him at his car repair shop. She had one final thing to say.

Ralph was lying on the mechanic's creeper, performing an oil change underneath a 1967 Chevy Impala hoisted by a car jack stand. As the oil was captured into the oil pan, Angelic boldly said, "Ralph, we need to talk."

Ralph rolled out from under the car. Lying on the mechanic's creeper, he sternly replied, "Angelic, of all the times you want to talk, you want to talk while I'm working after I have closed my shop? Here it is Thursday when you had all week to talk. You could've easily said what you wanted to say ten months ago when you asked for a divorce. We've had little conversation, haven't slept in the same bed, and spend time with the kids separately. I'm still paying all the bills and working two jobs while you spend the day doing anything you want to do. You should've spent some of that time filing for a legal separation since you're the one who asked for it."

"I have been a housewife the whole time we've been married. Our deal was for me to take care of the house and the kids. I've done that. Tony and Lorraine are pursuing their careers. I am left with no job and no money. I need you to agree to give me half of your retirement, business, bank accounts, and investments. I deserve it," Angelic stated in a wearisome tone.

"That was our deal since you didn't want to work. Your mother told me in front of you that her daughter didn't see her work and deserves a man who will work and care for her. The Bible says that man shall work while the woman gives birth to children. Tony and Lorraine have been on their own for the past six years. What have you been doing all this time? You could've gone to school, learned a trade, opened a business, or helped operate my business. But you chose to lay around at home, cook and clean less, withhold sex, and walk around with an attitude."

Ralph sighed and looked at his grease-stained fingers for a moment, then went on . . . "Now, because I have to work to pay the bills, I am getting back under this car to repair it so its owner can pay me tomorrow. You can go to the courthouse right now to file the legal separation; otherwise, I am going just as soon as this car is repaired." Ralph rolled back under the car to monitor the oil flow into the oil pan.

The words stung Angelic like five crossbow arrows. Calmly, she walked close to the car, placing her hips by the jack. "Ralph, you won't need to go to the courthouse. I'll handle all matters for you." She briefly fantasized about bumping the car and crushing Ralph, but she thought about the number of objects she'd already touched. Her fingerprints would be everywhere.

"Well, I'm glad you will busy yourself with that at least. Now we also agreed to tell the children together. We agreed peacefully to drive to Tony's apartment tomorrow night for dinner. Lorraine will be there. We can tell them about the divorce together. Now, if you will excuse me, I have a car to finish repairing,"

Angelic thought to herself, *It'll be the last car you'll repair.*

36

If You Love Me,
Then You'll . . .

Booker and Angelic just finished their second round of lovemaking at the One-Night Motel. Angelic was gazing at the alarm clock, hypnotized in the afterglow as Booker lay asleep with his penis inside her. Countee and his woman of the night left thirty minutes earlier to get something to eat. She shifted her body gently and purposefully, causing Booker to moan. She quickly closed her eyes. "Baby," Booker yawned as he slowly pulled his penis out.

"Hey, Honey. It looked like someone needed a nap," Angelic softly stated.

"Yeah, you made me put in a workout tonight," Booker admitted somnolently. "Where's Countee?"

"He and his girl went to eat. This is a perfect time for us to discuss the plan to get rid of Ralph. We need this $450,000 to start our lives together."

"So what were you thinking about?"

"We are supposed to go to my son Tony's house for dinner tomorrow night around 7 p.m. I will drive. You know where the four-way-stop sign at the intersection of Brown and Wyles Street off Highway 18 is?"

"Yeah, that's near the Haynes' grocery store, on the right."

"That's right. So I'll stop at Brown Street while you wait at Wyles Street. It'll take thirty minutes from my house to get there. I'll leave promptly at 6 p.m. so you can arrive five minutes before."

"Okay, so what do you suggest happens next?" Booker asked, intrigued by the plan so far.

"Then, I would flash my lights twice at your vehicle to signal you to turn left from Wyles onto Brown. As you turn, you block my car and go onto the passenger side. Tell Ralph it is a robbery, and you promptly shoot him, run to your car, and scurry off."

"It's not a bad plan, but I think I need another person to ride with me. He can be the driver while I carry out the shooting. He needs to be someone who needs money and will keep his mouth shut," Booker suggested.

"We have to do this tomorrow night, so you have to think fast. I think it needs to be someone who doesn't know you or me. Someone who will do the job for $1000 cash. Now, I can provide you with an untraceable gun, but you need to provide the person," Angelic reasoned.

"Then I need to see Reynaldo. He hangs out on the south side of the ghetto. About twenty years ago, he was in and out of prison for a variety of crimes, including murder or being an accomplice. Now, he works a 9-to-5 job but recruits hitmen for a fee. I'll tell him I need a guy to ride with me," Booker plotted.

"So once you pay Reynaldo, you'll also have to pay the gunman?" Angelic reasoned.

"Yes, after receiving payment, Reynaldo will tell me how to find the gunman. I'll ask him if he can send Quincy with me. I'll shoot Ralph so that we won't have to pay Quincy as much money."

"OK—as long as you can trust Quincy and Reynaldo. I have to make sure I have my story straight with the police since they will be asking me questions," Angelic thought out loud.

"Just tell them that someone tried to carjack Ralph and you, and you escaped by driving off after you heard gunshots," Booker suggested.

"I think we need to make it more convincing. I know this is quite a risk, but it is one worth taking. You have to shoot me too." Angelic nearly surprised herself when she announced it.

"Baby, I can't shoot you. I'd never forgive myself."

"It's not like you would kill me, Booker. After you shoot Ralph in the head and heart, if necessary, I need you to shoot me on the outside of my left thigh. It will be just a flesh wound. I need it done since the police would be asking me all sorts of questions and looking at me as a possible suspect. If I am shot, then the two of you can ride to the nearest payphone and call the police, disguising your voice. You can park away from the payphone. Make the call last less than 20 seconds, telling the 911 operator that the police need to come out to the location because a car is running and the people in it look slumped. Hang up the phone. I'll be taken to Saint Daniels' Hospital, a mile away south of Wyles' Street. Come to the hospital with Countee about two or three hours after the incident and have him inquire about me. I know Countee, and you are close, but don't tell him about this plan."

Insulted, Booker replied, "The fewer people that know, the better. Countee won't know a thing." Booker maintained a calm disposition that even surprised himself. "Show me where on your thigh you want me to shoot."

Angelic threw the duvet back and grabbed some skin from the side of her mid-thigh. "Shoot me right in between where I have grabbed the skin." Angelic pointed out.

"OK, let's get out of bed. I have to find Reynaldo, an unregistered gun, a getaway car, and a man to ride with me within less than 24 hours." Booker threw back the duvet and sat on the edge of the bed. "I'll meet you tomorrow at 6:30 p.m. at the intersection of Wyles and Brown."

"Baby, tomorrow will be the start of us being closer to marriage," Angelic softly stated.

Booker stood up and stretched. "Well, Mrs. Soon-to-Be Booker Johnson, we're going to take a shower together so your soon-to-be husband can execute his part of the plan. Now get up and come join me, girl," Booker stated playfully.

Angelic quickly ran towards the bathroom in the spirit of a giddy schoolgirl. Booker moved quickly behind her, grabbing her by the waist as she gave a hilarious scream.

37

Stealing to Survive

It was a sunny Saturday morning when Bart was cooking breakfast for the other eight boys in the house. His love of trying out new recipes and cooking meals complete with starch, vegetables, and sometimes dessert earned him the reputation as the best cook in the house. He took cooking seriously, especially since he felt he was protecting and providing for them. He socialized with the boys without allowing the boys to get to know him. He was still attending high school and working twenty hours a week at A & P grocery store Monday through Friday. He knew his days were numbered being in the group home since he would age out when he turned eighteen in a year. He was saving money to either go to college or get an apartment. Either way, the minimum wage of $3.35 an hour just wasn't enough. None of the other boys who were old enough to work held jobs; their parents sent money for them each week. Their parents would also visit, take them out, and hug them upon leaving. That was not the case for Bart, who hadn't seen Booker or Dreama for some time.

Within that time frame, Rodney told Bart that Booker was coming to visit on two different occasions, and he never actually showed up. The first time, Bart waited outside on the porch for six hours, longing for the other boys to see that a family member cared about seeing him. He was too embarrassed to walk back into the group home. The second time, Bart waited outside for eight hours in cold weather. He never let the other boys see him upset. He didn't want to form bonds with them only for them to disappear from his life, as people had done before.

Today was the third time Rodney had shared that Booker was coming to visit Bart at 3 p.m. Bart was not expecting Booker to come, and he wouldn't wait around for him. "Tell Booker that if he wants to see me, he can come to the A & P store," Bart stated indifferently.

"Booker is still your father. You need to refer to him as your daddy, not by Booker," Rodney reprimanded.

"He hasn't acted like my father in any part of my life. You do not know what hell I've had to endure living with him. And now that he makes promises to visit and doesn't keep them. You never did tell me why he didn't show up the first two times, yet you want to tell me why I need to refer to him as my daddy? I don't have a father," Bart stated resolutely.

"He assured me two days ago he was coming. I will call him now and place the call on speaker to confirm. It is best that you just listen," Rodney challenged.

"Call him. I will not say a word. But I can tell you now that you are wasting your time," Bart shared his annoyance.

The phone rang three times before Agnes answered. "Hi, Mrs. Johnson; this is Rodney with the Sentajo Group Home. Is Booker there?"

"Make what you have to say quick," Agnes quipped. "Booker! Come get the phone. It's Rodney from the Home."

Bart looked at the time as he sat in Rodney's office. It was 1:38 p.m. Bart knew that even if Booker started driving now, he would not arrive until close to 6 p.m.

Booker spoke quickly without waiting for a telephone greeting: "Hey Rodney, I won't be able to come up there tonight to visit Bart. I meant to call you before, but so much is happening. I'll call you again next week. Goodbye."

The click prompted Rodney to look at the stone-faced Bart and say, "I guess I can understand how you feel."

"His words and actions have made it clear that he never wishes to see me again. Now, if you will excuse me, I have to get to work. It is a 15-minute walk," Bart said, repressing his temper.

"I can take you to work. I'm so sorry, Bart. It is the least I can do to help."

"It's ok. I need to walk just to get some fresh air. I'll be back tonight at 8 p.m. I have to do some studying for my chemistry test tomorrow." Bart grabbed his coat and stormed across the yard to the main road.

As he walked on the left side of the road, he held his head down. *God, I don't have anyone that loves me. I don't have a family. It hurts me to be alone in this world with no one by my side. Booker is such a disappointment as a father; Dreama is nowhere to be found. Warren is surrounded by a family that loves him. I just want to kill myself. I wouldn't be missed anyway,* Bart cried profusely. Just then, he spotted an 18-wheeler truck coming in his direction. *"I may as well step in front of the truck to end it all. If I am wrong, God, please forgive me. I am ready to go,* Bart pronounced, then walked into the middle of the road to wait.

The driver honked the horn three times, and the truck's lights got brighter as it approached Bart. Bart braced himself for the hit. The driver turned left into the Creeklight Gas Station, annoyed that it took three honks for the taxicab to unblock the entrance. *Well, God, I guess it is not time for me to go,* Bart concluded as he walked back to the left shoulder of the road.

—⚏—

"Bart, I need you on register four," Rhonda Witfield, the manager at the A&P, directed. Bart was a favorite cashier at the store among customers and management. It was the fourth straight month Bart held the lead for being the fastest cashier. "Register four is now open," Rhonda announced. Bart greeted customers, asked them about their lives, secretly received tips, and smiled for five hours. Close to the end of his shift, Bart noticed the register's drawer held too much money for it to shut completely. Bart casually grabbed 30 one-dollar bills to make the drawer close and placed them in his pocket. He figured the store wouldn't miss it and muttered to himself, "I'll add this to what I'm saving so that when I turn 18, I'll be able to get an apartment."

Little did Bart know, Rhonda had noticed for the past three months that Bart's drawer was consistently short between $10 and $40. She was allowed to write off the losses per company policy, but the losses were adding up. She deemed it best that Bart did not know she was watching. She reasoned that other cashiers would use the same register sometimes, so she couldn't be certain that Bart was causing the shortage. *I have to get the Loss Prevention Department involved,* Rhonda thought to herself.

38

The Carjacking

Angelic's blue-jean knee-high dress and red three-inch heels made her feel like she was auditioning to be on the cover of a magazine. She checked her makeup with her compact in the driver's seat of her white 1978 Volkswagen. "If I am going to get shot tonight, I have to be at least beautiful," Angelic reasoned.

Ralph walked towards her car. "Angelic, you never drive when you and I ride together. All of a sudden, you want to drive tonight?" Ralph wondered as he stood by the driver's door.

"Ralph, it is not time to argue over pettiness. I am in the mood to drive. Get in the car. We do not want to be late; we should've left ten minutes ago," Angelic dryly stated.

With a heavy sigh, Ralph complied.

Angelic drove above the speed limit to make up for lost time; she even ran two lights.

"You are always late for everything. Why are you endangering us by driving fast and even running stop lights?" Ralph asked nervously.

"You and I are in the car in very close proximity, the closest we have been in a long time. I'm in a hurry to get you out of this car," Angelic retorted.

"I could've driven my car, Angelic, and left you to drive as fast as you wanted. Being with you is not a physical experience I'm treasuring," Ralph replied.

"Well, we are still showing our young adult children we can get along. That's why we are riding together, so just shut up about it and enjoy the ride. We will be at Tony's within 15 minutes," Angelic replied as she saw a white rusted Ford Grenada stopped at the four-way intersection of Wyles and Brown streets.

She slowed the Volkswagen down to a complete stop and flashed her bright lights twice to signal the Ford Grenada to move forward. The driver of the Ford Grenada slowly made a left from Brown onto Wyles Street. During the mid-turn, the driver quickly turned in front of the Volkswagen, blocking it from moving forward.

Two men in all-black coveralls quickly emerged from the driver and passenger sides. Ralph loudly whispered, "Angelic, back this car up."

Angelic, pretending not to hear Ralph, screamed.

"BITCH, BACK THIS CAR UP!" Ralph yelled.

Within seconds, Ralph and Angelic found the doors open. "Give me all your money NOW!" A rifle was pointed at Ralph, while a semi-automatic was pointed at Angelic.

Ralph was dumbfounded as he reached for his wallet. Something about this man was all too familiar. "Look, man, please don't hurt us. We will do anything you say."

"Hurry up, ma'am. We don't have all day," the second gunman said. Angelic tossed her purse to the man, and the contents fell out all over the seat while Ralph looked on nervously.

"Now, slowly get out of the car, man!"

"If something happens, Angelic, just know that . . ." Ralph stated nervously as he reached for the doorknob.

"SHUT UP, RALPH!"

"What? You know me!" Ralph quickly said, looking the man up and down. "This is a setup! I know that it is you, Booker Joh . . ."

The gunshot reverberated off the side of the dilapidated building in the wooded area as one bullet was released into the middle of Ralph's forehead. The bullet exited the rear of his head. He was dead instantly.

Booker gazed at Ralph's open eyes and mouth as Angelic called Ralph's name three times. Finally, Quincy, Booker's accomplice, called Booker's name. Booker shook his head twice.

"Quincy, get the bullet from the backseat," Angelic calmly directed.

Quincy attempted to shift Ralph's slumped body to lean the seat slightly forward as Ralph's blood gushed onto Quincy's clothes and splattered on his shoes. Booker's failed attempt to help yielded the same result.

"It'll be better for you to get out of the driver's seat so I can climb through the back. We don't need to move your husband's body," Quincy advised. Angelic obliged. Quincy scurried to retrieve the bullet just as Angelic was outside of the door. He dragged the blood-soaked bullet through the grass before placing it in a brown paper bag. Angelic got back in the car after looking over Ralph's body once more.

"Booker, hurry up and shoot me in my upper outer thigh. The bullet will exit from my inner thigh. Y'all have to get out of here before other cars come," Angelic rushed.

"Ok, baby. Here goes." Booker took one shot reluctantly. Angelic winced in pain as she doubled over the steering wheel. "Damn, that shit burns!"

"Baby, you ok?" Booker nearly screamed as he ran to her side.

"I'm fine. Now get the bullet and just go to the payphone to call the police!" Booker instantly retrieved the bullet from underneath the driver's door.

As Booker and Quincy ran back to the getaway car, Quincy told Booker, "Look, man, you are going to cough up some money for my time. You hired me to kill, not to be an accomplice."

"You will get your money from Reynaldo. Hell, I did all the hard work. All you did was point a weapon," Booker retorted.

"You will pay me, and Reynaldo will pay me the $2000 we agreed on," Quincy sharply advised.

"Don't worry about that right now. You'll get it when we get the life insurance payout. We have to take off these coveralls and shoes when we get to the gas station! We can leave the vehicle at the abandoned junkyard on Plank Road."

Booker and Quincy quickly left the scene of the crime; as Angelic thought seconds before passing out, *I just became $450,000 richer.*

39

This Wasn't Part of the Plan

Angelic awakened to a nurse's voice as she was inserting a needle in her arm. "You are really lucky to be alive, ma'am," the blonde-haired, oval-faced nurse softly shared. Her blue eyes hovered over her rectangular glasses as she spoke to Angelic, who was convinced that the nurse had more information that she chose not to reveal. You have been out of surgery for four hours now. Through dental records, we were finally able to identify you positively. "The doctor will be with you in a moment,"

Angelic thought to herself, "Whew! I'm glad that went off without a hitch. I hope Booker and Countee aren't in the lobby already." Angelic then reflected on what the doctor may say: "I bet she is going to tell me that Ralph is dead. I'll have to muster tears from somewhere. Anyway, I'll contact the insurance company as soon as I know when I am released. Let me see which soap opera I'm going to watch today."

As she propped herself up, Angelic realized that she could not feel her legs. "Maybe they are just numb for now," she considered. As she was channel surfing, Dr. Harrell walked in.

Without exchanging pleasantries, Angelic said, "Doctor, I need something for my legs. I tried to prop myself up on the bed, but I could not feel my legs. Perhaps they are just numb."

"You were shot in your lower back, Mrs. Custon. The bullet hit the nerves around your spine, causing a spinal cord injury and thus caused your paralysis from the waist down," the doctor stated.

"NO, NO, Doctor. It can't be!" Angelic shrilled. "Surely you can give me something to make them move again. Doctor, please!" She grabbed the doctor's coat lapels as tears fell.

"I have already written you a referral to undergo physical therapy," the doctor continued. "You can still live a full life, although you will have to be in a wheelchair for the rest of your life. I know this is a lot to hear all at once. Now, just relax. You are going to be just fine. It is time for your second dosage of medicine. I'll send the nurse to administer it. We have asked law enforcement to help us contact your next of kin since we were unsure if you would make it. You can inform the nurse and law enforcement when they arrive."

"Doctor, you need to run more tests or write me a prescription. Hey, I know. Maybe I should get a second opinion. DOCTOR, GIVE ME SOME OPTIONS!"

"I know you are angry. You do not want to raise your blood pressure. Our medical team examined you thoroughly. I am sorry."

As the doctor walked out of the room, Angelic saw the doctor was stopped by a female and a man dressed in a beige long-trench coat. When the doctor pointed to Angelic's room, she figured they were the investigators who would ask her for Tony and Lorraine's contact information and questions about the robbery. They will likely inform her that Ralph is dead. She decided to close her eyes to feign her attempt to rest, hoping they wouldn't ask too many questions.

"Mrs. Custon, we are with the Catticoro Police Department and are here to ask you a few questions. How are you feeling today?" the gap-toothed, red-haired officer asked, her speech soothing and empathic.

"I'm a bit groggy, I guess, from the medicine, but I may be paralyzed and need to rest," Angelic responded weakly. "What do you want to ask?"

The officer promptly responded, "May we have the contact information of your next of kin?" Angelic freely provided Tony and Lorraine's addresses and phone numbers.

"Thank you. We will contact them after we ask you a few questions. Can you tell us what you remember about the shooting at the intersection of Wyles and Brown Streets? Give us every detail," the burly, thick-mustached detective requested.

"I was driving, and my husband was the passenger. When I stopped at the intersection of Brown and Wyles' streets, these four men with masks emerged from the cornfield, pointing guns at us and demanding money. I sat in absolute shock as Ralph was trying to negotiate with one of the shooters. The next thing I know, I wake up in the hospital . . . That's it!" Angelic shared, wincing from the pain she was feeling.

"Can you describe the voices of the men? Do you remember their approximate height or weight?"

"Everything happened so fast. Only one of the men spoke. His voice was deep. He was the one who shot me. He looked to be about 5 five 9 inches, weighing 195 pounds or so. The other three men followed his lead without saying a word like it was organized. They were all dressed in black, wearing black gloves and ski masks. The other three men may have been around 6 feet 3 to 6 feet 5 inches. I can't tell you anymore about their physical characteristics," Angelic answered with fatigue.

"What kind of vehicle were they driving, ma'am?" the officer asked gingerly.

"It was a red Ford truck that was rusty," Angelic managed to say softly.

"Thank you for the information. We can tell that you need some rest. We do have to inform you that . . ."

"Oh, please tell me where my husband Ralph is. Is he okay? Have you talked to him?" Angelic interjected to feign interest in Ralph's whereabouts.

He shook his head before he said, "Well, ma'am, we're sorry to report that your husband didn't make it." Angelic immediately started thinking about her being paralyzed for the rest of her life. She started to murmur, "No, no! It can't be . . ." She gradually started yelling and wailing loudly.

Before the detective could get the doctor, a nurse came in and injected a sleeping agent in her left arm.

"We are going to have to interview her once she's out of the hospital. The information she just gave tells us nothing. There are no bullets at the scene of the crime. We are going to have to go to the news to ask the public to come forward if there were witnesses," the detective stated as he walked down the corridor with the officer.

"I don't know why someone would set up an execution-style killing of Mr. Custon but not Mrs. Custon. Do you think he had any enemies?" the officer asked.

"He owned his own business, was married for over twenty years, went to church regularly, had two adult children, and worked at Chev Mills. He doesn't have a criminal record. It just doesn't sound like he had any enemies. That's what we immediately found on Mr. Custon. We need to look into Mrs. Custon's background. I just sense we need to look closer to home," the detective confirmed.

"We've combed through the intersection of Wyles and Brown Streets, and all we've found so far was smeared blood in the grass, which we are testing," the officer added. "We had the intersection closed for the past five hours, attempting to find something that could give us a lead. We didn't even find any bullets. The captain radioed that he would open the streets shortly."

"In my thirty years of law enforcement, I have never found any evidence at the crime scene. I don't recommend that we put this in the news. We don't want to alarm the community since we just don't have enough information," the detective said as they walked towards the hospital's exit doors. "Now that we know who she is, we will have to notify her children."

Just then, Booker and Countee walked in. Booker was dressed in a navy blue suit and carried a teddy bear with a heart symbol on its chest. Countee was dressed in black clergyman garb, but he was not sure whom they would visit since Booker kept it from him. Countee went to the restroom, while Booker went to the patient-services desk, waiting in line to ask to see Angelic.

"Ma'am, we do not have a patient named Miranda Miller at this hospital," said the White-haired receptionist slowly. "I know it is the third hospital you have called, ma'am, but I am sorry. She is not here." The receptionist placed her left hand on the receiver and turned to Booker: "I'll be with you in just a moment, sir."

"No hurry, ma'am. Take your time," Booker politely stated.

Booker turned to look at a few of the brochures at the receptionist's desk only to faintly hear Angelic's name mentioned by two individuals at the hospital's entrance. They also mentioned the shooting and Brown Street. "I bet those two are undercover cops."

"My apologies, sir, for taking so long to assist you. Who are you here to see?" the receptionist stated cheerfully.

"Uh, I'd like to see Janice Smith. I understand she is a patient here," Booker mentioned out of caution. He saw her name on the receptionist's checkout list for the week.

"Sir, Janice Smith checked out two days ago," the receptionist confirmed.

"Ok, thank you."

Countee walked up to Booker as he walked away from the receptionist's desk. "You brought me here to minister to someone but never told me who? Why are we walking back out?"

Booker felt certain that the officer and detective had heard part of Countee's questions. He wanted to nudge him to keep his mouth shut. "Janice Smith is not here, so maybe we could go by her home to visit," Booker said patiently as they walked past the officer and detective standing by the exit doors.

The police officer asked the detective, "Did you hear any part of the conversation between the receptionist and the Black man as he asked about a patient named Janice Smith?"

"I heard a portion of the conversation. The man had the wrong location, apparently. What made you ask?"

"Janice Smith was badly beaten by her fiancé over being jealous of another man. I just wondered if he was the fiancé since he fits the general description. I know that Janice Smith is a common name, but we need to make sure he's not the guy we're looking for. I'll get his license plate number and run it." The officer wrote down the information just as Booker and Countee drove by. "Let's see what we can find out about this man," the detective suggested.

40

From Bad to Worse

It was Sunday morning. Vanessa set the breakfast table complete with a white tablecloth, freshly picked daisies, and white-cloth napkins. The menu consisted of fried bacon, buttered grits, scrambled eggs, wheat toast, and freshly squeezed orange juice.

"Darling, breakfast is ready," Vanessa called.

Countee came dashing down the steps in well-worn blue slippers, red sports shorts, and a white t-shirt. "Good morning, my love. Breakfast really smells good. I can't wait to eat." Countee gave Vanessa a quick kiss on her cheek.

"Today's breakfast is really special because you have become really special to me during the course of our marriage. Sit down at the table so I can tell you more," Vanessa cheerily stated.

Countee obeyed and looked at her as she was preparing their plates. He thought to himself, "I have a good woman. I really need to do more to be a better man to her."

"Here we are," Vanessa stated in a high-pitched soft tone as she placed the plates on the table. She went back to get the orange juice before sitting down and saying grace.

"What made you cook breakfast an hour earlier, honey? It is 8 am. We don't have to be at church until 10:45 am," Countee asked.

"Well, I wanted some pastoral advice," Vanessa calmly stated.

"Ok, I am your husband and pastor. What kind of advice do you need?"

"I want you to listen to a portion of this cassette, and then I'll ask you questions." Vanessa pressed 'Play' as Countee took two bites of bacon before dropping it back on his plate, unable to swallow.

Vanessa slowly chewed her food while watching the Countee's reaction as he heard the sexual acts he was performing on women and conversations with the women on how much their services cost. Vanessa stopped the cassette tape and then crossed her arms. Nervously, Countee stated with apprehension, "Whose voices are on the tape?" Countee's mind was flooded with wondering how much Vanessa knew and how the hell she got a recording.

"Now, now, Countee darling. Surely you know whose voices those are. I'm focusing on the voice that's been patronizing the One-Night Motel. In fact, I even was there one night dressed in a tawdry outfit, hoping you'd notice me, but you got a much younger woman. The next thing I see is Booker, Angelic, the younger woman, and you go into room 435 and stay longer than two hours. Were you all having another prayer session or couched meeting in a seedy motel as missionary work?" Vanessa asked sardonically.

Realizing she had absolute proof of his indiscretions, he knew he could not lie his way out. "I just made a mistake, and I'm so sorry, honey."

Vanessa replied, "Oh no, dear. You didn't *just* make a mistake. I've discovered that you've been fucking up for the past year and a half. I have more recordings of you and Booker and the sex you've had with a variety of women and what's been going on with Booker and you."

"So, what questions do you have? I am ready to be honest about everything," Countee said, trembling.

"I know all of what I need to know. This is what is going to happen. I am filing for a separation and a divorce uncontested. You will sign this house over to me. You will have one car and sign the title to the other cars for me. I will contact the creditors under which you opened credit accounts under my name to tell them that they were opened fraudulently. That is going to open an investigation involving the police department. I also get half of your pension from the church and spousal support. You are going to agree to everything I have presented, or else my attorney will go before a judge with the cassettes, AND I will ensure that your members EACH receive a copy, starting with Agnes Johnson," Vanessa commanded.

"Vanessa, baby, we can get counseling. I want to make this marriage work. I'm admitting I've done some wrong by you. Please, let's try it again. What about the church? They need to see us fight through our problems. Baby, don't leave me. We don't even have to sleep in the same bed. We just need to look like we are a happy couple so the church members can have hope," Countee pleaded.

"You hypocrite! We've been looking like we were a happy couple in front of the church members ever since the fifth year of our marriage. And I've been unhappy being married to you since then. Every wife wants to feel secure and like she is the only one. But you haven't appreciated daily home-cooked meals, total submission, active participation in your ministry, single-handedly raising our kids, ironing and washing your clothes, nor questioning your whereabouts because I put my whole trust in you, and the list goes on . . ." Vanessa maintained.

"Why did you have to do this today? You know I am preaching later today," Countee entreated, his head in his hands.

"Countee, why did you have to take me through lying, cheating, stealing, and falsifying every week for the past twenty-five years?" Vanessa pointed out. "And another thing, I am not stepping foot back into that church. I will tell the children why I have filed for a legal separation and a divorce soon after that. If I hear that you lied about why I am leaving your ass, I will provide the evidence."

"Vanessa darling— just give me another . . ."

"I no longer have the grace to stay in this marriage. And don't 'darling' me! You have put me through too much, Countee. And I am bowing out. That's the end of this conversation."

Vanessa retrieved three pre-packed suitcases from the hallway closet and placed them by the door. "You have four days to be moved out of this house, at which time you will sign the house over to me. Leave me a forwarding address. Give me everything I have outlined so we can have a quiet divorce. Today is the start of me being single."

"I will give you everything you want. I'll maintain on-time payments with the creditors. Just don't let the church know. I can't lose my church and marriage, either," Countee lamented.

"Good. I am going to stay with a friend. I'll be back in four days. My first order of business is to change the locks, so be sure you got all your things out because you won't be coming back," Vanessa warned before closing the front door.

Countee sat dumbfounded with the specially-prepared breakfast looking at him; his spirit was broken. "Church is just not going to be the same today," he thought as he cried silently.

Vanessa drove to the nearest pay phone and deposited $1.75. "Michelle, I am on the way to the airport to visit you in Texas. I finally told Countee he had four days to leave my house. I'll give you more details when I arrive, Girl!"

As Countee pulled his Cutlass Supreme into his reserved parking space, he heard Brenda leading the song *Have a Little Talk with Jesus*. After his surprise message this morning, he was an hour late, not knowing what he would preach today. He planned to preach on surviving the storm in light of the community still reeling over the loss of Ralph Custon and the hospitalization of Angelic. But he had his own personal thunderstorm and was not sure how he was going to survive it.

"Reverend, I know it's not a good time to say this, but . . ." Rosa said upon seeing Countee as he walked into his office. "You look dejected, Countee. What is going on with you?"

"I just didn't rest well last night," Countee lied. "What is it that you wanted to say?"

"Where is the First Lady?" Rosa asked curiously.

"She is going to visit some relatives out of state. Shouldn't you be in the sanctuary by now?"

"I got tired of people asking me where you were. I came into the office to call just before you walked in. I need to talk to you about something."

"Well, make it quick. I've got to pray about what I'm preaching about."

"We have $10 in the church's checking account, disconnection notices for the telephone, gas, and lights, and a tax lien on the church . . . We just have too many bills that are not being paid."

"Rosa, I can't deal with all of this right now. I have to preach shortly," the Reverend sharply stated.

"Let me tell you something, Countee," Rosa stated, trying to keep her anger under control. "You won't have a church to preach in if you don't. You will either deal with this now, or it will deal with you later—which is sooner than you think. Due to the sorry trustee board, you put in place, they have allowed you to spend as if this church has an unlimited amount of money, affording you to live in a nice house, have multiple cars, and take lavish vacations, all the while teaching the congregation that the blessing starts from the head of the church and then flows down to them."

"Rosa, you need to get out of my face now! I have had a hard morning, and I have a lot on my mind right now," the Countee's voice quivered.

"Fine Countee! Just know that the handwriting is on the wall. Nobody can tell yo' ass anything! You will be wishing for my advice when it is all said and done," Rosa scoffed as she walked past the window towards the office door. She took three steps back to look out the window as the tow truck hoisted Countee's vehicle onto the truck bed.

"Countee, are you up-to-date on your car payments?" Rosa stood with her right hand on her hip.

"The trustee board would know the answer to that question, Rosa.

Why are you asking me about my personal finances anyway?" Countee faltered.

"Well, because it looks like you're losing your car," Rosa stated as she craned her neck further towards the window.

Countee quickly ran to the window and flung the curtains away. Hastily, he said, "Rosa, have the choir sing two more songs while I go outside to handle this matter. Tell the ushers to try to stop the people from coming outside for thirty minutes. *Go!*"

Countee quickly exited his office to catch the tow truck drivers. Rosa feigned, rushing towards the sanctuary from Countee's office, but stopped in her tracks the moment Countee was out the door.

"We have a past due light bill, a past due gas bill, six months behind in the first mortgage, five months behind in the second mortgage, and people not being paid for services rendered. The bank is about to foreclose on this church, and this fool is more concerned about having the choir sing two more songs and have the ushers stop the people from going outside. I ain't doing shit. It is time the church found out about what was really going on. We have less than $10 in the bank; this has got to stop!" As soon as Countee stepped outside, the tow truck was driving off the church grounds just as the choir began to sing. *Jesus Can Work It Out*. Rosa just shook her head at the irony.

41

Holding Pattern

"You'll arrive at what time?" Rhonda asked as she shifted the phone from her left to her right ear. "We have had register shortages for the past five months, and I'm glad you are coming. I'll be sure to tell the manager. See you shortly." Rhonda breathed a sigh of relief before turning on A&P's intercom. "Pardon the announcement, shoppers. Mr. Kitchen, please come to the front office," she stated officially.

Mr. Kitchen, the store manager, approached the office heavily breathing twenty minutes after he was called. He was a 70-year-old balding White man who just wasn't ready for retirement. "Rhonda, what is it? I was lifting some boxes in the produce area and think I overdid it. Anyway, you call me for what?"

"Scott Kilwalter from the A& P Loss Prevention Department will be here in less than five minutes; he was just leaving the downtown store when I talked to him 15 minutes ago. He wants to briefly meet with you and me before he interviews the cashiers," Rhonda voiced above a whisper.

"Do we have all the cashiers here that he asked for?" Mr. Kitchen asked.

"I deliberately scheduled them to work during this time," Rhonda stated proudly as she looked down at her watch. "Looks like Scott arrived a few minutes earlier than I thought," Rhonda shared as Scott walked towards the manager's office.

After exchanging pleasantries and summarizing the missing monies, Scott was escorted to the break room to spread out some papers. Each cashier who shared a register for the first two months was interviewed one by one. Rhonda decided that Barbara, Bart, and Wendy used only their respective registers for the past two months. They were none the wiser. Rhonda knew who was taking the money but needed Scott's help to confirm.

Scott finished his interview with Barbara and Wendy at the end of their shift. He then sent word to Rhonda to send Bart to the break room. As she walked carefully to his register, an elderly customer said, "I've been coming to this store since it opened in 1936, and you have demonstrated the best customer service out of anyone who has worked here. You speak to customers very well, and you're always fast."

"Thank you so much, Ms. Jasper. Your kind words mean a lot."

Ms. Jasper turned to Rhonda as she spoke to Bart. "Is this your manager?"

"She is the assistant manager."

"I want to complete a customer survey on behalf of Bart," she told Rhonda.

"I'll be glad to get you one. We are very pleased to hear about customers' satisfaction with our service. After you complete the survey, I'll have one of the bagboys place your groceries in your car."

"Oh, that would be so wonderful," Ms. Jasper softly stated.

"So why don't you walk with me, and Bart, why don't you close your lane and take your 30-minute break?"

Bart was secretly pleased that Ms. Jasper spoke highly of him in front of Rhonda. It had been some time since he had been praised for anything. As he arrived at the breakroom, he felt uneasy. *Who is this man, and why is he here?* He quickly dismissed the thought as he put 45 cents into the drink machine and selected a Fanta Orange.

"My son likes Fanta Orange too. It has such a robust flavor," Scott stated while standing behind Bart.

"I like Fanta Orange and Fanta Grape better than other sodas," Bart replied kindly.

"Wow, so does my son. You are probably the same age as he is. How old are you?"

"17."

"He will be 17 next month. By the way, I'm Scott. What's your name?" Scott asked to make conversation.

"I'm Bart."

"Nice to meet you. How long have you been working here, Bart?"

"Almost five months."

"Well, I have a situation which I'd like you to help me work out."

"I'm glad to help."

"Won't you sit down so I can tell you all about it?"

Scott and Bart took their places at the break room bench, sitting opposite one another.

"So I have a situation that I have to solve. Two months ago, I received a call that money had been missing from registers for the past five weeks. Have you heard anything about it?"

"Rhonda has mentioned it to me once," Bart nervously answered.

"Well, I asked her, 'Who was the only person on the register on the following dates' that I'll show you here. Tell me whose name you see."

Scott presented Bart with a paper with 18 dates; the dollar amounts for the register were short, the times the register was counted, and who was working on that register. Bart's name was listed 18 times by each date.

"So, Bart, how many times do you see your name listed by each date? Go ahead, count them," Scott coerced.

"18," Bart replied nervously.

"Yes, and the amount of missing money totals how much according to the information at the bottom?"

"$1872."

"Correct again. Since it was your register, shift, and shortage, how do you think the money became missing?" Scott asked, crossing his arms as he looked directly into Bart's eyes.

"I don't know what happens to the money when the register is turned over to management," Bart responded, his face flushed with embarrassment.

"But what management knows is that each time since you've been working here, your register would likely come up short," Scott's voice projected. "'Bart, if we have to get law enforcement to investigate each day you've worked, the banking deposits you've made, and search your bedroom at the group home where you are staying, then that is what I will have to do."

Bart became teary-eyed. Thoughts of the police frightened him, and the idea of going to jail frightened him more. He didn't know what to do. "Jesus, help me," Bart managed to muster above a whisper.

"Jesus is here, and He wants you to tell the truth," Scott stated reverently.

"I took the money," Bart sobbed.

Scott handed Bart his handkerchief, which Bart declined as he wiped his face with his hands.

"Now, you know that today is your last day working here at A & P. You will be notified at the group home about the next steps. You are to exit through the delivery doors so you are not seen leaving. You are also banned from being on the grounds of any A&P stores throughout the country. I wish you the best." Scott extended his right hand to shake Bart's hand, but Bart quickly turned to escape the humiliation and interrogation A&P's break room represented.

Bart sat in the prisoner dock of the courtroom, reflecting on the events that led him there, hoping that he would be released today after being in jail for four months since he had no one to call to post bail. He thought about when he was permitted to spend the night at Sean's aunt and uncle's home. The moment Bart met them, they insisted he call them Aunt Jo and Uncle

Leroy. He considered them the cool family who gave free rein for Sean and Bart to watch, do, and eat anything they wanted.

But that ended three weeks after he was fired from A&P. He was arrested at the group home and immediately taken to the juvenile detention center. Rodney was quick to call Booker to let him know, but Booker told Agnes so that she would spread the news.

"Don't be surprised if you see Bart on the news for stealing $30,000; he probably did it so that he could go to prison just to be around men," Agnes shared with the church and community in the name of getting them to pray for her since she is going through tribulation for the cause of Christ.

He had been in one fight in which he broke the boy's arm. No one else bothered him. He enjoyed going to church; the missionary group members, especially Mr. Hayes, had been really kind to him.

Bart's thoughts were interrupted when he heard his name called. Once he stood beside his attorney, Judge Moses Kravitz said monotonously, "Susan West, you are the public defender representing Bart Johnson for the embezzlement charge."

"Yes, I am your honor."

"This is case number 86725. Your client is accused of one count of embezzlement. How does your client plead?"

"Guilty."

"The amount reportedly embezzled was $3742, which is punishable by two years in prison. The bail is still set at $12000."

"Your honor, the embezzled amount is $1872, according to what A&P's loss prevention officer presented to my client and what was shared in open court when my client was arrested three weeks ago."

"Then we need to be certain of the amount before we proceed. Does the defendant have the means to pay ten percent of the bail?"

"No, he does not, your honor. He has no family and no resources. I am petitioning that his bail is reduced."

"The request is granted. Please provide me with documentation of the actual amount the defendant owes. The bail has been reduced to $5000.

The defendant's next court date is three weeks from today at 9 am. The defendant is remanded in custody and returned to the county jail. Next case," the judge swiftly spoke.

"Does it mean I am getting out?" Bart asked anxiously.

"No, Bart, it does not. What it means is that your bail has been reduced. Instead of someone having to pay $1200 to get you out of jail, the person would only have to pay $500. Try your best to call someone to get you out. I'll work on getting a certified letter of what you owe to A&P.

I'll see you again in a few weeks. Hang in there."

Bart tried to make sense of all he heard when the officer reached for his elbow. "Back to jail, you go," the officer stated drily. As the officer escorted Bart down the corridor, he heard a hymn being sung from the jail's chapel. Bart asked, "May I sit in the chapel?" The officer walked Bart into the chapel without saying a word, making him the tenth inmate among twelve missionaries in the sanctuary.

The small chapel had several pews and did not indicate any particular religion. Before he left, the officer informed the men, "Today, our missionaries want to talk with you and pray with each of you. The warden has given us one hour. Feel free to share your stories; you matter to God," the minister announced as he paired each inmate with a missionary. Since just a few inmates were in attendance, the minister had the men spread out so the conversations would not be overheard.

Bart was paired with James Hayes, a deacon at the Seventh Baptist Church. James was one of the seasoned missionaries who gravitated towards Bart from the first time they met four months ago. James and his wife even remembered Bart when they visited Reverend Allison's church years ago. James admitted to Bart that he and his wife were saddened over how he and Dreama were treated during that one-time visit.

James was six feet tall, slim-built, caramel-skinned, and had a head full of salt-and-pepper hair. Bart grew to trust him completely because James treated him nonjudgmentally. James and his wife Darlene even accepted Bart's collect calls every day. Over the four months he was incarcerated,

James even brought Darlene and each of their nine children to the jail to minister to Bart and the other inmates.

"Bart, you look like you've been working out, son," James greeted him fondly.

Bart embraced being acknowledged as James' son. He knew that older men in James' generation called all boys sons because they saw the family as a village.

"I have been doing 150 push-ups and sit-ups each day," Bart said proudly.

"I'm proud that you're staying in shape. I know you were in court today because I asked a guard about you when the missionaries arrived. What did they say in court?"

"The judge lowered my bail, but I have to go back to jail. They have to get a letter from A&P about how much money I owe them, and then I go back to court again. My attorney tried to help me make sense of all of this," Bart admitted.

"Well, the lowering of the bail is good news. Is the issue that your mother and father do not have the money to get you out of jail?" James asked softly.

"I don't really have a family. My father dropped me off in a group home, and my mother left South Carolina and disappeared. There is no one I can call," Bart sadly stated.

"I know that you told my wife and me about your parents and the abuse you underwent. We even suspected it years ago when we visited Reverend Allison's church. I just figured that your parents would at least get you out of jail. As a parent, it's hard for me to imagine leaving my child in jail," James softly stated as he placed his right hand on Bart's right shoulder.

"I wish I had a dad and a mom who cared a little about me. I don't have anybody who loves me," Bart whispered, tears rolling down his cheeks.

James was moved so deeply that he also teared up. "Jesus loves you, and so do my wife and I. I'll tell you what—my wife and I will get you out of jail. You won't have to go back to the group home. You can live with us until after your court case; then, we can work on getting you some counseling. I will be there when you have your next court case," James consoled. "Just remain patient a little longer."

"It feels good to hear that. I know Jesus loves me, and thank you for showing your love. I thank God for sending you. I love you too," Bart mumbled as he continued to cry.

"Alright, it is time for us to go. I hope that everyone was moved and touched by the ministering of God's Word. We will be back to fellowship with all of you in two weeks. Let us grab hands and pray," the minister requested. As Bart grabbed James' hand, it marked the first time anyone treated him with complete care. "*God, I pray that you richly bless Mr. James and Mrs. Darlene for helping me out of this mess I got myself into,*" Bart prayed.

Bart was in a positive mood, excited about life even though he was in court. He mentally replayed his interactions with James repeatedly. He felt like he mattered since he had someone who loved, visited, and prayed over him. His thoughts were broken as he saw James, Darlene, and their nine children walk into court. James' smile greeted Bart as the family sat down.

"Docket number 45175 A&P versus Bartholomew Johnson. Bartholomew, please stand," announced Judge Brasswell, a white-haired, round-faced man whose flourished face always looked embarrassed. "Do you have an attorney? You do have a right to an attorney."

"Your honor, may I approach the podium," a well-dressed attorney asked.

"Yes, you may. Please state your name for the court."

"I am Donny Faraway, attorney for Bartholomew Johnson. I am here to request his release and the conditions of his release."

"Mr. Faraway, please approach the bench," the judge invited.

As they spoke in hushed tones, Bart looked at James with a camouflaged smile, expressing his thanks for doing what he said he would do. James' half smile reassured Bart that all would be well.

"I hereby order the release of Bartholomew Johnson. The conditions of his release are as follows: He is ordered to make monthly restitution to the court of the monies he admitted to taking from A&P. He must perform fifty hours of community service and be on probation for three months. Failure to complete any of these orders will result in a two-year sentence. If you complete these terms in their entirety, you will not have the charges posted on your record under youth adjudication," the judge stated monotonously. "Further, the charge of felony embezzlement has been reduced to misdemeanor larceny." Looking at Bart, the judge asked, "Mr. Johnson, do you have any questions?"

"No," Bart voiced happily.

"We have the Sentajo Group Home address on file for you. Is this the correct address?"

Before Bart could answer, James called out, "No, it is not the correct address."

"Sir, would you please stand beside Attorney Faraway and please state your name for the court," the judge asked.

"I am James Hayes. I filed for guardianship over Bartholomew Johnson two weeks ago. His probation officer can come to our home to monitor Bartholomew's compliance with the court."

"Ah, yes. We received the documents," the judge shared as he shuffled papers. He then asked for Mr. Faraway and James to approach the bench. He asked about Bart's parents, detailed what guardianship means, and what would happen if Booker or Dreama filed a case to resume custody of Bart.

As Mr. Faraway and James walked back to the podium, the judge shared, "I hereby order the release of Bartholomew Johnson and that James and Darlene Hayes have guardianship over him. Bartholomew is to report to his probation officer tomorrow morning and follow the conditions previously outlined by this court. Next case."

Bartholomew cried tears of joy as he was escorted out of court. *I am getting out of jail and going home to Mr. Hayes' family. God, please help me not to do anything that would lead them to kick me out of their house. I'll be 18 soon enough. I just need to finish high school and work to get my own place. I know they are not my parents, but I promise to honor them. Help me be good,* he prayed.

Everyone in the Hayes family interacted well with Bart. He was loved, chastised, and assigned chores just like the other nine children. He even attended the same church. Bart was pleased when he overheard people saying he was James Hayes's secret son. The family ensured Bart eventually completed all the court requirements to get off probation.

Six months later, the family celebrated Bart's 18th birthday with a cook-out, including plenty of ribs, hamburgers, hot dogs, and cake. James and Darlene's siblings and spouses attended. Bart was so excited; it was his first birthday party.

"May I have everyone's attention, please!" James piped into the microphone as he held Darlene's hand. "It is with great pleasure that we celebrate Bart's 18th birthday. Y'all know he has been a part of our household for over six months. We have grown to love him. He's never given us a moment of pain or regret being in our home."

Turning to Bart, James said, "Bart, we know the circumstances under which you have come to us. I have asked a family friend, Attorney Sarah Gains, to join us today because she is going to help us offer you a gift that our family hopes you accept. Come up here, Bart!"

The guests clapped their hands and chanted, "Happy Birthday!" as Bart walked up to James and Darlene.

"Darlene and I have spoken to Sarah about what we want to offer you. We know that you have been chosen to be in our lives. We publicly announce that we wish to adopt you legally as our son."

Bart collapsed in James' arms, causing him to drop the microphone nearly. Bart cried so profusely that James' shoulder was soaked. The guests waited patiently, some saying, "It's alright," "Get it all out," and "You have a wonderful opportunity." Bart then moved to Darlene and hugged her very tightly.

Bart was finally given the microphone and shared, "I have never been wanted by my biological family or any other family in that regard. To all members of the Hayes family, you have helped me in so many ways for which I could never repay you. I am a better person because of you. You sacrificed your time, money, and house just to ensure that I was well cared for. It is what you have done for someone who has been through so much, yet you didn't judge me for being different. It would be my honor to be your son."

There wasn't a dry eye in the crowd.

"Well, son," James said after clearing his throat, "we love having you. Darlene, do you want to say anything?"

"I feel the exact birth pains I felt when I gave birth to my other nine children, yet my tubes have been tied since the 1970s." The crowd laughed as Sarah moved towards the microphone.

"So, I already drew up the paperwork for Mr. and Mrs. Hayes. The only thing missing is your legal name and all three of your signatures. Once I have that information, I can file it with the court within an hour to make it official," Sarah said enthusiastically.

"Well, Darlene and I collaborated on what to name our children, and we did the same for you." Bart saw the document with his new name. He quickly signed it along with Darlene and James. Today, you are no longer Bartholomew Johnson; your legal name is now Montgomery Bartholomew Hayes. We will still call you 'Bart' since it is now a part of your middle name. Would everyone welcome our son Montgomery?!"

As the guests clapped and hugged him, he thought, *I will never have to go through being abandoned by a family again. I am with a family that genuinely loves me.*

42

Escaping the Reputational Baggage

Countee sat in his office of the recently named Fire Baptized Baptist Church, daydreaming about his days as pastor of Saint Elijah Baptist Church. Even after he gave Vanessa the house, half of his retirement, all of the money in all three bank accounts, all the cars, and alimony five years ago, she still spoke to Agnes Johnson about everything that happened between Countee and her. Agnes told four church members, and then the news spread like wildfire. Countee was bitter that he couldn't even confront Vanessa. Last he heard, her five children and she relocated to California, dating an up-and-coming pastor.

Countee was becoming relieved that the media was no longer flanking him at his church, studio apartment, and even the grocery store. The number of microphones surrounding him was accompanied by questions from news outlets regarding the allegations of adultery, misuse of church funds, and the murder of Ralph Custon. Countee touted to his church members that these were nothing but spiritual attacks on him, but most of the members were not convinced. His 500-member church was reduced to 32 members, most of whom were new members. He knew that to escape the reputational baggage surrounding Saint Elijah Baptist Church valiantly, he had to change the church's name. He hoped that this change also helped dust the dirt off his soiled name.

The ten members he called last week to ask them to come back only yielded one member saying she would come back. He maintained Ms. Rosa Lee as the secretary and Brenda as the soloist. He was even glad that Agnes and Author were still members. Since Angelic obtained the life insurance money from Ralph's death, Booker has been financing Countee's ministry. In exchange, Countee appointed Booker as the Associate Pastor and Angelic as head of the Deaconess Board. Booker and Angelic sold Ralph's home and business for hefty sums of money, plus they cashed out the $450,000 life insurance policies.

They taught Bible study every Wednesday night to help Countee bolster his church membership and popularity. They shared how their prosperity equates to holy living and used their lifestyle of a large house, four fancy cars, and the latest expensive 80s fashions to support their claim. They slept well at night, thinking they had gotten away with committing the perfect crime since detectives or Quincy last contacted them five years earlier.

That is until Booker, Angelic, and Warren were one day exiting their car at the Skylander Mall. "Hey, Booker!" a menacing man shouted as Booker closed the door. The moment Booker looked back, he recognized Quincy. "Warren, help Angelic to go inside the mall while I chat with this dude."

"Warren, why don't you go inside? Your daddy and I will be in shortly."

Warren noticed that the mysterious man had two others with him. Warren wasn't fazed since he was more excited that even at 25 years old, Booker was still giving him everything he wanted.

"Well, isn't this a surprise, honey? A blast from the past," Booker stated as he rolled Angelic's wheelchair towards the men, both short and scrawny. Neither Booker nor Angelic appeared nervous.

"Booker cut the bullshit! You know damn well that you owe me money for covering yo' ass while you eliminated the man who stood in the way of you and Angelic getting married. You promised to pay me my money when the insurance check arrived. I haven't seen a dime, man, and I want my money!" Quincy snarled.

"I don't owe you shit, Quincy. In fact, it turned out that I didn't even need you to get the job done. Exactly what work did you do that would justify why you should get anything?" Booker argued.

"For my time! The cops and detectives have been visiting me at my house, my mother's house, at my job, and shit. And I've told them I don't know anything about it. So you owe me for covering Angelic and *YOU!* Then I had to get some investigative help to find where y'all at! I've fallen on hard times, man. You know that Reynaldo was the one that would send me to do some jobs, but now that his best friend killed him, I ain't got no job and no money!" Quincy's voice escalated. "I ain't got time for the bullshit man!"

"Speaking of time, you are wasting ours," Angelic stated directly. "Now you were hired to do a job you did not do. So, as far as I'm concerned, you didn't work, so you didn't get paid. There is nothing else to say. And I suggest that all three of you do not wish to make a scene here," as she brandished the butt of her gun.

Turning to look at Booker, Angelic hissed, "Roll us in the mall. These gentlemen will not be bothering us anymore.

As Booker rolled Angelic towards the entrance of the mall, Quincy pondered: *Should I go to the police? Even if I have to do some prison time, I'll take pleasure in knowing that Booker and Angelic will be doing time with me.*

43

The Trek to Forgive

Bart had just ended the night shift at the Smithworthy Factory and arrived home with James and Darlene in time for breakfast.

"Ma, it really smells good. What is for breakfast this morning?" Bart asked as he greeted Darlene with a kiss on the cheek.

"Baby, I made you some pancakes, livermush, and scrambled eggs. Go wash your hands so that your daddy, you, and me can eat together before we run some errands," Darlene pleasantly stated.

After the three prayed over the food, Darlene stated, "How was work last night?"

"Oh, Ma! Guess what?" Bart remembered.

"What is it, son? Are they offering more overtime this week?" Darlene guessed.

"Well, that too. But I got an award last night for three years of quality service and never missing a day of work," Bart proudly stated.

"That's great news, Son! I'm proud of you. I'm instilling in you the value of hard work. You're a young man now. You're saving money, right?" James asked like a proud father.

"Yes, sir, I am. Next year, I want to go to a four-year college. I'd hate to stop working, but it'll work out."

"You know that we will help you in anything you want to do. The sky's the limit," James added.

"That's right, we will," Darlene added cheerfully.

"Thanks, Mom and Dad!"

"Those words sounded so good. James and I are so happy to have you in our family. I get so tickled when people ask me, 'How many children do you have?' When I replied, '10,' they were so surprised. As your parents, we will teach you and love you."

"Ma, I am the happiest I've ever been. Thanks to y'all, I finished high school, graduated community college, worked full-time, and attended church regularly. I have nine times as many siblings now. I have a place I can call home. I am the only one of your children who can say you're the best parents I ever had. I am really blessed," Bart shared in reflection.

"God chose you to be part of our family; all your brothers and sisters love you. Now, you haven't mentioned Booker or Dreama in some time. Have you heard anything from them or about them?"

"I don't really know what's going on with either of them. Last I heard, Booker remarried and lives in a big house with his new wife and my brother. Dreama left the state years ago. I really don't want to have anything to do with them. Booker has caused so much hurt in my life. I still don't know why he hated me so much. I'm not even in a place where I can forgive him. Dreama did her best, I guess, but she loved my brother more than me. But at least I knew she loved me." Bart was careful not to call Booker and Dreama 'Mom' and 'Dad' out of concern that he would offend James and Darlene.

"Bart, James, and I know that we are your parents. You are our child; there's nothing Booker, Dreama, or anyone else can do. So, it is ok to refer to Booker or Dreama by any name you wish. We are not offended," Darlene said with wisdom.

"Thanks, Ma," Bart stated as he looked down, eating the last of his pancake.

"Well, Son, God requires that we forgive; otherwise, he will not forgive us. Think about this past Sunday's message on forgiveness. Forgiveness releases you from being in emotional bondage with Booker. Unforgiveness has a way of impacting your relationships with other people. I know some unforgiving people who look for reasons to be unforgiving to others, though they don't realize it. They say, 'You remind me of my ex who acted just like you're acting,' or every dating relationship they have never worked out beyond a month since they are bitter, fault-finding, and mean to others," James coached.

"And they get a reputation for such," Darlene added. "Forgiveness gives you control and releases you from being a prisoner from whatever hurt you. You need to try it."

"Darlene, it's almost time for us to go," James mentioned after glancing at this watch. We have to get to the grocery store, then go by the hospital to visit some church members,"

"Oh yes! Let's go. But Mont, we challenge you to think about what we said. Read the chapters of Matthew 6 and 18. Then, reflect on writing a letter to Booker about your pain. By the time you get to the end of it, tell him the great things God has done. We can talk more when we get back. We love you, Honey!"

"Love y'all too."

Bart sat with paper, pen, and Bible on his twin bed, reflecting on the breakfast conversation. He said a prayer. Then wrote this letter to Booker:

Dear Mr. Booker Johnson,

I hope that all is going well for you and that you will read the contents of this letter in its entirety. I reflected on the years of physical, sexual, and mental abuse that you put me through. As far as I can remember, I worked to please and obey you out of wanting your love and approval. Oddly enough, I was like a mom. You abused her terribly, yet she stayed with you, seeking to satisfy you despite your moods at the moment. I watched how you did not allow her to get her driver's license, did not allow her to go to college for nursing, did not allow her contact with her siblings, and did not allow her to have a say in any decisions you made. She was under your absolute control.

I was under your absolute control; you'd have sex with me then openly call me faggot and sissy. Now I have to face a world that hates gay people; I survived facing you; I can survive facing them. I was so embarrassed for Mom—not so much me—but for the time the apostle called us out from the congregation only to say that we have sexual sins. She and I both covered you. To my knowledge, she's never cheated on you, yet she stood the shame of being called out and confronted you with Warren and me. You shaped my sexual identity as gay, yet I covered you by not telling anyone in the church about it. The thanks Mom got was a divorce, loss of her children, loss of reaching her siblings, and loss of the life she knew with you. There is no telling how she is living after you threw her away. She was totally submissive to you. You hated me because I reminded you of her.

You threw me away in a group home, which marked the last time I saw you when you dropped me off going on ten years ago, which was around the same time you were divorcing Mom. I remember asking myself, 'What did I do that was so terrible to make my own father place me in the group home?' Looking back, you treated Mom and me as disposable. And between Grandma and you, y'all used the Bible as a basis for spreading how evil Mom and I are and corralled the church members into believing the same thing.

Well, the good thing that came from that group home is that I met a family that loves him just as I am. Way beyond what you prophesied over my life, I graduated from a two-year college, worked a full-time job, and gained a new family. If you never placed me in that group home, I would've never met James and Darlene, who loved me through the pain you put me through, and they legally adopted me and gave me their last name. They are my parents and will support me as I attend a four-year college next year. God turned things around for me. He found it fitting for me to experience losing what I never had. I never had your love, support, rearing, or encouragement. I chased after those things from you no matter the physical, psychological, or sexual cost.

I owe it to God and myself to forgive you wholeheartedly. I have much healing to undergo, and it may take a lifetime. But God's grace is sufficient. I forgive you. I hope you will allow God's grace to transform you into the best man you can be. I love you! Bart Johnson, as you know me.

Bart cried softly as he put the pen down. He recalled Booker's last known telephone number. He placed in a code whereby James and Darlene's number would not be received prior to his nervously dialing it. *I want to make sure I have the correct address,* Bart reasoned.

"Hello."

"Warren? This is Bart."

"Hey, Bro, what's going on? Your voice has really changed since I last heard from you."

"Many things have changed since the last time you saw me."

Bart and Warren talked about classmates and recent births and deaths of people from their former church for about twenty minutes. Then Bart stated, "I have a letter to mail to Dad. Can you give me the address?"

"It's funny that you asked about that. He and Angelic left the house about five minutes prior to you calling," Warren stated just before he gave the address. "Now, if Dad asks you how you got this address, don't tell him I gave it to you."

"Don't worry, bro. I won't tell him. Just make sure he gets the letter," Bart said as he wrote the address on the envelope.

"Great talking to you, Bro. Why don't you come to the house to visit? Dad and Angelic are usually home after 5 p.m. I'd like to see you. You're the only brother I have. You think you can visit in two or three weeks?" Warren asked anticipatingly.

"You know that I'm not Dad's favorite person. I would have to be in the right mental space to see him."

"How about this? You can call me two weeks from today at around 4 p.m.; I'll answer the phone and tell you whether he got the letter. Then we can plan your visit here. I miss you, bro!"

"That sounds like a plan, 'lil Bro. I miss you too! Bye." Bart sealed the letter and prayed over it as he walked to the mailbox and raised the red flag.

44

An Unwelcome Visitor

Bart turned right into the upscale community and was enamored by the palatial houses. "Look at the columns on that house!" he exclaimed as he passed the two-story brick house with the matching brick driveway.

However, the largest house on the street was the only one in the cul-de-sac. It was a white stucco house with a basketball court and a three-car garage. "This must be the house," Bart confirmed as he looked at the address in the mailbox.

He took a deep breath as he rang the doorbell.

"Hey, Bart! Come on in," Warren said cheerfully as Bart took three steps in. "It is good to see you, bro. Give me a hug!"

"It is good to see you, too. Daddy and Angelic are in the dining room. We were just about to eat."

"Who was that at the door, Warren?" Booker asked inquisitively.

"I'm going to let you see for yourself," Warren shared as he walked into the dining room.

Booker and Angelic looked up from the dining table in total surprise when Bart followed in after Warren.

"Well, look who is in my house! The prodigal son has come to visit," Booker dryly blurted out.

"Yes, it is," Angelic mustered. "We were just about to have dinner? Won't you join us?"

"Thank you," Bart voiced reluctantly.

Angelic had prepared Booker's favorites: Fried chicken, smoked ham, chitterlings, macaroni and cheese, apple pie, and sweet tea. *I see Booker still doesn't eat vegetables,* Bart thought. Booker turned on the television as background noise and to make the day's news a part of the conversation. He had no idea what Bart would say or what he could talk to him about.

"So what brings you to town?" Booker asked gingerly, feigning to have a semblance of interest in Bart, who was standing before him.

"I just wanted to visit to see how Warren, Angelic, and you were doing. I haven't seen you in some years," Bart casually shared. Booker was pleased with his response.

During dinner, the foursome discussed news, politics, recent deaths of church members, and life among family members. There were even a few moments of laughter. As dinner drew to a close, Angelic and Warren went to the kitchen to wash and dry dishes. "Let me take you on a house tour, Bart," Booker offered.

Booker showed Bart the upstairs area with pristine, spacious rooms accessorized by family pictures and fine art. The windows were state-of-the-art and covered with expensive-looking drapes. As they came downstairs, Booker asked Bart, "Why don't you and I take a ride to see your great-grandmother? She's been asking about you. I can drive."

"Well, I have to be at work later tonight and need to start to head home to rest," Bart said.

"Ahh, it won't take long. It's just 20 miles away. We would stay all of 15 minutes and then come back," Booker bribed. "Think about it as we walk to the entertainment center on the ground level," Booker added.

Bart recalled the times when he witnessed Booker screaming and degrading Dreama at the top of his lungs, arguing with her over something very petty, only for him to put her out of the car after cocking his gun to her head. "I sure as hell hope that he does not do that bullshit today,"

Booker thought as Booker talked about the art in the entertainment center.

"Sure, I'll ride with you. I don't know if she'll recognize me since I may have been twelve when I last saw her," Bart blurted.

"She knows you don't look like the twelve-year-old you once were. Come on, let's go."

Booker and Bart sat silently for the first five minutes of the drive as the AM/FM radio played music from the 1980s. Booker turned the music down and said sternly, "So I got your letter filled with lies."

Bart sat erect in the passenger seat. "What do you mean lies?"

"How dare you falsely accuse me of abusing you and your mother!" Booker stated in an elevated voice. "I have nothing to do with your mother choosing to abandon her family or going to school. Hell, you saw your aunt Mabel go to school with me transporting her. I was a good provider. And another thing, you were sent to the group home because *YOU* reported a lie to social services. To prevent them from continuing to investigate me, I signed over my parental rights."

"Have you really lost touch with reality?" Bart asked, befuddled. "Let me get this straight! You have no recollection of cocking your gun to mom's head? Bashing her head against the car door? Writing cryptic messages on bathroom mirrors? Not working since I was six years old when you lost your job at Chev Mills? Being behind the plot of Mom and me being called up to the altar for sexual sins when it was *YOU* who forced me to perform sexual acts with you, only for you to call me disparaging names in public? And as far as Aunt Mabel goes, don't think I don't know that you are Lee's father—or should I say his father and uncle. So don't all of a sudden claim you have amnesia just because you got remarried."

Seething, Booker pulled up to the stop light. "Everything you said is a lie. You were a liar as a child, and now, as an adult, you're a bigger liar. The pastor, bishop, and apostle said that you have a demonic spirit, and they couldn't cast it out. I am a holy man and couldn't stand being around you or your evil mother." The light turned green, only for Booker to make a

U-turn. "We can't even have a damn decent conversation. I can't drive to great-grandma's house with you saying some stupid shit. I'm taking your ass back to my house."

"Well, you do what you deem necessary. You have definitely made it obvious throughout my life that you never wanted me as your child. But I am not here to argue. Just know that I have forgiven you wholeheartedly. I have been adopted into a family that loves me; I will be going to college very soon. I am working on building my relationship with God. I came to you in peace. I love you," Bart carefully stated.

"I don't give a damn about that," Booker hollered. "You have always been fucking delusional, living in a fantasy world. Your new parents will grow to hate you, too. You'll wind up in the streets wishing I was a part of your life. I have money now. Look at Warren! He is enjoying life living with me and Angelic in our large home in an exclusive neighborhood that you'll never enjoy," Booker argued.

"I don't care about your house or money. For the first time in a long time, I am loved. I am very happy. There is nothing you can say that would dampen my spirit," Bart politely stated.

Booker turned into his housing development so quickly that Bart slid inches away from him. "Slide your sissy-ass over, boy!" Booker snapped as Bart slid back to the center of the passenger seat. "My fucking day is ruined because of you," Booker stated just before the car made an abrupt stop one block away from their destination. Booker looked Bart squarely in his eyes and balled his fist as he hollered, "I FUCKING HATE THAT THE DAY YOU WERE BORN." He quickly swung his arm to backhand Bart, but Bart grabbed his wrist just an inch from his face.

"Just because I have forgiven you doesn't mean I will not defend myself against you. Despite you calling me all kinds of derogatory names, I am a grown man. Don't put me in that position ever again," Bart sternly asserted. Bart controlled Booker's arm away from him and placed it on the seat.

Booker realized instantly that Bart was physically stronger than he was as they pulled into the driveway. "DON'T you EVER come to this house again! I told you years ago that I NEVER want to see you again. Warren has always been my only child, you filthy piece of shit! Haul your ass out of my car, and don't bother trying to reach any member of my household. God HATES sissies, and so do I! I HATE you! Be gone FOREVER!" Booker said in an attempt to get an emotional reaction from Bart.

"At this moment, I realize that I can't lose what I never had. In you, I never had a father, provider, intercessor, or protector. I hope you allow God to transform your heart and mind," Bart calmly stated as he exited the vehicle.

Booker moved quickly out of the car and into the house, slamming the door. Angelic and Warren had retired to their respective bedrooms. As he looked out the window, Bart was driving away. "I really should've shot that son-of-a-bitch!" Booker whispered as the doorbell rang.

"WHO IS IT?" Booker attempted to sound threatening.

"Quincy! Open this door NOW!" Quincy stated assertively.

Booker quickly swung the door open and stepped outside. "How the fuck did you find where I live?" he asked menacingly.

"Don't be asking me a bullshit question. I am asking the question now. You seem to be avoiding me. So, I parked a block up the street. Where is my fucking money? I have been quiet over what really happened to Ralph Custon for the past seven years. We had a deal!" Quincy stepped closer to Booker's face.

"I just got rid of one asshole! Now, I am getting rid of another. Get yo' ass off my property. I don't owe you shit!" Booker looked him up and down.

"I'm taking Angelic and you down! You have 24 hours to cough up my money." Quincy said as he walked out of the driveway toward the next block.

"Do the best you can! Ain't nobody got shit on us!" Booker yelled as his across-the-street neighbor opened her door wide-eyed. "The nosey bitch," Booker murmured as he closed the door.

"Honey, who was at the door?" Angelic asked as she rolled her wheel-chair towards Booker.

"It was Quincy, but I took care of him."

"How did he find our home, Booker? We need to do something about him. He is a nuisance. What did he want?"

"He wanted money. I didn't give him any. He left with an attitude. I'm not worried about him," Booker stated nonchalantly.

"That's my baby. Now, come to bed. That queer son of yours kept you from getting in the bed. You've got to get up to work the night shift in four hours," Angelic softly mentioned as she caressed his back while rolling her wheelchair alongside him.

Quincy sped out of the upscale housing development, fuming over Booker's treatment of him. "My next stop is to see my attorney and then go to the police station!" he avowed.

—m—

Attorney Sylvester Calhoun and Quincy walked timidly into the police station. Noticing that three people were ahead of them, Sylvester asked Quincy, "Why don't you have a seat while I stand in line to speak with the officer?" Quincy nervously sat down, pondering whether he was making the right decision. "The detective will be right out. And don't worry; you'll be fine," Sylvester whispered to Quincy.

As Sylvester was getting water for Quincy, they heard, "Quincy Miller!" Sylvester replied, "This is Mr. Miller, and I am Sylvester Calhoun, attorney for Mr. Miller."

"I'm lead Detective Brookshire. It was a pleasure meeting both of you. Won't you come to my office?"

The office walls were bare, and there was a table that seats six. "I've asked Detective Maurice Kelly, Detective Shawn Bradshaw, Police Chief Gordon Carter, and prosecuting attorney Stacy Wallsensky to join us as we collect a statement from you," Detective Brookshire stated gentlemanly.

"I understand that your client has information on the Ralph Custon murder."

"Yes, my client does. But do know that we have to discuss immunity."

"Okay, we have to see what information he has, and then I can consider it," the prosecuting attorney said.

The interview was three hours of the officers interrogating Quincy on the details of Booker's role in the murder of Ralph Custon and how Angelic arranged it so that she would benefit from the life insurance policy. They discussed Booker shooting Angelic to make the carjacking appear legitimate, leaving her a paraplegic as a result. Upon request, Quincy presented the gun, bullets, and the clothing they wore during the commission of the crime. He even shared where the getaway vehicle was—despite the damage it endured when Booker deliberately set it on fire.

"So, with all of the information you presented, you mean to tell us that the only thing you did was ride in the vehicle with Booker?"

"That's right," Quincy curtly stated unintentionally.

"And that all you did was witness the events you described?"

"Yes."

"Ok. We will send these items to the lab for analysis and collect whatever DNA we can from the van. Now, we do have to arrest you for being an accessory to murder and have you processed through the jail. You do understand that, right?"

"My client understands that. I will speak with the judge about the bail and then arrange to get him out. After the DNA evidence is confirmed, I would like to speak to you privately, Mr. Prosecuting Attorney, about my client receiving a lighter sentence in exchange for testifying against Booker and Angelic."

Gordon Carter thought, "I will get justice for Ralph Custon. I will have to get some of my best officers to pay Angelic and Booker a visit to bring them to the station for questioning. And I'll be at the station waiting on their asses."

Quincy was arrested without incident and read his rights. He knew he would only be held for two hours maximum. His experiences the few times he'd been in jail taught him that. As he walked away from his attorney, he thought, "Going to jail for a few hours in exchange for testifying against Booker and Angelic is well worth it."

—⚏—

Booker hit the snooze button twice before struggling to get out of bed. "Honey, wake up."

Angelic rubbed both of her eyes as she turned on the lamp. "What's wrong, dear?"

"I'm feeling lightheaded. My right arm is feeling uncomfortable, and also . . ." Booker stopped mid-sentence as his eyes rolled towards the back of his head.

"Booker! Booker!" Angelic cried out as she shook him for 20 seconds.

"What? What? I'm just fine," Booker stated quickly.

"You went out of it. I wasn't sure what was happening."

"You know I'm a trooper! Now, I better get up and get ready to slave from 11 p.m. to 7 a.m. at the cardboard factory," Booker slowly stood up.

"Tomorrow, I am taking you to a doctor. You haven't been to a doctor once during the years we've been together."

"Doctors can't be trusted. God has kept my body strong throughout my adult life. I'm not going to the doctor," Booker commented as he grabbed his truck keys.

"Well, you are the head of this house and your body. If you change your mind, I am happy to go to the doctor with you," Angelic submitted.

Booker drove in complete silence, replaying the discussion between Bart and him. "That bitch-ass sissy has some gall to tell me I was abusive to his mother and him!" Booker spoke aloud. "I told him that he was gonna go crazy reading the Bible all the time! Looks like it already started." Booker merged onto the highway, exceeding the speed limit. "I've got to stop and get a soda. My chest feels tight. Probably due to the stress Bart put on me today."

The moment Booker looked into the rearview mirror, he saw the blue flashing lights. "Why the fuck are these cops riding on my ass?" he asked with annoyance. "Now I'm going to be late for work." Booker suddenly started to sweat profusely as he pulled his truck along the shoulder.

"Sir, I need your license and registration," the officer gently stated.

"Why did you pull me over? I did nothing wrong," Booker defended himself.

"This highway has a fifty-five-mile-per-hour limit, sir. You were driving twenty miles over the limit. Hand me your license and registration."

Frowning, Booker complied.

"Just stay put while I run your information. I'll be right back."

Booker thought, "This day has been one of fucking surprises. Bart stressed me out with his lies, Quincy wanted money, and this cop stopped me over some bullshit!" He breathed heavily as he glared in the rearview mirror. "It's so hot," Booker said aloud as a second officer arrived, pulling his cop car in front of Booker's truck. Both officers returned to Booker's vehicle.

"Sir, we need you to come down to the station for questioning," the second officer boldly stated.

"What! I have a right to know why!" Booker's voice projected.

"We want to ask you some questions about Ralph Custon."

"I DON'T know who you're talking about. So I have nothing . . ." Booker's voice trailed off as his eyes rolled to the back of his head.

"Sir! Sir!" The first officer opened the truck door, only to have Booker slump heavily in his arms.

"Help me get him on the ground," he commanded the second officer. They carefully placed Booker's body on the grass. "Quick! Check for a pulse while I give him CPR."

Despite their life-saving efforts, Booker was dead.

45

The Concealed Revealed in Order to be Healed

"YOUR DADDY died of a broken heart because you were a disobedient child. It caused him to pray for you without ceasing until his heart gave out! And now you've got some nerve to show up at this funeral. God will deal with you!" Deacon Chuckie openly accused.

"Deacon Chuckie, please have a seat. You know that we are in the house of the Lord, and we must act appropriately," Reverend Countee Allison commanded. Chuckie eased in his seat as the congregants looked at Bart. "We HAVE reached a point in the service where if anyone wants to say anything more about the life of Booker Johnson, please do so at this time."

Bart stood up slowly but with confidence. "I am Montgomery Bartholomew Hayes, and I did not kill Booker Johnson. But those of you who were once members of Saint Elijah Baptist Church may remember me as Bartholomew Johnson," Bart stated confidently as he walked to Booker's open casket to face the congregants. Some of them were astonished, especially those who knew him. They wondered where he had been all these years.

"Why do I now have a name change, some of you may ask? I have been legally adopted and renamed by a family that loves me just as I am." He continued, "Now, while I didn't know the Booker that Reverend Allison described, I do know that this church needs to get to a place where it tells the truth about the living and the dead."

"Gurl, it's about to be some drama," Suella Mathis whispered to Erma Cowhune.

"One truth I've learned is how important forgiveness is. My reality with Booker was years of sexual abuse, physical abuse, and emotional abuse, not only to me but also to Dreama, my biological mother. Booker would reference the Bible to justify his actions against us. And when the outcome was his calling me hurtful names, ridicule from the church, taken to a group home and left for dead. I hated Booker because I kept losing at the game where only he knew the rules. But that all changed when the Hayes family taught me that I had to forgive to have productive relationships with friends, co-workers, my new siblings, and my new parents. God forgives me for all my sins, and I had to do the same. Forgiveness is about building my relationship with God and not allowing what others say or do cause me to become a lifelong bitter person."

Some congregants nodded in agreement while others sat on the edge of their seats.

"I told Booker I forgave him, and I also forgave Dreama who often fell under Booker's wrath and was powerless in delivering me from it. I have so much joy and peace because I confronted the hate I had for Booker and allowed God to turn it into love through forgiveness. May everyone under the sound of my voice, think about who they need to forgive. Decide to forgive today. Thank you."

Bart heard the parishioners say several "Amens". One by one, people stood to applaud his message of forgiveness as he walked away from Booker's casket up the aisle towards the exit.

As he walked to the fourth right pew, Christine Mullinax held her arms open. Bart hugged her tightly. "I always prayed that things would work out for you. I am glad to hear that my prayers were answered."

"Thank you so much for your prayers and support, Ms. Mullinax.

Continue to make a difference in the lives of more children," Bart stated as he released her.

As he walked towards the vestibule, he heard: "BARTTTTT, I'M SO SORRY!" Dreama screamed as she emerged from a back pew and ran into Bart's arms.

"I know that you did the best you could. I forgave you long ago; I needed you to hear it. I'll always love you." Bart held Dreama as she sobbed. They walked out together to the vestibule, and the parishioners were still applauding Bart.

"Bart, baby, thank you for forgiving me. I know that I wasn't the best mother to you; I felt guilty giving Booker both of my children during the divorce," Dreama said.

"Perhaps we can start a new chapter. Meanwhile, you need to forgive Aunt Mabel, just as you have been forgiven," Bart added. Dreama immediately looked stone-faced. She changed her appearance when Warren walked up. "Warren, come give Mama a hug," Dreama said apprehensively. Warren and Dreama walked out of the vestibule to the parking lot. "Meet us at the Burger Joint three blocks from here. From what you just said, brother, we need to say what needs to be said to become a family again."

"Cool, I'll meet you, but Booker's service hasn't ended."

"Right now, it is important to focus on the living. Dad doesn't need me to stare at his body to prove my love for him. Mom and I will meet you in thirty minutes?"

"Absolutely."

Warren waved at Bart as he helped Dreama into his car.

Bart considered turning to look through the glass back in the sanctuary for one last look at Booker. *I have all the closure I need. It's unfortunate that he didn't live to see the man I have become, thanks to the guidance from the best parents I ever had.*

Reverend Allison continued the service, stating, "We have had an adventurous service. Is there one more that would like to share something about Booker before we transport his body to the gravesite?"

Police Chief Gordon Carter and his colleague were dressed in black suits. They walked down to Angelic. "Brother Carter, do you wish to say something about Booker."

"Not at this time. We are just offering our condolences to Sister Angelic," Gordon replied. The plain-clothes officers walked up to Angelic, where Gordon whispered in her ear, "You are under arrest for insurance fraud and the murder of Ralph Custon. Now, we can have you roll your wheelchair as we walk to the unmarked car, or we can arrest you in front of everyone. Which would you prefer?"

"Well, since no one else has words to say, let's move on to a song, and then we will go to the burial site," Reverend Allison concluded.

"NO, NO, NO! This can't be happening to me," Angelic hollered as Gordon positioned her to roll out of the church. The congregants and her children thought she was so overwhelmed with grief that she needed to be taken out.

As Bart stood near his sportscar reflecting on the day's events, he was met by a tall, dark-skinned man with white teeth. His black suit outlined his athletic build. "Hey Bart, remember me?"

He couldn't hold his excitement: "Oh my gosh! Glen! I can't believe it is you." Glen held Bart as he cried. Glen cried, too.

"I told you years ago that I would find you. And now that I have, I am not leaving you again," Glen stated softly as he held on to Bart without regard for who might be looking.

Upon releasing Glen, Bart smiled. "You look really good,"

"Yeah, you do, too," Bart complimented.

"Thanks. I'm sorry to hear about your dad. How do you feel considering what happened?"

"I feel like I'm losing what I never had and gaining in what God has called me to have and be."

"What do you mean?"

"I never had in my father a protector, teacher, guide, positive example, role model, nor someone who loved me. God blessed me with my adoptive father who are all of these things and more to me. He still takes time to teach me what it means to be a man though I have only been his son less than ten years now."

"Wow. That's profound. I am very happy for you. And to celebrate, why don't we go and get something to eat? I would love to catch up with you," Glen invited.

"I'd like that too. Let's stop by the Burger Joint. But I just don't want to go out in this outfit," Bart pointed out.

"Don't worry about that. You still look good. We can take my car."

"Thank you. But I'd rather wear something that doesn't remind me of what I have left behind," Bart mentioned as an idea came to mind.

"I think I have a change of clothes. Why don't you go to your car and pick me up at the corner?"

"Sounds great! I'll be at the corner within two minutes."

Bart went to the woods' opening next to the church. Recalling his childhood heroine, Wonder Woman, he spun around three times before a bright light flashed. He then found himself in a new outfit, just right for his outing with Glen. He was running quickly just as Glen was pulling up at the corner.

"Wow, that was fast! I love what you changed into," Glen flirted as Bart got to his convertible. "Looks like you're ready!"

"I'm ready to face a future with everything that life has to offer," Bart stated. "Let's go!"

Acknowledgments

I thank God for giving me the courage to write this story. This book is a labor of love dedicated to Randall, Kris, and Naomi. It has been my greatest achievement raising you.

To Deborah, your feedback on my book gave the content greater heft. To William, thank you for pushing me to tell this story for years.

To Darius and Solomon, you have made time in your home to listen to my dreams of this book. To Joseph and Dorothy Heaggans, thank you for adopting me and teaching me the value of forgiveness. You are the best parents I have ever had.

To my nine siblings, thank you for embracing me as your brother. To Corey, you were the impetus that led me to become your brother. It changed my life forever. To Katika, our conversation on our respective life experiences had a great impact on me telling this story.

To Derrick, you have been laser-focused in asking what the drama of the day is in my book. Thank you for being there for me every step of the way.

To Rich, you have been a critical friend and active listener.

To Ronald and LaFreda, you opened your home to me when I had nowhere else to go. To Henrietta, you supported me while I was in graduate school. To Charles Squared, the two of you have been very instrumental in helping me share my story with others. You have been among my biggest cheerleaders.

To the Uncle's Outside Travel Club members, thank you for listening to a modicum of my story and demonstrating your immediate support.

To Chad, my favorite cousin, you have been there through thick and thicker. To Matthew, you have influenced me to pass the torch to those who come after me. To Rasheen, you have been that friend who has supported every life decision I've made.

To Scotty and Dwight, thank you for being among my biggest cheerleaders. To John, you challenged me to role-play what I would say; it gave me greater courage to write it in this book.

To Linda, I am telling your story, too; I just wished you revealed what you concealed so you could be healed. To Pablo, thank you for supporting me in telling the story. I am glad you were protected. To Richard, I grew spiritually and have a story because of your influence.

And to all people who have faced religious trauma, I encourage you to use this book as a springboard to boldly discuss your pain. Writing this book helped me to develop even greater courage to be the me I am divinely called to be.

About the Author

Dr. Raphael Heaggans is an educator, public speaker, father, and author. He has presented his writings across the United States, Canada, France, Belgium, Germany, and the Netherlands to engaged audiences. He is a recipient of the *Barack Obama Award* by the National Alliance of Faith and Justice. In his other life, he is a real-estate agent, notary, and bartender. He lives in Washington, DC.